All My Love, Always

A NOVEL

All My Love, Always

A NOVEL

SARAH ARCURI

Paisana Press

For information about this title or to order books and/or electronic media, contact the publisher:

Paisana Press
P.O. Box 32841
Palm Beach Gardens, FL 33420

Paisana Press

Artwork: Nicholas Galetta
Cover and interior design by The Book Cover Whisperer:
OpenBookDesign.biz

Library of Congress Control Number: 2025910214

979-8-9989692-1-8 Paperback
979-8-9989692-0-1 Hardcover
979-8-9989692-2-5 eBook

Printed in the United States of America

FIRST EDITION

Per la mia anima gemella.
In ogni storia che racconto, ci sei tu.
Hai tutto il mio amore. Sempre

For my twin soul.
In every story I tell, there are you.
You have all my love. Always

"We were together.
I forget the rest."

— WALT WHITMAN

"You must know,
surely you must know,
it was all for you."

— JANE AUSTEN,
PRIDE AND PREJUDICE

THE SOUNDTRACK OF *ALL MY LOVE, ALWAYS*

Music lives in the bones of this story. *All My Love, Always* was born that way—sparked by a single song, that sparked a single scene.

From Pia's soaring soprano to Enzo's Eros Ramazzotti obsession, from Scarlett—the only one in the family who loves Fleetwood Mac—to the timeless *canzoni Napoletane* that echo through kitchens and car rides, music pulses through these pages. These songs shaped the emotions, memories, and moods of the Valenti family's journey. Now, they're yours to hold.

Let the music take you to Montauk, to Little Italy, to the places where love bloomed and secrets unraveled.

To listen, open Spotify, click the camera icon in the search bar, point your camera at this code and, Spotify will take you straight to the official playlist.

My beloved Francesco,

I hope you're still getting a kick out of me up there in heaven. Did you laugh this morning when I sobbed like a baby over Emilio's college graduation card, my tears smearing the ink? Did you shake your head as I stared at Pia's senior picture, wondering how seventeen years passed by in seventeen seconds? Oh, Francesco, honey, our babies are growing up, and I'm so not okay with it. I wish you were here to see who they've become.

Tonight, I'm hosting a celebration at our restaurant for their graduations. I presume it'll feel like all the other gatherings—warm and inviting, yet missing something. Because no matter how full the room is, there's always an empty space where you should be. And yet, I put on a brave face. For our children, to let them know that they can live fully despite their grief. For myself, so maybe I'll believe I can do the same.

So much of my life has been telling myself something, true or not, until I believe it. Did you do that, too? Did you have these little lies you whispered to yourself in the shadows of night until they stitched themselves into the fabric of who you were?

Lately, I've been telling myself that I'll be fine on my own, without the kids to dote on. I've gotten used to Emilio being out of the house—four years is enough to dull the sting.

But it's Pia who scares me. My precious girl, sweetness and fire all the same, she's a wild card. All I want to do is hold her close and protect her, but she's got these big wings, and I have a sneaking suspicion they'll take her places I've never been before. If I'm being honest, I think I've managed widowhood as well as I have only because I've had to keep it together for Pia's sake. When she leaves, will I fall apart?

All I have left is our restaurant. Maybe now that the kids are grown, I can give the place we built, from nothing into everything, the pieces of me it deserves. Our history is carved into every inch of that restaurant, your stamp marked on every detail. I promise I'll continue to honor your legacy with all that I am.

*I owe that to you, Francesco. I owe you more than you'll ever understand, for things you'll never know **anything** about.*

All my love,

Always,

Scarlett

CHAPTER ONE

SCARLETT

Summer, 2011

Though we're told not to judge a book by its cover, I much prefer to be taken for the woman I pretend to be rather than the disaster I am inside. Laughter, chatter, and Sinatra hum in the air as I weave through the dining room of my restaurant, flashing smiles. In the mirrored wall behind the bar, I catch a glimpse of myself. June has arrived, blanketing Manhattan in a relentless humidity, but seasons do not dictate the way I dress. A structured black blazer clings to my frame; a diamond-encrusted collar necklace rests cool against my skin. At its base, a gold leopard with black diamonds for eyes bares its teeth in a silent growl, poised to pounce. A show of power. A bluff. My wedding rings catch the dim light overhead as I reach up to smooth back any hairs that have dared to stray out of place. They should know better by now. I've been sporting the French twist for more years than I'd like to admit.

That's the thing about me. I'm not fond of change. Certainly not when it comes to an image that suggests I'm much more in control than I really am.

My stilettos dig into the fleur-de-lis patterned carpet as I reach my destination. Twenty-five of my closest friends and family mingle around the U-shaped table at the rear of the dining room for my children's graduation celebration. A *Class of 2011* banner is taped to the wall, flanked by gold, black, and silver balloon arrangements. My gaze sweeps over the gathering. Everyone appears happy, munching on breadsticks and transparent strips of prosciutto, marinated artichokes and folds of mortadella—the traditional Italian antipasti laid out with care. I stop a busser passing by to clear away used silverware and empty plates. Even though it's a family event, I can't turn off my hostess brain that demands I be hyper-focused on the most minute of details. I take a deep breath, steeling myself to enjoy the night, and stop by the ice bucket where I whisk up a half-empty bottle of Dom Pérignon and pour myself a flute.

"Alright, everyone," I announce. At once, all eyes are on me. I'm no performer, but I've lived most of my life at center stage. "Please find your seats. Our appetizers will be out any minute now."

Before I reach my seat, I make the rounds, exchanging warm words with each guest. Fausto, one of my oldest friends, is slowly adjusting to the time difference, having flown in from LA for the occasion. My mother, Lana, seated beside her boyfriend Tony, chides me to sit down and enjoy the party—advice I want to heed but can't. My daughter and her gaggle of girlfriends savor the few sips of champagne I've allowed them, while my son and his friends indulge in an expensive label of Chianti. Finally, I reach the empty seat beside my best friend, Julie. Before I sit, I press my fingertips to my lips, then to Francesco's portrait. My ritual. My invitation.

"I'm not letting you get up again," Julie warns, her baby-blue eyes taking on a sharpness that lets me know she means it.

"Someone has to make sure everything goes smoothly," I remind her as I drape a napkin over my lap.

"Please." She rolls her eyes. "What's a family party without a little chaos?"

Right on cue, food runners emerge in single file from the kitchen and artfully arrange family-style appetizers around the table. I slip into owner mode, watching their every move, not just for the sake of the party, but because their aptitude is a reflection of mine.

Conversation floats around the table as the mounds of Italian fare disappear: burrata al tartufo, beef carpaccio, charred octopus, and langoustines that trick me into believing we're closer to the Mediterranean than we are. After our plates are cleared and the table is reset, I clutch my champagne flute that's been refilled for a second time, smooth down my pencil skirt, and rise. A hush falls over the party, though the few patrons at nearby tables continue their quiet conversations, the clank of their silverware punctuating the stillness that's gripped my guests.

"Oh, Lord," my mother says. She makes a dramatic show of retrieving tissues from her purse. She looks around the table and says, "Trust me. You'll need these."

"Right on," Emilio chimes in, raising his glass to his grandmother. "The Scarlett speeches are legendary."

Legendary. My smile falters for a split second, too brief for anyone to notice. I know my son, along with the throngs of people who have used that same adjective to describe my restaurant, mean it as a compliment. But all fail to understand the weight it carries. Becoming legendary requires passion, tenacity, and unwavering dedication. But remaining legendary is the true test, one of tremendous responsibility. Because it's not just a status; it's a legacy not of a place, but a person. Of their character, of everything they spent their life building. One wrong step, one moment of faltering, and it all could come crashing down. Did I know, deep down, when I married a man with a bad heart, when I spent my thirties and early forties preparing his cocktails of medications and accompanying him to cardiologist appointments, that one day I'd be his widow left to keep him alive even after he was gone?

As I draw in a breath to tell my friends and family just how proud a mother I am, I try to shake off the weight of Francesco's legacy that rests on my tired, fragile shoulders.

"I want to start by thanking all of you for being here tonight," I start, shifting my weight to one leg. "When you own a restaurant, everyone wants to be your friend. It's amazing what the prospect of free food will bring out in people." This garners a few laughs. "That's why I learned early on to keep my circle tight. Most of you have been in my life for more than twenty years, so you know firsthand just how obsessed I am with my children."

A warmth envelops my familiar group. As I glance over at Emilio and Pia, the two halves of my heart, my pretenses disappear and my emotions, however complex they are, take over.

"Emilio Gaetano." I focus my attention on my son who is the splitting image of his father, with a frame standing more than six feet tall and chestnut curls that complement his bronze skin and caramel-colored eyes. "The man you are today is who you've always been. Reliable. Sensible. Hilarious. Kind. Thoughtful. Dependable. No matter what's going on, you have a way of putting everyone around you at ease. These last four years, you've been my rock, even though I didn't ask you to be."

A lump forms in my throat as the world shrinks to me and the boy who made my dreams of becoming a mother come true. Emilio has always been my strength. Now, as the man of our family in his father's absence. Then, when he was just a rambunctious toddler, and my marriage was teetering on the edge of falling apart.

"I still can't believe a kid that *I* made," I continue, "is an Ivy Leaguer and future attorney."

Laughter ripples around, a welcome reprieve from the weight of my memories. Out of the corner of my eye, I spot Jeffrey, one of my veteran waiters, hovering with unspoken urgency, his palpable energy suggesting I'm needed. Whatever it is, it can wait. Right now is about my family. I wink at my son before looking at my daughter. Anticipation shines in her endless eyes that are so dark, I can't make out her pupils. Her white shift dress pops against her tanned skin, and her silky blanket of black hair drapes over her shoulders.

"My baby girl," I say no louder than a whisper. The dam has burst open, and I know if I don't get a handle on my tears now, I'll end up in the bathroom in a fit of uncontrollable sobs. Julie squeezes my hand, reminding me that I can do this. "I don't know how seventeen years have gone by since you came into the world, but all I know is that they went by way too fast. You've always been my little best friend." Pia's tears mirror mine, skating down her cheeks. "When I was pregnant with you, Daddy wished that you'd be an artist. A painter, dancer, singer—he didn't care. He just wanted you to love art the way he did. Daddy got his wish and then some. When you sing, it's like magic." I think of how I haven't heard that magical voice floating around the house in a long time, something that worries and frustrates me to no end. I can't let my daughter squander her gift, so for good measure, I add, "And I hope you make magic with that voice of yours for the rest of your life. You two are my everything, and I'm so, so proud of you. I know you're all grown up now, but you'll always be my babies. Both of you—you have all my love. Always."

Emilio and Pia glance at each other before rising from their seats and rushing to my sides, enveloping me in a hug that's so filled with love, it forces me out of my head and into the moment. This moment, with my kids' arms around me, their love pouring out; this time and place before things like careers and spouses and cities of residence change who we are as a family. I raise my glass in the air, facing my group once more. "To Emilio and Pia."

But my mother holds my gaze from across the table, her green eyes glistening. "To you," she mouths, and I take it for all it means. *For keeping it all together.*

As my kids give me kisses on the cheek and tell me they love me, Jeffrey approaches with an urgency in his step.

"Something wrong with main course?" I ask in hushed tones as we step away from the table.

"No, no." Jeffrey says. The concern in his eyes tells me it's something far worse than a hiccup in the kitchen. "Saverio is here. Says he needs to talk to you. I told him you're having a family party, but he said it couldn't wait."

My brows knit. "My landlord?" Jeffrey nods. I blink, stumped. As a fellow Italian, Saverio knows just how sacred family gatherings are. What could possibly be urgent enough to trump that? "Where is he?"

"By the host podium."

I thank Jeffrey and cross the dining room, past the bar, until I reach the entryway. The front windows frame the view of tourists meandering up and down Mulberry Street, their laughter and banter permeating the glass barrier between us. Saverio leans against the host podium, a white envelope dangling between his fingertips. My worries dissipate; he must've heard through our mutual neighborhood friends about the kids' graduations and wanted to bring them a gift.

"Saverio," I greet him, "how are you?" He gives me a kiss on the cheek. A twenty-five-year landlord-tenant relationship, we're well past handshake territory. "We're about to eat. Happy to add an extra chair if you'd like to join us." I turn to lead the way, but his hesitation stops me.

"You'll have to pardon my bad timing," Saverio says, without much apology in his voice, "but I have some business I need to discuss with you."

A pit forms in my stomach. I lead him through the dining room and up the service steps to my office on the second floor. As my landlord, he could want to discuss any number of things—a rent hike, structural issues, perhaps? Scenarios I use to talk myself down as I close the door behind us and perch on the edge of my desk.

"So, what business is so important that we need to discuss it during my kids' graduation party?" I say in teasing tones, though my message gets across loud and clear.

"As you can see, I'm getting old," Saverio starts, his worn leather loafers dragging across the hardwood floors as he paces. I don't mock argue with a tongue-and-cheek quip; I want to get this over with. "I'm selling my properties here in Manhattan."

"Wow," I exhale. "That's a big decision."

Saverio nods and glances at the envelope in his hands. "As you know, you've been floating a bit of back rent for the last few years."

A bit is putting it kindly. Try a quarter million dollars in back rent, late fees, and repairs I couldn't afford. Given our long-standing relationship and Saverio's soft spot for Francesco, he'd graciously accepted my meager, sporadic payments toward the mountainous debt over the last four years.

"And I've so appreciated your patience," I say, keeping my nerves in check. "As you know, things haven't been the same around here since Francesco passed."

"I know," he says, a little firmer than he needs too. He draws in a big breath that makes his shoulders rise as if he's winding himself up. "Scarlett, I really hate to do this, but I have to settle all my tenant matters before the sale of the building can go through."

My throat tightens. "Could you spell it out for me?"

He approaches and hands me the little white envelope. With great reluctance and shaking hands, I open it, pull out the single sheet of paper, and unfold one of the trifolds, hoping I'll find a settlement offer. Instead, printed in black and white, is a threat I never expected to face: I'm being evicted unless I can come up with a quarter million dollars in ninety days. My head shoots up and suddenly I've lost all control of my emotions.

"Saverio," I say as a plea, my voice cracking, "you can't be serious."

His stoicism fades to sympathy, a gesture I've been on the receiving end of all too often. "I don't want to do this, but I have no choice. The buyer won't take on a tenant with this much unpaid rent."

"I don't have that kind of money." A fuzzy picture becomes clear. In ninety fleeting days, Amanti is going to cease to exist. My life's work, gone in one fell swoop. My husband's legacy destroyed because his wife isn't competent enough to carry it on. Though my children have no interest in taking over the family business, they'll resent me for destroying the last tangible link they have to their father. My staff will be out of a job. And me?

I'll be totally and completely lost. Frankly, I have no idea who I am without this place, and I never planned on finding out.

A knock at the door startles both of us. "Who is it?" I call out.

Julie pops her head in. "Just making sure everything's okay?" But one look at me, and she knows it's the precise opposite. Her smile fades and her curious eyes dart between me and Saverio. "We're almost done eating. I told them to keep your dish in the kitchen, so it stays warm."

"Thanks, babe." I force a smile. "I'll be right down."

Once the door closes again, the heaviness of the news falls between us once more.

"Scarlett, I really am sorry." But if anything, Saverio looks relieved. "If you have any questions, my lawyer's information is in that document."

It's all pretty clear to me, I want to say, but instead, I rest the eviction notice on my desk where it joins a graveyard of overdue bills and collection threats. "Congratulations on your upcoming retirement. It's well deserved." I flash a tight smile that lets him know we're done here, and mercifully, he takes the cue.

With him gone, I lean my backside against my desk and go still. I don't like to do this; stillness gives me too much time to think. Ruminate. When I do that, my heart pounds and I'm flooded with ugly emotions—guilt and shame and regret. So I hide, most of the time, behind the chaos of raising a teenaged girl, of making sure my popular son stays on track, of managing the sinking ship that is my restaurant. I glance over at the notice, wanting to wallow in the reality it's dragged me into, when Julie rushes back in. Her heels click-clack at an quick pace until she reaches me and wraps her arms around me.

"I tried to eavesdrop," she says. "But I'm not sure I heard things right."

"You did," I say into her shoulder. "It's over. I'm being evicted."

We break apart and I look into her eyes. I know I'm the woman in charge in all respects, but right now, I long for someone to take the lead and guide me out of this mess.

"No," she says. "You're going to fix this."

"How?" The beginning signs of a panic attack hit me—cold sweats, racing heart, dizziness. I want to run home and dissect this news with Julie, but I remember the party going on downstairs. At the thought, I'm met with resentment. What should be a joyous day will forever be tainted with the stain of my failures.

"We'll figure it out." Julie squeezes my arms. Then, one of her brows arches higher than the other. "But I'll tell you one thing. That Saverio? I can't believe him, dropping this news in the middle of your kids' graduation party."

"I know." I swipe my fingertips beneath my eyes, not allowing my tears to go any further. I have friends and family and my children to be strong for. I can't fall apart yet. "I guess he's just doing his job. Something I evidently don't know how to do."

"Come on." Julie links her arm through mine as I push away from the desk. As we walk downstairs, I try to shake off the news and step back into mom mode; I don't want anything to ruin this day for my babies.

But as the table comes into view, I feel every bit of the seismic shift that's occurred. While everyone around the table is laughing and eating and drinking, blanketed by an ease that's far from my reach, I am reminded that this problem is solely mine to deal with. Instead of seeing the people who I love and who love me, I see who's missing.

If Francesco hadn't died, *eviction* wouldn't even be part of our vocabulary.

If Enzo had stayed—if he hadn't vanished after that gray, rain-soaked funeral where we buried his *kid brother*—maybe we wouldn't have landed here at all.

All I know is, the two brothers whose last name I bear have left me with a problem I don't know how to fix.

As I plaster on a fake smile, downing copious amounts of champagne that numbs my mind and my limbs and does nothing more than delay the inevitable, I let myself fantasize that Julie is right. Maybe I can fix this.

Oh, who am I kidding?

That's just another lie, like all the rest on which my life is built.

CHAPTER TWO

SCARLETT

Summer, 2011

"I think I have a solution," I say to Paul, my accountant, who sits behind his large oak desk scattered with paperwork like a money oracle. He came on board as the official Valenti family finance manager in the early nineties, around the time Francesco received his Michelin star, which led to lucrative book deals and a hit PBS series. I straighten my blazer and meet his gaze. "My townhome. Emilio's out of the house. Pia's off to college in a few months. I'll be devastated to sell, trust me, but I know I have to make some sacrifices."

"Your townhome," he says, sliding on a pair of readers, "is tied up with home equity loans. Even if you get top dollar—which, given the market, would be a stretch—you won't clear enough to cover the debts."

My shoulders slump at his dire news. The loans had covered payroll, taxes, and utilities when Amanti's cashflow ran dry. But they also went toward Pia's private voice lessons, therapy, Francesco's over-the-top funeral that landed a write-up in *The New York Times*, and a high-end espresso machine, as if better coffee could fill the voids my husband left. Remembering it all now, I realize I wasn't keeping things together. I was laying the groundwork for my life to implode.

"So where does that leave me?" I ask, folding my hands in my lap.

"Your only real asset is the Montauk house," Paul tells me.

At the mention of the beachside palace that once symbolized the pinnacle of success, of all that my marriage could be, my chest twists. Our eyes meet briefly before I look away.

"I can't sell that house. What about the education trust?"

"It became irrevocable when Francesco passed," Paul reminds me. But it's more than a legality. It's proof that Francesco never fully trusted me. He hadn't made the fund off limits to me so I couldn't use the money for something else, but to punish me for my supposed incompetence. So I'd mixed up the dates for Emilio's entrance exam to The Browning School, and he ended up at a lesser prep academy instead. Did that one little mistake really warrant Francesco locking me out of our children's future forever? "You said you were willing to make some sacrifices."

I cross my legs and bounce my foot, forcing myself to meet his gaze. "You know that Francesco's brother owns half of that house."

Paul nods. "Enzo."

A single word. Two syllables that strike like lightning. "Yes. Enzo." I don't tell him that we haven't spoken in four years, or that we didn't part on good terms, to put it mildly. "I'm not sure he'd want to sell."

"Let's play devil's advocate and say he would," Paul says as he shuffles through some papers. The phone on his desk rings and I wish he would answer it so I could buy myself some time. So I could rack my brain for another solution. Anything but selling my beach house.

Anything but needing Enzo.

But Paul draws in a breath and reads from a sheet of paper. "The home was purchased in 1992. You all took out a mortgage of $800,000, and you've paid off about half of that. Current value is anywhere between three and four million. Even after splitting that with Enzo"—Paul glances up at me—"you'd have more than enough. Pay off your debts, renovate, bring in a marketing expert, hire a renowned chef."

"I know what I have to do to turn the restaurant around," I say, sounding more defensive than I intended. "My daughter went through a very difficult period after Fran died. I focused all my attention on her and Emilio. That's why things fell apart. Not because I don't know what I'm doing."

Paul raises his palms, as if I've spewed darts at him rather than words. "I don't doubt it."

I relinquish further into the chair. "Look, all I need is to pay off the back rent and some of my vendor debts to buy myself some time. I don't need millions. Four hundred grand, tops."

"And the simplest way to get that money is by selling the house. I understand its sentimental value," Paul says, sounding anything *but* sentimental. "But to me, it seems like a no brainer."

That's because you don't know everything. He makes it sound as easy as signing a piece of paper, as if I haven't spent every summer of my adult life with my feet buried in that sand, as if every one of Pia's seventeen birthdays weren't celebrated in that stunning cedar shake house overlooking a pristine beach. He doesn't know that house represents exactly what my marriage to Francesco was: a beautiful façade that weathered relentless storms.

Paul doesn't know what I'll have to face if I decide to sell.

But I do, and as long-buried thoughts and fears and memories bubble to my surface, my heart rate multiplies. The facts are plain as day. I'm drowning. Montauk is my only life raft, and I'll have to swim through everything I've been running from to save myself. I swallow my tears and rise.

"Thank you for meeting with me," I say and extend my hand. "I'll let you know once I make a decision."

"I feel like I'm pinned against the ropes," I say, uncorking a bottle of wine. The pop echoes before I pour two generous servings. "I'm not sure I've got much fight left in me."

"Slow down, Rocky Balboa," Julie teases, reaching for her glass. "There is a solution here. You just don't like it."

"I would've preferred to sell my townhome."

"Beggars can't be choosers, sugar."

"Shut up, bitch." A smile tugs at my lips as I lean back in my chair. Jeffrey drops off a plate of roasted artichokes, though nothing seems appetizing right now. "You know why. It's not just a house."

Julie serves me a helping of grilled octopus with potato wedges, whether I want it or not. "You know you can't bullshit me, right? I know too much," she adds with a wink.

Rather than respond, I take a bite of octopus and chew, holding her gaze.

"You just don't want to deal with Enzo," she presses.

I stiffen. And change the subject. "Pia turns eighteen this year. I've been planning a big party for her."

Julie shrugs. "So you have the party. Doesn't mean you can't list the house for sale. Plenty of people live in their homes while it's on the market. You're making excuses."

"Can you stop?" I set down my fork and reach for the much-needed wine. "You know damn well I can't reach out to Enzo."

"And why not?"

"Because I promised him and myself that I'd never speak to him again."

Julie's mouth twists into a smirk. "You're really going to let your *pride* destroy everything you've worked for?"

Before I can respond, Stassi, my bartender, approaches. "Sorry to interrupt," she says, tucking a spiral curl behind her ear.

I force a smile. "What's up, honey?"

"We're out of Jameson."

My shoulders slump. Our primary liquor vendor stopped delivering last week. Another gargantuan balance I can't afford. Another reminder that selling the house is inevitable.

Stassi shifts. "This couple at the bar is complaining."

I can't count how many testy customers I've tamed over the years, but this one strikes me differently. It's nothing but proof that I've fallen short of everything I'm expected to be. Looking for a quick solution, I scan the stock of bottles that line the bar. "Offer them Macallan. No extra charge."

Stassi's eyes widen, but she accepts the offer before I can change my mind. It's a costly decision on my end, though the prospect of making someone's night, plus a potential good Yelp review, makes it worth it in my eyes.

With Stassi gone, Julie's stare burns a hole through me. "You realize that's your problem, right?"

"What is?" I ask.

"You give, give, give. You don't care what it costs you, even when it wrecks you. And that's what you're doing with this Montauk house. You're hanging on for dear life, because you think you owe it to the kids. To Francesco. But where does that leave you?"

"Anxious, depressed, and addicted to Xanax," I deadpan.

But Julie doesn't crack a smile. "Let me ask you something. What about what you owe yourself?"

"*Me?*"

"Don't make me repeat myself," she mutters, swirling her wine. "You've spent your life making sure everyone else is okay. Happy. Satisfied. What about you? When's the last time you made sure *you* felt that way?"

"*I* come last," I say, sarcasm slipping into something humorless and painfully true.

"Exactly. That's a big problem, Scar."

I grab my wine glass and rest my back against the chair. "You're trying to tell me that if I sell the house, I'll magically be happy and satisfied and all those good things?"

"What I'm telling you is that I don't think you know how to let go." She sets down her glass. "Your whole identity is wrapped up in Francesco. In the kids. In your very complex, very unresolved feelings for Enzo," she sing-songs. "And I get it. I know why you are the way you are. But at some point, you've got to realize that you are more than your mistakes. Sometimes I just wish you'd live for you. Not as a wife, or a widow, or as a mother. As a woman."

I wait for her words to spark something, for me to have some big *aha* moment, but all I feel is the same unbearable weight I carry every day. How do you let go of the things that hold you together, even when they're the very things you've been running from?

Across the restaurant, a food runner emerges through the kitchen doors, and as they swing back into place, I swear I see Francesco behind the line, clad in his usual white chef's jacket. But I blink, and the image is gone. He's everywhere and nowhere. It's just his ghost that haunts me, that lingers in every brick of this place that we laid together.

This place that made me. Not love. Not marriage. Not motherhood. Here, I'm someone else entirely. An equal. Francesco and I built

Amanti on nothing but grit, sheer will, and ideas, when the future still felt like something we could mold with our own hands.

And yet, I still feel him watching. Waiting for me to repay a debt I'll never be able to satisfy.

I trace the stem of my wine glass. Without Amanti, without Francesco's image on the walls, without the carefully crafted mask I wear, what would be left of me?

The truth is, I'm too afraid to find out.

Just like I'm afraid of Enzo. The man I swore off four years ago.

"I know Enzo disappointed you," Julie says softly, drawing me back to the present. "But he's not a bad guy. Besides, you're not inviting him back into your life. You just need his signature. Is that so scary?"

I shake my head to appease her, but of course it is. Because Enzo has always been the one person who knows just how to make me unravel. He's the only one who knows the parts of me I never want to face again.

Yes, it's terrifying to face the truth, especially when it has a name.

———

THE TRUTH IS, I don't have a choice. If I want to save my restaurant and all that it means to me, Enzo it is. And so, while Pia is out with her friends, living the carefree life I've worked so hard to give her, I head to the basement and switch on the light. I have to look up his address. That's how far removed we are from each other's lives, a fact that both shocks and saddens me. I wake the computer, open Google, and type his name. *Lorenzo Michael Valenti.* The blinking cursor taunts me, daring me to go ahead with the search. A few clicks, a deep breath, and a $65 charge later, there it is. His Florida address proves that he's still out there, living a life that has nothing to do with mine. At the sight of his unfamiliar zip code, I'm flooded with imaginary images of what Enzo's life might look like there. I wonder if he ever thinks of me the way I still think of him.

But like Julie said, this isn't about reconnection. It's about facts and figures. Reaching out to Enzo has nothing to do with our history and everything to do with my future. And that's why I reach for the stationery I haven't touched in years, nestled in the top drawer of my desk, right where it's always lived. The pages are still pristine, like they've been stuck in time, waiting for me. I hesitate, my fingertips grazing the edge of the drawer. I will myself not to dwell on the past. Then, pick up my pen, and I bleed.

Dear Enzo,

The last thing you heard me say was that I'd never speak to you again. That was four years ago. Can you believe it? With every year that passes, the details fade. Your laugh is like an old song I used to love whose melody I can no longer place. I can't remember your voice. Isn't that crazy? I know it's a rich, velvety baritone that always sounds like you know something the rest of the world doesn't. I know which vowels you draw out thanks to your Neapolitan-turned-New Yorker accent. But the sound itself is gone, sand slipped through my fingers. I can't believe this is where we are because I know where we have been.

I want you to know, Enzo, that I had every intention of upholding my vow to never speak to you again, but life has a funny way of making us eat our words. I thought I'd left you in my past, but a circumstance has pulled me back to a place where you and I still exist in some fashion.

Montauk.

I'll keep it brief, because putting it on paper makes it real, and you know me, Enzo. You know I don't do real. You know that I'm a great pretender, a master of crafting beautiful façades no one can see past. But here it is. I've mismanaged things, and Amanti is ninety days away from eviction. I owe a quarter-million dollars to Saverio, and I have another mountain of debt owed to my various vendors. The only way out of this mess is to sell our beach house. I know this is a big ask, Enzo, but I hope like me, you don't want to witness the extinction of Amanti. I suppose you've moved on, but I'm still here at the intersection where you left me, waiting. Waiting for what, I do not know. Maybe for life to return to normal, though I know that day will never come. That's why I cling to the past. I know how the story goes, imperfections and all. I'm scared the best is behind me and that's why, though life is moving forward, I'm still looking back with wistful eyes and a longing heart.

Because I'm scared to face a future that doesn't look anything like the one I'd planned.

You and I have always had this thing, Enzo. This inexplicable, indescribable connection tethering the two of us together by some invisible, unbreakable string. Even when I want to hate you, which is often to tell you the truth, I can't. Because I know we're something that can't be explained. I've always been able to feel you, like you're this living, breathing entity within my soul. For some reason that evades logic, I have an Enzo-shaped hole in my heart. I think you feel the same way about me, and I can't help but wonder if you're

sitting there, reading this, knowing that although I don't want
to, I need you, Enzo. I'm tugging on that string between us.
Can you feel me?

So I'm asking you to please allow me to sell the house. A
week from today, I'll leave for what is hopefully, unbeknownst
to my children, our final summer at the house. I know you and
Francesco bought it as an investment together, so that our fam-
ilies might be intertwined against the backdrops of hazy beach
days and pastel sunsets. We had those good times, watching our
kids build sandcastles and ride waves and tell stories around
the fire eating s'mores. Beautiful times I'll forever cherish. But
like everything else, those times are gone. And now, it's up to us
to come together despite our bad blood and save the one thing
your brother loved most—Amanti.

We owe this to him. We let him down before, Enzo. Are
we really going to let him down again?

All my love,
Always,
Scarlett

Time stills as I set my pen down and scan my swirling, loopy
cursive. It's just me and this letter. Writing it was a catharsis, but
sending it is another. An invocation whose consequences I'm not so
sure I'm prepared for. Despite my reservations, I reach for the envelope,
scrawl Enzo's address, and stick on a stamp. I eye the bar cart when I
reach the main level of my home, knowing a glass of wine or three is
in my future. Grabbing the keys off the hook on the wall, I head out
of the house and down Bank Street where I come face to face with a

mailbox. I stare at it. Does this blue metal box have any idea what it's holding? The catalyst it's about to propel?

Once I let go of this letter, it's out of my hands and into Enzo's. And then? I don't know, but as I pull back the latch and deposit the envelope, there's no turning back.

And just like that, I've invited the past into the present. Not just Enzo.

But Francesco, too.

CHAPTER THREE

SCARLETT

Fall, 1992

The slap came so fast, neither of us saw it coming.

He didn't mean to do it. That was the story we told ourselves, just mere moments after it happened. I sat at my vanity, my face still stinging, tears drying against the patch of skin my husband had struck with his open palm. The same hands that cradled our son. The palm that cupped my cheek with sweet tenderness. Tonight, he'd used it to hurt me.

But he didn't mean to. There was no way.

I squeezed my eyes shut, but all I saw was how it had happened. I had looked innocent enough, minutes before Francesco walked through the door, sitting on the couch in a trance as I watched our son's round belly rise and fall in sleep. But my mind was someplace else. Looping. Obsessing. Drowning in the rumors. Were the whisperings of Francesco's infidelity just that? Idle gossip? Or were they the reason he'd become so distant, so disinterested in my domestic sphere? I'd never expected Francesco to be an equal partner when it came to parenting; I knew, even before we made our vows, that my husband possessed a special quality, a prolific talent that he was both blessed with and enslaved by. But life had changed since we got married. The Michelin star catapulted him into the culinary stratosphere. The cookbook deals bought this gilded cage of mine and all the shiny, expensive fixings inside of it. The PBS specials and morning talk show appearances sealed him as a household name, drawing people from near and far to dine at our restaurant. But while our life was growing more glamorous on the outside, inside, in the places no one else could see, our marriage was crumbling.

Not because of the success itself, the new demands placed on Francesco, but because he'd become addicted to the most dangerous drug of all. Fame. Louder, sweeter, more intoxicating than I ever could be, fame had become the high he couldn't stop chasing, and I was just his soft place to land.

Yes, Francesco was a star now, and that meant he no longer just belonged to me. To our son. Now, he belonged to the world. But that didn't stop me from trying to reel him back. I was his wife. The mother of his only child. I deserved the pieces of him that no one else had a right to. But when I begged for those pieces tonight, he didn't answer with words. He answered with his hand.

"How was work?" I'd asked as he reached for his pill bottles, twisting the white caps with muscle memory. The ticking clock echoed loudly, reminding me that Francesco had worked even later than usual.

"Good. Busy," he replied, not looking at me, his voice flat and far away.

I leaned my elbows on the counter, trying to catch his eye. "Emilio learned a new word today. *Garden.*" Lighthearted tones clung to my voice, trying to make Francesco care. "He asked why we didn't have one. Got me thinking, we should put a little herb garden on the rooftop for him. Don't you think that'd be cute?"

He gave me a curt nod as he lifted a water bottle to his lips, tilted his head back, and gulped down some water to wash the pills into his system. He set it down with a thump. "I'm gonna go shower." He started past me, but I stepped in, pressing my palms to his chest.

"Francesco, wait." He looked down at me, brows arched, eyes already irritated. I had his attention, but no sense of victory.

"I'm exhausted," he said. "Can this wait?"

I swallowed. Where *was* he? The man I used to adore, whose heart beat in sync with mine? I was desperate to find him. "Not really," I said, mustering up the courage to say what had been on my mind for months. He sighed and crossed his arms, poised to hear me, but not to listen. "I know your life is different now. You're famous. I get that. But you can't forget about us. You live here, but you're not *here.* Emilio's growing and changing every day and you're not around to see even glimpses of it. And me. I'm...I'm..."

A lump lodged in my throat. My eyes fluttered shut. He was already annoyed. Bringing up the rumors would only make it worse.

"You what, Scarlett?" he snapped. "You said this couldn't wait, so say whatever you need to say."

I opened my eyes and looked at him. A few beats skipped between us. "I've heard all these rumors that you're cheating on me," I said, sounding as small as I felt.

"Oh, Scarlett, come *on.*" He smacked his palm against the counter. I jumped and worried that Emilio would wake in the next room. "I'm killing myself, taking advantage of every opportunity I can to provide for you and our son. And you have the nerve to accuse me of cheating?" He paced the length of the counter, his brooding energy darkening by the second. In one swift motion, he scooped up his pill bottles and hurled them against the counter. "I should stop taking these pills and let my heart give out."

"Please don't say that."

"No, I *am* gonna say that," he shot back, pointing at me. "They're the only thing keeping me alive. My work's killing me, and I've got no one to help me. Enzo's all for Enzo, and you're here being a mommy. It's all on me. It's all fucking on me." He ripped open the fridge, grabbed another water bottle, and slammed it shut so hard, all the items on the door rattled. "Cheating on you," he muttered under his breath, shaking his head as he drank.

My heart pounded in my ears as I watched him, though he refused to look at me. He continued pacing, stewing in a rage that seemed to go far deeper than any cheating allegations. I was wracked with confusion; he was the one who might've been unfaithful, and yet somehow, I felt like the guilty party. "Fran, I'm sorry, I didn't mean to upset you."

"Yeah. Right. That's all you do is upset me." Finally, his eyes met mine. "Do you realize what kind of life you have? Do you know any other woman who has what you have? You're so *lucky*, and all you do is complain."

I scoffed. "I'm *lucky*? What's so lucky about my life? My big house that my husband never spends time in? My child who my husband barely knows anymore? My famous husband who's screwing other women behind my back?" I yelled, my anger rivaling his. "Where there's smoke, there's fire, Fran. And mark my words, if it's true, I am not going to be one of those Italian wives who looks the other way. I refuse. I'll take Emilio and I'll leave. I'll go back to waiting tables if I have to, but I am not staying with a cheater."

He rushed towards me, his eyes wild. "You sure about that? You wanna say that again? Say it one more time, that you're gonna leave me."

"I'll leave!" I shouted. "I'll leave you right now!"

And then, he slapped me. Right across the face with his open palm. And as a silent sob escaped my chest, as I sunk to the ground numbed by shock, staring up at Francesco's stunned expression, I knew deep in my bones that I wasn't going anywhere.

I shook myself out of the memory, like it was a bad dream I could wake from. Numb, I traced my fingers over the welt, knowing it would bruise by morning. Knowing I'd ice it, cover it with makeup, and head to work like nothing happened. But this physical blow would leave marks that couldn't be healed. I was damaged goods. Our marriage, once a place of pure, unadulterated love, was now tainted. The man I married, the one I saw as my home, the man I trusted with my life, was suddenly a stranger. A monster.

From the bathroom, I heard the bedroom door open. His heavy footsteps neared. I gave myself a hard look in the mirror. I wouldn't cry. I wouldn't make this bigger than it was. It was the first time. An isolated event. If I just held onto that, if I believed it hard enough, it would be true. Wouldn't it?

"Hey," Francesco said, his voice sounding foreign. His red eyes told me he'd been crying. "Can I come in?"

I nodded. He sat on the floor in front of me, taking my hands in his, staring at them, tracing a finger along the teardrop-shaped diamond he'd given me six years ago, when I was twenty-four and believed we'd always be as in love as we were then.

"You don't know how sorry I am," he started. Tears soon followed and when he retreated his hands from mine to cover his face,

I sank to the floor to be near him. "I didn't mean to. The second it happened, I wanted to take it back. I don't know who I was in that moment. It was like someone else took over. I just—I need you to believe me."

"I want to believe you." My voice wavered, revealing the war inside me. Between the part of me that wanted to run, and the part of me that wanted to believe this was an exception. A one-time deal. I hesitated, unsure if I should say what was really on my mind, yet unable to stop myself. "I'm so proud of you, Fran. Seven years ago, when you took me on a date to the Rainbow Room and I told you that I wished you could see you the way I see you, this was what I meant. That you could *be* somebody. And you are, Fran, but…but it's changed you. You've changed. It happened so fast and so easily, and it terrifies me."

As his eyes searched mine, I wondered if he could see it. The shift in me. How this had changed me in some irreparable way I could not yet name.

"I haven't *changed*," he said quickly, the words tumbled out. "I'm just under so much fucking pressure. The book, the filming schedule, the restaurant, it's too much. I come home, and there's nothing left of me. Nothing left to give you. I know that's no excuse," he muttered, running a hand through his hair. His jaw tensed, as if he didn't want to voice his next thought. "What happened down there—that wasn't about you. That was about me, and me taking on more than I can handle, as much as I don't want to admit that. And I'm sorry I took it out on you. You have every right to hate me."

"I don't …" I swallowed hard, forcing myself to finish the sentence. "I don't hate you. And I don't mean to add more pressure, Fran, but Emilio's growing up so fast. I want him to know his father. I want you to see what I see every day. The little details of you in him."

Brushing a stray curl out of his face, I cupped his face in my hands, an irony that was not lost on me.

"All I want is a family," I continued. "You, me, and our son. That's all that matters."

"I know." He nodded, his voice barely audible. "I know I need to get my priorities in check."

We were quiet for a while, the incessant ticking of the grandfather clock in the hallway breaking our loud silence. Loaded, questioning glances were exchanged, before remorse overtook him.

"You're my heart," he whispered as his face wrinkled.

I, too, dissolved; it was something he'd said to me before we got married, words forever sewn into my heart.

"I know."

"I can't lose you."

I thought only of Emilio. "You won't."

"Do you think you can forgive me?"

I squeezed his hands. When that horrible, ugly moment flashed in my mind again, I rerouted my thoughts once more to my son. My son who needed a father. "I'll try like hell."

Silence enveloped us again. The clock kept ticking, his hands interlaced mine like we were trying to hang on to something that had already slipped through our grasp, and we remained planted on the floor, like if we moved, it would all fall apart.

But the truth was, I knew it already had.

***

"WHO COULD THAT BE?" I said to Emilio.

The doorbell's chime echoed as Emilio continued to work on his Lego tower, uninterested in the colorful cartoon flashing on TV. My knees crackled as I pushed myself up from the floor and went to answer the front door. There stood Enzo, leaning against the railing, a Valenti's take-out bag in hand, the maple trees lining Bank Street rustling in the early autumn breeze.

"Hey, you," I said as I opened the screen door and motioned for him to come in.

"Delivery." He handed me the bag and kissed me on the cheek. But then he did a double take. My stomach dropped. I hadn't bothered with concealer; I was staying home and didn't feel the need. "You get in a bar fight?"

I feigned laughter. "Your nephew's got quite the arm, and those Legos are lethal."

Enzo glanced over at Emilio, and at the sight of my sweet, innocent son playing, guilt surged through me for casting the blame on him.

Enzo's gaze lingered on me, his eyes narrowing, like he was trying to connect the dots. "How about that?"

I straightened the hem of my sweatshirt. "He's gonna make a mean pitcher. Or wrestler." I looked past Enzo. "Emi, come say hi to your zio."

Emilio tossed his toys and ran to Enzo, who scooped him up and covered his full cheeks with kisses.

"Hey, *bello guaglione*, who said you could wrestle with your mother, hm?" Enzo tickled his round belly, sending Emilio into a fit of giggles that delighted my ears. "You gonna be a Yankee when you grow up?"

"No," Emilio said, drawing out the word as his mouth curved into a mischievous grin. "The Mets."

Enzo's eyes went wide and his mouth fell open. "We don't say that word around here."

Laughter filled the room as Emilio returned to his blocks. Enzo focused in on me again, and feeling the heat of his scrutiny, I walked toward the kitchen, bag of food in hand.

"How's the restaurant?" I asked.

"Slammed," Enzo answered as he followed me. "We had a full house at five. Fran asked me to drop this off before the next seating."

At the counter, I unpacked steamed langoustines, branzino served with a lentil confit, pasta *alla nerano*, and a slice of his famous strawberry tiramisu that made my mouth water. My favorites. Beneath it all was a note scrawled in Francesco's tight, familiar cursive: *I love you more than anything! Kiss the baby for me, and I can't wait to kiss you later.* I set the note down, feeling slightly pathetic that such a small gesture could stir up such hope in me.

"Is he okay?" Enzo asked, breaking me out of my thoughts.

I glanced up. "Fran?"

He nodded. I reached into the drawer, grabbed a fork, and slid it into the creamy, layered square dessert. Leaning my elbows on the counter, I took a bite, buying some time to compose myself.

"He's stressed," I finally said. "He's past due with some recipe testing, and the filming schedule is crazy. It's a lot on him."

"That's what I was afraid of."

I took another bite and raised my brow, urging him to continue.

"After the star, all these opportunities fell into his lap all at once. I knew he was going too fast. He didn't want to say no and miss out on anything. I just …" Enzo trailed off.

I stood up straight and dropped my fork into the sink. "You can say it."

Emilio's bubbling laughter interrupted our conversation, and for a moment, I wanted to abandon it entirely and go bask in my child's simple joys.

But Enzo caught my eye again. "I'm worried about his heart."

I ran my fingers through my hair. How many things had I let slide because of that very fear? Wasn't that why I buried my own feelings and held my tongue as often as I could, because I didn't want to be the thing that sent his heart out of rhythm, or worse?

Was that why I let him get away with hitting me?

"I am, too," I admitted.

Enzo drummed his fingers against the counter. "I think I'm gonna talk to his manager. See if there's a way to push some of his deadlines so he can slow down."

I was grateful that Enzo had the foresight to do something I hadn't thought of. "Thanks, Enz. That would mean a lot."

Enzo started down the hall at a wandering pace. He snapped his finger and pointed at Emilio. "No more Mets. You hear me?"

Emilio giggled, coaxing a smile from two adults who loved him beyond measure.

I put my hands on my hips as we came to a stop in the entryway. "Thanks for bringing that over."

"No problem."

"And listen," Enzo said, digging his hands into his pockets, "if Fran starts taking out his stress on you, you let me know. He might be the *Pasta King,* but he's still my kid brother."

A small, sad smile spread across my lips. As we stared into each other's eyes, as our long-ago buried connection rose to the surface, I knew Enzo knew. My heart swelled with affection, not because I could tell him the truth, but because I didn't have to.

Sometimes the greatest act of love is letting someone lie.

Two Months Later

"Can I open my eyes now?" I asked as gravel crunched beneath the tires. Finally, the car came to a stop. I didn't know where we were; Francesco had woken me up this morning by telling me he had a big surprise, and I'd been under strict orders to keep my eyes closed since we left Manhattan. "I'm starting to get dizzy."

"One second," Francesco said. Excitement burst from his voice, the click of his seatbelt unbuckling acting as an exclamation point. A few moments later, he opened the passenger side door, helped me out of the car, and guided me forward. "Okay. Now."

I opened my eyes. A cedar shake Hamptons-style home stood before me, its wraparound porch hugged by bright blooms of purple, pink, and blue hydrangeas. Its grandeur was demure. It wasn't massive; it simply was. Serene. Content. Perfect. The roar of the ocean wasn't far.

"Fran," I started, "you could've told me we were going on vacation. I didn't even pack a bag."

"This isn't vacation, babe," Francesco said. He reached his hand out for mine and I grabbed it, though my gaze remained focused on his proud smile and eyes sparkling with anticipation. We walked up the few steps leading to the porch, and the front door swung open.

Enzo greeted us, dressed in dark wash jeans and a tan cable-knit sweater with the sleeves pushed up to his elbows. I was surprised to see him on what I thought was a romantic getaway with my husband. Enzo's smile was impossibly wide as he said, "Welcome home, kids."

My brows raised as I looked at Francesco. "What's going on?"

"Just what he said." Francesco reached into the pocket of his khakis and handed me a set of keys. "Welcome home, honey."

I blinked a few times, my eyes darting between Enzo and Francesco, both of whom appeared to be waiting for me to catch the punchline. "You bought a timeshare?"

"Not quite," Francesco said.

"Rental property," I tried again.

"Getting warmer," Enzo chimed in, but then he corrected himself. "Actually, not really."

What was left? By process of elimination, the only other possibility was that Francesco had purchased this home. Were my suspicions correct? Was this home, so beyond my wildest dreams, ours?

"You … You bought this house?"

"Bingo," Enzo said with a snap of his fingers.

"*We* did," Francesco clarified. "For our families."

"Oh my God." I stared at the keys in my palm, letting myself feel the weight of them. Of this gesture that far surpassed *grand*. "Oh my God!"

"You haven't even seen it yet," Francesco teased. He motioned for me to go inside. I quickly kissed Enzo on the cheek before moving further into the house.

I was greeted by a large living room, whose hardwood floors were topped by a rattan area rug and a coffee table decorated with driftwood and a large ceramic vase. Beyond that was a dining space with an oblong table large enough to seat twelve. I wandered up to the windowsill in the spacious, sparkling kitchen, and gasped when I saw the view. The endless Montauk beach that I'd loved since I was a girl unfurled before me, unobstructed, all mine.

Francesco's arms wrapped around my waist and his body pressed against the back of mine. He kissed the top of my head and led me away from the window and up the stairs. After a quick tour of the second level—four bedrooms, three bathrooms—we reached the master suite.

"And this," Francesco said, my hand in his, "is ours." He closed the door behind us. A four-poster birchwood canopy bed anchored the room, with white sheer drapes cascading to the floor. There was an en suite bathroom, featuring the same white marble that made up the kitchen. I peeked into the walk-in closet that Francesco had thoughtfully filled with a small selection of clothes and shoes, but Francesco reached for my shoulders and swiveled me back around.

"There's something in there for you," he said. As I walked into the closet, he followed me in, leaning against the wall and crossing one leg in front of the other. "It's in an orange box."

I looked up at one of the shelves. A bright, beautiful Hermès box stared back at me. Francesco joined me, grabbed the box, and held it out. I tore open the lid and layers of tissue paper, undid the drawstring of the dust bag, and gasped at the cognac-colored Birkin bag in my hands.

I clutched the bag to my chest. "Two questions. Am I dreaming, and are you insane?"

Francesco put the box back on the shelf and kissed me. "I wanted you to fit in with the Hamptons crowd."

"Oh, babe, that'll never happen," I said as I stared at the soft leather bag with gold hardware. "But I appreciate your willingness to try."

Francesco led me back into the bedroom, where floor-to-ceiling windows allowed sunlight to bathe the room in a hue of yellow gold, presenting the home as it was. A gift. Francesco wrapped his arms around me and laid me back on the bed. I let his body sink into mine as we held each other's gazes. It had been two months since the incident. Two months since I convinced myself I was strong enough to forgive him. Two months since swept it under the rug and vowed to never speak of it again. Like ice slowly thawing, every day that we didn't argue, that he didn't hit me again, led me to trust him more. He traced my jaw and kissed me, his lips lingering.

"Do you like it?" he asked.

"It's unbelievable."

"You remember what you said to me, that first time we came out to Montauk together?"

Tears stung my eyes, because it was so vivid. On my twenty-fourth birthday, we'd come out to Montauk with some friends; we weren't even a couple yet. Beneath the hot, afternoon sun, as the ocean roared in front of us, as the music of the eighties rang from our boom box, I'd told him that if I ever had a house out here someday, I'd know I'd made it.

"We made it," Francesco whispered. But it had nothing to do with our financial success. It was about survival. We'd made it through, and maybe we weren't on the other side just yet, but we were on our way. Trying. He was proving it was a one-time mistake, and I was trying to believe him.

He stretched my arms above my head and interlaced his fingers with mine.

"I just want you to know how much you mean to me," he continued. "When Enzo and I came out here last month to see the house, we talked a lot. About family. Marriage. Having a home. And that's all I want to focus on from now on."

For a moment, my doubts quieted. There was such earnestness in his eyes, such conviction, I knew he meant what he said. Sure, his fame and wild levels of success had gone to his head. How could it have not? But the man in my arms felt like the one I fell madly in love with. The man I adored and trusted with everything in me.

"You know what else you said that day?" Francesco asked. "That you wanted two kids."

I giggled as he kissed a trail down my neck, but I unraveled my fingers and sat up. "Later."

We joined Enzo on the deck, who was smoking a cigar and sipping on whiskey. When I noticed the infinity pool, I tossed my arms up.

"It just keeps getting better," I said, the afternoon wind picking up, blowing my brunette locks in all directions.

"How'd we do?" Enzo asked.

"Well, you boys certainly know how to pick a home, I'll give you that."

Enzo rocked on his heels and pursed his lips. "We're gonna have a lot of good summers here."

Francesco draped one arm around me and kissed my cheek before clapping his hands together. "I'm gonna get us some champagne."

As he disappeared inside, I soaked in the view, the salty air, the flock of seagulls traveling overhead, the family a ways down the beach, covered by a striped umbrella. I only looked away because I felt Enzo's stare on me.

"You happy?" he asked. It was a loaded question, and he knew that, no matter how innocently he framed it.

The house was stunning. A dream come true. It gave me hope for my future with Francesco; we were planting more seeds together, talking about growing our family. He was keeping his promises, and I was falling back in love with him. Later, my mother would tell me that the house was a trap and not a gift. I'd grow to resent that my home was filled with handbags instead of my husband, and I would one day realize that I wasn't falling back in love so much as I was falling for his manipulations. But in that moment, planted in a dreamscape, I was happy.

As happy as someone bleeding out from walking on eggshells could be.

CHAPTER FOUR

SCARLETT

Summer, 2011

"Come on, Pia," I say over the music, glancing in the rearview mirror. Emilio drives us down the winding curve of Old Montauk Highway. In the backseat, Pia is curled up beneath a Hello Kitty blanket, her eyes shut in a defiant protest. But I'm determined to make this final summer the best one, reminiscent of times past, redolent with new memories we'll cherish forever. "Sing the next verse for your mamma."

I turn up the volume, letting Stevie Nicks's voice swirl through the car as she croons "Dreams." But when I look in the mirror again, Pia's scowl taints the sweet melody.

"Absolutely not. You have the worst taste in music," Pia groans, reinforcing her displeasure by crossing her arms.

"Fine." I sigh. "You're in for a solo, then."

Before I even open my mouth, Emilio is laughing and shaking his head. Pia's disapproval is palpable as I belt out the lyrics as loud as I can, as off key as possible, though that's not a difficult feat for me. Pia's glittery, gaudy, operatic voice is purely from the Valenti side. Finally, she caves and joins in, and when the rich, elegant boom of her voice fills the car to the brim, I stop singing and savor the sound. Even Emilio's smile fades as he resigns to enjoy the gift that is his sister's talent.

Her talent, that she's put on the shelf since her senior recital. I don't know what's gotten into Pia—she's every bit the clichéd teenager who won't talk to her mother about anything—but the melodies that used to fill our home and rule her world have gone silent. I tell myself she's resting her voice so she'll be in tip-top shape when she starts at NYU Tisch in the fall, but I know my delusions are just that. Delusions.

I add Pia's vocal hiatus to my list of things to worry about as Emilio pulls into the driveway. Gravel crunches beneath the tires as the car comes to a halt. I stare at the house and soak it all in, taking as many mental snapshots as I can of the lush hydrangea bushes and the wooden swing where I used to rock my babies and nestle close to Francesco. The ocean's song rings loudly from just around the bend, greeting us the way it always has. *Come on in.*

This time it adds: *One last time.*

I stand there for a moment, trying to memorize the lines and angles that make up this place. It's as if the house itself is holding its breath. Like it knows this is our final chapter, too.

Emilio hops out of the SUV and unloads our bags. Pia sheds her blanket and joins me in the driveway, putting her hands on her hips as she stops, tilts her head toward the sky, and basks in the summer sun. Emilio buzzes with restless energy, the kind only the ocean can settle. Montauk made him a surfer at a young age, and I know he's already itching to hit the waves. Pia, my daughter of fire and ice and nothing in between, for once seems to have reached a peaceful middle ground.

And I'm going to be the one to shatter their visions of the perfect summer to come when I say the words out loud. That this is the end. That we'll never come back to this house or the life we've lived here. I'll argue that Montauk will always be here, that we can rent a house next year, but I know the truth. Once you leave a place like this, you don't get it back. As I turn the key and walk into this slice of serenity, when I'm greeted by the blue, roaring ocean just beyond the floor-to-ceiling windows, I'm met with memories that are etched into every crevice of this house.

Memories, many of which I never want to forget, others, I wish I didn't have to remember.

While I open windows to let in fresh air, and Emilio dutifully carries our luggage upstairs, Pia sinks into the couch, glued to her cell phone. I feel the tug of the beach, of the late afternoon heat and the sparkling sea surface, and decide I can work on opening the house later.

"Want to lay out with me?" I ask, refolding blankets and fluffing pillows in the living room.

"Can't," Pia says, tapping away at her phone with acrylic nails that are far too long for my taste. "Athena and Maggie want to meet up at Egypt Beach."

"I'll go too," Emilio calls as he descends the stairs. "Just need to strap my board to the car. Cole's already out. Said the conditions are great today."

This is typical; the kids were always in and out of the house during our trips. But I feel greedy for their time. I realize the only way they're going to understand the importance of experiencing this summer together, as a family, is if I tell them that it's our last. I had planned on giving it a few days, maybe telling them over a dinner of fried fish and beer, but now that we're here, I feel like the clock has started ticking, and every minute counts.

"Okay, guys," I start, drawing in a breath, trying to remember the speech I prepared after I wrote to Enzo. My mind goes blank, and my hands go clammy, and not from the hot, stuffy air. I'll have to speak from the heart and tell them the truth.

Sort of.

"I have to tell you two something. Something important. And I don't want you to get upset, because even though it's sad news, we're going to be okay."

Emilio's hands fly to his hips and his broad presence towers over me. Pia flings her phone aside, disregarding the multiple *pings* that emit from its speakers. I have their full attention, which, regardless of the circumstance, is a rare gift.

"You know Daddy and Zio Enzo bought this house together." I'm met with fast nods that say *get to the point*. "Well, your Zio Enzo has decided he wants to sell it. And if everything goes through, this is going to be our last summer here."

I swallow, though my throat is dry. I hate lying to my kids, really, I do, but as a parent, sometimes slight twists on the truth are necessary. I want my kids to remain kids for as long as possible. They don't need to carry the burdens of my business financials, certainly not the summer before college and law school begins.

As expected, Pia is the first to react. "Can't you, like, say no?"

"Maybe you can talk him out of it." Emilio interjects. He strokes his chin with his palm, and all I see is a boy trying hard to be a man. "Or," he says, snapping his fingers, "you can buy him out. Problem solved."

I let out a laugh, trying to appear light, unfazed. "Hate to break it to you, sugar, but I don't have that kind of money."

"Did he say why?" Emilio presses.

"We haven't had much contact," I say, hoping it sounds casual.

But then Pia's big, innocent eyes brim with tears. "My birthday."

"Sweetie, we're still going to have your birthday here this year," I assure her. "I'm planning something special."

"Yeah, because it's my last one." She swipes the tears from her cheeks. But soon after, her sadness is replaced with rage. "I hate him. First, he just *vanishes* after Daddy's funeral, and now this?"

I should correct her. Tell her not to speak like that about a family member. But the trouble is, I hate him, too.

"I know Enzo has made some"—I pause, searching for a word tame enough to use in front of my children—"questionable decisions. But he's still your father's only brother."

"I don't care who he is. He's a complete asshole."

"Pia!" I yell, though every part of me agrees with her angry assessment of Enzo's character.

"This is our *home*," Pia adds for good measure.

"No, New York City is our home. This is vacation. This is where we come to escape." As the words pour out, I wonder if I'm trying to convince myself more than I am my daughter. "Look, I know it's disappointing. But Montauk isn't going anywhere. We can rent a house every summer and still enjoy it just the same."

"It's not the same!" Pia storms upstairs.

"I just want to make sure you understand what this means," I call after her. "I want us to spend this summer together, as a family."

Her response is a slamming door. Emilio approaches, glancing at his phone, but he tucks it into his pocket when he reaches me. "I'll cancel my plans," Emilio says, his brow furrowed, but I hold up my palm to stop him.

"I still want you to have a good time. I'm just asking for balance, that's all. The older you two got, the less time you spent here at the house. I want us to enjoy whatever time we have left here together, as much as we can."

Emilio nods. Wise beyond his years, I can tell he understands where I'm coming from. We both know that Pia does not. "I'll talk to her."

"I'll order dinner from Clam Bar?" I ask as Emilio takes the steps two by two. He flashes me a thumbs-up.

I retreat to the kitchen. The house hasn't changed an inch; its airy hues and floods of natural light provide a feeling of peace and stillness. Though nothing is ever right in the world, I've flocked to this sandy, salty slice of the earth since I was a girl because it tricks me into thinking maybe it could be. But the energy has shifted. When we used to come here, the moment we kicked off our shoes and ran down to the ocean's shore, time stopped completely. Now, it feels like the clock is moving at double speed, propelling us toward an inevitable outcome we all know will break our hearts in different ways.

But when I stand at the kitchen sink, looking out over the windowsill—a place I've stood many times before, watching my kids play in the sand, seeing my husband jog down the beach for an evening dip in the ocean, soaking in the snowfall, blanketing the earth in an eerie peace when I came here to seek refuge from my real life—as I stare out at that endless, far out horizon, I'm bathed with a thought that exhilarates and terrifies me all the same.

It's sweet, sweet summertime, and for the first time in a long time, I don't know what happens next.

———⁓———

"How does this never get old?" Emilio says mid-chew. A sky painted with pastels hangs above us as we sit around the deck's picnic table, feasting on fish and chips, lobster rolls, and copious amounts of French fries.

I'll regret the swell from the sodium come morning, but I, too, can't deny that there's something to the combination of this meal, this beach, and this company, that tastes like magic. I squeeze a lemon wedge over my helping while Pia eats one fry at a time, staring out at the beach with a glum expression. She spent the day barricaded in her bedroom, only emerging to gather junk food Emilio had picked up at Stop and Shop, while I dove headfirst into housework to keep my mind occupied. By the time the sun started its descent, there wasn't a knickknack left to straighten. Now, as the ocean breeze takes on a coolness, it becomes clear. I'm the head of this family. I have to turn this ship around, me and me alone.

"Hey, chickadee," I say to Pia, interrupting the quiet lull, "I don't want my final memories of this house to be you sitting on the deck, eating fried cod with a puss on your face. Got it?"

She narrows her eyes. "You're insufferable." Emilio kicks her beneath the table. "Ow!"

"Can you not be such a bitch to Mom?" Emilio says, his hands occupied by a heaping lobster roll. "You don't think this is tough for her too?"

"Then she should do something about it."

I set my fork down with a clink. "I'm right here, by the way." Beyond the house, the distant hum of cars whisking by breaks through the evening air. "I want us to have the best vacation we can, given the circumstances. So if there's anything special you want to do, or even if it isn't special, even if you just want to watch a movie all together in the living room, speak now, or forever hold your peace."

Emilio leans in, hesitates, then finally says, "I'd like to cook a Sunday dinner or two."

A startled laugh bursts from my throat. "You? Want to cook?" Pia and Emilio exchange a glance, one of those silent sibling conversations that's loaded with information I'm not privy to. "Would anyone care to catch me up to speed?"

Emilio takes a bite and chews. "Forget it."

My head whips between my kids. What are they hiding from me? "Am I missing something?"

"Uh, yeah," Pia says with an eyeroll. "You're totally clueless. Emilio doesn't *want* to cook. He's *been* cooking."

Slowly, I turn to my son. "What's she talking about?"

He wipes his hands on a napkin, avoiding my gaze. "Nothing. I cooked for the guys in college. There were eight of us in one apartment. Someone had to make sure we didn't survive on ramen and cereal. But you're right." He finally looks at me, and the heaviness in his eyes catches me off-guard. "It's ridiculous."

"No." I place my hand on his arm. My eyes flutter closed for a second before I open them again. "It's just, Daddy was adamant that he didn't want you to feel like you had to follow in his footsteps."

Emilio shrugs. "I don't."

I can't help but admonish myself. I've drilled it into their heads that they can come to me with anything; I've prided myself on knowing my children better than they know themselves. So how could this have slipped through the cracks? What else don't I know about my kids, and why don't they feel like they can tell me everything? I want to press the subject further, but the sounds of gravel crunching and breaks creaking cut through the moment, the sounds too close for comfort. "Did you two order more food?"

It was something they used to do, ordering delivery behind my back and watching me fork over cash with fits of bemused giggles. Now, all I get are silent shakes of the head.

A sharp knock at the door prompts me to rise.

I take a sip of Diet Coke and walk to the front door, already prepared to tell whoever it is that they have the wrong house. But when I
swing open the door, my breath catches. At first, I don't register who's
standing there. I see the dark shape of a man against the fading sun,
the cut of his shoulders, the way he stands, a presence so familiar yet
far away. So impossible. It can't be. But then, my vision catches up
with my heart.

It's just me and him.

Enzo Valenti.

And the million secrets between us.

CHAPTER FIVE

SCARLETT

Fall, 1992

The martini was starting to taste dangerous. Two down, and if I had it my way, three more to go. Maybe then, I could stop thinking about the label life insisted I be branded with.

Victim.

I scoffed as I topped off my glass. The word felt dramatic. My mother had called it verbal and emotional abuse, but what couple didn't fight? What husband didn't explode every now and then, taking out his life's stress when his wife forgot to pick up a prescription? Couples fought. People yelled. Who didn't want to kick and scream sometimes? I'd be a good girl. I'd let him believe I had forgiven him. I wasn't going to be some strong woman who left the man whose hands and words had hurt her. No, I was even stronger than that. I was going to stay. I wasn't about to let a few mistakes, a couple of lapses in judgment, dismantle everything I was building.

I drained the last of my drink and poured another. The ice clinked as I stirred, my gaze fixed on my warped reflection in the curve of the glass. I wanted to smash it to shards. I hated the woman staring back at me.

I had fallen into Francesco's trap, willingly. I'd let him convince me that the house meant something. I let him make love to me on fresh sheets in a room swathed in golden light while he promised me *a new beginning*. I let him drape a Birkin bag on my arm, a trophy of my forgiveness, as if that hunk of soft leather could erase what he'd done.

I took it all, like a fool, wanting to believe that the man I married was somewhere still inside of him. Wanting to believe we weren't irreparably broken.

That had gotten me here, alone in the restaurant we'd named *Amanti*—Italian for *lovers*—while my husband was out playing one.

He was in Miami, making fresh pasta for a house full of celebrities by day, and probably, making fresh promises to the girlfriend he had down there by night. I had no tangible proof he was cheating on me, but rumors were swirling that he had women in every city he traveled to for work. The thought made my throat tighten. What if, despite my misery, he left me? What if he discarded me and the life we were building for someone new and young and shiny?

I tilted my head back and drained my glass like I was in a rush. I couldn't go down the *what if* path, because it always led me to the same, forbidden place.

To Enzo. The first man I'd ever loved even though I wasn't supposed to.

But I was a girl from a chaotic, unstable home, born to a mother who abused martinis in the same manner I was tonight. Enzo opened my eyes to see that anything was possible, no matter where you came from, no matter what you thought of yourself. He was living proof of that, with an inspiring tale of achieving the American Dream of owning his own business. It was easy to fall for someone like that, who could make you feel like you were the center of the universe.

Especially for someone like me, who'd grown up feeling like it didn't matter whether I existed or not. I never thought about how he was married at the time. How he discarded me for the sake of his family. How he broke my heart, only for Francesco to pick up the pieces and put it back together several months later. All I seemed to remember was the way Enzo made me feel.

Happy. Something I hadn't felt in a long time. It was like my mouth forgot how to smile, like my throat no longer knew how to laugh. And that was what sent me on to another martini.

But a creaking sound, followed by footsteps stopped me in my tracks. My motor skills were inebriated, so in the event that someone had broken into the restaurant, I was screwed. I stood up as straight as I could and grabbed a vodka bottle, hiking it above my shoulder, but then I lowered it.

There he was. The man I was daydreaming about.

"Jesus, Enzo," I said with a sigh. I tried to set the bottle down gently, but it landed with a thud. "What are you doing down here?"

"I heard music." His voice sounded gruff, and he was dressed in a pair of gray sweats and a wifebeater tank. Since his messy divorce, he'd been renting the small apartment above the restaurant where Francesco and I used to live. He had a bottle of Macallan in his hand. An empty bottle.

I hadn't even noticed the music until he pointed it out. He joined me behind the bar and lowered the volume, but faint swells of Italian music droned on, softer now. Enzo paused to study me. Me, and the empty glass next to me.

"Why aren't you at home?" I didn't appreciate his accusatory tone. He dropped the empty bottle in the trash bin and fished out another, uncorking it and pouring himself a generous helping.

"Since when can't a woman enjoy a drink alone?" I countered, refilling my own glass.

He arched one of his inky, angular brows. "Looks like you've enjoyed more than *a* drink to me."

I punched his chest with my fist, though he didn't so much as rock backwards. Looking into his eyes, I noticed how bloodshot they were. Half-moons hung beneath his eyes. "You look like shit."

"Thanks, honey. You're looking marvelous yourself." Enzo's throat moved as he downed the whiskey at record speed. "Who's watching Emi?"

"My mom. She stays with me when Fran goes away. She hates me being in that house all by myself."

Enzo refilled his glass.

"What's the matter with you?" I asked.

"What makes you think something's the matter?"

He wiped his mouth with the back of his hand. I raised my brows to say, *You better spill whatever it is you're hiding.* He looked past me as a headlight beamed in through the sheer curtains and a honking horn made a rhythmic song.

"I can't tell you," he said in a low tone. "I haven't even told Fran yet."

"Even if you tried, I bet he wouldn't listen." I uncorked my bottle of vodka. "The *Pasta King* is very busy these days, don't you know?"

"Cut the shit, would you? He's busting his ass to pay for your *homes*. Plural."

I held my tongue and looked away. How tempted I was to confirm his suspicions that his brother was *busting his ass* so much, he had to take out his frustrations by slapping me across the face. But Francesco had made it very clear to me that no one, under any circumstance, was to know. If word got out that America's favorite

Italian chef hit his wife and hurled horrible insults at her, we'd lose it all and then some.

I whisked my glass and the bottle from the bar and walked away. "Enjoy your drink."

"Fine," Enzo said, making me turn on my heel. His glass dangled from his fingertips, and he hung his head back, like he was debating his next move. "It's Claudia."

I rolled my eyes. It was always Claudia. "What'd she do now?"

Enzo reached into a drawer, fished out a pack of cigarettes, and lit one. Smoke curled between us as he came out from behind the bar and leaned his elbows on the back of a barstool. "She wants to move." Enzo nodded, as if he were just learning this information. "She wants to move to Maryland, and she wants to take the kids with her."

"Maryland?" I asked, sliding onto a barstool. "She can't do that. You have a custody agreement."

"I know." Enzo took a drag on his cigarette. I reached out, with a desperate craving, and he placed it between my fingers. "But she wants to be closer to her brother and sisters and their kids. And if I don't agree, she's going to be miserable, and she'll make me and the kids miserable, and who's going to look like the asshole?" He took the cigarette back from me. "You're looking at him."

While Enzo smoked, I drank, like we were on a twin mission to self-destruct. "So what are you gonna do?"

"I'm thinking about following her." He didn't look at me as he said it, as if he knew I'd have some visceral reaction that he didn't necessarily want to deal with. Enzo was trying to forget his problems, not compound them. But eye contact or not, panic started to set in. Enzo was leaving. He was leaving me alone with Francesco. And even though Francesco hadn't laid a hand on me since, my marriage was about as steady as a table with a missing leg. Still standing, but should one more thing be placed on us, we'd collapse.

"You can't." The words fell out of my mouth before I realized what I was saying.

"I what?" Enzo finally looked at me, startled. "Scar, they're my kids. I can't just let Claudia take them from me."

"I know." Logically, I understood. But this wasn't about logic. "But you can't leave."

My chest heaved with a sob and I knew now that the tears had started, there was no turning back. The vodka had worked its magic. I was loose. Even the parts of me I didn't want to slip out. I kept telling Enzo he couldn't leave and somehow, I ended up with his arms wrapped around me while I cried into his chest, the cold metal of his gold chains kissing my skin.

"Hey," he said, gentle as a feather. "Who knew you'd miss me this much?" But he could see it in my eyes that this was no teasing matter. "There something you need to tell me, Scar?"

"I can't." I darted my eyes away. I was afraid he would be able to see the truth there, that it was obvious in my brown irises alone that my husband had hit me.

"You can." His words were like a balm, soothing, calming, exactly what I needed. I looked into those midnight-colored eyes and I was safe, just like I was seven years ago, when I was a young girl with nowhere to go but in his arms.

"You can't tell Fran I told you. I'm serious, Enzo. Promise me."

He took another puff on his cigarette as he nodded, focusing all his attention on me. With my face cupped in his hands, with his eyes peering into mine, the song of New York fell away, as did the memories that haunted the rooms of the restaurant. It was just me and Enzo, the safest place I'd ever known.

"Emilio didn't hit me with his Legos," I said, both my body and my voice trembling. A cold sweat covered my body and adrenaline coursed through my veins. I was making a verbal admission, but it felt equivalent to committing a physical act of murder. Enzo's features blurred as I said, "Your brother did."

"I knew it," he said, quiet. He backed away and slammed his fist against the marble bar. "I fucking knew it." He pointed at me. "You had that look in your eyes, Scar. Like you were scared. Not even of him. Just to be talking to me, to answer my question when I asked you what happened."

"He made me swear not to tell anyone."

"I'm gonna kill him."

"No." I stood up and threw myself against Enzo. "You can't tell him I told you. He'll kill me. He's afraid if this gets out, we'll lose everything."

"Everything?" Enzo held my arms, and it wasn't the alcohol swirling in my bloodstream that made me unsteady, but the intensity of his gaze. "You know what's everything? You. Your son. Your family. I tried to tell him that. Tried to help him learn from my mistakes." He pinched the bridge of his nose and closed his eyes. "I was a shitty husband, but I never laid a hand on my wife."

"He said it would never happen again." I recognized how pathetic I sounded as soon as the softspoken words left my mouth.

Enzo's eyes drifted upward, like he was fitting a final piece into a puzzle. "It all makes sense now. He was so adamant about buying that house. It had to be in Montauk, and we had to buy it *now*. I told him I wanted to look around. Wasn't sure I could swing that big of a down payment right now. What did he do?" He tossed his hands up. "Convinced me, like he always does."

"I'm sorry," I offered, though it came out weak. Now my marriage was costing Enzo, too.

"You have nothing to be sorry for, you hear me?" Enzo's head tilted, sympathy written in his wrought expression. But all he said was my name, like a whisper, like a vow. "What are you gonna do?"

Like two magnets, we inched closer to each other until my hands rested on his shoulders and his on my waist. "Nothing. I can't leave him. He's the father of my son."

"Scarlett, he hit you."

"It's okay."

"It's not. You don't deserve that." Silence danced between us. "Don't you want to be happy?"

Enzo had no idea how badly I wanted that. But there were things more important than happiness. "I want a family more."

"I'll stay if you want me to. If you don't feel," he paused, not wanting to say what came next, "safe. With Fran."

I shook my head, sure. "I would never ask you to stay when I know you need to go."

Enzo's teeth grazed his bottom lip. His eyes bore into mine and I tried to focus on everything else. The smoke curling from the cigarette in the ashtray. The lyrics of my favorite Eros Ramazzotti song, "Un'altra te," humming from the speakers overhead. The wail of a siren on the distance. But it was all in vain. Nothing, no human force, could stop what I had with Enzo.

"So I'm chasing a woman I don't love to another state, and you're staying with a man who smacks you around. All in the name of being good parents. That's some racket, isn't it?"

"How'd we get here?" I whispered as my hands traveled to the nape of his neck.

He leaned his forehead against mine. His breath was warm, whiskey-laced, and all over me. I could feel the rise and fall of his chest, matching mine. "I don't know, but I don't like it here," he said with a dry, humorless laugh.

I could taste it on my tongue, the desire for forbidden fruit. The most delicious varietal, the one I was craving with pure desperation. Everything I wanted to feel, Enzo could make me feel it. Wanted. Important. Worthy. Happy. It was all in his hands and his mouth, and I wanted both all over me. His flame had lit me on fire, and I'd burn to ashes if I didn't satisfy my craving. I could still taste Francesco's last promise on my lips, but all I wanted was for Enzo's mouth to erase it.

"Take me somewhere else," I said, the words barely escaping my lips before his mouth met mine.

Shame would forever scorch me. Guilt would ride my coattails for the rest of my life, and regret would haunt me in the shadows of night. But none of it mattered then, when I closed my eyes and fell into a rhythm like we knew it by heart. Later, when I'd replay the scene in my head, I wouldn't remember who kissed whom first; I would think of it as some magnetic force that pushed us together at the same precise time. I'd think of how delicious that forbidden fruit was, how my craving only grew more intense as he tore my clothes off and carried me upstairs where he laid me down on his bed like I was something precious.

I'd remember the exact moment that I sealed my fate as a sinner: when I screamed out a name that most definitely did not belong to my husband.

CHAPTER SIX

SCARLETT

Summer, 2011

"What the hell are you doing here?" I snap, still trying to register that Enzo is here. Standing mere inches away from me. After four years of *nothing.*

I don't mean for my words to come out so sharp, but I'm not exactly in tune with my motor skills right now. Enzo tends to have that effect on me.

He clears his throat, his gaze flickering past me before meeting my eyes again. "You get one last summer here. I thought I deserved one, too."

I don't have a chance to respond. My kids flank either side of me, ogling their uncle like he's a celebrity.

"Wow, did you two grow up fast," Enzo says.

I soak in the sound of his voice. It's the same as it always was. Rich like velvet. Smooth like olive oil. Pleasurable. Like sex.

"No," Pia starts, and I already dread whatever comes next. "You just haven't seen us in four years."

Enzo exhales, but he doesn't argue. He can't. "Can I come in?"

He steps inside and instinctively, the three of us move back, not just giving him space, but making room for his presence which somehow fills the entire house. And then I see it. A suitcase. A duffel bag stacked on top. My pulse rages like a wild bull. Enzo's not just here to pop in. He's staying.

Here. With me and my kids. At my house.

Our house.

Emilio, being my saving grace, breaks the tension. "Hi, Zi. Good to see you." They do that *bro*-style hug-slash-handshake thing. Enzo pats Emilio's cheek and takes a good look at him.

"Bello guaglione," Enzo says. It's Napoletano for *beautiful boy*, and it's what he's called my son since the day he was born.

I instantly go to war with myself not to cry.

He tries to greet Pia with the same level of affection, but she backs away and crosses her arms. "I'm mad at you."

Enzo blinks those long black lashes that frame his equally as black eyes. "For?"

"For deciding you want to sell our beach house," Pia says. She's a tough cookie, my girl, and though her voice betrays her, she squares her jaw and lefts her chin. "How could you do this to us?"

My heart sinks. Enzo's confusion is written all over his face, and it sends me into a panic. I can't get caught in a lie in front of my children. They'll never trust anything I say ever again. I lock eyes with Enzo, silently begging him to *go with it.* Because we've never needed words to communicate, he does.

"Look, why don't we all sit down, have a drink, and catch up before we get into this house business?" Enzo offers, glancing at me for approval.

"I'm good," Pia says, a coldness in her voice as she tosses her hair behind her shoulder and sashays away. I massage my temples, mortified by her brashness. I raised her to be tough, but I also instilled the concept of respect.

I glance at Emilio. "Why don't you pack up the leftovers, and I'll show Enzo to his room," I suggest.

Emilio nods and takes off, as if he can't escape this awkward interaction fast enough. With the kids gone, I study Enzo. He's dressed in a polo and dark-wash jeans, a far cry from the pinstripe suits he used to live in. Tattoos peek out from beneath the sleeves of his shirt, and I'm ravenous with curiosity. What could have been so important that he felt the need to document it on his body in permanent ink? I have a hard time reconciling the more rugged version of Enzo with the coiffed man I used to know, but there's remnants of the old him—the inky black hair slicked away from his face, his self-assured stance, that devilish, borderline arrogant smirk that I want to smack away.

"Come with me," I say before turning on my heel and leading the way upstairs. Though Francesco and I always occupied the master suite, Enzo claimed the second largest bedroom—a space with an unobstructed view of the beach and a sleek fireplace. The décor mirrors his masculine taste, with a modern, matte-black four-poster bed anchoring the room. Though this house is just as much his as it is mine, I reach the room first, grip the door handle, and close it behind us. "And I'll ask you again, what the hell are you doing here?"

Enzo digs his hands into his pockets and stares out the window. Stars speckle the dusky sky that's still hanging onto the last remnants of daylight, while a family down the beach struggles to launch a kite. "You told the kids selling was *my* idea?"

"I couldn't exactly tell them that their mother is a complete financial disaster."

Enzo swivels around. He doesn't say anything, but I can see it in his eyes. He's scanning me, searching for changes in a woman he knows far too intimately. "You look great."

"Thanks," I say coolly, trying to conceal the spark of warmth I feel at his compliment. "I know."

He lets out a short, amused exhale. "You're as vain as ever."

If I'm wax, Enzo is a flame thrower. But I stay rooted where I am, refusing to soften. "Look, I don't have the time or energy to play this little reminiscing game. I came here because I wanted to enjoy one last summer with my kids. I will not let you ruin it."

"Scar," he says, his voice low as he inches closer, "we're family."

I scoff and cross my arms, feeling as defiant and immature as my daughter. "And you really act like it."

Enzo closes the space between us, his hands cupping my arms. That's when I catch it, his signature scent of citrus and musk. One whiff, and it's a bright, spring day in 1986. I'm twenty-three, looking for a way to change the hand life has dealt me. I land at a restaurant named Valenti's and a man named Enzo changes my life, not just because he offers me a job, but because it's him. The stranger I recognize the instant we lock eyes. In a split second, my world tilts off its axis.

Twenty-five years later, and he still has the same effect on me.

And judging from the spark in his eyes and the way his smirk unfurls into a devastating smile, he knows it, too.

"Hi, Scar," he says, our eyes truly meeting for the first time tonight. It's disarming, to feel his skin on mine, to breathe the same air, to peer into the eyes of someone who's been nothing more than a memory for four years. I want to hide, because I know Enzo can see it all. My weaknesses, my worries, all the places I'm most vulnerable. That's the thing about Enzo.

I've never been able to hide from him, no matter how hard I try.

I bite my bottom lip. "Hi, Enz," I say, begrudging the way his name slips past my lips as if no time has passed at all, as if all the resentment I've been harboring has drifted out to sea, never to be found again.

"How are you really doing?"

"Isn't it obvious?" I dart my eyes away. "Just swell."

He squeezes my arms. "Hey, everything's gonna work out." I watch as Enzo whisks his duffle bag off the floor, drops it onto the bed, and unzips it. He's nine years my senior, but he looks like he stopped aging at forty-five. In fact, his arms are more defined than I remember, his stomach tauter, his skin a radiant bronze, like the years have only multiplied his good looks.

A string of expletives runs through my mind like a ticker tape.

But marvels of his appearance fall to the wayside when he pulls an open envelope out of his duffle bag.

"Your letter," he announces, as if it needs an introduction. No, I recognize the swirls and curves of my own handwriting in a split, and instead of melting from Enzo's flame, I ignite.

"Why would you bring that here?" I gesture toward the letter and find myself backing up, as it's a living, monstrous being. "I wrote it. I don't need you to remind me what it says."

He pulls out the sheets of paper decorated with my innermost thoughts and squints, holding it several inches away from his eyes. *"But like everything else, those times are gone. We owe this to him. We let him down before, Enzo. Are we really going to let him down again?"* Enzo holds up the letter like it's evidence. "This is not the Scarlett I know."

"That's because you don't know me anymore."

Enzo inches closer at a slow, wandering pace. "Oh, yes, I do." Now, he's so close, we're nearly nose to nose. "The Scarlett who wrote all the other letters you sent me—and I know you probably don't want me to bring those up—*that's* the real you. Not this hopeless shell. Not this pious widow."

Enzo's right on one count. Our secret letters are the last thing I want to talk about, especially with my kids lurking around. A few months before Pia was born, before the age of texts and emails, Enzo had moved to Maryland to be near his adolescent children. The letter-exchanging began shortly after, and I'd be lying if I said it was just a simple way to stay in touch.

The truth is, Enzo was there for me when no one else was.

Our letters are tangible proof of that. Proof that my life wasn't as pretty as I made it seem, that my marriage wasn't as strong as I pretended, that I wasn't as happy as I let on. Talking about them after all this time drags me beneath the murky waters of shame and guilt and regret.

How foolish was I to think that I could cross a line and not pay the consequences?

I hear my children's voices drifting up from the deck below, though the drum of my pounding heartbeat drowns them out.

"I have news for you, Enzo," I say, swallowing, though my throat is bone dry. "That letter in your hands is the real me. The new me, okay? And sure, maybe I leaned on you in the past. But *this* Scarlett thinks you've got a lot of damn nerve thinking you can just waltz back into my life like nothing happened, and everything'll be peachy keen."

"I know you're mad at me."

"Mad doesn't even begin to cover it."

Enzo puts his palms up in surrender. "And that's why I won't object to you selling the house. I know you're in a bind. But come on, Scar. It sounds like you need me."

"I have never *needed* you." I say it slow, deliberate, like I want him to feel every syllable. Like I want the words to cut. For a flicker of a second, I see my statement land in the way his jaw tightens, how something in his expression wavers. My stomach twists. Because it's so not true, and we both know it.

"You've never been a good liar."

My chest rises and falls, unsteady, as my lungs refuse to draw in a deep breath. Centimeters separate our noses, and in Enzo's eyes, I see the man I used to know. The one who could fix anything. The place I'd go to when I needed to feel safe. The way he left four years ago erased all of it, every good thing I used to think of him. "I can't be in this house with you. I'll put you up at a hotel."

"With what money?"

"Fuck you, asshole."

"I've missed you, too, Scarlett."

The heat between us is so tangible, thick like summer humidity, I feel like I could reach out and grab it with my fist. "You are not to breathe a word of *anything,* and I mean *anything,* to my kids. You got that? Not the restaurant, not the fact that I wrote to you, not those godforsaken letters that I wish I never wrote. Do you understand me?"

"Loud and clear, Mrs. V," he says, rocking on his heels.

But as I turn to leave, something stops me. I turn around and clock his expectant glance. "What did you ever do with those letters I sent you?"

He shrugs. "I kept them."

"All of them?"

He nods.

My entire being goes aflame. "Where?"

He smiles as he shows me out of his room. "Don't worry, honey. Not here."

His stare burns into me as I leave, but I don't look back. I retreat to my room and slip into my closet. Beneath a cabinet, I pry loose a taped key. I stab it into the lock and pull open the door. There they are. Every single piece of correspondence Enzo has ever sent me. I sift through them, and the various dates stare back at me, spanning more than a decade. For a moment, my anger flickers into something else. Awe. Amazement, even.

Our letters are the only tangible proof of what we have, and evidently, that means something to both of us. I kept his and he kept mine.

All, except the one I never sent.

"KNOCK, KNOCK," I SAY as I step into the church office at St. Therese of Lisieux.

Father Tom glances up from behind rimless glasses, his eyes lighting up when he sees me. His office is a mess of books stacked in uneven piles and mounds of loose papers.

I place a large box of pastries on top of it all with a knowing smile. "Ferrara's finest."

Father Tom leans back in his chair and pats his round belly, as if making room for what's to come. "Ah, now summer has officially begun." He gestures to the chair opposite his. "Have a seat."

"How are you doing, Father?" I ask, tugging at the hem of my linen shift dress before sinking into the worn leather chair.

"Better, now that I've got *sfogliatelle*," he says as he cuts the string. The room fills with the aromas of powdered sugar and almond paste. "We're blessed with great bagels out here. Italian pastries? Not so much." I laugh as he digs into a mini cannoli. "And how are you doing? The kids?"

"We're hanging in there," I say, shifting in my seat. "I was hoping we could talk. About something personal."

"Of course." He raises a powdered sugar encrusted index finger. "Though you didn't have to bribe me with pastries."

"Hey, that's our tradition, not a bribe." He lets out a polite laugh as I clear my throat and try to calm my racing heart. I avert my gaze, but his calming presence lets me know I don't have to. "You remember Enzo, my husband's older brother?"

He nods. "The dark one."

I smile at his description of Enzo, because it's so simple yet accurate. While Francesco looked like he was drenched in a hue of gold, Enzo was all dark, from his hair to his eyes, to his olive skin. "Yes, that's the one."

Father Tom leans his elbows on his desk. "What about him?"

"Well, we didn't exactly leave off on the best of terms. After my husband died, Enzo ran off without a trace. Never checked in on me or the kids, or the restaurant." This version of events is abbreviated, but enough to paint the picture. "I was angry."

Father Tom narrows his eyes. "Why?"

A bitter laugh escapes me. "We were always …" I pause, my throat constricting, "close. Not to mention, he left me with everything. Raising my kids, running the restaurant. I had no choice. But he chose to walk away when my kids and I needed him most."

"You feel abandoned," Father Tom supplies.

I'm overcome with vindication. I gesture sharply, as if presenting cold, hard evidence. "Yes. Exactly. He abandoned us."

"But was it his *job* to stick around?"

I feel like we're in a dance and I'm on my toes and don't know the choreography. Just as I open my mouth to argue, the church organ cuts through the silence, its dark notes curling around us like a warning. What am I doing here, spilling my guts to my priest of all people? But his light gray eyes are focused on me.

"We're Italian, Father. Family is what we *do*. No matter how hard it gets." I scoot to the edge of my seat. "The restaurant's struggling. The only way to save it is to sell our home out here. And Enzo—who owns half of it, by the way—has shown up out of nowhere. He wants to spend this last summer in the house with me and the kids. But I'm just so…so angry."

"Do you blame him for the restaurant's troubles?"

"I'm a savvy businesswoman, but I've been a bit preoccupied these last few years. I can't say it's *all* his fault. But I don't think we'd be in this predicament if he'd stuck around. He could've picked up the slack if I needed to take some time off to grieve."

"But perhaps he needed time to grieve, too," Father Tom counters. He sits back in his chair and opens his hands. "We all handle grief and loss differently. Some of us like to lean on a support system. Others seek isolation. A fresh start, if you will. It sounds like Enzo was of the latter."

"But he hurt me."

Father Tom presses his lips together. "How often do people hurt others due to their own self-interest? Knowingly and unknowingly?"

The question zings me, not because I've been on the receiving end of that hurt, but because I've inflicted it.

"Scarlett," he continues, his tone warm and compassionate, "what our faith really boils down to is forgiveness. We're forgiven, yes, but we're also called to forgive. If I may be so bold, I'd say that this summer is one of chances. Some people have to find forgiveness in silence, but you have the opportunity to actively forgive and mend this relationship."

My gaze falls to my lap. I gnaw on the inside of my cheek. I've forgiven the unforgiveable before, and it's never benefited me the way Catholicism touts. "I don't know if I have it in me to forgive him."

"None of us do. We have to ask God for the strength. He forgives us, no matter *what* we do," he reminds me. An odd feeling settles in my gut. I *know* this, but I'm not so sure that unfathomable blanket of forgiveness applies to me. Not when I've done the unforgiveable. Not when I can't even forgive myself.

"I know it's not easy to let things go." Father Tom stares at me until I meet his gaze. "But make no mistake about it, Scarlett. This summer? It's a gift."

But I leave St. Therese feeling no more peaceful than I did when I entered.

Because this summer doesn't feel like a gift at all.

Enzo's unannounced arrival is a gust of wind against my fragile house of cards. And even though it's still standing, I can hear it. The rumble, the rattle, the tremor of something about to give way.

The inevitable collapse to come.

CHAPTER SEVEN

SCARLETT

Summer, 2011

"Hi, boys," I say as I step onto the deck and slide the glass door closed behind me. When I left this morning for church, the beach was vacant. Now, it's speckled with chairs and umbrellas and people walking along the shoreline. I raise my hand to shield my eyes from the sun and join Emilio and Enzo, who are seated at the table playing two-card poker. An ashtray sits between them, and the scent of cigars permeates the air. "What are we playing for?"

"If I win," Emilio starts, eyes still focused on his ace and two, "Zio's going to attempt surfing. If Zio wins, I have to clean out the shed."

"By yourself," Enzo adds for good measure.

I rest my hands on my son's shoulders. "Make sure you wear gloves. God only knows what's in there, and I don't want you needing a tetanus shot."

Emilio swivels around to reveal an exasperated expression. "Have some faith in me, Ma."

I hold up my hands in defense. "I'm just saying, your uncle was a gambling addict."

Enzo bites his bottom lip and looks away, muttering something under his breath.

"What was that, Enzo?" I ask.

"It just amazes me," Enzo says with mock sincerity, "the way you know exactly how to make a man feel good about himself."

I laugh and step aside. "Have you seen Pia?"

Emilio nods toward the beach. "She's been laying out since ten."

"Without sunblock, I'm sure." I drift away from their card game, whisking a bottle of sunscreen out of the trunk where we keep pool noodles and goggles that haven't been used since my kids were little. I kick off my sandals and start down the beach. Halfway down, I spot my daughter, worshiping the sun on a neon pink-and-green beach towel. I reach her, envious that her olive skin has already turned brown, though her cheeks and nose are red. I twist the cap of the sunblock and spray her, sending her jolting up.

"Are you serious?" she whines, wiping the shine with the corner of her towel.

"Scoot." As she sits up and shifts to the top of her towel, I sink down beside her and hand her the bottle. "Skin cancer is real, and I don't want you to get it."

She rolls her eyes and flips onto her stomach. "You're just jealous because I tan easier than you."

"Oh, Pia." I sigh as I lean back on my elbows, squinting beneath the beaming sun. "I wanted to see how you're feeling."

"Do I look sick to you?"

"I mean about Enzo being here."

She hugs her knees to her chest and glances at the house. Emilio and Enzo are still hunched over their cards. "I'm still pissed." But when she looks at me a moment later, her eyes brimming, I see sadness rather than anger.

"Honey." I reach out and draw her close. "What is it?"

"This is the first time that Zio's been here since Daddy died. Remember they used to come together on Tuesdays?"

I rest my chin on top of her head as the memories come back to me, of Enzo and Francesco barreling into the house together, quipping back and forth in their native Napoletano dialect as they escaped the stresses of our life back in Manhattan, even if just for a few days during the quiet lulls of the week. "I didn't even think about that." The truth is, when Enzo showed up, I was too overwhelmed by the shock of his arrival to think about what, and who, was missing. But now that I know Pia's anger is only a mask for sadness, my concern grows. "You haven't been feeling any attacks coming on, have you?"

Pia stiffens. We haven't talked about her panic attacks in what feels like forever. After Francesco passed, Pia's anxiety became so intense, her attacks so frequent, that she slept in my room for two years. Thanks to a very good, very expensive therapist, she was able to put her body's physical reaction to such a great loss behind her at the start of junior year. "No," is all she replies, barely putting my own anxiety to rest.

Families and couples and morning joggers pepper the beach as the sea sprays its mist and the seagulls call out, alerting one another of stray fries and chips, providing a brief distraction from the weight of Pia's admissions.

"So that's why you're avoiding Enzo," I conclude. "Because it makes you miss Daddy?"

Pia shrugs against me. "I guess. He reminds me of Dad. Not the way he looks, obviously, but him and Dad were like a package deal. I just—" She cuts herself off and retreats.

ALL MY LOVE, ALWAYS

"Tell me."

"I don't know if this is bad," she says, her voice low, "but I try not to think about Daddy."

I tuck a lock of hair behind her ear and cup her face. "I understand. Because when you think about him, it upsets you." Like a fuzzy picture becoming clear, it all clicks. "Is that why you haven't been singing lately? Because it makes you think about him?"

The thought horrifies me. Music has been my daughter's life since she was eight; it's as if she thinks in melodies instead of words. Songs live at the tip of her tongue. Or at least, they used to. Music, particularly opera, was the shared language between Francesco and Pia, their secret messaging system I wasn't included in. My mind reels back, trying to remember when the shift started, when her vigor for her art started to fade. I only noticed it in the last few months, but there's a chance I was too caught up in my own grief that I failed to notice.

Pia gives me a small, reassuring smile. "I just need a break, Mom."

"A break is fine." My shoulders relax an inch. "And if you need more time to warm up to Zio Enzo, I understand that, too. Why don't you and Emi go out with some friends tonight?"

"But you said you wanted to spend as much time with us as possible."

I wave away her concern. "That was before Enzo ambushed our summer."

As Pia laughs, a loud shout comes from the deck. We turn to look, and Emilio stands, smacks his palm against the table, and throws his arms up. "What's his deal?" Pia asks.

My mouth twists into a wry grin as Enzo wraps an arm around my son and rustles his hair, as if no time has passed at all.

"Looks like your brother just lost a bet," I say as Pia stretches back out, a deliberate rejection of watching her brother bond with the man who's unsettled her in ways neither one of us is willing to admit.

But while my kids are on opposite ends of the spectrum about Enzo's return, I'm caught somewhere in the middle. I curse the soft spot in my heart, damn the curiosity raging in my mind. I try to remember that this summer isn't about reconnecting; it's about business. Cold, hard numbers. A transaction.

I shouldn't enjoy the ease at which Enzo has slipped back into the house, how effortlessly he falls into conversation with my son. I shouldn't be anticipating tonight, when the kids will go out and leave us alone, together. I shouldn't care about Enzo at all.

But oh, oh do I.

WE MAKE RESERVATIONS, BECAUSE neither of us can cook. Ironic, I realize, for two lifelong restaurateurs to lack the skills to boil water, but when it came to Amanti, Enzo and I brought the charisma, not the cuisine. In my bedroom, I glance at the large, shiplap clock on the wall to see how much time I have left to get dressed. Thirteen minutes on the nose, all of which I'll utilize. I peel off yet another dress and toss it to the pile of rejects on the ground, huffing and slightly sweaty from trying on different outfits. Sifting through the hangers, I pull out a floral maxi dress with an open back. I lift the straps over my shoulders and glance at my reflection in the full-length mirror. I look different out here in Montauk. My black hair is down, air dried to its natural wave, and I can afford to wear less makeup thanks to my slight tan, though I'll never forego my winged eyeliner. I can't say it's the truest portrayal of myself; I'll always see myself as the blazer-clad lady with a French twist. But I can't deny, as I slip into a pair of nude sandals and pluck out a matching clutch, that this version exists, too.

This version, who cares way too much about what she looks like. I go into the bathroom for a final onceover. With two minutes to spare, I spritz some Hanae Mori perfume on my neck, add a pop of blush, and swipe a fresh coat of gloss over my lips. I try to tell myself, as I switch off the lights and close my bedroom door behind me, that vanity has always been my Achilles heel, and it has nothing to do with the fact that I'm going out with Enzo.

To dinner.

Alone.

Music drifts through the house as I head downstairs. I recognize it as an old Eros Ramazzotti song. It comforts me that not *everything* has changed; the Italian pop idol's unmistakable voice has been part of my family's musical rotation since the early nineties. I find Enzo in the living room, sipping on a glass of wine as he sifts through our CD collection. He swivels around and we scan each other up and down. Vanity is his cardinal sin of choice, too, and it shows. A knit polo hugs his frame, the creamy tan color popping against his brown skin. One hand is shoved into the pocket of his jeans, and the gold chains that have always lived around his neck still reside there. He's as sharp as ever, but there's one thing about this new Enzo that still jars me.

"I just can't believe you have tattoos now." But more, I can't believe they suit him. I tilt my head as I approach, trying to read one of the inscriptions on his arm, but it's partially covered by his sleeve.

"And I can't believe you're wearing your hair down for once," he quips back, feigning wide-eyed shock. He hands me his glass of wine and I drain the last of its contents. He grabs the keys from the side table and swishes the key ring around his index finger. "You ready?"

I nod, and he locks up behind us. Ever a gentleman, he opens the car door for me, but he doesn't immediately close the door. "Nice dress."

He lingers a moment longer, his fingers curling around the edge of the door, his smirk half endearing, half daring. When I lean back and feel the warm leather against my bare back, I feel ashamed. *Definitely too much.* I want to run inside and change, but Enzo hops into the driver's side and takes off, sealing my fate. Our night is already in motion, and I'm stuck in it, bare backed and burning.

Scarpetta Beach bustles beneath a periwinkle sky, the fire pits surrounded by people munching on bar snacks and sipping overpriced cocktails. When Enzo's fingertips graze the small of my back as he leads me toward the host stand, my senses heighten.

I can't wait to sit down and have a drink.

"Reservation under Valenti," Enzo tells the pretty hostess with brown ringlets for hair.

"Ah, *tu sei Italiano*," she replies as she taps away at the reservation system.

"*Napoletano*," Enzo says with pride. "*Di dove sei?*" he asks her as she leads the way to our table. Is she strutting like that on purpose, or do all Italian women have an effortless allure? Except for me, of course—the half-Italian anomaly that I am, for whom nothing comes effortlessly.

"Calabria," she tells him. Our table overlooks the beach, and she pulls out the chair for me to sit.

Enzo taps his forehead. "*Capa tosta.*" Hard head, the stereotype of everyone who hails from the tip of Italy's boot.

"*Veramente.*" The girl laughs a little too hard as she hands us our menus, and her high-pitched harmony grates my nerves. Enzo's still got the deadly combo of movie star looks with movie star charm. "*Buon appetito.*"

I watch Enzo watch the girl strut away and roll my eyes. He's older now, but he clearly hasn't matured. "I see you've still got it," I say as I pretend to read my menu.

"It's always nice to meet a *paisana.*"

I shoot him a look that says *yeah right*, and he responds with a wink that lights up his eyes.

The bastard. I focus on the menu. Really focus on it, from every ingredient to the absurd prices. Then, a waiter approaches to take our drink order.

"My …" Enzo starts, his smile faltering just enough for me to notice. I feel every moment of that split second of hesitation, of him trying to figure out what to call me. But just as quickly, he recovers. "She'll have a Grey Goose martini, shaken, extra dry with a twist, and a little bit dirty."

He rattles it off like it's second nature, like he's been ordering on my behalf for years. I freeze, soaking in his proud smile. He raises his brows in a silent question. *Did I get it right?*

My mouth parts, but no words come. I nod, though I'm frozen.

"And I'll do a Manhattan," he orders for himself.

The waiter takes off and Enzo leans forward, resting his forearms on the table. The space between us shrinks. Suddenly, we're not in a crowded restaurant overlooking an endless beach. It's just us, and our little world that no one else knows about.

I swallow and force my voice to come out even. "How the hell did you remember that?"

"It's only the most complicated martini order known to mankind," Enzo says with a shrug, trying to be casual. "Hard to forget."

But there's a softness in his eyes I can't ignore, and something tightens in my chest. I trace the edge of the empty glass in front of me, soon to be filled with something strong enough to make my reservations fade, if only for a night.

I look away and exhale, "Oh, Enzo," not realizing I had been holding my breath. At once, the thickness lifts and though we might look like we're on a date, we're just two grown adults having dinner together out of forced proximity. "So you've spent the last four years breaking hearts, hm?"

"Breaking walls," he corrects me as he leans back in his seat. "I'm in construction now."

I pluck a piece of bread from the basket between us and arch a brow. "I didn't think the mafia existed anymore."

He lets out a snort as he drapes his napkin across his lap and swirls his cube of focaccia in olive oil. "Can you ever be serious?"

"Now why would I want to do that?" The waiter drops off our cocktails and we raise our glasses to each other.

"To catching up," Enzo toasts.

I bite my lip, swallow my pride, and clink my glass against his. "Damn, that's good," I say after savoring that first crispy sip that never loses its luster. "So go on. You're in construction, and that's not code for something else?"

"Just sort of fell into it," he explains. "Bought myself this little bungalow in Sarasota when I first left New York, a few blocks from the beach. Fixed it up, added an addition, and sold it for more than twice what I paid. I kept flipping houses, a few at a time, and then I started buying lots. Built and sold six homes from the ground up. Got my own crew and everything."

This information sinks me deeper into my chair. Enzo's always been resourceful, savvy when it comes to business. He took a small *trattoria* gifted to him by his then in-laws and turned it into the grand restaurant that was Valenti's. When his ex-wife, Claudia, won it in the divorce, he joined me and Francesco at Amanti, elevating what was already a successful restaurant into a legendary Manhattan establishment. But maybe I never gave Enzo enough credit. I'd thought his talent was limited to restaurants. Evidently, everything Enzo touches turns to gold.

A fact that reels resentment back to the forefront. If Enzo hadn't abandoned me to build his fortune in Florida, we wouldn't be sitting here right now, offloading our joint investment just so I can claw my way out of a canyon of debt. But it's not just resentment. It's envy, sharp, stinging. Because while he's been out building something new, I've been stuck holding on to what was. Is that why he looks so carefree? Why, despite his age, his face has barely lined, and his black hair is speckled with only a few strands of gray? Because he has a freedom I don't?

Because he let go while I held on?

"That's wonderful," I force out in my most genuine of tones.

He gives me a look that says he knows there are far less pure emotions behind my perfunctory smile.

"Enough about me," he says after he orders our meal—halibut for him, seared scallops for me. "What have you been up to these last four years?"

Like a turtle shrinking into its shell, I avert my gaze, trying to hide. "Same old."

"Come on."

"I'm serious. Mothering my kids, mothering the staff. That's it." But there's a seriousness to his expression, maybe even a hint of remorse.

I draw in a jagged breath through my nose. "Pia had a difficult time after Fran died. She would have these attacks. A few times she even fainted. She thought something was really wrong with her, like that she got Fran's bad heart or something. I knew she didn't, but I had to prove it to her. I spent the first two years after he died taking her to doctors and therapists." Unloading this to Enzo feels like taking a Mack Truck off my chest. Is it my imagination, or am I breathing deeper? "Then slowly, she got better and started sleeping in her own room again. Emilio was our rock. Still is."

"He's such a great kid," Enzo agrees with a rueful grin. "They both are."

I take a drawn-out sip of my cocktail until I can no longer handle the vodka's sting. "And that's my sad little story. Can we move on?"

I set my drink down and rest my hand on the glass's base. Enzo covers my hand with his, a silent reminder that I haven't been touched by a man in four long, lonely years, a tether to something I lost. My pulse spikes, but I don't pull away. "I'm sorry, you know."

"For?"

"For leaving you." He runs his thumb across my knuckles and electricity moves up and down my spine. "Sounds like you went through a lot with the kids, and that's probably why things fell apart at the restaurant."

"That's exactly why." When our appetizers arrive, neither of us dares to pick up a fork. "I'm only one person. You know how crazy I am about my kids. I had to prioritize Pia. By the time I went back to work full time, everything was already in shambles. The debts were racking up, covers dwindling. All I could do was try to survive. I know what I need to do to turn the place around," I tell him, my voice growing stronger. "I just need the money."

"And you'll get it," he assures me. "I found this realtor, and she's supposed to be amazing. Came highly recommended. She wants to come by tomorrow afternoon for a tour of the house."

I draw back my hand, remembering what this is. The end. "Sounds great."

We spend the rest of our meal catching up on other topics. Enzo fills me in on his kids' lives—Little Enzo, who's not so little anymore, is married with a child and lives in New Jersey. He still has a touch-and-go relationship with his middle daughter, Antonella, and his twenty-six-year-old baby, Maria, lives in Baltimore City with three other girls, to which he admitted, he worries about her safety incessantly. It's all very civilized, and dare I say, comfortable, until we reach the topic I've been avoiding all night.

"There's been no one else since Fran?" Enzo asks me, glancing up at me from behind the dessert menu. "Really, I'm not trying to butter you up, but look at you."

The wine has loosened me up. I toss my hair behind my shoulders and say, "Irresistible. I know."

He gets a kick out of this, but he still expects an honest answer.

I feel the weight of my wedding rings on my left hand. I haven't made an attempt to stop wearing them, and as I twist them around my finger, I'm not sure I ever will. "I'm not as good at moving on as you."

His smile fades, and is replaced with a slow, revelatory nod. "I deserve that."

"You never thought about me?"

"Try all the time.".

"Then why didn't you reach out? I was right there, waiting. The whole time."

"Scar—"

But our waiter interrupts us. Shaken out of his thoughts, Enzo orders us espressos and dessert, and hands back the menu. I'm grateful for the interruption; it's better we don't have this conversation.

"Look at that, you lucky bastard," I say, downing the last remnants of wine. "Saved by the semifreddo."

———

IF THERE'S ONE THING I hate more than anything, it's silence. My greatest foe, the monster that haunts me, lurking around every corner. Because where there's silence, there are thoughts, none of which do me any good. And right now, as the dark two-lane road stretches ahead of us, silence wraps its arms around me and whispers all the things neither of us dare to say.

Enzo drums his fingertips against the steering wheel, and soon after, he hums the same tune that was playing when we left.

"Still like Eros, hm?" I ask, desperate to cut the tension.

"Saw him in concert a couple of years ago in Rome. It was nuts," Enzo tells me. "You wouldn't believe the size of the crowd."

"You went to Rome?" Disappointment stings me. What else have I missed? What else has he experienced without me? Which parts of him are still unknown? He tells me he went with a cousin of his from Naples, but I don't hear the funny recounting of their Roman adventure. I hear the broad strokes of stories I'll never truly know; I see a picture that'll never be fully colored in.

I know, deep in my bones, that Enzo and I will never know each other the way we used to.

The car rocks above the uneven gravel as Enzo pulls into the driveway. My limbs feel languid, and I don't trust myself to get out of the car just yet, so I sit, leaning back against the headrest. I bask in my slight inebriation, and I dream of taking a Xanax to calm the racing thoughts that have penetrated the efforts of the alcohol I consumed.

"Scar?" Enzo says.

I turn my head and blink a few times. "Yes?"

"You drank too much, didn't you?"

A smile tugs at my lips. "Mhm."

He gets out and comes around to my side. When he opens the door, he leans over, undoes my seatbelt, and puts a hand on my thigh to twist me out of my seat, though my flesh is concealed by the drapery of my dress. He holds my waist until my feet hit the ground, and his hands don't leave me as he guides us to the door, unlocks it, and gets us safely inside. The house is dark and still—more silence that I detest—and the tension returns to its rightful place. Between us.

There's always something between us.

"Want me to help you upstairs?" Enzo asks.

I look down the hall at the kitchen and point. "I'm just gonna—"

"No you're not."

"You don't even know what I was going to say."

"But I know what you want to do. Pop a Xanax and go to sleep. Not happening."

The ocean rumbles in the near distance, echoing the way my brain sounds right now. Angry. Thrashing. Filled with longing. I cross my arms in front of my chest. "You can't boss me around. I'm not your wife."

"No, but you're my—"

"Your what? What am I, Enzo? Because you couldn't think of what to call me earlier, and you're still struggling to find the word." He doesn't answer. I inch forward, daring him to say it, to tell the truth. "What am I to you?"

Enzo's eyes search my face. He swallows hard. "You're someone I care about. Deeply."

I scoff and drop my arms. "Coward."

"Takes one to know one."

"What are we—in fifth grade?"

"If there's anyone who's an expert at evading the truth," Enzo says, staring down his nose at me, "it's the woman I'm looking at right now."

I stomp away to the kitchen where I swing open the cabinet containing ibuprofen, Dramamine, and my beloved tranquilizers. With great defiance, I make a show of opening the bottle and depositing a little peach-colored pill onto my tongue. It's tiny and bitter, and I don't even need water. My body knows this act all too well.

"Scarlett, the only person you're hurting by doing that is yourself," he yells after me as I brush past him and jog up the stairs. He doesn't follow me, and like my own shame burned my back earlier, now it's replaced with his stare.

My vision blurs and I barely make it into my room before the dam of my tears bursts open. Because it's not just the substances that are hurting me.

It's the secrets. The ones that have been tied around my ankle like a heavy anchor, dragging me down for far too long.

The ones, I know, are rising dangerously close to the surface.

CHAPTER EIGHT

SCARLETT

Fall, 1992

I knew two things. I was extremely hungover, and I wasn't where I was supposed to be. My vision was blurry as I blinked awake. Sunlight snuck through the slats of the blackout shades, though the room was still dark. My head pounded with a relentless headache, and as I stared at the ceiling, I became keenly aware of the feeling of circles being drawn on my bare skin.

I glanced down. Slices of black hair peeked through my fingers. A gold chain was draped across my stomach.

Enzo. Enzo was the one tracing my skin with his fingertips. An overwhelming panic surged through my body as the reality of what I'd done hit me all at once.

I screamed. It was completely unintentional yet unavoidable, the only appropriate response given the situation. There were no words to rectify this. No rationale. I reached for the comforter and covered myself as Enzo woke out of his deep slumber. Blinking away the sleep in his eyes that were still puffy from the whiskey he'd consumed a few hours ago, he took a good look at me.

"Shit." Enzo scrambled away from me as if the bed was on fire. "Oh my God."

"Oh, no, no, no," I said, waving my index finger. "One of us has to remain calm and it sure as hell isn't going to be me." He said nothing else. The only sound was that of my shallow, uneven breath. "Did we really—"

"You don't remember?"

"I was drunk!" Outside, the city sounded alive and awake, going about its normal bustling routine, completely oblivious to the irreparable mistake I'd just made.

"So was I." He looked shaken as he smoothed his hair away from his face. "I slept with my brother's *wife*."

"I'm the one who's *married*. I'm an adulteress." I flopped back into the pillow. "We're both going to hell for this, I hope you know that. It's over for us."

"We have to tell him."

I bolted upright. "What? Are you insane? We can't do that."

"He's my *brother*. I can't lie to him for the rest of my life."

"You don't know that," I snapped. "You haven't tried. And that's what you need to do. I need you to try, Enz." I reached for his arms and squeezed them for emphasis, but he pulled away as if my touch repulsed him. Tears sprung to my eyes. "I know you don't want to lie to him, but please, do it for me, Enzo. If he finds out, I'll lose everything that matters to me. My baby," I whispered. "Do it for my Emilio."

Enzo went quiet, as if he too were trying to wrap his mind around the fact that we'd done the unthinkable. The unforgiveable. By the time I looked at him again, he was fully dressed, standing by the dresser, lighting a cigarette like it was an ordinary morning. "Alright, stop with the drama, would you? We used each other."

I let his words linger, trying to make sense of them. "We did?"

He nodded as he waltzed over to my side of the bed. He pressed his palms into the mattress and leaned in until our eyes were level.

"What did we use each other for?" I finally asked.

He gestured with his cigarette, drawing lines of smoke through the air. "To escape our mutual misery."

"Enzo," I said as I sat up, pressing the comforter against my chest, "I admire your talent for justifying sins, but this isn't funny."

"Didn't say it was, honey."

"Don't honey me!" My gaze drifted past Enzo as I mulled over his sentiment. "So what does that mean if we used each other? Does that change anything? I mean, we still did what we did."

"Yeah." He shrugged. "But if we were just using each other, it didn't mean anything. And if it didn't mean anything, we don't have to talk about this again. Not even in private. We can act like it never happened."

"That's your trick? Act like it never happened, and poof, it didn't?"

He took a slow drag, exhaling toward the ceiling. "A little advice, Scar. The longer you're married, the more pretending you'll do."

He turned around and gave me privacy while I redressed. What was the point, when he'd seen the parts of me that were only supposed to be enjoyed by my husband? When I finally had myself together, or as together as I could be given the circumstances, he faced me again. This time, his cool façade had fallen away.

"I can pretend last night didn't happen," Enzo said, "because I know you want your marriage to work. I don't want to be the thing to destroy it. But I can't pretend he didn't hit you."

"I told you, Enz, it's fine. It was a one-time thing."

He went quiet, like he was in a game of chess, plotting his next move. "My offer stands. If you want me to stay, I will."

The backs of my eyes stung with tears. "Now you really can't stay." I pressed my fingertips to my lips, like I wanted to shut myself up, but the words came out anyway. "I know Fran and I are going through a bad time. Really bad. But I didn't mean for last night to happen. I mean, you know me, Enzo. *I* know me. I'm not a cheater," I added with a scoff, like it was an utter impossibility. "I'm not a bad person."

But as Enzo bid me farewell with a tight smile, and as I lingered outside his apartment door for far too long, I was left with one looping question.

Am I?

WHEN I RETURNED HOME, my mother was pacing in the entryway with my son on her hip. It was disorienting, the way everything looked just the way I'd left it. My life had been upended, but my home remained intact, at least at face value. My mother set Emilio down as I closed the door behind me, and after a hug and a kiss, he ran off to the kitchen. I noticed how haggard she looked, no doubt from taking care of my toddler for far longer than she was supposed to.

"Where the hell were you?" she yelled, her raspy voice confirming her exhaustion. "I was worried sick! I can't count how many times I called the restaurant. You're a mother now, Scarlett."

"I know."

She pointed at me, her stare sharp and authoritative. "Before you do *anything,* you have to think about your son."

I couldn't hold it in any longer, not when I'd done the precise opposite. I dissolved into tears—the hysterical, uncontrollable kind. Last night, I'd acted like I wasn't a mother at all. I'd traded a few hours of pleasure for a lifetime of regret. And if Francesco ever found out, it wouldn't just be my marriage on the line. It would be my son's future, and that's what killed me most.

My breath came out in jagged gasps as my shaking hands covered my face. I sank into the couch, trying to hide, but that's the conundrum of humanity. We can't hide from ourselves. My mother brushed my hair away from my face as she tried to console me with kind, calming words. But nothing was going to work. I knew what I had to do to free myself. Confess.

"I …" I started, though I relinquished at the thought of discussing sex with my mother, "with Enzo."

"You what with Enzo?" she asked, her brows furrowing. "Full sentences, babydoll."

I glanced down the hall to make sure Emilio was still in the kitchen, glued to his cartoon. Then I looked my mother in the eye and whispered, "I slept with Enzo."

Her hands flew to her mouth as she sank into the spot next to me. "Scarlett Marie."

"I know." A fresh bout of horrible feelings rose in my throat. "I'm nothing but a disgusting little whore."

"Scarlett—"

"Who *does* that? This has to be a mortal sin, Mom. Those are unforgiveable. Do you know that?" My skin felt like it was scorched with fire. I wished I could crawl out of my skin and become someone else. Someone clean. "I'm going to rot in hell for all of eternity." My mind reeled, trying to comprehend just how long eternity really was. I went faint and sat back against the cushions. Glancing up at my mother's green eyes, I waited for her judgement to rain down on me. But instead, like Enzo last night, she looked sympathetic.

"Scar, baby, you go to confession, pay your penance, and never do it again. You're a human being. You're gonna make mistakes."

"I *slept*," I hissed, "with my husband's *brother*." The words alone made me nauseous, never mind that I had committed said sin. "That's so far beyond a mistake, there's not even a word for it. There's just a destination." I tossed up my hands. "Hell."

"Stop thinking about hell, would you?" my mother said as I drew my knees to my chest. "But I gotta ask you—what the hell were you thinking?"

"I wasn't," I replied, but it wasn't entirely true. I *was* thinking, of how Enzo could fix everything that was wrong with me. Sure, last night was spurred on by the turmoil in my marriage. How abandoned I felt by Francesco. How deep down, I really was afraid of him, not just of his hand but also of his words and the way he lashed out at me, and Enzo made me feel safe. The way I felt like I was married to a monstrous stranger, forever bound by our son and the vows we made before God. But it was more than that. What I did last night went far beyond Francesco or wanting to escape my own life.

I pressed my lips together, trying to keep my thoughts contained where they belonged—in my mind. If I said it, it would be real, and I didn't want it to be. But my mother sat there, patient, neutral, as if she'd half-expected her only child to do something so abhorrent.

"I think I still love him," I admitted, bracing myself for a long lecture about how warped my brain was.

"Well, no shit," she said—two words that made my eyes bug out. "He's your first love. You never get over the first one."

"I'm sorry. What?"

"Your first love is special," my mother continued, as if her theory were scientifically proven. "You give them *everything*. And when you break up, well, you don't really get all of yourself back."

"You knew this," I said, "and you didn't warn me?"

"I didn't want you to marry Fran thinking you'd be all hung up on Enzo for the rest of your life."

"Newsflash, I am." But then I scanned the numerous family photographs on display around my living room. I listened to the sound of my son's sweet giggles coming from the kitchen. "But I love Fran, too."

"I know you do," she said with a sigh. I wasn't imagining the disappointment in her voice. Her wistful expression disappeared. "Look, I've gotta be honest, because I'm your mother. I don't think you're very happy with him. I mean, besides the obvious"—she pursed her lips—"you don't smile. I don't remember the last time I heard you laugh. Really laugh. And he always looks so distracted. Like he's a million miles away."

It scared me, how transparent my life was to my mother. Her blonde hair looked bright like sunshine, but there was genuine concern in her eyes, like she'd been wanting to bring this up and didn't know how or when she could.

"That's about as accurate as it gets." I swiped the tears from beneath my eyes as Emilio barreled into the room.

"Mommy," he said, still in his dinosaur pajamas, his mouth stained with various colors from the sugary cereal I let him eat when his father was away. "Can we go to the park?"

"Sure, sweetie." I plastered on a smile. "Why don't you go up and change, and Mommy will be ready soon, okay?"

Satisfied, he hurried up to his room, my guilt mounting with each of his little steps.

"Honey," my mother said, pleading with me to look her in the eye. "I don't even want to bring this up, but I hear things. I don't know if they're true, but people say he's got girlfriends. Lots of them, all over the country. Is it true?"

"I don't know." I looked away, just like I looked away from my husband's cheating. I'd become exactly who I said I'd never be—one of those stereotypical Italian wives portrayed in the movies. Worse, I didn't care to do a thing about it. I didn't want to know. What would I do if it were true? Or rather, what wouldn't I do? Would I look the other way and pretend, just like I always did?

"Is that why you did it? To get back at him?"

I hugged my knees to my chest, feeling like a teenager again. The truth was, I needed my mother, and I needed to tell her the truth. Not because I felt like I was in any grave danger, but because I couldn't carry this burden alone. "Fran hit me, Mom."

Her face drained of color, and fury filled her eyes.

"It was one slap," I told her. "Got a little bruise, that's it. I was complaining about how little time he spends at home, and I threw in a dig about the rumors of his cheating. I riled him up, and he didn't like it."

Tears skated down her cheeks as her eyes fluttered shut. "My baby," was all she said, and I understood how she felt. If someone ever hurt my Emilio, I'd tear them apart with my bare hands, consequences be damned. She opened her eyes and reached for my hands. "I don't care what you said to that man. You don't deserve that." I opened my mouth to respond, but she cut me off. "You have to leave him."

I shook my head. "I won't. He's my son's father."

"Scarlett—"

"It's not going to happen again."

"That's what they all say, until the next time, and the next time."

"He means it, Mom. I mean, come on. He bought me a beach house."

"And that's supposed to impress me? That he bought another house to trap you in?" Her voice rose, and I kept eyeing the staircase to make sure Emilio wasn't eavesdropping. It was incredible, the information a three-year-old could retain. "That husband of yours shuts you up with gifts and promises he has no intentions of keeping. Look around, Scarlett. You've got this big, beautiful house, and he's never in it."

"He's working to pay for it," I said in his defense.

"He's stealing your life!" She stood up as Emilio jogged down the steps, his backpack containing his baseball and glove slung over his shoulder. "That man is so insecure he has to put you in a cage so you won't realize what a zero he is. He's *nothing* without you and everybody sees it but you. Wake up, Scarlett. You deserve more than this. You want to know the truth? I'm glad you cheated on his sorry ass. That's exactly what he deserves."

My cheeks aflame, I ran toward Emilio, who remained frozen at the landing. I didn't know how much he heard, or if I was imagining the shift behind those big, innocent eyes. I told him to wait for me in his room, and later at the park, I'd tell him that everything that happened while Daddy was away was our little secret. But now, I had to deal with my mother and her apparent distaste for my husband that she'd been keeping from me.

"I thought you liked Francesco," I said, reconvening with her in the entryway.

"I did, in the beginning. Guess he had me fooled, the way he fooled you." She scanned all the grand fixings that were supposed to make my house a home. "He doesn't appreciate what he has in you.

And you? I don't know what was so bad in your life that you think this is all you deserve."

"I cheated on my husband, Mom." Then came the truth I hadn't even dared to admit to myself. "This is all I deserve."

CHAPTER NINE

SCARLETT

Summer, 2011

I feel like I've been struck by a freight train, multiple times, and the worst part is, I brought this relentless hangover on myself. Morning light streams through the shades, suggesting today is a fresh start with no memory of yesterday. As if. I peel myself out of bed, my head pulsing with a headache, and grab my robe from the hook behind the bathroom door. After I twist my hair into a claw clip, I shuffle downstairs.

Italian music blares from the living room stereo system, and the melody takes to my headache like a sledgehammer. Pia is slouched over the kitchen table, looking as ragged as I feel, while Emilio pours glasses of orange juice with eyes still glazed from sleep. Enzo is at the helm, making eggs three different ways at the stove—scrambled, poached, and soft-boiled. Spices, herbs, and paper towels cover the countertops, and it all looks so normal, it takes me a moment to register what's going on.

Enzo is cooking breakfast for me and my children. For a moment, I wonder if I'm still asleep and this is just one of those domestic dreams

I used to have—of what everyday life might've looked like if it had been us. Me and Enzo.

"Morning, sunshine," Emilio says, laughing as he gives his disheveled mother a onceover.

Enzo, too, glances my way. He steps away from the stove, reaches for a mug, and fixes a coffee just the way I like it. "Morning." He hands it to me, holding my gaze a moment too long. "How are you feeling?"

"Great," I chirp, lifting the mug to my lips. "You?"

He nods as he turns back to the stove and shuts off the burners. "I'm great, too."

Feeling Emilio's curious eyes on me, I shoot him a smile and reach for a glass of orange juice. I join Pia at the table, and she slinks upright when I hand her the glass.

She groans as she massages her temples. "Why is alcohol so evil?"

"Next time you want to drink," I tell her, "I'm going to remind you that you said that."

She takes a moment to size me up. "You look hungover, too, you know."

"The family that drinks together, stays together," Enzo quips, three plates balanced on his arm like the restaurant industry veteran that he is. He arranges them around the table, while Emilio adds a platter of fruit and extra slices of sourdough toast.

"Since when do you know how to make a spread like this?" I ask.

"Since I became a divorcé who had to learn how to feed himself," Enzo cracks. "Everyone good on drinks?"

I nod, satisfied with my coffee. "But can we please lower that God-awful music?"

Enzo draws in a gasp. "Adriano Celentano is a legend."

"One that I don't care to listen to," I say, "over poached eggs and orange juice."

Enzo turns away to refill his own mug with coffee. As he pours, he opens his mouth and the lyrics ring out in his rich, commanding baritone. His eyes dart to me, defiant, daring, and I work hard to suppress a smile. Pia, on the other hand, looks impressed.

"You're pretty good," she tells him when he returns and sits at the head of the table.

"*Pretty* good?"

"I mean, compared to me."

Enzo laughs as he reaches for my plate and loads it up with a large helping of breakfast.

"That's my girl," I say, smoothing her hair back behind her shoulder.

Enzo hands me my dish. Something flickers between us, an apology perhaps. My shoulders relax as I try to convey with my eyes that I, too, am sorry for the way things went down last night.

"So," Enzo starts, miraculously energetic compared to me and my children, "what's everybody up to today?"

"Recovering," Pia grumbles as she eats with vigor. "I'm going to take a long nap. On the beach. Until sunset."

"I'll be right there with you," I say in between bites. I glance out at the beach that's already buzzing with activity. "Why, did you have something in mind?"

"The realtor's coming by," Enzo reminds me.

"That's right."

"I can handle it."

Feeling Emilio and Pia's stares on me, I say, "No, I'd like to be there for that." But while Pia and Enzo munch away, I sense something in my son. "Yes, Emi?"

"I didn't say anything." But his rosy cheeks say everything.

"But you'd like to."

He sets his fork down with a clink. "How would everyone feel if I cooked dinner tonight?"

His question hangs in the silence that falls between us. Pia glances at me, as if she's weighing my reaction.

Enzo leans back in his chair, brows raised in surprise. "You cook?"

"Yeah," Emilio says, trying his best to sound casual. But I know every nuance of this child of mine, and I know that for some reason, this is a big deal to him. I try to brush it off as his way of connecting with his father, but my intuition tells me it's deeper than that.

But in the event that my son wants to dedicate his life to the culinary arts, I'd have to shut it down. Not only because I worked just as hard as he did to get him into law school, wining and dining every contact I had at Columbia University, but because his father and I never wanted that life for him. Francesco had been a slave to his craft, and the kitchen ravaged his already fragile health. As his wife, I suffered alongside him—every exhausting shift, every illness. But Francesco and I worked so hard to conceal our hardships from our children, they now have no idea of the realities behind our profession. It's my job to protect them from the things they're still naïve to.

Enzo reaches over and squeezes Emilio's shoulder, rocking him back and forth in his chair. "Well now you have to make dinner. I don't know." Enzo looks over at me. "Something tells me he's gonna put his old man to shame."

I shift in my seat and a trace of understanding dances across Enzo's face as he narrows his eyes. "We'll have to see about that."

Emilio glares at me, able to hear the undertones of doubt in my voice.

"What are you gonna make?" Pia chimes in, breaking the tension.

"I don't know yet. It's a surprise."

"I really hope there's pasta in my future," Pia says as she gets up, taking her empty dish with her. Before she stops by the sink, though, she heads to the stereo and lowers the volume. "Sorry, Zi. But you've got just as bad of taste in music as Mom."

Enzo laughs, shaking his head as Pia sits back down and leans her head against my arm. I lean over and kiss the top of her head.

"You know what you are?" Enzo says, pointing his fork at Pia. "You're a mini Scarlett."

"Hell no," Pia snaps. "I'm way prettier."

My jaw falls open at her dig, but I'm reduced to laughter when I see Pia's satisfied, sheepish smirk.

"Damn," Emilio remarks. "You got Mom on that one."

As laughter settles over the table, Enzo takes command. "Alright. What time's dinner, chef?"

"How's seven?" Emilio offers.

"Seven it is," Enzo confirms. He slides his chair out and gathers the empty dishes.

"Take my card," I tell Emilio. "Go to Citarella. Get whatever you need."

Emilio seems moved by this, as if my financial contribution is a subtle blessing. I'm not sure if it's a blessing so much as it is a reaction to facing the inevitable.

I sit back in my chair, tightening my robe around me, grasping my still warm mug in my hands. Pia breaks off a piece of a croissant to satisfy her insatiable sweet tooth. Emilio packs away leftovers, and

Enzo loads the dishwasher. That damn Italian music still croons softly as the backdrop to what appears so foreign yet so familiar, it takes my breath away.

We look like the family I used to dream we could be.

———

"Scar," Enzo yells down the hall, "she's here."

I've spent the day thus far cleaning every nook and cranny of the house, shoving things into closets, and rearranging knickknacks so the house looks elegant rather than cluttered. I dash into the living room to fluff a rogue pillow before joining Enzo at the door. He opens it, only to reveal a bright, sunny blonde with perfect white teeth—veneers, if I had to put money on it—and fake boobs propped up as high as they could go. I suddenly wish I were wearing something other than my tired Lululemon activewear, a stark contrast against her structured shift dress that is tailored to her curves. I shoot Enzo a side glance. Did this realtor come highly recommended, or does he have the hots for her?

He dismisses me with a look that says, *Come on, give me some credit,* as the woman starts her show.

"Hi guys," she starts, extending her hand to me first. "I'm Tinsley Astor."

Of course you are, I think. Her name sounds like it belongs to a beauty pageant contestant rather than a top-rated realtor. "I'm Scarlett. This is Enzo."

"We spoke on the phone," she remarks as she shakes his hand. It's firm and sure—everything I'm not. "The exterior is just stunning. That porch swing makes the house look like it's right out of a story book."

"Well, let's show you the rest of it," I say, turning into the house. We slowly pass by the living room framed by crisp, linen curtains billowing in the breeze let in through the open windows. I try to see the stone fireplace and cozy, lived-in furniture through her eyes. She nods in approval, and we move onto the dining area that boasts the table I set with rattan placemats and stoneware dinner plates. She runs a hand along the marble-topped island and makes a comment about the impressive Viking stove range and state-of-the-art appliances, all of which were hand-selected by Francesco to create what is still a chef's dream. But it's the view that stops her in her tracks.

"The view alone is worth a million," she tells us. She and Enzo quickly tour the deck while I peer out at the view through narrowed eyes clouded with nostalgia. It's 2011, but it might as well be 1990-something. I can still see Francesco jogging out of the ocean, his sopping wet body emerging like a mirage behind windblown beach grass, his muscles slick like a Greek god as he approached the house slightly out of breath and hungry for me. A smile pulls at the corners of my mouth as I picture Pia and me building sandcastles, her big brother mastering the art of surfing, when I think of late nights spent floating in the pool beneath the stars. The image of Francesco flipping food on the grill while he enjoyed a beer beneath a cotton candy sky is so vivid, I can almost taste the char of the steaks and vegetables he fed us summer after summer. But as Tinsley and Enzo slip back into the house, I'm reminded that those are pretty brushstrokes of a very messy piece of art.

"Can I ask you two why you're selling?" Tinsley asks as we head upstairs.

I open my mouth to respond, but Enzo puts a hand on my arm.

"We have some other projects we're looking to invest in, and we only use this property a few months out of the year, if that," Enzo says as Tinsley tours Pia's room, which is an organized mess topped with a shabby chic rose-patterned quilt.

"And do you all have a timeline?" she asks, examining Enzo's bedroom next.

"We'd like to get it listed as soon as possible," Enzo says. "Ideally, I'd like to accept an offer by the beginning of August."

"I think you'll have offers rolling in much sooner than that," Tinsley says, flashing a flirtatious smile squarely in Enzo's direction. What is it about him that us females find so irresistible?

Next, we tour my bedroom. It looks straight out of a magazine, much like how my marriage looked. We were one of those couples everyone else idolized. *Made for each other,* was what they wrote about us when we gave joint interviews to magazines or newspapers. *Power couple.* But the power was one sided. The *Pasta King* wasn't just the American leader of Italian cuisine; he was the all-powerful boss at home. His moods dictated mine, and his whims determined where we went and what we did. He held all of me in his hands, as the father of the children for whom I'd die, and he crushed me until I was nothing but shards.

But when I remember the past, I don't see his angry outbursts, the way he projected what he hated about himself on me, how he burdened me with blame for things that were never mine to carry. Looking at these walls and the life we lived within them, I realize I've been choosing to see what everyone else saw: the perfect couple, with their perfect homes, their perfect children, and their perfect restaurant. The beautiful package we presented ourselves as. And as Tinsley and Enzo lead the way downstairs, and Enzo gives me a questioning glance that I dismiss, I know it's time for me to take off the rose-colored glasses through which I see my memories and view this house for what it truly is.

A four-thousand-square-foot broken promise.

A bribe. A peace-offering made in vain. A way to keep me quiet. And now, it's nothing but a gorgeous reminder that my husband wasn't who I wanted him to be.

"You've got quite the property here," Tinsley says as we convene in the kitchen. The future of my restaurant rests in the hands of this blonde bombshell whom I admittedly envy. She sets her designer bag down on the counter and clasps her French-manicured hands together. "Let's get into the nitty gritty, shall we? This house is really a dream. The location and view are out of this world. It's classic Montauk. With a few tweaks for staging, it's ready to list."

"What kind of tweaks?" I ask.

"Put away all personal photographs, tidy the bedrooms, and stage the deck for entertaining," she suggests. "Simple things."

"Speaking of entertaining," I say, shifting my weight from one hip to the other, "my daughter's birthday party is on the 17th. No showings that day, if that's alright."

"Not a problem."

"What are you thinking pricewise?" Enzo asks. He looks all business as he folds his arms and rests his index finger against his lips.

"Being that you're motivated to sell," Tinsley says, glancing between the two of us, "I'd say somewhere between three and four million."

I maintain a poker face, but inside, relief floods me. Even after we pay off the mortgage, closing costs, and split the profits, I'll be in the black again. I'm ready to sign whatever I need to, to get the listing on the market, but the sliding door opens, and Pia, wrapped in yet another neon towel, tiptoes into the house.

"Sorry," she says as she passes by. "Just going up to shower."

I gesture to her beet red chest, but I'll chide her for her reckless defiance toward sunscreen later. Tinsley greets her with a smile and a wave.

"That's your daughter?" she asks us.

"Mine," I say. "So, when can we get some photographs done and get the listing up?"

"Well, we'll need to agree on a listing price, you'll sign the contract, and then I'll have my team out here early next week to take photos."

"$3.995 million," Enzo says with finality. "We'll go as low as $3.2, but try to get us top dollar. If we get multiple offers and it's between a cash and a finance, let's go for the cash, and push for a quick closing."

"Almost all of the offers in this price bracket are cash," she assures Enzo with a practiced, professional smile.

"A friend of mine said you're one of the best out here." Exerting every ounce of his masculinity, Enzo leans in and his voice is low and firm. "I want to make sure you have the network to move this in the time frame we've given you."

"Obviously, I can't make any guarantees," Tinsley says, putting her hands up, sending her bracelets jangling toward her elbows. "But I think my record speaks for itself. I have a ton of contacts, and I actually have a few people in mind that I want to show this to."

As they finalize the details, I retreat, not because I'm uninterested, but because, despite the independence I cling to, it feels so good to have someone else handle the details for me. After Enzo shows her out, we meet in the living room and sink into the couch, facing each other.

"You happy with how that went?" Enzo asks.

"Very." I prop my elbow against the cushion and rest my chin on my knuckles.

"I'm surprised you're taking it so well, Mrs. V," Enzo teases.

"Stop calling me that." I rub my face with my palms, like I'm trying to wake myself out of a stupor. "I'm just starting to see this house for what it really is. And it reminds me of how pathetic I was for accepting it."

He looks at me like there's something on the tip of his tongue, words he won't let slip out. But just as quickly, he blinks it away, erasing whatever was there a moment ago.

"You weren't pathetic," he says instead. "You were being a good mother."

"I wasn't *being a good mother* when I accepted the handbag that came along with the house."

His mouth twitches, fighting back a smirk before he delivers the punchline I've walked right into. "I always did peg you as a gold digger."

"First class," I deadpan. I swat him with a throw pillow as we laugh. But before we can veer back into serious conversation territory, a honking horn outside breaks us apart.

Pia barrels down the steps and heads outside, the sound of her flipflops trailing in her wake. Together, my children unload Citarella-branded grocery bags from the car and lug them inside. I massage the nape of my neck as my smile falters. The rhythm of our days is picking up, and summer's end is staring down its barrel at me. I hate to admit it, but I'm enjoying this. All of it. The ease of our banter, the way our laughter harmonizes into the sweetest sound, how we all fit together as if we aren't made of jagged edges. But as Emilio carries in the last of the bags and locks the door behind him, I'm reminded that this isn't a summer of building something new.

It's a summer of saying goodbye, to so much more than a house.

CHAPTER TEN

SCARLETT

Winter, 1992

It was the night of the last supper. Enzo was set to move to Maryland—his house had been purchased, his belongings transported down, his children already settled at their mother's new home—and tonight was our final Christmas Eve together. While we typically celebrated holidays at the restaurant, seeking more privacy from his adoring and sometimes demanding fans, Francesco and I opted to host this year's dinner at our house. The tree was placed before the bay window in the living room, strung with incandescent multicolored lights that cast a cozy glow. Emilio, clad in a hunter-green Christmas sweater, khaki pants, and little driving loafers that were too cute for words, kept circling the tree, shaking the boxes, trying to guess what Santa had brought him. Most of our guests had arrived, but Francesco was still in sweats and a wifebeater, slick from the day's work in the kitchen. I was putting the finishing touches on the table, perfecting my festive plaid and gold theme, when Francesco called me into the kitchen.

"Yes?" I said, my heels click-clacking against the tile floor.

"I need the big *sculabast,*" he said as he wiped his hands on a *mappina* draped over his shoulder. Beside him, Julie sliced a loaf of semolina bread, the serrated knife tearing through its golden crust.

After I retrieved the colander from a closet in the basement, though the kitchen was a chaotic mess with sauce splattered all over the counter, and rogue ingredients speckling every surface, Francesco found a moment to snake his arm around my waist and kiss me. He kept his face close to mine, his eyes sparkling with the warmth that enveloped our entire home.

"I love you," he said before kissing me again. It felt natural, as if he was always like this, but I couldn't ignore the snagging thought that he wasn't. In fact, the bigger the audience, the bigger the show when it came to Francesco's affection. Still, I took it, hoping he'd still be as warm and attentive when the curtains closed and we were left alone.

"Get a room," Julie teased as she transferred the thin slices of bread from the cutting board to a serving platter.

"I love you, too," I said to Francesco. I kept my eyes on him as he placed the colander in the sink and strained what had to be four pounds of linguine. Warmth spread throughout my chest as I tuned out any lingering doubts. Something had drawn us back together.

Perhaps it was the baby I was eight weeks pregnant with.

I glanced toward the door as Enzo entered, his arms laden with bottles of wine. Joining him in the entryway, I plucked the wine out of his arms, and he removed his scarf and coat.

"Merry Christmas," I said.

"Hey, it's *Buon Natale* around here." He bent down to kiss me on the cheek, his scent of citrus and musk enveloping me like a warm hug as we headed for the kitchen. "What's up, everybody?"

"*Guaglione!* Now the party can start," Francesco said as he poured a gorgeous red crab sauce over a large mound of pasta.

Enzo made the rounds, greeting everyone with a kiss on the cheek. He appeared jovial, considering he was about to leave the city he adored for an unspecified length of time, if not forever. I had a hard time believing Enzo was leaving New York behind for good, but maybe that was my delusion, or rather, denial, talking. When he reached Francesco, I watched them embrace, reading between the lines of their tight, lingering hug that neither one of them wanted to let go of. Afterward, Enzo uncorked a few bottles of wine and Francesco plated the last of our meal that would be served family-style, and we all convened in the dining room. Steam billowed from the hot plates of the traditional feast of the seven fishes, the scents of fresh seafood and garlic filling the room. Emilio chased Julie's sons, Bobby Jr. and Nico, around the table until Francesco scooped up our son and propped him on his hip. He stood at the head of the table and motioned for me to join him.

I straightened his wifebeater. "That was really nice of you to clean yourself up for the family."

Laughter rang around the table. Francesco kissed my forehead and raised his glass of wine, and as he looked out at our small family of ten, I noticed a sadness to Francesco's smile.

"Family is the most important thing in the world," he started, glancing around at each of our guests, "and we're so blessed to be sitting down together to enjoy this meal tonight."

"Amen to that," Julie agreed, raising her glass.

"To my brother," Francesco said, making eye contact with Enzo. "I haven't been apart from you since I was a kid, but I think we can all agree that what you're doing, moving to be near your children, is a tremendous sacrifice, one that pretty much sums up who you are."

My eyes flicked to Enzo to catch his reaction. Beyond clenching his jaw, he remained stoic, though I knew it was a front. But I didn't have time to dwell, because Francesco was toasting to me, now.

"And to the best gift of all, my stunningly beautiful wife." Francesco wrapped his arm around me and drew me to his side, kissing my temple. I rested my hands on his waist and looked into his eyes. "I don't know where the hell I'd be if it wasn't for you, but I know it wouldn't be as amazing as this." Francesco paused, his eyes glittering, his smile impossibly wide. "Don't kill me, babe, but everybody, we're having another baby."

I didn't have time to process how I felt about him breaking the news because at once, everyone gushed over us. Francesco bent over to kiss my belly, which had yet to round with a bump, while Julie swiped away tears of joy, and her husband, Bobby Sr., raised his glass to us. My mother gave me a loaded glance that I tried to ignore, while her boyfriend, Tony, applauded. Enzo was the one to break the celebration with a final toast.

"*Alla famiglia,*" he said. *To the family.* Then, he knocked back a large sip of wine, and I couldn't help but wonder if it had anything to do with our announcement.

"I'm only eight weeks," I reminded everyone as I sank into my seat beside Francesco. "So let's keep this under wraps."

"You ruined my plan," my mother chimed in as Francesco loaded her plate with a helping of *baccala*. "I was going to call the *Enquirer*."

"Very funny, Mom." I adjusted my napkin across my lap, fighting to maintain a placid expression, though everything in me was irritated. With Francesco, for announcing my pregnancy too soon, not to mention stealing the spotlight that was supposed to be on his brother tonight. And with my mother, whose burning stare said it all without words—*Are you serious?*

After our meal, I laid out platters of desserts and pastries from Ferrara's, and Francesco went around, serving demitasse cups of espresso accompanied by sambuca. As we indulged, conversation drifted to the elephant in the room: Enzo's impending departure.

"So," Julie said as her youngest, Anthony, climbed onto her lap, "what's the plan tomorrow?"

"Taking the train out of Penn at eight," Enzo said, pausing to sip his espresso. "Claudia's brother's picking me up down in Baltimore City, and Claudia's hosting dinner at her house."

"It's nice you two get along so well," my mother said as she loaded her fork with another bite of tiramisu.

"In front of a crowd, we do," Enzo teased. "It's when we're alone that she turns into *strega*." That part, he was not kidding about.

"I think Bobby would agree I turn into a witch when we're alone, too, wouldn't you, honey?" Julie asked.

Bobby shook his head. "I'm not touching that one."

"And you have a job lined up?" Tony inquired.

"Claudia's family is in the food business, but I'm going to look into doing my own thing." Enzo ran his index finger around the rim of his glass. "Maybe open a small restaurant, or a *salumeria*. They have a Little Italy down there, too. Not like ours, but what are you gonna do?"

"You'll show 'em how it's done," Francesco said.

"I'm sure your kids will be so excited to have you there," I offered, trying to ignore how permanent his move seemed all of a sudden. What felt like a temporary solution to be near his children now felt like he was starting his life over, and he didn't look too thrilled about it.

Enzo had switched to whiskey somewhere in the middle of dinner, and he downed the rest of his pour until he winced. "The things we do for our kids, right?"

When we looked at each other, it was like lightning struck, destroying everything around us. All that was left was me and him and our dirty little secret, and all the ways we were trying to let go of it. But it wasn't just that night we were trying to let go of. It was each other, and all the things we weren't supposed to feel.

I remained quiet for the rest of dinner, for fear that my emotions might spill out. After Julie and her family left, the air fell serious. The festivities were over, and it was time to say goodbye.

In the kitchen, Francesco drew in a big breath, his shoulders rising and falling. "Alright," he said, his eyes focused on his brother, "you be good. Take care of yourself."

"You too," Enzo said before they embraced. They each held on tight, not wanting to be ripped apart by the different directions their lives were now unfurling in. Enzo cupped Francesco's face and patted it, a melancholy expression written on his own. I knew that they weren't seeing each other as they men they'd become, but rather, the inseparable kids they once were. Enzo then picked up Emilio. "You be good for Mommy and Daddy, you hear me?"

Emilio nodded, his eyes sleepy as he rested his head against Enzo's shoulder.

"I'll walk you out," I said after he said goodbye to my mother. She, Francesco, and Emilio remained in the kitchen as my heels created an echo against the tall ceilings in the entryway. Though we could've said goodbye in the house, by some unspoken sixth sense, we convened on the porch outside. I didn't have a coat on, and winter's bitterness enveloped me, but I needed a moment with Enzo, alone.

"You okay?" I asked.

He shrugged. "It is what it is."

"I know I've said it before, but I think what you're doing is really amazing. Your kids will never forget that you sacrificed your life here for them."

But Enzo seemed disinterested in talk of his heroic character. As New York's melody hummed around us, Enzo dug a hand into his pocket and pulled out a cigarette. "You're sure you're okay with me leaving?"

I nodded confidently, that dark, isolated incident feeling so distant, I wondered if I'd imagined it. "Everything's fine now." My hands flew to my belly. Did the little life inside of me know it was my protector? "And now with the baby, it'll never happen again."

Enzo's eyes flitted to my stomach. He pressed his lips together, and I wasn't sure if it was because I was worried about it, or because I knew him better than I should've, but his concern was apparent. Would he spend his train ride to Maryland calculating the days and weeks and minutes just as I had since the moment I'd discovered I was pregnant?

"Congratulations," Enzo finally said, though the single word was loaded. As a thick silence filled with things we didn't dare to say fell between us, tears lodged behind my eyes.

I didn't want to speak, because that would've meant I had to say goodbye, and I wasn't ready. I was never going to be ready. I took a breath to speak but stopped myself. Enzo tilted his head as if to say, *Let it out.* "I just feel like I'm never going to see you again."

"It's Maryland, not Mars," he said in lighthearted tones as he inched closer to me. He hesitated before reaching out to swipe a tear from my face, letting his hand linger on my cheek. "We still have Montauk."

I nodded as I caught my breath and steadied my emotions. The Montauk house had been presented to me as a gift, a fresh start to my rollercoaster of a marriage. Now, it was the only tether I had left to the man I wasn't supposed to love.

Enzo patted my cheek. "You don't have a coat on." When he dropped his hand, I knew it was time.

I wrapped my arms around him and drew him into a hug. "Call us when you get settled in." I squeezed him close until I could feel his heartbeat against my chest.

"Get inside," he said once we parted, gesturing toward my house. "This cold can't be good for the baby."

I smiled and waved as he walked away, acting like I was okay, when in reality, it felt like the universe was ripping out a part of me I didn't know I couldn't live without. I slipped back inside the house, still frigid despite the warmth of my home, and pressed my face against the glass until Enzo disappeared down Bank Street, though I lingered there long after he left my line of vision.

"He'll be back," my mother said. I whipped around to find her in the first set of doors that led to the small corridor I was in. She joined me, the wintry air slipping through the cracks of the front door, chilling my legs. I glanced through the windows of the French doors, though my home appeared vacant.

"Where's Fran?"

"Getting Emi ready for bed." Though she was dressed in a festive sweater and matching kitschy bow earrings, my mother's face was anything but cheerful. "Really, Scarlett?"

"Really *what*?" I tossed my hands up. "He's my husband, Mom. I'm sorry you don't like him and what he did to me, and I'm sorry you don't like the fact that I'm having another child with him."

"That's my question, chickee. Is it with him?"

Fear gripped every part of me. Besides Enzo, only my mother and Julie knew, and this was the first time my concerns about the paternity of my unborn baby were being voiced aloud. Even still, Enzo was gone, and I was one hundred and ten percent committed to making my marriage work. "Listen to me, Mom. I don't care if this child comes out looking like a carbon copy of Enzo. It's Francesco's. That's the story. That's the *truth*. Do you understand me?"

She looked away, annoyed.

"This is *my* life. You don't have to like the way I live it," I added.

Though her neck was craned in the other direction, her eyes shifted to me. "Maybe so. But let me warn you, little girl." She grabbed her purse from the coat rack, slung it over her shoulder, and leveled me with truth that would linger with me far longer than our heated exchange. "Living a lie is a lot harder than you think."

I ALWAYS HATED GAME shows. The chimes, the cheers, the corny set designs, I never understood the appeal. But my husband had a penchant for *Wheel of Fortune,* and as the late-night rerun flashed on the TV in our bedroom, the joyful sounds grated against my nerves. I was anything but joyful, and despite it being Christmas, I felt like I was in mourning. I didn't know why, but it felt like everything had changed, forever.

Enzo was starting a new life, I was bringing a new child into the world, and Francesco seemed swept up in the tornado of change. After showering and changing into a fresh set of pajamas, he paced in front of the TV, the glow of the spinning wheel casting multicolor shadows on his face. He stopped at the dresser, sifting through the clutter like he had lost something.

"Whatcha looking for?" I asked from my side of the bed.

"You keep your tranquilizers up here, right?"

I propped myself up on my elbows. "You never take those."

Francesco ran his hands through his curls, until his hair was a wild mess. "I just need something to take the edge off."

Noticing how jittery he was, I waved him over to join me in bed. "Come here."

With reluctance, he flopped down next to me, keeping his gaze fixed on the TV. He rested one arm behind his head, the other on his taut abdomen. I snuggled close to him, trying to provide a sense of calm, but his heart continued to race.

"Hey," I said, rubbing a circle with my palm on his chest, "take a deep breath."

"I feel weird," Francesco admitted, sitting upright against the pillows. His eyes darted to mine, wide and worried.

"You think it's your heart?" I asked, sitting up, too, trying to conceal the concern in my voice.

"I don't know." He exhaled hard, but his shoulders remained tensed.

"I think you're just nervous." I rubbed his shoulder and interlaced my free hand with his.

"About what?"

"Fran, your only blood relative in this country is moving away." The game show chimed with the upbeat sound of a puzzle being solved, similar to how I'd cracked the code on what was causing Francesco's anxiety. For the first time in a long time, I saw the man I married—the one who was earnest and tenderhearted, who saw me as his insular world—rather than the culinary god everyone else worshipped. "It's only natural you'd feel this way."

"I feel like a wuss. I'm a grown man. I run my own business. I have my own family. Now I'm nervous because my big brother left me by myself?" He bent his knees and arched over, his head hung low. "This is embarrassing."

"Babe, no it's not. Come on. It's just me."

Finally, he let his defenses fall. When he glanced over at me again and rested back in my arms, he gave into his vulnerability, glossy eyes and all. "I haven't been apart from him since I was a teenager. I didn't want him to go to America because I didn't want to be alone, but he promised me he'd come back and get me."

"And he did," I reminded him. The story never ceased to amaze me, how Enzo had ventured to America all on his own at the age of sixteen. He'd stayed with some *paisans* who lived in Little Italy, both of which led him to his now ex-wife, Claudia. When he was established, he fulfilled his promise to Francesco and went back to Naples, and when they returned to Manhattan as a pair, they were a sensation. Similarly, even though Francesco and I had started Amanti together and saw it to success, we'd reached new heights as a trio when Enzo joined us. The truth was plain: Enzo and Francesco were stronger together. What would life bring, for all of us, now that they were apart?

"He didn't promise me this time," Francesco said, sounding like a boy. "He's starting a whole new life down there."

"I know. But we have our beach house together, remember?" As he rested his head on my chest, I ran my fingers through his mop of curls. "We can spend summers together."

Francesco looked up at me. "What if he never comes back?"

The question seemed to rock him just as much as it rocked me. My stomach hollowed out, but I had a role to play—that of the strong, stoic wife who by some intuition knew the future would work itself out. Tonight, it felt like I was performing for the both of us. "Then I guess you're stuck with me."

He gave me a weak smile that faded quickly. My hopes dimmed; I had failed to put his worries to rest. Maybe he could feel that my optimism was a mask and that I, too, couldn't fathom the rest of our lives without Enzo in it. His eyes still watery, he rolled himself up.

"I just need to be alone right now."

But I tugged on his arm. "If you want to cry, I'll cry with you."

It took him a minute, but he silently agreed when he wrapped himself in my arms and sought refuge in the crook of my neck. My tears melded with his, and though we were grieving the same person, we had different reasons. Francesco was missing the person who'd been his constant in life. His anchor and his home.

I was missing the person who felt like the other half of my soul.

And yet I remained there, committed to my husband, to what we were building, to the future we were scared of, to the child I'd raise as his no matter what. Like the age-old toast *alla famiglia* goes, everything was for the family, no matter the lies and pretending and sacrifices it took to uphold such an institution.

As I laid my head down that night, eyeing Francesco's chest for even breath, I told myself that sooner or later we'd stop missing Enzo and start focusing on what we did have—each other. But I recognized it for what it was. Another lie.

Yes, I was already finding it difficult to live a lie, and I'd only just begun.

A MONTH HAD PASSED. Enzo had called a handful of times to check in, though most of his conversations were with Francesco, meaning I received information secondhand. According to Francesco, things were off to a rocky start. Enzo's youngest, Maria, wanted to live with her father full time, while his middle child, Antonella, was all but refusing to go to Enzo's new place. Little Enzo, his oldest, was the peacemaker, trying to keep some sense of order among his siblings. I couldn't imagine the toll it must have been taking on Enzo, the complicated dynamics of his children on top of starting a new life at the age of forty.

But I wanted to know. I wanted to know everything.

It was that curiosity that drove me to the basement, to sit down at my desk and pull out a notepad, to put pen to paper and let my heart bleed.

Dear Enzo,

I realize writing letters might seem a little old fashioned, so I hope you don't find this strange. I know you're busy, and when you call, your time is for Francesco, but I want to talk to you, too. I thought this could be our way of keeping in touch. What do you think? Maybe I shouldn't be so presumptuous, that you want to keep in touch with me. But I wanted you to know that despite the distance, I'm thinking of you.

I'm sure Francesco hasn't told you, but he was a wreck the first two weeks after you left. He cut back his hours at work, and I think it was because he didn't like walking into Amanti and not seeing you there. But then we had a big party that required his attention, and ever since then, he's thrown himself into work to keep himself distracted. Extremes. I think that describes all three of us, tell you the truth. We only know hot and cold. Don't you agree?

Francesco mentioned that things are off to a rocky start for you. I've been worried about you, thinking of how you're trying to get on your feet with a new line of work and a new home, and at the same time, make your kids happy. I'm so sorry to hear that Antonella's giving you a hard time. Maybe Maria, that adorable little girl of yours, will rub off on her and she'll grow to love spending time at your place. I hope so. All we want is for our kids to be happy. That's what this is all for, isn't it? Our lives, everything we work for, it's all for them.

If you'd like to, write me back. Tell me how you're feeling about things down there. What's your day to day look like? What's your neighborhood like? Francesco wants to visit you in the coming months, before I'm too far along to take the long drive, but tell me anyway. I want to be able to picture your house as you sit there reading my words. I know you're a man in every sense of the word, but I have to imagine that, like your brother, you've been feeling a little uncertain about things too. Scared, even, though I'm not sure you'd be willing to admit to that. Whatever you're feeling, I just want you to know that you can tell me. I might be hundreds of miles away, but I'm also right here.

All my love,

Always,

Scarlett

CHAPTER ELEVEN

SCARLETT

Summer, 2011

"Saverio?" I call out, my Blackberry perched on the bathroom counter while I make up my face. "It's Scarlett."

"Scarlett, how you doing?" comes Saverio's gravelly voice through the speaker. "I understand you're out east for the summer."

I wonder if I've imagined the twist of judgement in his voice, or if he is, in fact, implying that I'm enjoying a life of leisure while I should be in the city, working my ass off. "Yes. That's actually what I'm calling about." I set down my blush brush and reach for this new thing called a Beauty Blender—a pink sponge shaped like an egg—and dab concealer beneath my eyes. "I wanted to let you know I've listed the house for sale. God willing, I'll have your money by September, if not sooner."

I lean in closer to the mirror and blend, as if makeup alone could cover the years of emotions that have drawn the lines on my face.

"That's great," Saverio says flatly. Then there's a pause. A long one. "I suppose now's a good a time as ever."

"For?"

"A restaurant group has expressed interest in buying your place. I told them you're away for the summer, but they're eager." I set down all my beautifying accoutrements and face my reflection of an agitated, middle-aged woman who's had enough. "I didn't want to bother you, but since you called—"

"I'm not selling," I cut him off. "I just wanted to show some good faith. I'll have your money by your deadline. Don't you worry."

A knock at my door draws me from the bathroom. I take the phone off speaker as Saverio offers more hollow pleasantries. My stomach tightens as I hang up. Here I am, delusionally enjoying this final summer with my family, while vultures circle my restaurant.

I open the door to find Enzo, dressed sharp for Emilio's home-cooked dinner. A gesture I find sweet.

"What's wrong?" he asks.

"Nothing," I snap.

"Okay." His expression says *yeah right,* but beyond a lingering glance, he doesn't push it. "Dinner's ready."

"I'll set the table."

Enzo's mouth expands into a proud grin. "Pia took care of it. Wait 'til you see."

Enzo guides me to the stairs with a hand on my back. As I descend, I shake off Saverio's conversation and threats of the Manhattan vultures. I'm as sure this house will sell in time as I am that the sky is blue. Focusing on the scene awaiting me, I smile.

Candles flicker, Mina croons from the stereo, and the kitchen is alive. Containers and mixing bowls clutter the counters. At the helm of it all is my son. With a *mappina* draped over his shoulder and an apron tied around his hips, Emilio carries a platter of delicate zucchini flowers, their golden batter still glistening with olive oil, paired with a small bowl of fresh tomato sauce. He sets them beside a beautiful arugula salad on the dining table. At the stove is a large bowl of—judging from the bright strips of green and creamy parmesan—pasta *alla nerano*, a dish from his father's home province. He shoots me a quick smile as he plates a whole roasted branzino topped with sea salt, herbs, and lemon slices.

My heart swells as I watch my son work with both ease and efficiency. He looks so at home in the kitchen, like he's been doing this for years, and I can't help but think of Francesco. What would he think of his son, putting his hand to his father's old recipes? Francesco never taught Emilio his craft. Instead, we pushed other interests on the kids—sports, the arts, academics—never the restaurant business. And yet, it's in him. Innate.

Enzo catches my eye. He doesn't need to say anything; I know the same thoughts are looping through his mind, too. "He looks just like him."

The sentiment coupled with Enzo's sweet if not sentimental tone draws tears to my eyes, but Pia appears before us with a pep in her step.

"Come see the table," she insists, reaching for my hand. I squeeze her to my side as she shows me her handiwork. Candles are nestled in large cylinder vases filled with sand, and she's layered a rattan table runner over a white linen tablecloth. Aquamarine goblets sit atop matching placemats I haven't used in years, and her lush, breezy tablescape makes me wonder why.

"Pia," I say, "honey, it's so beautiful."

Pia puts her hands on her hips and looks at Enzo. "How's that *mini Scarlett* for you?"

She leaves us laughing in her wake as she helps Emilio transfer dishes to the table. It's strange, to be in my home, ahead of a meal, and not be *doing* something.

"Need my help with anything?" I offer, unable to resist.

Emilio waves his hand. "You two sit down."

Enzo sits at the head and I to his right. But as I drape the floral-patterned napkin across my lap, I feel Enzo's stare on me. "What?"

"You're glowing," he says, his eyes soft.

I look at my babies, the two halves of my heart who live outside of my body, the two human beings whose lives I'd trade my own for. Seeing them get along, working together, *enjoying* this time as a family makes me want to sing, though I'll spare my family from such a spectacle. "I love them so much it hurts."

"Last, but most importantly," Emilio says as he approaches, his hands full of orange-colored cocktails, "Aperol Spritzes for everyone."

"I feel like I'm in Positano," I marvel.

Emilio raises his glass and for a moment, everything stills. "I just wanted to say thank you for letting me cook this meal, and if it's terrible, I'm sorry in advance." He winks at me, and I hope he knows that there's nothing terrible about him nor the things he produces. "I don't think any of us expected this to be our last summer here, and I certainly wasn't expecting to spend it with you," he says to his uncle, "but it's been pretty fun so far. So cheers, and *buon appetito*."

"And," Enzo says, his glass mid-air, "*alla famiglia*."

Emilio nods and clinks his glass against Enzo's first. I wish I could stop this moment and bottle it up—just us, warm and tucked away from the world. Because I know all too well, it's fleeting. After we've all toasted and had our first sips, Emilio serves us, starting with the salad and zucchini flowers, though Pia opts to dive headfirst into the pasta. The ocean roars outside and the music transitions to a Dean Martin song, the perfect punctuation to Emilio's old school meal.

I brace myself as I pick up my fork, realizing this is no ordinary dinner at the beach. This is the very first meal my son has ever cooked for me, and I have a gut feeling it won't be my last. Stabbing the fork through leaves of arugula and slices of citrus, when I take my first bite, flavor explodes in my mouth. Flavor, and nostalgia. How many summers had Francesco combined these same exact ingredients? How had my son managed to get the measurements just right, so that it tastes exactly the same? My eyes dart to Enzo's first, and though he's eating, he's remembering, too.

"Tastes just like Daddy's," I say to Emilio, who's not eating, but eagerly awaiting our feedback.

"Like, *just* like it," Pia adds for emphasis. They look at each other, their glances full of knowing, exchanging one of those telepathic sibling communications.

Enzo reaches over and squeezes Emilio's shoulder, rocking him back and forth a few times before patting his cheek. "What'd I say, hm? I knew you'd give him a run for his money."

"I don't know about that." Emilio shrugs, though I know he's feeling anything but nonchalant. As I take a bite of the pasta, whose sauce he's perfected in both flavor, composition and texture, I'm riddled with both pride and insecurity. I'm amazed that my child was able to foster such a talent all on his own. But I'm also blindsided. How had I not noticed Emilio's interest, or rather, obsession, with food, and why hadn't he ever told me about it?

"You thinking about culinary school?" Enzo asks, a possibility that jolts me into hyperawareness.

"I don't know," Emilio says, avoiding eye contact with everyone.

"He can't," I answer for him. "He's already enrolled in law school."

"Plans change, Scar," Enzo says in a half-mock.

"Not for my kids, they don't."

"Oh yes they do," Pia corrects me. Her eyes are like laser beams, boring into mine. "You want me to *enjoy my twenties* as a single girl, and that is *so* not happening."

My fork lands with a clink. "Oh, really? Is there something you'd like to tell us, missy?"

"I am going to get married as soon as I meet Mr. Right," she announces. "And I have a feeling I'm going to meet him soon."

"Why the hell would you want to do that?" Enzo asks.

"Look at Mom." Pia gestures to me. "She got married young. Her life's been pretty fabulous if you ask me. The trips, the houses, the clothes, and oh my *God,* her jewelry collection."

My jaw clenches so hard, my teeth grind against each other. "I earned everything I have, Pia Rose."

My words land like a lead balloon, bringing on a tense silence. Enzo knows what I mean. Sadly, Emilio does too, to a certain degree. But by my own design, Pia has been shielded from the uglier parts of my life, hence her false perception.

Enzo looks at Pia and says, "Marriage isn't fun. *Like,* at all. It's a job."

I cover my face with my hands. "Please don't give her that speech."

"No, they both need to hear it," Enzo says. He points his fork at Pia. "Your mother and I come from a different generation."

I clear my throat. "I'm nine years younger."

He shoots me a side glance. "You get the point. Anyways," he continues, "everyone back in our day got married young, but it didn't make anybody's life easier. Made it harder, if you ask me. I was twenty-five when Little Enzo was born. Few years older than you," he says to Emilio. "Can you imagine being a father right now? Giving up your freedom and partying to wake up in the middle of the night to a screaming baby, arguing with your wife about who forgot to buy formula?"

Emilio raised his palms. "I'm not the one who wants to get married young."

Enzo cocks his head in agreement. He focuses in on Pia. "It's just like a job, P. At first, it's all new and shiny, and then when the shine wears off, it all goes to shit. Every day, you get up, and it's the same thing. The things you once found so endearing about the other person agitate the shit out of you. I had a fight with Claudia once over the way I *chewed*. But you're committed, for the rest of your life, so you have to eat it. Bills, health problems, disagreements over the smallest things and forgiving when you really don't want to. That's what marriage is."

Wide-eyed, Pia blinks and looks at me. "Is he for real?"

I pick up my glass of wine. "I think that's what marriage is like when you're not in love."

"Nobody stays in love," Enzo says before taking a bite of branzino.

I catch his eye. Is that what he really thinks? Because if that's true, why, after over two and a half decades of knowing him, does my heart still skip a beat when he walks into a room? "Pia," I say, forcing myself to end this conversation on a positive note, "it's not that I don't want you to fall in love and live happily ever after. I just want you to know who you are before you do all that. And that takes time. You have more freedom than I did. Better opportunities. I just want you to make the most of them. Both of you." I look at my son, hoping he can read between the lines, that this speech of mine isn't just for his sister with a vagabond spirit.

For a moment, everyone goes still. The playlist veers from Dean to Laura Pausini, and the ocean sings freely to its vacant beach. I glance at the mess in the kitchen that I itch to tidy up, but my gaze falls to my Aperol Spritz that's now a mound of orange tainted ice in a glass slick with condensation. What was supposed to be a pleasant evening has left me riddled with worry. How and why are my children changing so fast? All I want to do is retreat to my room and devise a plan to keep them on track. But Enzo, ever the smooth talker, breaks the awkward silence first.

"Hey almost birthday girl," Enzo says to Pia as he eats the last bites of his meal. "What's on your wish list this year?"

"Diamonds, a Birkin bag, and a yacht," she says with a shrug and zero hesitation. Her mouth forms a smirk that mirrors Enzo's.

"Oh, Pia," Emilio says as he rises and starts clearing plates.

"Well," I chime in, rising from my seat as well, though to retrieve wine rather than gather dirty dishes, "at least I raised her right on one account."

———

THE SAND IS WET and cold beneath my feet as Enzo and I start down the shoreline at a wandering pace. The waves kiss my feet every so often as we walk, the ocean's rhythm keeping time with our comfortable quiet. Hands dug into the pockets of my linen pants, I steal glances at his profile, one half of his face illuminated by the crescent moon hanging high in the black sky speckled with twinkling stars that we never get to enjoy in Manhattan. It reminds me of when we were young and very much in love, when he'd drive me home in his Cadillac and I'd stare at his profile like I was desperate to commit it to memory. His features are still sharp and severe, his essence still the same, but this new Enzo lacks something the old him was full of. Hope. Ambition. A tenacity no one could stifle. All I want to know is, why.

"Earlier," Enzo says, breaking the silence, "before dinner. You seemed antsy."

"I called Saverio." I let out a deep sigh. "Wanted to show some good faith and let him know about us selling the house."

"And?"

I press my lips together, hesitating. "And he told me there's a restaurant group interested in buying me out."

Enzo's brows shoot up. "Are you serious? That's amazing."

"Amazing? I have no interest in selling."

Talking with his hands, now, he says, "That would solve all your problems. What do you need this restaurant for anyway? What more do you have to prove? It's nothing but a headache."

"It's not up for discussion, Enz."

"Because of Fran, right? And his legacy that you're so worried about?"

"That restaurant was his life's work. It was his art."

"And you haven't suffered enough for his art?"

I draw in a sharp inhale and let him know I'm annoyed by looking in the opposite direction, toward the row of beachside homes evoking warmth with cozy lighting and family activities. But knowing how fleeting this summer is, I don't want to waste a second of it, so I change the subject. "I'm still recovering from that speech of yours."

He gives a weak smile, his gaze falling to the sand beneath us. "Hope it wasn't too much."

"It was," I say with a laugh. I inch closer to him and nudge his arm with my elbow. Finally, he looks at me. "Is that really how you feel? That no one stays in love?"

"Guess that's been my experience."

"Really?"

"You're telling me you never fell out of love with Fran?"

"I'm not talking about Fran right now."

A wave crashes with force as Enzo comes to a halt. His almond-shaped eyes are like two big question marks. "Then who are you talking about?"

I don't realize the word *us* escapes my lips until he asks me to repeat myself. "Us," I say, though the moment it's in the air, I want to snatch it back.

"What about us?" Mirroring my body language, he shoves his hands into the pockets of his jeans, too.

I regret opening my big mouth. Why would I willingly choose to veer our conversation into this territory? And now, I'm trapped with no way out. "I never stopped thinking about you. Ever."

"We were never married," Enzo reminds me. "I wasn't talking about us either."

He turns and we start down the beach again. In the distance, what looks like two teenagers are enveloped in each other, resting against a lifeguard chair.

"I do have one question for you," Enzo says. "Why don't you want Emilio to cook?"

"How much time do you have?" I joke, but a bitterness spreads over my tongue. "You know how that life is. I don't have to tell you. It's not your own. When you own a restaurant, you're married to it. You're a slave to the people who sit in those chairs. I never had Fran all to myself. Always had to share him, whether it was with our customers, or celebrities, or with his *fans*. With his girlfriends. It's not a life."

But Enzo stops again and this time, he puts his hands on my arms to stop me. His endless eyes are enough to coax the truth out of me.

"You know better than me how Francesco was as a young man," I say, my voice wobbling all over the place. "My Emi is so *good*. He's so gentle and considerate and kind, and I don't want the world to harden him. I don't want him to become cynical like us." I narrow my eyes against the wind. "I don't want him to become the monster your brother became."

"And the whole thing about Pia staying single?" he inquires softly.

"I don't want her to end up like me," I confess. I dart my eyes away, envying the two teenagers who exude a carefree energy I've never possessed, the one I worked so hard to provide to my children. "I was so naïve when I got married. I didn't understand all the ways a person can change. And yes, I was in love with Francesco." I glance up at Enzo. "But after he fell out of love with me, I spent the rest of our marriage trying to win him back. Do you know what that did to me? Spending years of my life trying to win the approval of my own husband?"

"I have news for you, sweetheart," Enzo says, a sternness to his voice and a darkness in his eyes. "The way you're holding on to everything, trying to keep up this façade that everything's perfect, trying to preserve his *legacy*, you still are."

I want to argue. I want to tell him that I'm hanging on for myself, that I've worked too hard to give up on Amanti. But the thing is, he's right. He just doesn't know why. Enzo doesn't know I've been putting up a façade for him, too.

And I'm holding onto that façade with all I've got. Should I let the curtain fall and should anyone see what's behind it, I'm not sure anything would survive.

Not the restaurant. Not my family.

And definitely, most definitely, not us.

CHAPTER TWELVE

ENZO

Spring, 1993

The Maryland air was different. Mourning doves replaced taxi horns, and distant dog barks replaced sirens. Everything here felt still, like it had no interest in going anywhere. But New York? New York rushed like it had something to prove. Manhattan ran through my veins. Living anywhere else felt like my oxygen had been cut off.

My jog slowed to a walk, and I stopped at the mailbox at the end of my driveway, flipping through the envelopes of junk mail and bills as I headed for the front door. I didn't like to admit it even to myself, but I was disappointed when there was no letter from Scarlett. Since that first letter, we'd been writing consistently; sometimes I'd hear from her twice a week. It wasn't so much what she said that I was so eager to receive a note from her, but every time I saw that familiar swirl of her handwriting, something in my chest loosened, like I hadn't realized I'd been holding my breath. Her letters weren't just my tether to home. They reminded me of the *real* me, who still had a place in New York. Who was missed. The one who was replaced with this new version of Enzo I was trying to be.

Entering my house, I dropped the mail on the console table in the entryway and headed for the kitchen. Claudia had warmed my bachelor pad with decorative pillows and generic artwork that wasn't my taste. I knew she did it for the kids, so they'd feel some sense of her presence when they stayed with me. I might've been *Dad*, but Claudia, no matter how she treated me, was their everything. However, despite her efforts, six months in and the place still felt like a waiting room to me.

To drown out the silence, I flipped on the kitchen TV. The local news droned in the background while I whisked some eggs. I was due into work at ten; upon arriving in Maryland, I'd decided that my hospitality wasn't a match for this kind of crowd, so I'd joined Claudia's brother in his produce business. I flipped on the espresso maker and downed a shot before pouring berries and protein powder into the blender to make a shake. Once everything was done, I sat down at the kitchen table, though I preferred standing. Sitting at the table with five empty chairs around it reminded me of what this was.

A hollow haven I saw no way out of.

A loud banging at the door jolted me. The knocking became frantic as I neared the door, and when I peeked through the window and saw Claudia and my girls standing there, my heart sped up.

"What's wrong?" I asked, soaking in all five foot two inches of my ex-wife. Her pajamas alone told me something serious was going on; Claudia was from the generation who didn't leave the house unless they were all dolled up. My daughters flanked her, clutching their mother's hands, tears streaking their perfect little faces.

"Your—" Claudia started, but she couldn't get the words out.

"My what?" I asked. My heart sank. Had something happened to my brother?

"Your son," she let out, her voice hoarse. "He ran away."

I opened the screen door wider and gestured for them to come in. "Go sit down," I said as I closed the door behind us and placed my hands on Claudia's shoulders, squeezing them to let her know that despite our differences, our kids were *ours*. Without a word, we all convened in the kitchen. The girls plunked down at the table, Maria clutching a tattered doll to her chest, while Antonella folded her arms and looked everywhere but at her hysterical mother.

"Claud," I said, loud enough to get her attention, "tell me what happened so I can fix it."

She didn't sit. Instead, she placed her handbag on the table and pulled out a handwritten note, torn from a tablet as told by the jagged side of the page. "He left me this. Saying he loves me, but he wants freedom from his *family*. My baby." I took the letter from her, scanning over my son's sharp, almost illegible handwriting, while I drew Claudia into me with my free arm. "He could be anywhere," she said, her voice muffled as she talked into my shoulder.

I looked over at my daughters. "Did he say anything to either of you?" Maria shook her head, but I stepped away from Claudia when I noticed the hesitation in Antonella. "Nella," I said, "did your brother tell you he was leaving?"

My brown-eyed eleven-year-old with long waves of chocolatey hair looked away. Claudia and I exchanged a glance.

"Nella!" Claudia yelled. "What the hell did he tell you?"

"Nothing," she muttered.

"Antonella, this is serious! Your brother could be in danger!"

I crouched down in front of my middle child and held her arms. "Honey, as you can see, your mommy's very upset. Whatever Little Enzo told you, you have to tell us."

Her eyes darted between her mother and me. "He made me promise. And Mommy always tells us if we make a promise, we have to keep it."

"And under normal circumstances," I said, "that's the case. But your mother's right. He could get hurt if you don't tell us what you know."

Claudia joined me in front of our daughter with a pleading expression. "Come on, Nella."

"He went to Ocean City," Antonella finally told us. "He said some friends of his have a place there for the summer. He's going to get a job and save up until he can get his own place."

Claudia drew in a sharp inhale, pressing her lips together.

"Did he say it was just for the summer?" I asked.

Antonella shook her head. "He doesn't want to come back. He said if I was good and didn't tell you guys, that I could go live with him at the beach when I'm sixteen."

My knees crackled as I stood up. I reached out my arm and helped Claudia rise, though she needed me for support, falling into my chest. As I consoled my ex-wife with a kiss on top of her head and rubbing circles on her back with my palms, it dawned on me that our daughters had never seen us this way. As a couple. I wondered what was running through their little minds as I continued to let Claudia know that I would handle it.

"I think he's hooked on something," Claudia whispered.

"Girls," I said to our daughters, "why don't you go watch TV in your room?"

"You just don't want us to overhear what you're saying," Antonella said with a huff as she rolled her eyes and obliged. She took Maria by the hand and they jogged up the stairs. Claudia and I went quiet, the sound of the local news reporting yet another homicide in Baltimore City filling the silence between us, a cold reminder of the vicious world my son was now navigating alone.

Once I heard the bedroom door close, I continued, though I kept my voice down. "Hooked on what?"

"That white powder you used to shove up your nose," she said, her tone changing now that our children were out of earshot. "Like father, like son."

"Can you not go there right now? That was a long time ago. And I never did anything like that around the kids."

But it was too late. The guilt was old; it lived in my bones. I stared at the tile floor, remembering the times I'd stumbled home, smelling of whiskey and another woman's perfume, my kids already asleep, Claudia pretending I wasn't crushing her with my recklessness. I'd given our son every reason to want to escape. My actions were the driving force behind my son's poor grades, lack of interest in everything, and overall evasiveness. And it was my job to fix it.

"Why aren't we in the car right now?" Claudia asked.

"What are we gonna do? Drive up and down Coastal Highway until we spot him? We have to play this right," I told her. "The more stifled we make him feel, the more he's going to want to rebel."

"He's only sixteen."

"He's a smart kid, Claud. I know my son. This is bullshit, but the kid's got common sense where it counts. And trust me, he's gonna learn real quick how hard it is to be on his own. He'll come back before you and I even find him."

"He's my baby," she whispered.

"I know." I brushed her wiry black hair away from her face. "But sometimes we have to learn things the hard way, no?"

Claudia sat down at the table while I fixed her a cup of coffee. Though my back was turned to her, I could hear her trying to stifle her cries. Guilt mounted with every tear that fell from her tired eyes. I'd married Claudia not because I was in love with her, but because we made sense. I knew she'd give me the family I was supposed to want, though what I wanted and what I needed had never been the same thing. Still, was that so wrong? Didn't people marry for all kinds of reasons? Or did marrying for something other than love, even with the best of intentions, always lead to destruction? Was the absence of that kind of all-consuming adoration, no matter how hard I tried, the reason I simply couldn't be faithful to her?

Placing the coffee in front of her, I rubbed my hand along her tense shoulders. "I want you and the girls to stay with me until this gets sorted out."

"But what if he comes home and I'm not there?"

"He's got my address, too."

She glanced at the phone attached to the wall.

"And he's got my phone number. I know I made a lot of mistakes," I said, holding her gaze no matter how difficult it was to admit my wrongdoings, "but I am still their father. And you"—I pinched her cheek, coaxing a small smile from her lips—"you're still the one and only Mrs. Enzo Valenti."

ONE DAY BLED INTO the next, until days became a few weeks. Claudia and her family put calls out to every last person they knew from Salisbury to Fenwick Island to keep a look out for Little Enzo and eventually, we had a lead. He was working at a pizzeria, owned by a friend of a friend. We had eyes on him and knew he was safe, but I wanted to play our hand right rather than drive him into further rebellion. I asked Claudia and the girls to stay, telling myself it was easier this way—no phone tag, no frantic drives, no one sleeping alone. I woke up unsure what day it was, coffee already brewing, while Claudia got the girls ready for school in the mornings and spent the afternoons ironing shirts I no longer wore, and cooking feasts too big for us to consume in one sitting. All the things she used to do when we were married.

All the things that made me feel like maybe this could, in fact, become my home.

The thought tugged me back to Scarlett, though I wasn't sure why. Maybe it was because like Claudia, she was the woman who'd made that beautiful townhouse a home for my brother. I still hadn't heard from her, something that both worried and disappointed me. Being that I finally had something newsworthy to report, I sat down at the desk in my bedroom and wrote her a note.

Scarlett,

    I haven't heard from you. Is everything okay? He hasn't touched you again, has he? If he has, you let me know. I'll be on the first train up there to knock some sense into him. Is everything going okay with the pregnancy? Here I am, worried, and it's probably the postal service's fault. I live in the fucking boonies. I bet your last letter got lost or something.

    Things aren't so hot down here right now. Little Enzo has run away to Ocean City, trying to start a new life for himself without us. Claudia is beside herself. I'm concerned, too, trust me, but I don't want to pounce on him. Maybe he needs a taste of the real world to realize how good he has it at home. That's certainly what happened to his father. Claudia and the girls have been staying with me since this all went down, and it's reminded me of how good I had it when we were married. I took it all for granted. Having her here, making coffee in the morning and dinners at night, makes me realize just how empty this place feels without her.

I want to find my son and smack him silly for making us worry like this. But I know he's like me, Scar. The more he's pinned down, the more someone tries to tell him what to do, the more he'll want to rebel. It scares me, how much he's like me. I did things I know I'll regret 'til the day I die. And right now, the number one thing I regret is destroying my family. I should've tried harder. I should've had more respect for Claudia as the mother of my children. But I was a selfish bastard, as you know. But the fact that I moved here, away from everything and everyone I love, makes me think maybe I'm not anymore. Who knows. I don't know if someone like me can change that drastically, but I like to hope so.

Anyways, I know you're big on those novenas, so say one for my boy, that he comes home to us in one piece. Squeeze that little nephew of mine and give him a kiss from me, and let me know how my brother's doing. We both know he likes to hide things from me, that sneaky bastard who I miss like hell.

All my love,

Always,

Enzo

Though the letter made me homesick and ravenous with curiosity about what was going on back home, when I went back downstairs and found Claudia, I was back in the present moment. The countertop was scattered with ingredients, while my boombox emitted the soft hum of Sinatra. I looked around for the girls, but the house was in order, free from the chaos of two little ones.

"Where are the girls?" I asked.

"At my sister's," Claudia said as she scooped up empty cans of tomatoes and deposited them in the trash. "All the girl cousins are having a sleepover. Movies, junk food, playing—just the distraction they need."

I leaned against the wall and crossed my arms, watching Claudia flip the meatballs sizzling on the stove. "They've been through a lot with this whole thing, poor kids. As if I didn't have reason enough to want to give our son a beating."

Instead of chiding me, she nodded. "I know."

"You need help with anything?" I moved further into the kitchen, grabbing a bottle of wine from the rack on the counter and pulling a wine key out of a drawer. "It's just us. We could've ordered in."

Her lips curved into a smile. "I don't do take-out."

I laughed as I poured us two glasses of wine, suddenly turned on by Claudia's no-nonsense approach to domesticity. The things I used to find boring about her now excited me—her ability to mold ingredients into something delicious, how she filled my hollow home with a warmth that never existed without her. It jarred me, how this woman I'd known since I was a teenager, freshly immigrated from Naples, seemed new and shiny to me, with a *mappina* draped over one shoulder and a wooden spoon in her hand. I thought of how I'd disappointed her in the past, broken her heart even, and I didn't want to open the door to Claudia unless I was sure I wouldn't do it again. But like I'd said to Scarlett in my letter, I'd changed. I'd left behind a life I loved for the sake of my family. That selflessness didn't exist when I was married to Claudia. Maybe I had left it all behind—the gambling, the cheating, the fast-paced living.

Maybe I could have this now, this perfectly mundane life made better by Claudia, a woman with the remarkable talent to make my rootless self feel like I had a stable home. I'd given my son something to run away from. But maybe I could give him something to come home to. A real family. Maybe, for the first time, my wants and my needs were one in the same.

I turned up the volume on the boombox and took a sip of wine, mustering up the courage to be romantic with her. Standing behind her, I snaked my arm around her waist and swayed her to the gentle music humming all around us. Her laughter filled the kitchen.

"What are you doing, Lorenzo?" She turned around and looked up at me, confusion resting between her brows.

All the women I'd philandered with over the years, outward beauty aside, suddenly paled in comparison to this one. This one I'd taken for granted and tossed aside, and now desperately wanted back. I had to try. I had to try and be the man we both wanted me to be.

I traced the plane of her face with my thumb, my eyes searching hers. "Ever since I got here," I said, my voice gravely, "I felt like it didn't matter one way or another if I'm here or not. I don't know." I shrugged as the labels I'd attached to my ex-wife melted away, and I saw her not as my adversary, but as an ally. "You make me feel like this might be where I belong."

She remained still as she registered my admission, as if she had to make sure the words had truly left my lips. With my arms still around her, she reached behind to shut off the stove before grabbing my face and kissing me. It wasn't some frantic, mad explosion, but between us was a fire that had never before been lit. Had I ever desired her more than I did right now? When we reached the living room and sank onto the sofa, the television bathing Claudia in a hazy red glow, I undressed the body I used to betray. Her lips found mine, her skin warm against me, and I promised myself I'd never let her go. But as we moved together, a thought snagged me, a warning that I shouldn't be making promises I couldn't keep. It hit me too late that I hadn't changed at all.

I was just running away from what, and who, I really wanted.

WE LOUNGED IN BED until eleven the next morning. Claudia rose first, eager to make breakfast and start our day together. I, too, suddenly felt brighter. With the dawn of a new day, I shook off any doubts and focused on what this reunion meant. My days didn't promise to be as mundane, not when I had this new relationship with Claudia to explore and a family to rebuild.

After a quick shower and change of clothes, droplets falling to my neck from my still-wet hair, I jogged down to the kitchen. Claudia was seated at the table, though no breakfast was to be seen. Instead, she had a sheet of paper in her hand and a ripped envelope to her side.

"Is that from Little Enzo?" I asked, rounding the table to stand behind her.

Claudia didn't answer. She just sat there, clutching the pages, her lips pressed tight and her body stiff. I slowed. Then, I saw it. That big, loopy handwriting I could spot a mile away. Scarlett. Of all days for her letter to arrive. Before I could stop it, I felt the familiar flush I got when I saw her innermost thoughts scrawled across the page for my eyes alone. *Not now,* I thought. *Not when things are finally falling into place.*

"Claudia—"

But Claudia whipped around and stood, cutting me off. "Why would you start anything back up with me when you have *this* going on? Did you not hurt me enough the first time?"

"There's nothing going on," I assured her. "She likes to keep in touch with me. Fran hit her, Claudia. Talking to me makes her feel safe."

"Nothing going on?" She held up the sheet of paper, covering her tear-streaked face, and read. *"Mi manchi. It doesn't mean 'I miss you.' It means 'you're missing from me,' and that's exactly how I feel about you, Enzo. Like you're this vital piece of me that I can't function without."* She lowered the sheet of paper so I could see every inch of her enraged, no, heartbroken face. "You call that nothing?"

I ripped the paper out of her hands and tore it to shreds, the pieces fluttering to the ground like wrinkled confetti. "I don't want her," I insisted. "I want this. I want this so fucking bad, Claudia."

"Listen to yourself, Enzo," she yelled. "You don't want *me.* You want *this.*" She opened her arms, gesturing to my house that had become what appeared to be a home in the last few weeks. "You want this, alright, but you want it with her."

My chest heaved up and down as I stood there, defenseless.

"We got divorced, right after you stopped seeing her, you remember?" Claudia went on, not so much with anger, but something worse. Pity. "And you know why, Enzo? It wasn't because I'd finally had enough after a thousand times of you cheating on me. It was because I knew she was different. I knew that you loved her in a way you'd never be able to love me."

I opened my mouth to argue, but no words came out.

"And I don't get it," she said, her voice heavy with exhaustion, her eyes glistening with tears. "I don't get what's so special about her that both you boys are so nuts about her."

"She's not special. Claudia, honey, listen to me," I said, reaching for her as she pulled away, slipping through my fingers like sand. "She's nothing to me. She's—"

"Oh, Enzo, give it up already. She's everything to you," Claudia said, all knowingly. "I don't know if maybe you're embarrassed to admit it, or maybe your ego can't handle the fact that she married your little brother, but I have news for you. Whether you like it or not, she's the love of your life."

Claudia left soon after, taking her warmth with her, leaving behind words that both taunted and haunted me. Not because I didn't want to hear them, but because they were true. I hadn't made Maryland my home because I didn't see it as home. It was a temporary fix, a waiting period, all until I could get back to her. *Anch'io mi manchi*, I thought, as if Scarlett could read my mind a hundred miles away.

She was the missing part of me, too.

CHAPTER THIRTEEN

SCARLETT

Summer, 2011

"**H**er middle name is Rose," I tell the florist as we walk around the deck that will soon be unrecognizable beneath layers of candles and blush-colored blossoms. Pia's birthday marks the true midpoint of summer, but it feels like it's arrived overnight. July has disappeared into salt-slicked beach days, late-night dinners with Enzo and the kids, and efforts to keep our house tidy for showings. Tinsley has foregone a sign in the front yard per my request; the last thing I want to do is spend Pia's party explaining why I'm selling off my slice of paradise. The sun presses down on me, hot and insistent, as I adjust my oversized sunglasses and smile. "And her favorite color is pink. Need I say more?"

"I get the vision," the florist, clad in overalls and Birkenstocks, says with a laugh as she surveys the space. She motions to the area where the dining tables will be set up. "So I'm thinking we do pink gauze table runners that drape to the floor, and we'll do small vases of tight arrangements so people can see each other across the table."

"Good idea," I say as Enzo emerges from the sliding door and brings us two glasses of iced tea. "I would like one big arrangement for the cake table. Something tall."

She nods. "I can do that."

I hesitate, but it's my baby's birthday. "How much would white orchids cost? The kind that cascade down the vase? I just love that look."

"Those would run you about forty a bunch." She gives me a knowing look. "You've got the eye, don't you?"

I do, but sadly, I don't have the bank account to support said eye. I feel Enzo's stare on me as I decide to be a fiscally responsible adult. "Let's stick to the garden roses."

After leaving the florist with a hefty deposit that makes my heart race, I call the caterer to confirm my order for the umpteenth time. Pia, Emilio, and Enzo enjoy the bright beach day as I rattle off the details to the receptionist—passed crab cakes, Caesar salad shooters, seafood towers, and a three-course meal that'll set me back a few thousand dollars I don't have. I painstakingly relay the details of the cake—three tiers of white buttercream, baby pink piping, and enough sugar roses that would bankrupt me if I weren't already. And yes, that's Pia with a P, not Mia with an M. Then, I call the DJ to go over the song selections. I realize selecting songs is his job, but I'm nothing if not a meticulous hostess who insists on having her hand in everything. I've instructed him to start with Bossa Nova, Sinatra while we dine, and we'll dance the night away to classic oldies, a few Italian hits for good measure, and Pia's favorites, Lady Gaga, Katy Perry, Miley Cyrus, and the Black Eyed Peas.

I'm still going down my checklist when Enzo comes in. He's so tan, his skin glows, and it's so shiny with sweat, it's almost reflective. A black tank clings to his stomach, tighter than it has any right to on a man his age. My fingers tingle with the urge to lift the hem, just to see if the abs I remember are still there.

"Jesus. It's that hot out?" I ask.

He's tries to slow his breath as he approaches the sink. "Went for a jog." I clock his sneakers as he turns on the tap, runs his hands beneath it, and splashes his face, getting water everywhere. I rip off a few paper towels and hand them to him to wipe his face and chest, while I clean up the water that's landed on the counter and floor. "What are you still doing in here? It's gorgeous out."

"This birthday party's not gonna plan itself." I sigh as I look out at the beach. He's right. There's not a cloud in the sky and it all looks glorious. "It's also not going to pay for itself. I'm damned if I do and damned if I don't. I feel guilty for spending the money on the party, but if I skimp, I'll feel even guiltier. She's my baby. She deserves the orchids."

Enzo laughs as he discards the paper towels and grabs a bottle of water from the fridge. "No one's going to notice the lack of orchids. Certainly not an eighteen-year-old."

"Oh, this eighteen-year-old will." I shouldn't even be splurging as much as I am, but that doesn't stop me from considering hocking a piece of jewelry to pay for more luxurious flowers.

"She knows you love her. Orchids or not."

Enzo's throat moves as he chugs the water, and his brief distraction gives me a moment to study him. All five-feet-eleven inches of him that've become this hunky, rugged man with sculpted shoulders and bulging biceps and strong legs, all peppered with tattoos. When we make eye contact again, I blink a few times.

"Yes?" he asks me, his eyes narrowing as he smirks.

I hesitate, but he's got me pinned with his curious glance alone. "You're in pretty great shape for an almost-sixty-year-old."

"And you look great for fifty."

I smack my palm against the counter. "Forty-fucking-nine, thank you very much."

"Knew that would get you all riled up." He tosses the water bottle in the garbage. "You coming down to the beach?"

I look out the windowsill with longing, but my responsibilities tug at me. I still have to wrap Pia's present and write a card, something I'd like to get done before my chaotic relatives arrive. Then, I have to check on things at the restaurant … "I can't."

"Scar, summer's halfway over."

Both of our expressions shift, to one of realization. Whatever *this* is, it's halfway gone.

"Well, when you put it that way," I say, trying to recover, "I'll go put on my bikini."

"I'm going boogie boarding," Pia announces. We've been sunbathing for the better of an hour and my daughter's tan rivals Enzo's. She gets up from her beach chair, dusts the sand from her legs, and grabs her board.

"Please be careful," I call after her. As she treks down the beach, her feet creating divots in the sand, I look over at Enzo, who's baking under the sun next to me. "One time she wiped out so bad, we thought she broke her nose."

He winces. "That would've been a shame. She's got a Valenti nose."

The sentiment seizes me. I realize she's half a Valenti, but for so long, especially since Francesco died, I've thought of Pia solely as my own, down to her aquiline nose.

Emilio wakes up, having been asleep on his stomach, stretched out on a towel. "I'm gonna go for a swim too." He stands and stretches his arms overhead. "When's the last time you went in the ocean, Ma?"

"I think when I was your age. Never did find my sea legs."

"Come on," he says in his easygoing way, dragging his boogie board behind him.

Bathed in a coat of sweat, I agree, though only to cool off rather than to explore the ocean's currents. I stand and wriggle out of my coverup, carefully, lest an inappropriate body part slip out. I feel the heat of Enzo's stare, and though he's seen the parts of me that are concealed by my shimmery brown bikini, I feel exposed. I put my hands on my hips and cock my head. "Make your comments now, or forever hold your peace."

He laughs, his eyes hidden behind a pair of Ray-Bans. "I have nothing appropriate to say."

"Get the hell out of here," I laugh. "You coming too?"

"Why not," he says with a huff as he pushes himself out of his chair. But as he starts down the beach, curiosity that's been tugging at me finally wins.

"Alright," I say, falling into stride next to him, "what's with you not wanting to take your shirt off? We're at the beach."

He pats his stomach. "Always gotta leave a little mystery, Scar."

But as we head down the beach, rife with activity—families perched beneath umbrellas sharing snacks, kids hopping waves, couples going for strolls along the shoreline—I can't help but wonder what he's hiding. A scar, maybe? A tattoo he doesn't want me to see? The Enzo I knew was a showoff in every sense of the word. But now, as he slips into the ocean with ease, I want to know what's stolen his bravado. A seagull dips down, too close for comfort, shaking me out of my thoughts. I shriek and jump back a few steps.

"Forget this," I shout. But Emilio sloshes out of the water and grabs me, and before I know it, I'm waist deep in the ocean. I kick and protest the whole way until Emilio's got me out to calmer waters, what feels like miles away from the shore. My heart thuds. "I don't like this."

"Relax, Ma," he says. He helps me onto my back so I float, though I don't relax. And when he leaves me to catch a wave with Pia, I panic and fall back into the water, treading in place.

"I never knew you had such a phobia," Enzo says, coming to my rescue. He adjusts me so I'm flat again, floating, blinded by the sun. Seagulls swoop and sing, and laughter rings in the near distance against the crashing waves, but despite it all, my heart races. I close my eyes, trying to tune everything out and focus on the steady current of the ocean thrumming against my body. "You know what your problem is right?"

"Enlighten me, Lorenzo."

"You have no control out here."

I open one eye. "I'm trying not to die by rip current at the moment. Can we save the life lessons for later?"

"*Tranquillo,*" he says with a low laugh. "I've got you."

It's those three words that calm me, rather than the flow of the sea. It's his hands keeping me steady, and his presence that lets me know no matter what, he's there. *He's got me.* I shouldn't be reeled in like this, into needing him, wanting him, but he's here and I do. More, he's right. Control is what I crave, and it's not just in this rough ocean that I have none. It's every aspect of my life. My restaurant has spiraled, my kids have their own ideas, and though I'm older now, I still can't get a grip on my forbidden feelings for Enzo. That's why I cling to things like Pia's party, little moments in time where I can act like a maestro.

The kids join us, floating, suspended in time and space, and for a moment, everything stops. My racing thoughts, this summer, my to-do list—none of it matters as the sun begins its descent and the sea glitters gold. I breathe in the salty air and my shoulders relax. When I open my eyes, Enzo's looking at me, a placid smile on his face when he realizes the effect he, and this moment, are having on me. Soon after, we all swim toward shore and I awkwardly find my legs again, droplets falling from my body as I return to my chair. Pia towels off and rings out her inky hair, while Emilio stretches back out on his towel.

"Hey, Zio?" Pia says, standing over us.

"What's up, P?"

"Obviously I'm not in charge of my own birthday party," she says with a purse of her lips, "but I was wondering if my cousins are coming."

"My kids?" Enzo clarifies. Pia nods. Enzo glances at me like he's asking for permission.

"You want them to come?" I ask her.

"Yeah. I mean, I haven't seen them since Daddy's funeral. It'd be nice to spend a little time with them here before the house sells."

"I'd love that, P," Enzo says with pride. "I'll give them a call, see who can come."

"Cool," Pia squeaks. "I'm gonna lay out some more."

I toss her a bottle of sunscreen. "Lather up."

She sticks her tongue out at me before laying out next to her brother, lazily spritzing sunscreen over her chest and arms. With a smile planted on my face, my chin resting on my knuckles, I look over at Enzo.

"She's such a great girl," Enzo says. "You're one hell of a mother, Scar."

The words, paired with his tender expression, bite me. I think of the letter I never sent, the one without a stamp, and my stomach twists. One hell of a mother.

One hell of a mother, indeed.

CHAOS IS MY FAMILY's specialty. Luggage has been dropped in the entryway, unpacking saved for later. Wine is flowing, as is conversation, a combination of catching up and reminiscing about summers past. Julie's laughter booms, filling up the entire kitchen, while her boys and Emilio pick out cigars from the humidor to smoke by the fire pit outside. Fausto, our dear friend and former Valenti's coworker, has flown in from LA for the occasion, and it's as if we haven't skipped a beat.

Upstairs, Pia is in her bedroom with three of her closest girlfriends, the blaring pop music seeping through the walls. Enzo is rattling off a story in his quick Napoletano dialect to Fausto and my mother's boyfriend, Tony, while Julie's husband, Bobby, laughs along like he understands a word.

My mother and I work side by side at the counter, washing the dishes, the clink of plates and silverware blending with the evening's soundtrack. Emilio cooked yet another stellar meal tonight, much to the fascination of our relatives. Outside, the sky is painted with stripes of pastel as yet another day of this fleeting summer comes to a close. Inside, however, it feels like things are just getting started.

"Scar," Enzo calls from the kitchen table, "we got a pack of Scopa cards laying around anywhere?"

I close the tap and dry my hands. "We should. I'll look."

I head to the living room, the flurry of activity swirling behind me, and start searching for the traditional Neapolitan card game that my husband and Enzo used to play for hours on end. But as I'm going through the armoire that holds our stereo system and CD collection, a knock at the door pulls me away. No one else seems to have noticed, not above the storytelling and laughter and incessant Italian music that rings through this house like a heartbeat.

I open the door, and there they are. Two faces I haven't seen in four years.

"Oh my God," I say as I pull open the screen to welcome Enzo's children—his oldest, Little Enzo, and his baby, Maria. I want to see the kids they used to be, running around this house with my own, but instead, two grown adults stare back at me, proof that time is sprinting by.

Maria steps in first, and I wrap her in a hug. She's tiny like Pia, no more than five feet tall, and she squeezes me tight.

"Hi Zia," she says, her voice still sweet and high-pitched.

"Look at you," I say, cupping her face in my hands. "I don't know how it's possible, but you got even more beautiful." She smiles in response as I turn to Little Enzo. "And you. I keep forgetting you're not *little* anymore."

His voice is low and velvety like his father's, his hair the same shade of ink. Enzo joins me in the entryway, and though he's appeared happy all summer, something shifts in him when he sees his kids. It's a glow I understand completely. Maria greets her *daddy* with such warmth, it draws tears to my eyes. And when Enzo hugs his son, who is the same age Enzo was when I met him, it's like timelines have collided.

"God," I say to Enzo, "did you clone yourself?"

"He's a handsome devil, isn't he?" Enzo teases, but his eyes linger on Little Enzo with a softness that betrays his tough front, giving way to a tenderness he tries to keep under wraps most of the time.

"Nella couldn't make it," Maria tells us as we head toward the kitchen, though the dip in her voice suggests *couldn't make it* is a polite cover up for *didn't want to come.*

"Sorry, Pop," Little Enzo adds.

Enzo stiffens for a second before waving it off. "Two out of three. All good. Let's have a drink."

"I'm gonna go get Pia," I say. "She'll be so excited you came."

I jog up the stairs and knock twice before opening Pia's bedroom door. A wall of techno music nearly knocks me backward, the bass thudding in my chest. Pia and her girlfriends jump up and down on the bed, hands in the air, lost in the beat, while an episode of *Jersey Shore* flashes on the TV.

"Mom!" Pia shrieks, mortified, as she scrambles down from the bed. "What the hell?"

"I knocked," I say, laughing as she wrestles me into the hallway. But I grab her arms before she can escape. "Your cousins are here. Not Antonella. She couldn't make it. But Maria and Little Enzo just got here."

Pia rolls her eyes. "Nella's always been such a bitch."

"Pia Rose—" I start, but she's already halfway down the steps by the time her name leaves my lips. I hurry after her, just in case she decides to broadcast her thoughts about her missing cousin to the entire house.

"Hey, *cugi*," Little Enzo says as he draws Pia into a hug, her head barely reaching his chest. My mind flashes back to all the times he hoisted her onto his shoulders, carrying her into the ocean while us grown-ups lounged, oblivious. "You're finally a legal adult."

"One more day. Honestly, it's not easy being the baby of the family. I can't catch up to you guys."

"Trust me," Maria chimes in, "you don't want to."

When they hug, their matching blankets of black hair tangle together, and for a fleeting second, they look like twins. Coos of *Aww* and *How sweet are they* pepper the room, but the moment is quickly zapped by Pia's sharp tongue.

"I see Nella's still a total nightmare," Pia snaps, dragging out the last word with relish.

"Jesus, Mary, and Joseph," I mutter, covering my face with my hands.

But Little Enzo and Maria burst into laughter. "Yep," Little Enzo says, shaking his head. "That about sums her up."

Behind me, Enzo slips his hands onto my shoulders, his fingers warm and grounding. A soft chuckle rumbles in his chest before he leans in closer. "It's okay," he whispers in my ear, his breath sending a shiver down my neck. "I think she's a trip."

As everyone crowds around to greet Enzo's kids and Pia's friends file in from upstairs to see what all the ruckus is about, Enzo claps his hands together, his voice rising above the noise.

"Come on, everybody. Let's have a little champagne."

"Woohoo," Pia whistles, throwing her arms in the air. "Let's get this party started!"

"Half a glass for you, missy," I say, pointing at her with sternness. "You are *not* going to be hungover on your birthday."

She groans, turning to her cousins. "See what I mean? Torture."

Corks pop and glasses clink against bubbling laughter. A half-hour later, the champagne has done its job and the house hums with a second wind of energy. Voices grow louder, stories more animated, and the night seems endless.

I pinch the back of Julie's arm. "Get Fausto. Let's go down to the beach."

The three of us slip out the back door, unnoticed by everyone except Enzo. He leans back in his chair, his eyes catching mine through the glass slider. Despite his watchful gaze, he gives me a small nod that says, *Go on. Have some fun.*

"It's just like the old days," Fausto marvels as we sink into the sand, halfway between the dunes and the ocean. "Except we have better liquor now."

He passes me a bottle of Dom and I take a sip, my fingers curled around the bottle's slick neck. We certainly didn't enjoy such a pedigree of alcohol back in our heyday, when we'd huddle in the alley behind Valenti's after closing to gossip, pour our hearts out, and console one another with cheap booze and even cheaper advice.

Julie laughs as she rests her weight on her palms behind her, crossing one leg over the other, looking eternally at ease. "The booze has changed. But *other things* have not," she says, flicking sand toward me with her foot.

I take another much-needed sip before passing her the bottle. "Like what, Julie?"

"Don't *Julie* me," she says, grinning. "And don't play dumb, either. We're talking about you and Enzo whether you like it or not."

"Ah, yes," Fausto adds with dramatic flair, as if announcing an opera. "Let's get right to the good stuff."

I glance between them. "Sorry to disappoint, but there's nothing to talk about."

"Oh, *please*. There's always something to talk about when it comes to you two," Julie protests.

"The chemistry," Fausto adds, "is still very much alive, I must admit."

"Chemistry aside, you lunatics, Enzo is what he's always been. A fantasy. Off-limits." I pause, letting the words sink in. Am I trying to convince them, or myself? "He's my husband's brother, for Christ's sake."

"That never stopped you before," Julie sing-songs.

"Bitch," I mutter.

"*Late* husband," Fausto corrects. His sweet, bright blue eyes pierce right through me, the teasing slipping away. "And I get it. For a while, you wanted to play the good Italian widow. Loyal. Stoic. Honoring Francesco. But you're still young, and you're still beautiful, and I know you, Scarlett."

My breath catches. The words hit somewhere raw.

"I *know* you still want to be in love now," he continues, "the same way you did all those years ago, when we'd sit in that alleyway and you'd cry over those Valenti boys."

The tears come before I realize I'm reacting to his words. I swipe at them fast. "Thanks a lot, Faus."

He reaches out and squeezes my shoulder as I take a long gulp of champagne, the bubbles sharp against my throat.

"We're best friends. And best friends are honest with each other." His raised brows dare me to meet him there, that terrifying place of truth.

I hug my knees to my chest, the cool sand clinging to the soles of my feet. For a second, I feel like that girl again, the one they pulled into their tight-knit circle all those years ago, when I was naïve enough to be driven by my desire to matter to someone.

"I made a lot of mistakes in my marriage," I start, my voice barely rising above the sound of the waves. "Did things I regret. Things Fran never knew about. And no matter how much champagne you feed me," I say, handing him the bottle, my limbs growing number by the second, "I'm not going there tonight."

"Regrets are one thing, Scar," Julie says, refusing to back down. "But the fact is, he's gone. You're still here."

"I know," I snap. The words tumble out of me before I can catch them. "But I can't forget what I did. I can't believe I was that person. That I betrayed him. That I *cheated*. That I lived a lie." At their charged silence, I continue, though my voice wavers both from my admission and too much alcohol. "Every day, I think if I just try hard enough, if I throw the perfect party, save the restaurant, stay single, I can make up for it. I feel like I owe it to him. If I can just keep doing what I'm doing and not be as *bad* as I was, I can erase what I did."

"But he's not here to see it," Julie reminds me.

"But I am." I meet her eyes and draw in a shaky breath. "And I need to prove to myself that I'm not that woman anymore."

Julie and Fausto exchange a glance as if I'm speaking a language they don't understand. Beyond us, the ocean draws and crashes in its relentless rhythm. Behind us, what's ended up being a lively night rages on with laughter, music, life. But here, in this small, quiet pocket of the world, I'm suspended in the middle, one foot in the past, the other tepidly testing the waters of the future.

"So in your mind," Julie says, "being with Enzo would make you a bad person?"

My eyes drift to the flat horizon. "Montauk isn't real life. It never has been," I say with a scoff. "My life is in the city. His is in Florida. And when this summer is over, we're going back to our real lives. This isn't a beginning." The breath leaves my lungs as I realize, "This is where we end."

The statement draws a coverlet of silence over us, and we sit like that for a while, soaking in the stillness of the beach, the nearly full moon overhead, the twinkling stars dancing around it. Fausto looks like he's about to say something to break the thick tension that's fallen between us, but his gaze shifts past me. I glance over my shoulder to find Enzo approaching.

"What's up, boss?" Fausto says, hopping up to his feet with impressive agility.

"I haven't been your boss in a long time," Enzo jokes, his cheeks flushed from the champagne.

Julie rises and dusts the sand from her. "Guess we should get back to the party." She extends her hand to help me.

"Party's over," Enzo announces. "Everyone crashed."

I manage to stand, but stumble right into Julie's shoulder. I press my palm to my forehead and close my eyes, dizziness swirling through me. An arm wraps around me, strong and familiar. I don't have to look to know it's Enzo.

"I got her," he says, his chest pressing against my back, his arms snugly wrapped around my shoulders, pulling me back to gravity. We get ourselves back in the house in one piece. Through my champagne-induced haze, I take in the aftermath. Empty glasses, stray playing cards, and crumbs litter every surface, and I'm already dreading the work that awaits me come morning. The sofas are claimed by Emilio and Julie's boys, blankets haphazardly draped over them. Upstairs, Julie slips into the guest room, Fausto bids us goodnight, and the house settles into quiet.

"Where are your kids?" I ask as Enzo nudges open my bedroom door.

"On air mattresses in my room," he says, closing the door behind us. When he loosens his grip, I stumble forward, but he reacts quick enough to keep me upright. "Did you take something?"

I steady my eyes enough to meet his narrowing gaze.

"Just champagne. This is why I stick to martinis and wine. None of this bullshit happens."

He laughs, more fond than amused, as he guides me to the en suite bathroom and manhandles me into the shower. Before I can protest, he flips on the water, grabs the showerhead, and sprays me with a blast of cold droplets. My hands fly up, trying to block the icy spray that causes goosebumps to blanket my body. A gasp escapes my throat.

"You asshole." I wrap my hands around his wrist and twist the showerhead, so the water drenches him instead.

He drops the showerhead and braces one hand against the tile. His soaked shirt clings to every line of him as he wipes his eyes dry. Water continues to pool at my bare feet, but the goosebumps disappear. The laughter vanishes. Enzo's gaze isn't playful anymore. It's fire.

I touch the back of my hand to his rosy cheek, warm beneath my fingers. "I remember champagne used to give you a headache."

"Never stopped me from drinking it."

He hasn't touched me, but my heart pounds as I wonder what comes next. I can feel the kiss before it happens, suspended in the space between our mouths. All it would take is a tilt of my head, a surrender, and I could have him right now. I want to have him, to give into every part of my being that's screaming for his. And for one dizzying second, I almost do. I want to feel something real and reckless and alive. I wonder what life would be like if I wasn't living six feet beneath my late husband's legacy.

But instead, I close my eyes and swallow hard. *This is where we end.* Why would I set myself up for heartbreak, when I know exactly how to avoid it?

"What are you doing, Enzo?" I whisper, my eyelids heavy as I blink against wet lashes.

His eyes search my face, his gaze soft. "Just trying to sober you up. Tomorrow's our girl's birthday."

He shuts off the shower and leaves, but those two words stay with me. *Our girl.*

Has he even realized what he said?

As the saying goes, *In vino veritas.*

In wine, there is truth.

CHAPTER FOURTEEN

SCARLETT

Summer, 1993

July 17th, 1993, at 6:03pm was the greatest moment of my life. My family was complete, and my biggest dream had come true.

I had a daughter.

The little girl I'd long dreamed of dressing up in pink outfits and bows, of taking to ballet classes and buying baby dolls for, had arrived. All seven pounds and fourteen ounces of her was pure perfection, from her thick black hair to her button nose and pouty lips. I couldn't stop staring at the little girl in my arms, as if her features were changing by the minute. She'd been in the world just a couple of hours, but I'd already forgotten the agonizing labor that brought her here. Instead, all I felt was the most incomprehensible, overwhelming love I'd ever experienced. A baby girl.

A baby girl we had nine months to name, but in the moment, couldn't decide.

"The big brother is here," Francesco said as he came back into the hospital room. Emilio looked unsure as his father guided him forward, maybe even a little scared. He had a bouquet of flowers in his little four-year-old hands, but he stopped at the foot of my bed.

"Look at those flowers," my mother, who sat in a chair beside my bed, said. She opened her arms and gestured for Emilio to come closer. "Come show them to your baby sister."

Emilio glanced up at Francesco. He gave a nod and a wink, giving our son enough courage to join us. My mother propped him in her lap, giving him a better view of his sister.

"Oh, wow," I said, glancing between my two children. "Babydoll, look at those flowers," I said to my daughter. "Aren't they beautiful? Say, *Thank you, Emilio.*"

I was so focused on making sure my son wasn't terrified of the baby in my arms, that I didn't notice Francesco on the other side of me. He bent over and kissed our daughter's forehead, then mine. Then, he produced a small velvet black box. "Mommy deserves a present, too."

"What did you do?" I asked, my cheeks aching from smiling so much. He snapped open the box to reveal a heart-shaped solitaire diamond perched atop a white gold band that was so gargantuan, it took my breath away. "Francesco!"

"Let me put it on you." He reached for my hand, but I was reduced to laughter as he tried to wiggle the ring on my swollen finger.

"I'm going to love wearing this, thirty pounds from now," I teased.

But he managed to get the ring onto my pinkie. Satisfied, he cupped my face in his strong hands and kissed me a few times, his gaze hooked on mine when he pulled away. A current pulsed between us, stronger than ever, unending, unyielding.

"I love it," I said, glancing at the diamond before tucking my hand back beneath my baby for support. "But I love you more."

"I'm crazy about my girls." As Francesco leaned over us like a covering, I savored his presence, his attention that was solely on us. His family. I wanted to hold onto the moment, to ignore my mother's unimpressed expression, but the door opened. In walked Enzo with a bouquet of what looked like three dozen white roses.

"*Guaglione,*" Francesco said, clapping his hands together before drawing his brother into a hug. "You made it."

"Congratulations," Enzo said, patting Francesco's cheek. "*Come state?*"

"*Tutto a posto,*" Francesco said, breezing his hand through the air echoing the Neapolitan sentiment, *Everything's alright.*

"Now you're gonna understand what I go through." Enzo just his chin toward the baby swaddled in my arms. "I'd be a rich man if I didn't have daughters."

Laughing, Francesco ushered Enzo over to the side of the bed. "Come see our girl."

Enzo held up the roses to me before resting them on the windowsill overlooking lower Manhattan. "For the Valenti girls."

"Thank you, Enzo," I said as he leaned over me to soak in his first glimpses of my daughter.

He ran his palm along her black hair, his fingertips against her tiny knuckles. "God," he whispered, "I forgot how small they are. She's beautiful. Absolutely beautiful." I fought off my raging emotions while he continued to admire her. "What's her name?"

"We don't know," I said.

"I'm liking Domenica," Francesco chimed in. "But Scar's not a fan."

I shook my head, scanning over every inch of my baby's features. "She doesn't look like a Domenica to me."

I glanced up at Enzo's profile. His brows were knit as he focused on the baby, as if he, too, were trying to pluck the perfect name out of thin air. Meanwhile, I was busy trying to decipher any similarities between my baby and him. The black hair wasn't a clear enough indicator; I was a dark brunette, too. Dismayed, however, there were no clear signs pointing to whom the other half of my daughter was comprised of.

"I'm still voting Rose," my mother said, keeping Emilio busy with his toy trucks. I looked over at the roses Enzo had brought in—my favorite flower. Was it a sign? Monitors kept beeping, the TV hummed, and chatter floated in from the hallway as all of us huddled together in silence, trying to put a name on this little perfect being.

"She looks like Mamma," Enzo finally said. He stood up straight and looked at Francesco. "Don't you think?"

Francesco leaned his hip against the side of my bed. "The hair, for sure. And her eyes, they're almond-shaped."

I tuned out their back and forth and focused on the name their mother bore. "Pia," I said aloud, testing it. Two sweet syllables that, in an instant, I knew suited my baby girl. I glanced over at the roses. "Pia Rose." I burst into tears. I wanted to blame my hormones, but I knew it ran deeper than that. It was the fact that my precious daughter had a name, and it was brought to me by Enzo. It was that it felt *right*. Surely, I was reading too far into things to think that meant he was her father, wasn't I?

"Pia Rose," my mother echoed. "That's it."

I opened my arm, gesturing for Emilio to come by me. "What do you think?" I kissed his forehead and drew him as close to me as I could over the barrier of the hospital bed. "Is that your sister's name?"

He nodded, his eyes lighting up as he finally reached out and touched Pia's hand with his index finger.

"She's tiny, isn't she?" I said, waiting for my son to look me in the eye before I continued. I wasn't sure he'd remember it, but I wanted to make the moment special for him, too. "She is going to be your best friend, forever. You two are going to love each other so much, you know that?"

And to the joy of my mom heart, Emilio leaned over and kissed the top of her head, melting all us adults into a puddle. We all went still, and I swore we were all thinking the same thing. Why couldn't it stay like this? Why must life's joys be balanced out by sorrows?

But I was thinking something else, too. Why must the miracle of my daughter's life be overshadowed by its muddy origin?

"Where are your kids, Enzo?" my mother asked.

"In the waiting room," he said. "We're gonna head out to Montauk tonight."

"Bring 'em in here," I said.

"You sure?"

"She's gonna have to get used to being part of a crazy Italian family someday," I joked. "Might as well start her young."

As Enzo's children filed in and marveled over how tiny their cousin was, and Maria promised she'd teach Pia how to braid her hair when she had enough of it, I searched my nieces for similarities. Did their noses dip in the same place as Pia's? Were their cupid's bows as pointy, their faces as round? My mother had brought up getting a paternity test more than once during my pregnancy, and each time, I'd shot her down. But now, possibilities all around me, I hated the looming question mark over my daughter's life. More, I hated that it was there because of my own recklessness.

I leaned back against my pillows, exhaustion hitting me all at once, consoled by only one thought.

Something so perfect couldn't have been created from sin.

Could it?

IT WAS THAT DOUBT, that fifty-fifty chance, that led me to go through with the test. A lock of my daughter's hair tested against my husband's—that was all it would take to shatter the illusions I'd worked so hard to paint. The results came a week after she was born, delivered by a nurse in pink scrubs in a sealed envelope. I didn't open it. Instead, I'd tucked it into the side pocket of my handbag and carried it with me when we drove out to Montauk as a family, as if time alone could bend the truth in my favor.

Now, a few days into our stay, I sat in my bedroom while Pia slept soundly in her bassinet, her belly full and her lips slightly parted. Outside, the sun was setting, and the boys were playing volleyball with Enzo's girls on the beach. I figured it was as good a time as any.

The fireplace in my bedroom crackled as I stepped out to grab my mother from the guest room. She closed the door behind us, and I dug out the folded envelope from the zipped side pocket of my Birkin. I sat cross legged on my made bed while she perched on the edge, her gaze fixed on Pia.

"Scarlett," my mother said, resting her hand on my leg, "I know I pressured you into this. But now that I see her, I feel so foolish. She's perfect. It doesn't matter who her father is."

"I want to believe that, Mom," I said, watching Pia's belly rise and fall with even breath. "But yes, it does."

My hands shook. Violently. Adrenaline snaked its way up from my belly to my throat where it threatened to choke me. I knew, no matter the results printed in black-and-white on these pages, that Francesco and I would raise Pia as a couple. That Enzo and I would uphold our vow to keep that fleeting night of sin a secret until the end of time. Nothing on the outside would change. It was me who would undergo something I'd have to endure alone. If Pia was, in fact, half of Enzo,

I'd have to live with that secret for the rest of my life, a thought that felt akin to being sentenced to solitary confinement.

My only solace was sharing this with my mother, who was growing more worried by the second. "I'm right here, honey. And whatever that paper says, you're going to be okay."

At her encouragement, I slipped my finger beneath the lip of the envelope, the sound of the tear cutting through the thick quiet, punctuated only by the sound of the waves just beyond us. The envelope fell to the ground as I undid the trifold. The thin pages felt as fragile as I did as they shook in my slick hands.

It was all very scientific, a chart of numbers and letters that I couldn't decipher, all except for the figure printed at the bottom.

Probability of Paternity: 0%.

I blinked to make sure it was really there. And it was, staring back at me, until it was permanently seared in my memory, an image forever branded on my brain.

"No," I whispered. I slammed the pages down and looked at my mother, desperate for her to make things better. "Mom, no." Cold sweat broke over me. The room tilted. This couldn't be. I couldn't spend the rest of my life being punished for one mistake.

I couldn't spend forever looking at my daughter, that sweet, innocent, perfect being I'd brought into this world, and be reminded of my one night of both sin and regret every time.

Voices filled the house, spiking my panic. My mother grabbed the sheet of paper, glancing at the results as she got up from the bed. She curled it into a ball and tossed it into the fireplace, where it was reduced to smoke and ashes, as if it never existed in the first place.

I sank into the pillows, my hands covering my face as if that would conceal the sobs that leapt out from my body that was still swollen from carrying my daughter. My mother grabbed me.

"Look at me," she demanded. "Get yourself together, Scarlett. It doesn't matter how she got here, alright? She's here, and she needs you. All of you. The very best of you. You owe that to her. You want to right your wrong? Raise her the best you know how."

I wanted to absorb everything she was saying, but not a moment later, the doorknob turned and the door creaked open. Francesco poked his head in. "Didn't want to wake anyone," he whispered. But when he saw my tear-streaked face, his face fell. "What's wrong?"

"Baby blues," my mother announced, a bold-faced lie she had no qualms about making. She patted his arm on her way out. "Good luck, buddy. You're gonna need it."

Francesco's gaze trailed after her as my mother sauntered out and closed the door behind her gently, so not to wake the baby. Shirtless and bronzed from a day spent in the sun, he studied me for a moment before sinking into bed next to me. He wrapped me in his long arms, and I inhaled the salty air and sunscreen that clung to his skin.

"You didn't have this with Emilio," Francesco said after a while, leaning his forehead against mine. He smoothed my hair back with his palms, holding me with a tenderness that brought forth a fresh wave of guilt. Yes, Francesco may have strayed. And yes, there was the time he hit me. There were the fights when we used our words as weapons. But those were the low points, not the whole story. Not the throughline that defined us. Looking into his eyes, it hit me all at once.

I thought I was punishing him. But the only person I'd punished was myself, with a life sentence I couldn't escape. I couldn't tell him. It would kill him. Destroy us, not to mention, ruin my children's lives.

And, I realized, I couldn't tell Enzo, either. Watching his brother raise his daughter?

It would kill him, too.

I had too many people to protect. No, this was mine to carry, and to carry it alone.

"What is it, babe?" he asked.

I turned into a blubbering mess, my hormones mixing with the revelation that I was still reeling from. "I feel so fat," I complained, my sobs messy and endless. "And look at you." I punched his chest. He didn't so much as rock backwards. "You look like a Greek god. You're gonna get a young hot girlfriend who looks like a Greek goddess."

He tilted his head and let out a lazy grin that made him look like the young man he was when I first fell in love with him. "*You're* young and hot, and I don't like Greek girls. I like half-Italian women from Hell's Kitchen who curse like sailors."

I laughed through my tears, though the reprieve was short lived. As Francesco enveloped me in his arms and drew me back with him into the pillows, I felt confined. To him, to the secret I was now forever laden with, to the future that felt claustrophobic where it should've felt endless.

He swiped my tears with his knuckles and held my chin between his fingertips. "I know I haven't been a perfect husband," he said, his voice soft and low, "and I'm sorry. I'm so sorry."

He drew his lips to my face, kissing the precise spot that had bruised from his slap.

"I promise, babe," he continued, "nothing will ever tear us apart like that again. I won't let it. I don't know why, but I feel like this baby gave us a second chance. Don't you?"

My heart felt heavy. My secret, my sin and its result, already felt like it was ripping me apart at my seams. I didn't know how, or if, the ache would ever dull. Still, maybe Francesco had a point. Maybe this was a fresh start. A second chance where I could leave my past with Enzo behind and start anew, focused purely on my family.

My tears slowed and I smiled. "I feel the same way."

We both looked over at Pia, who was blissfully unaware of the tumult that plagued her mother. And if I had it my way, it would stay that way, no matter my silent suffering.

My mother had warned me about the weight of my lies, but it was nothing compared to the crushing pressure of the truth.

———

PIA'S CRIES WOKE ME. I wondered if Francesco really was able to sleep through her wailing, or if he was just pretending so he wouldn't have to get up. Not that I would've made him go downstairs to mix her bottle in the wee hours of the night. The truth was, every second with my baby girl was sacred to me. Even when exhaustion tugged at me, I knew from having raised Emilio that these moments were fleeting, that they'd all blur into months and years I'd wish I could relive. I lifted her from her bassinet and rested her against my chest, taking each step to the kitchen careful and quiet so I wouldn't wake the rest of the family. The house was rarely silent, and in the stillness of the night, the ocean sounded ferocious.

I flipped on the light when I reached the main level of the home, but when I saw Enzo on the couch, squinting beneath the sudden brightness, I cringed. "Sorry," I whispered, quickly lowering the dimmer.

Enzo sat up. His hair was unruly, black spikes sticking out in all different directions. All he wore was a wifebeater and boxers. He rubbed his eyes, stood, and met me in the kitchen where he reached out his arms and took Pia from me.

"I know," he said as he rocked her, "I want to cry when I'm hungry, too."

I smiled as I gathered her bottle and mixed the formula with water, stealing glances of them. Them—my daughter and her father.

There it was again, that panic, sharp like lightning to the chest. I fought my way through it, focusing on wiping the dusting of formula powder that landed on the counter, and on getting Pia fed so I could go back to sleep. Without taking his eyes off her, Enzo reached out and I placed the bottle in his hand. As if he'd done it a million times, he placed it at her mouth, and she latched on immediately.

I forced myself to remember this tender, intimate moment. This was what it would've been like, wasn't it, in some other lifetime? One where Enzo and I could've been together, where I could've experienced the softer sides to him, feeding the baby he didn't know he fathered. His inhibitions gone, sleep still in his eyes, he looked at Pia as if she were a precious jewel. Had he looked at all his children with the same splendor, or was he, deep down, wondering if the jet hue of her hair and the curve of her nose were derivatives of his DNA?

One day, when she was all grown up, would the two of them look at each other and see a mirror in their eyes?

Would the truth be written on my daughter's face, or would she turn out to be a blend indistinguishable to all?

"Pretty Pia," Enzo said as she sucked on her bottle. "Pretty like her mamma."

I shared a smile with Enzo and ran my hand along her soft whispers of hair. "I love her name, by the way. Suits her perfect."

"Someone had to save her from *Domenica*," he teased. But as our gazes locked, the playfulness left his eyes and instead, all that was left was wonderment. How did we get here after where we had been? So close, so interlinked, only to return to a place of friendly distance?

"All done," Enzo announced as he took the empty bottle and set it on the counter.

I draped a *mappina* over my shoulder before propping Pia up to burp her. "You don't have to stick around for the fun part."

His laugh was forced, and he lingered longer than he should have, but we both knew it was time for him to go. "I'm gonna go up. The couch kills my back."

"Night, Enz," I said as I patted Pia's back.

He paused at the bottom of the steps, his fingers drumming against the banister. He stared at us: the woman he was never supposed to love, the baby we weren't supposed to have. Centimeters parted his lips, but it was enough for me to notice, to hope, that he might ask.

Please, Enzo, I thought. *Ask me.* I yearned to tell him the truth for my own selfish reasons; it was a heavy burden, and I wanted his help carrying it. But his expression smoothed over and he nodded one last time, soaking in an image he'd never see twice. Me caring for our newborn child in the middle of the night.

"Night, Scar," he said back, and he drifted upstairs taking all the *what ifs* running through my mind with him.

The next day, I'd sit in my bedroom alone, beside my sleeping baby, and I'd write him a letter. I'd stop and start and stop again and look at the fireplace and want to torch it, but I'd get the words out regardless. As summer faded to fall, I'd find pockets of time where I'd consider giving him the letter, but in the end, I'd tuck it away, never to see the light of day again.

It didn't matter. Every time I looked at my daughter who grew more beautiful by the day, who made my heart grow and swell far beyond measure, whether she was Francesco's or Enzo's mattered less and less. She was mine.

And she had all my love. Always.

CHAPTER FIFTEEN

SCARLETT

Summer, 2011

Sunlight streams through the windows, highlighting the aftermath of a summer night well spent. I weave through the living room, stepping over abandoned shoes and half-empty glasses, careful not to wake the boys sprawled across the sofas. As I take it all in, instead of being overwhelmed by the mess, I'm met with something else. Melancholy. Nights like last night are what this house was intended for; to be lived in, to be filled with laughter, a haven for making memories we'll recount for years to come. And as I switch on the espresso maker and brew myself the first of many shots, it's not lost on me that last night will be one of the final memories we make in this house.

As will tonight. My daughter's eighteenth birthday.

I'm loading the dishwasher when my mother joins me at the sink. She whispers *good morning* as I fix her an espresso. While she downs it, she scans over the disarray I have yet to clean.

"Well, we're all good at one thing," she says in hushed tones. "Making messes."

I wonder if she means something by it, or if the shoe simply fits.

"Everyone enjoyed themselves," I say as I wet a rag, wring it out, and wipe down the countertop. "And messes don't last forever."

"Oh, I don't know about that." She raises her brows as she heads over to the dining table and gathers up the Scopa cards. So, she definitely meant something by it.

I work in silence, stacking dirty dishes. "There something you'd like to say to me, Mother?"

She glances over at the living room, no doubt to make sure the boys are still asleep. "Maria and Pia look like sisters."

I exhale through my nose. "And? They are family."

"Yes, they are. Close family."

"Mom," I say, the single syllable laden with my most threatening tones. "I am spending a lot of money that I don't have on this party. I'd like to enjoy it without thinking about a mistake I made eighteen years ago."

"Oh come on, Scarlett," my mother hisses as I straighten the chairs around the table. "You're not the first woman with a baby daddy problem and you won't be the last. What's the big deal?"

Stirring sounds come from the living room. My head snaps to see whose curious ears might be tuned into our conversation. Emilio is stretching, but his eyes are still closed. Still, too close for comfort. I rush outside and my mother follows me, sliding the door closed behind us. I snatch up plastic cigar wrappers and lighters around the firepit.

"Why are you bringing this up?" I say, my voice raised now that we have the barrier of the waves and the windows to muffle our voices. "Are you trying to punish me for what I did?"

"What did you do? You had a baby. A beautiful one, and she's eighteen today. It's a day of celebration."

"Exactly." My chest is hot and my heartbeat echoes in my ears. "So why can't you just let it go?"

"You want to talk about letting go?"

I toss my arms up before storming over to the pool, gathering stray noodles, inner tubes, and goggles. The boys must've enjoyed a midnight swim.

"I just want you to lighten up, babydoll," my mother goes on.

"Lighten up?" I say from my squatted position next to the pool. "There's nothing funny about my life."

"That's the problem." With great effort, she crouches down to my level. "You want to see your kids happy, right? Well, you're my kid. I know you're a woman, but you're still my baby girl, just like Pia's yours. So imagine how I feel, watching your life fly by and seeing you not crack a smile. I want you to *laugh*. The kind of laughter that brings tears to your eyes. Your best friends are here. Your children are happy and healthy. All I'm saying is, let go. Enjoy it."

I glance toward the kitchen window, trying to escape the swell of tears behind my eyes. Emilio is awake, brewing himself an espresso at the counter.

"Bad things happen when I let go, Mom," I mutter, the words barely escaping my tight throat.

"Pia happened, the last time you let go," she says softly. "There's nothing bad about her. Just think about it, alright? Can you do me that favor?"

The slider opens, breaking us out of our conversation. Emilio's footsteps are heavy as he squints beneath the beaming morning sun.

"Morning, ladies," he says, waving at us from across the deck.

I help my mother to her feet, and we approach Emilio.

"What the hell happened last night?" he teases, his voice groggy.

"I don't know, but you better shake off that hangover," I tell him. "We've got a party to get ready for."

LET GO. IT'S WHAT I try to do as my house once more turns into a circus. From all corners, music battles for control—Fausto's disco anthems pulse from one end of the hall, Pia's modern pop thumps from the other, Stevie Nicks sings about landslides and changes in my room, all while a vintage Italian ballad croons from downstairs, its melody cutting through the chaos as if its age gives it more dominance.

Laughter and conversation bounce off the walls, mixing with the snap of hairspray cans clinking against the counter, and the high-pitched whir of blow-dryers. For some odd reason, the women have taken over my bathroom as their communal vanity. The mirror is crowded with faces, framed by a sticky cloud of hairspray that stings my eyes as I step inside. The countertop is a warzone of dirty makeup brushes, compacts, and lipsticks, while dresses are draped over the bathtub, my bed, and every available surface.

I reach to turn on one of the *his and hers* sinks that have long been just *hers,* but Julie's hand stops me before I can turn on the faucet.

"Curling iron's plugged in," she says, saving me from setting the house on fire.

While she resumes spraying and teasing her hair that will fall quickly from the humidity, I reach for a tube of mascara to apply another coat. I try to think through all the noise. The caterer is in the kitchen, plating the food, while the florist sets up the deck. The DJ is set to arrive within the hour, and Enzo handled the alcohol—

"Mom!" Pia's voice cuts through, garnering my attention.

At her worried expression, I swirl my mascara shut. "What's wrong?"

"My hair looks like *straw.*" She reaches for the ends and holds them up. Sure enough, the humidity has blanketed her hair in a coating of frizz that ruins the sleek, straight look she so loves.

"Come here." I wave her over to the counter and reach for a tube of blowout cream. I squeeze a dollop into my palm, rub my hands together, and smooth down her strays. Then, with the curling iron that Julie's momentarily abandoned, I round the ends with a soft bend, sealing it all with enough hairspray to send me into a coughing fit. "Better?" I ask once I've finished.

She squints her eyes as she inspects her reflection with a critical eye before giving me a subtle nod of approval. She glances up at me. "Thanks, Mom."

She hangs around, perusing through my lip gloss collection while I fiddle with my own hair. I'd love to try something new, but I have to make sure all of the details are handled downstairs. So, with one hand, I twist my locks up and reach for a bobby pin to begin my French twist, but my mother storms over.

"No, no, no. Don't even think about it," she says, grabbing the bobby pin out of my hand.

"What?" I ask.

"Let your hair down for once." Her voice is light and playful, though I know her suggestion is anything but.

Julie appears in the doorway, holding up a dress I forgot I had against her body. "And wear *this*."

I run my hands along the heavy bandage material of the baby pink Hervé Léger minidress I bought some time in the nineties. "Bold of you to think this'll still fit."

"I'm wearing pink." Pia gestures to her own skintight dress I'd never let her wear outside of the house. "We could match," she offers, her tone hopeful.

Julie shoves the dress in my arms. "Try it on, bitch."

"Fine." I laugh as I retreat to my closet, let my robe fall to the ground, and shimmy my way into the dress. Though the scale says my weight is nearly the same as it was in my thirties, it's distributed differently now. My hips have widened, pulling the hem a little shorter than it used to be, and my breasts are fuller. But as the fabric snatches my waist in and I catch a glimpse of myself in the full-length mirror, I can't deny how good I feel in this dress.

How *alive* I feel. When was the last time I allowed myself to feel this way?

I pluck out a pair of strappy silver heels and fasten the clasp. I shift my weight, pressing into the arch, feeling the power that comes from a good pair of stilettos. I poke a pair of hoops through my earlobes and fasten a dainty heart-shaped diamond necklace around my neck. But when it comes time for me to slide on the two rings that have lived on my left hand for twenty-five years, I pause. With this dress clinging to my skin, my hair kissing my shoulders, tonight I just want to be *me*. Not Francesco's widow, nor the woman crumbling beneath the weight of his legacy. I have this itch I need to scratch, to know what it would feel like to simply be Scarlett.

Stepping back a few feet, I take in my appearance. I don't see the girl I was who wore this dress a handful of times. I see the woman I am now, forever marked by things younger me could've never imagined we'd go through.

I step out of the closet, my hips adopting a natural sway from the heels, and strike a pose for my three favorite ladies. "What do we think?"

"Hot mamma," Julie yells, clapping her hands together.

"That's my girl," my mother says with a wink.

I catch Pia's eye. I want to ask her if she thinks it's too much;

it's her night, after all, and I don't want her to feel like I'm trying to overshadow. But much to my surprise, her eyes brim with tears that she doesn't let fall, lest they smear her carefully applied makeup.

"You look beautiful, Mom," she says, but I can't ignore the twist of sadness in her voice.

I cup her face in my hands. "What's wrong, dolly?"

She shrugs, glancing over at Julie, then my mother, before looking into my eyes. "You haven't gotten this dressed up since before Daddy died."

This stops me in my tracks. I'd thought I'd maintained my appearance, but it dawns on me what she really means. I haven't dressed like *this* since before Francesco passed away. Like a woman. Like a sexy, confident one. This dress, this night, this moment, it's the first time in a long time I've felt like more than their mother. More than a widow. More than the person trying to keep everything from falling apart.

Tonight, I feel more like myself than I have in ages.

"Only the best for my baby girl," I say, gently resting my forehead against hers. "Alright, are we all ready?"

Emotions brushed aside now, everyone stands up a little straighter. "Let's party," Pia says, squeezing my hand before leading us out of the bedroom.

Downstairs, preparations are in full swing. Every surface is topped with artfully plated summer fare. Beyond the window, tucked in the corner of the deck, the DJ is finalizing his setup, a moody Bossa Nova remix already spinning, its rhythm lazy and sultry. Pia at my side, we step out onto the deck that's been transformed into the lush rose garden of my dreams. Blossoms are everywhere, in every hue of pink, climbing trellises, spilling from vases, tucked into every free corner. And as if God himself ordained this evening, the sky above is a perfect, hazy pink.

"Oh my *God,* Mom," Pia marvels, her mouth agape as she takes in the details, from the floral arrangements to the twinkle lights strung overhead, to the three-tier cake perched elegantly on its own table, with votives surrounding it.

But when my eyes land on the arrangement next to the cake, I let out my own *Oh my God.* White orchids spill out over the top of the vase, dramatic and striking against the sea of pink. But I'm not stunned by their beauty. All I see are dollar signs.

Shit, I think, itching to go find my Blackberry and let the florist have it. Did I not make it clear I couldn't afford them? Pia drifts away, already snapping photos by the pool with her cousins and friends. But before I can escape, footsteps approach behind me. I swivel on my heel.

"Don't look so upset," Enzo says, his baritone voice carrying a hint of rasp. He's got a cocktail in one hand, the other, dug into the pocket of his jeans. The first few buttons of his linen collared shirt are undone, left to expose his deep tan accented by the gold chains he never takes off, and the sleeves are rolled up, revealing muscular forearms decorated with tattoos, all Italian inscriptions, only some of which I understand. He's all effortless confidence and cool ease as he stops just a few inches from me—everything I'm not.

"I thought I told the florist no orchids—"

"Just say thank you, and don't think another thing of it."

My eyes widen. "You did this?" I ask, motioning toward the extravagant blooms.

He shrugs, giving the flowers a onceover as he takes a sip of his drink. "I knew you really wanted them."

"I want a lot of things, Enzo."

"Can you just shut up and accept the gift?"

My mouth curves into a smile I can't suppress. It's so *him*. All of it. The lavish flowers, the sharp comeback. When I look at him again, I find his gaze sweeping over me, slow and deliberate.

His eyes start at my heels, trailing upward with lazy intent, over my legs, the curve of my hips, the way the bandage dress hugs my waist. Higher, past my collarbones, lingering for a beat too long at the bare expanse of my neck, before finally reaching my face. He has no qualms about mentally cataloging every detail of me, and for the first time this summer, I have no qualms about letting him see me.

Something shifts in his expression, like he's let his guard down, too.

I swallow, feeling heat in places I shouldn't.

"You're staring," I say, my voice quiet as I glance around the deck to see if anyone's caught our exchange. "Hard."

"Look at you," he says, exhaling a short laugh through his nose. He shakes his head slightly, like he's trying to snap himself out of a trance. "Can you blame me?"

I cross my arms and lean my weight into one hip. I want to say something flippant to cut the chemistry between us, but he's paid me a genuine compliment. I figure I owe him one back.

"And you've still got the good looks and charm to make us women go weak in the knees."

But he doesn't take the playful bait. His eyes darken as he says, "There's only one woman whose knees I'm trying to bend."

We both freeze. His jaw clenches and his eyes widen as if he, too, is surprised he said such a thing. I wonder if he's already had enough to drink to let accidental words roll off his tongue. I, on the other hand, have yet to consume any alcohol, and as the words linger in the thick, hot air between us, I'm glad I haven't had anything to dull my senses.

It's been four years since I've been desired by *anyone*. Four years since a man has looked at me the way he's looking at me now.

I should be running from this. I should shut down the way his words alone have propped me up and given me a new lease on the way I see myself. But instead, I want to feel every second of it.

And that's what terrifies me the most.

"Mom?" Pia's voice carries through the breeze and within a few seconds, she's standing next to us.

I struggle to tear my eyes away from Enzo, but I manage to put on a smile that suggests everything is of the ordinary. Pia, on the other hand, falters with a brief flicker of confusion, but she moves past it quickly.

"Come take pictures with us," she says. "Both of you."

At the edge of the pool, our family gathers before a photographer who squats, stands, and rises on his tiptoes, angling for the perfect shot. Thankfully, Enzo is standing on the other side of Pia, wedged between his children, allowing me some time to cool down from whatever it is *that* was. An accident, I tell myself. A slip of the tongue. I'm sandwiched between Emilio and Fausto, and from behind me, Fausto leans in close.

"And who are you all dressed up for tonight?" he murmurs.

Through my smile, still poised and posed for a photograph, I hiss back, "Shut up."

But laughter, that contagious kind, spreads between us and mercifully, the photographer dismisses us to shoot candids of Pia and her friends. Before Fausto, or anyone else for that matter, can tease me about my outfit, lest I lose my courage and run upstairs to change, I head inside and signal the caterers to bring out the appetizers.

In the words of my daughter, let's get this party started.

A half-hour later, the sun has finished its grand descent and the twinkle lights glow bright above our party. I've made the rounds, sipping sparkling water to cool myself down from combination of the thick humidity and my adrenaline. Some people get their kicks jumping out of airplanes; I get mine from hosting. When I catch glimpses of guests marveling over the food, admiring the décor, or swaying their hips to the moody pulse of the music, that's when I'm happiest. That's when I'm doing what I was made to do.

As the catering staff clears away empty plates to make room for the next course, I approach the DJ booth. He hands me the microphone.

"Okay," I say, my voice booming from the speakers. "If you know me, which, all of you do, you know I can't throw a party without a little speech."

I'm met with whistles and applause as the crowd quiets and focuses their attention on me. I walk over to my table, a long stretch lined with my most beloved, and reach for Pia's hand. She stands and joins me, anticipation sparkling in her dark eyes.

And just that easy, I lose it.

Tears blur my vision before I can get a word out, and the second I blink, they spill. The parents in the crowd cheer, knowing exactly how I feel, and laughter ripples through the party. I shake my head, trying to collect myself.

"I swear, I haven't had a drink yet," I say, "but clearly I should've." Laughter builds again, warm and indulgent, and I exhale, steadying myself before I start again.

"Oh, Pia Rose." I squeeze her hand. "I always say you're my biggest dream come true, but I was thinking about it today. I could've never dreamt up something as perfect as you. Your sassy one-liners, the way you love with your whole heart and then some, how you light up every room you walk into, you're beyond my wildest dreams."

I pause, letting the words settle before glancing out at the crowd. My eyes drift, unintentionally, foolishly, to Enzo.

"People like to talk about soulmates," I continue, tearing my gaze away. "And we always think about them in the romantic sense. But I think there's another kind of soulmate." I look into my daughter's eyes and say, "And I think they're called daughters."

Pia lets out a glowing smile before she wraps her arms around my waist and snuggles close. My mother and Julie weep side by side, and Enzo, judging from his wry grin and soft eyes, seems touched by this public display of affection.

"You're the color in my life, Pia," I say as the rest of the party falls away and it's just me and the little girl might never know the impact she's had on my life. "You mean more to me than I'll ever be able to put into words, and in as many lifetimes as we get, in all of them, you have all my love, always."

Cheers erupt like a vigorous roar as Pia and I embrace. As I cradle her face in my hands, I see it: eighteen birthdays flashing by in a rapid-speed montage, a life measured in cake candles and wishes made in secret. And now, here we are. The very last one.

The thought barely has time to settle before I shove it away. Not tonight. Tonight is as close to perfect as it gets, and nothing, not even the inevitable waiting for me on the other side of this party, is going to ruin it.

As we savor our main courses to the soundtrack of the rough sea and Sinatra, Emilio disappears inside, returning moments later with Pia's gifts stacked in his arms. Like an eager child, Pia wiggles her fingers as she reaches for the first box.

"That one's from me," Emilio says. His exchanges a quick, knowing glance with me as Pia tears off the floral print wrapping paper to reveal a small velvet box.

"Wonder what this could be," Pia sing-songs.

"Don't get too excited," Emilio teases.

Pia pops open the box to find a delicate gold bracelet sparkling with ten tiny diamonds. The second she sees it, her smile falters, not in disappointment, but in something quieter, close to awe.

"I wanted diamonds," Pia says, staring at the bracelet.

"I know. And the only way to make you shut up about it," Emilio says, "was to buy them for you."

Tears shine in Pia's eyes. Nearby, a few of her friends catch a glimpse of her jewels, gasping and pointing as Emilio fastens it around Pia's wrist. "Love you," Pia says as they embrace. "What the heck is this?" she asks a moment later, reaching for the larger box.

"That one's from me," I tell her, though she's already tearing open the wrapping paper. She freezes the moment she sees an iconic shade of orange accompanied by a thin, brown border.

"I really hope you're not pranking me," Pia says as she continues to draw back the paper, revealing the Hermès logo. Her hands fly to her mouth. "Oh my God."

Our family's attention is on us now as Pia lifts open the box, pulls open the dust bag, and lifts out the cognac-colored Birkin bag that rested in the crook of my arm a handful of times. Her jaw falls open and she stares at it like she's never seen it before.

"I hope you don't mind my hand-me-downs," I say as she continues to examine every square inch of the bag. "I know if Daddy were here, he would've bought you one. They cost a little more now than they did in the nineties, and there's a waiting list, so that's why—"

"I love it," she interrupts me, clutching the bag to her chest the same exact way I did when I received it. She tears her eyes away from the bag and her head tilts to one side as she stares into my eyes. "I can't believe you're giving this to me."

"You're my daughter, Pia. Everything I have is yours," I say, though I wonder if she understands that I'm no longer talking about a handbag.

Pia's friends gather around her, marveling at the bag as she turns it so the gold hardware gleams beneath the twinkle lights. Enzo comes around to our side of the table and he hands Pia an envelope.

"Happy birthday, pretty Pia."

I catch his eye as sounds of Pia tearing open the envelope ripple between us. Pretty Pia. I wonder if he, too, is remembering that moment in the middle of the night when he held my baby in his arms and fed her.

Our baby.

The thought seizes me, swallows me whole.

"A yacht!" Pia squeals. "Zio, what is this?"

She holds a sheet of paper in her hands, printed with a photo of the yacht she spoke of, plus a confirmation number.

"Well, you said you wanted one," Enzo says. "I rented one for the day. Captain, crew, everything you could want to take you all around the Hamptons. You can go with your girlfriends—"

"No," Pia says, shaking her head. "I want to go with you guys. My family." My daughter's eyes travel from the yacht booking, to the Birkin, to the bracelet on her arm, and as her expression softens, tears roll down her cheeks. She glances up at us with those big eyes so full of love and says, "You guys made all my birthday wishes come true."

She rises and draws us into a group hug. Emilio and Enzo laugh, but like my daughter, I can't stop crying. Because I love these three individuals so much, I feel like my heart is going to explode, because I haven't felt this perfectly content maybe ever. Enzo reaches over to swipe away my tears with his thumb, and as our eyes lock, I have only one wish.

That he knew. That I could tell him. That I could tell him without ruining absolutely everything.

I wish I could tell him that he didn't rent a yacht and buy orchids for his niece. He did those things for his daughter. I want to look into those eyes that feel like home and say it, the words that have been stuck in my throat for eighteen years. *Look at her, Enzo. This girl made of magic and beauty and everything wonderful. She's half of me and half of you. The love that's tormented us all this time, she's the culmination of what we couldn't share.*

She's my eternal tether to Enzo, and maybe that's why from the moment I learned I was carrying her, I've felt so fiercely protective of her.

As we part, the DJ amps up the music and "I Gotta Feeling" by the Black Eyed Peas kicks off the party's second wind. I wipe my face dry with my palm and dismiss Pia and Emilio with a wave. "Go dance and have fun."

Emilio draws me to his side and kisses my temple, while Pia wraps her arms around my waist and squeezes me tight.

"Thank you, Mommy," she says, just loud enough to be heard above the music.

I hold her face in my hands and tell her I love her before weaving my way through the party and slipping into the house, unnoticed. The music pulsates through the windows, though its sound is muffled. The catering staff works on the dessert course and I give them a smile as I pass by before reaching the living room. Nostalgia settles in my chest. Enzo's favorite, Eros Ramazzotti, is crooning away. My body falls into a gentle sway as I run my fingers along the extensive CD collection that's been compiled by me, my kids, Enzo, and Francesco—our personalities in music form.

"Now *this* is music."

I look over and find Enzo striding toward me. His familiar scent overwhelms me with comfort, drawing more tears to my eyes, though I somehow will them not to fall.

"You okay?" Enzo asks, his brows raised, his smile sweet and caring.

I draw in a breath. "I'm not this emotional when I drink. I hate it," I joke. "But I wanted to remember everything tonight, exactly as it is."

Enzo nods, his gaze drifting outside where the party rages on. "It's been perfect." Looking at me again with inquisitive eyes, he says, "You've always been an impeccable hostess."

"Thank you, Enzo. Learned from the best."

"That you did," he cracks. He looks over his shoulder one last time before reaching his hand out. "I think we deserve a dance, too."

I raise my palms. "I don't dance."

In a split, he interlaces his fingers with mine and says, "You do now," and before I know it, our bodies have drifted closer to each other, inches apart, and we move in a rhythm only we can feel. He sways me to a song called "L'aurora" that I've heard a million times, but tonight, I truly listen, understanding enough Italian to know what it means.

The dawn.

And suddenly, this summer that has felt like one big goodbye feels like a dawn, like the new beginning this house was supposed to provide.

Enzo must've felt it too. Maybe that's how we ended up here, in my bedroom. My back hits the door and before I can catch my breath, he locks it behind us lest one of us lose our nerve and escape. Enzo and I have never shared those pretty, soft, slow kisses like the ones in the movies. No, we're messy, mad, maniacal. Desperate, because all our lives, this has been so scarce, this thing between us. It's been fleeting and forbidden from the start, and yet, as he lays me down on top of my comforter, as his body rests on top of mine, it feels like we've been doing this forever. He stretches my arms overhead and threads his fingers through mine, and though we've been here before, I'm ravenous for Enzo, like he's something I've been starving for my whole life.

His mouth moves against my lips like he's trying to memorize me, while I clutch at his shoulders like I'm trying to make his flesh part of my own. As my hand snakes down his back, I feel the absence of my wedding rings. Lighter, freer, without the weight of that jewelry and everything it means, I can do anything I want. His lips leave mine only so he can kiss the length of my neck, down to my collarbone, and his fingertips ever so gently brush the strap of my dress to the side. So slow and deliberate, it's agonizing.

His name escapes my lips in a whisper, but I jolt up when there's a knock at the door.

It doesn't matter who it is. It's reality. This—this fantasy almost come to life with Enzo—is not. We both still, though my heart thrashes in my chest like I'm running a marathon and every cell in my body pulsates. I gesture toward the closet, and he takes off while I straighten the hem of my skirt and return the strap of my dress to its rightful place. After a quick glance in the mirror, I crack the door open.

My worst nightmare. My daughter.

"We're ready to cut the cake," she says, "but I couldn't find you."

"Oh, the cake," I say. Still out of breath, I shove my palm against my forehead. "Sorry, baby. I'll be right down."

Her brows knit. "Why are you out of breath?"

"Jogged up the stairs. Just need to change into some flats. These heels are killing me."

My excuse satisfies her enough to send her back downstairs. I close the door, lock it, and rest my back against it, steadying my breath. Then, I find Enzo in the closet. I kick off my heels, having to make good on my word to change into flats, but before I can, Enzo grabs my waist and leans me against a wall of shelves.

"Come on," he whispers, his mouth brushing against my ear. "Real quick."

I press my hands against his chest and push him back, glaring up at him. "Real quick? Maybe you've had some fun in the last four years, but I haven't had any. And when I finally do," I say, plucking a pair of sandals off the shelf, my legs wobbly beneath me, "there won't be anything *real quick* about it."

And so, we slip back into the party like nothing happened. We cut the cake and toast to the daughter he doesn't know we created together, and when the party gets a little wild and we all end up in the pool, fully clothed, as the stars flicker above us and the moon glows against the sea's surface, I lean my head back against the water and close my eyes. Even though I know time is fleeting and life is like a vapor, and dawn always, always comes, I wish this night never had to end.

A wish, I know, is made in vain.

CHAPTER SIXTEEN

ENZO

Winter, 1999

"You made it," I said as I swung open the door. On my patio stood my brother, Scarlett, and her kids who barreled into me and peppered me with *We missed you, Zio.* I hadn't seen them since last summer. Scarlett greeted me with a kiss on the cheek before Francesco acknowledged me by squeezing my shoulder.

I tried to take a deep breath as I closed the screen behind us, but it wouldn't come. My brother and I hadn't had a falling out so much as we fell apart. While every year of my life blended into the next since I'd moved to Maryland six years ago, Francesco's had continued to be littered with glamour and excitement, two ingredients I used to indulge in on a daily basis. His cooking special on PBS had led to five seasons of *A Taste of Italy with Francesco Valenti,* which led to three more cookbooks, countless daytime talk show appearances, and a restaurant with a yearlong waitlist. I wanted to cast the blame for us drifting apart on his busy career, but the truth was, Francesco changed the moment he had his first taste of fame. Once he had that first bite, he was hooked.

He was different.

The January air was biting, but the heat warmed us as we all convened in the kitchen. At the stove, preparing a lavish feast, was Angela.

My fiancée.

"Angela, sweetheart," I said, beckoning her over, "come meet my family."

Angela wiped her hands on a *mappina* and untied her apron. Her heart-shaped face flushed as she rushed over. "Gosh," she said, giving me a side glance, "I wish I had a second to clean myself up."

Scarlett dismissed her concern with a wave. "Don't give it another thought. It's so nice to finally meet you," she gushed. "We've heard so much about you."

"You must be Scarlett," Angela said, smiling ear to ear, greeting Scarlett with a kiss on the cheek.

Scarlett grabbed her left hand. "Let's see the ring!"

Francesco leaning over Scarlett's shoulder, the pair examined the round diamond ring that I'd given to Angela last week. We'd met just over a year prior, shortly after Claudia married her new husband, Ralph. I'd dated here and there over the last six years, but seeing Claudia solidify that she'd moved on by marrying Ralph was the push I needed. I wasn't getting any younger. My kids, despite my efforts to make my house a home, still preferred their mother's. Then came Angela, a thirty-two-year-old born and raised here in the suburbs of Baltimore, who, in true Italian American fashion, made it her mission to unite my family.

She'd succeeded to a point. Little Enzo was twenty-one now, still living in Ocean City after the stunt he pulled all those years ago, but he enjoyed coming around more often, staying longer periods of time.

Maria took to Angela right away, and I'd have been lying if I said that didn't have some impact on my decision to propose. But Antonella was still a tough nut to crack. A fully fledged teenager now, she spent most of her time at my house holed up in her room on instant messenger, chatting with her friends.

Looking at my brother's children, I couldn't help but compare. Would they present the same issues for their parents as my kids did for me, come their teenage years?

"So you cook?" Francesco inquired as Angela returned to the stove. While they babbled about her culinary skills, Scarlett surveyed the house with a keen eye.

"Nothing like a woman's touch," she teased as we wandered to the edge of the living room. "Look at that TV system. You're already in the next millennium."

"Had to give the kids a reason to like coming here."

Her arms folded in front of her chest, she looked over at me and lowered her voice. "You said the girls really like Claudia's new husband."

"Ralph," I said with a deep sigh. I'd kept her up to date on everything through our letters, that had remained a constant exchange since they started. "Mister wonderful."

She tsked her tongue against the roof of her mouth. "I knew when you told me he took them to Disney for New Year's, he was playing hardball."

"He's a nice guy. Too nice. Makes me look like an asshole in comparison."

"Nice guys finish last, Enzo," she said as she kept a watchful eye on her children who curiously sifted through my kids' selection of video games. "Angela seems really sweet."

"She is. She is a sweetheart."

"I promise, I won't interrogate her, but I want to get to know her better."

"I told you all about her," I said, referencing our letters without saying it.

"Telling is one thing. I want to see it with my own eyes. Make sure she's not a Claudia in disguise."

Her comment took me by surprise; I'd never seen this side of Scarlett applied to me. Her protectiveness. It'd always been the other way around. I didn't have a chance to respond before the front door opened. Maria walked in, all bright eyes and black hair and a sweet semi-formal outfit for tonight's family dinner. But when Claudia filed in after her, my senses went on high alert. Claudia never came in when she dropped off the kids.

"Oh, hi Claudia," Scarlett said after she'd gushed over how beautiful my Maria was. "Congratulations on your nuptials."

Claudia responded with an eye roll, accompanied by a scoff.

Barely suppressing her shock, Scarlett retreated to the kitchen.

"You can't pretend to be nice for five minutes?" I said to Claudia.

"I'll never be nice to that little *puttana*," Claudia sneered. "I need to talk to you."

"Where's Nella?"

"That's what I need to talk to you about, genius." Claudia turned on her heel and led the way to my home office. I hadn't yet closed the door behind us before she started. "I don't want you to get all riled up, or make a big thing of this, but Nella doesn't want to come here anymore."

Digging my hands into my pockets, I shrugged. "What do you mean *anymore*?"

"I mean, she doesn't want to come here. At all. She doesn't like the back and forth, and she wants to live with me and Ralph full time."

It hit me like a slap. My face went hot and I saw red, but I refused to give Claudia the rise she was expecting. "Last time I checked, Antonella is only sixteen. Our custody agreement is valid until she's eighteen."

"Enzo, come on. Give it a rest, would you? She's practically a woman already."

"She's a teenager with a bad attitude."

"She's a girl who hates you for what you did." Claudia's voice boomed, her words piercing right through me.

"I'm her father."

"But Ralph is her dad. And those are her words, not mine."

I thought of the nights I returned home from the restaurant in those early days of owning Valenti's, well past the kids' bedtimes. I'd sneak past their rooms and kiss the tops of their heads, though they'd have no recollection of it come morning, as if it didn't happen it all. I'd do all of that before reaching my room where I shared a bed with a wife I wasn't in love with. I thought of every Sunday when Claudia would spend hours at the stove, only for me to scarf down my meal in a matter of minutes before jetting off to a poker game or an evening of debauchery with my mistress of the month. It was as if all of my mistakes were multiplied to equal this horrific consequence. Still, I couldn't bear all the blame. I'd made mistakes but so had Claudia.

"You poisoned her to hate me! You and I didn't work out. Fine. That's one thing. But I've changed. I've been a good father to her. I'm trying, Claud. So tell me, what have I done that's so unforgiveable?"

"How much time do you have? Or do you have to rush back out there because that poor, dumb girl is cooking dinner?"

I pushed one of the leather chairs on its side, landing with a thud. "Did you ever ask yourself *why* I was such a shitty husband? Why I practically lived at the restaurant, and why I saw so many women on the side? Maybe because you were a shitty wife."

"Oh, save it, Enzo," she said, dismissing me with a wave of her hand. "You're a selfish bastard to your core."

She'd struck a nerve and she knew it. It echoed all the things my mother used to say about me, her *piccolo diavolo*—little devil—the nickname that haunted me to this day. Was I really that bad? Was my innermost core made up of only evil things? I could've done better. I should have done better. Regret was eating me alive. But what was done was done. I could only try to salvage the now.

Heat rising in my chest, I pointed at her. "You are not going to take my daughter away from me. Do you hear me? I'll fight you tooth and nail, Claudia. I'll spend every dime I've got on lawyers. She's half of me."

"Yeah, well, she wishes she wasn't."

Anger pulsed through me. My head pounded, and my fingers curled into a fist like a bad reflex. I grabbed the lamp off the desk and smashed it to smithereens. I'd tried. I'd tried so hard to make Maryland my home, to show my children that I'd sacrifice anything for them. Had it all been for nothing? A complete waste of time? "Fuck you, Claudia."

"Likewise, Lorenzo."

"What's going on in here?" Angela's sweet voice came from the doorway, a stark contrast to Claudia's brash New York-ness. My chest heaved up and down as she rushed to my side.

"I hope you're aware of what you're getting yourself into," were Claudia's final words to Angela. After the front door slammed closed behind her, Francesco and Scarlett stormed in, too, wrought with concern.

"Go finish making dinner," I said to Angela as I perched a seat on the edge of my desk. "Let's try to salvage the evening."

I could tell Scarlett wanted to say something. She wanted to be the one to comfort me rather than Angela, who cupped my face in her hands and kissed me, a silent way to let me know she wasn't going anywhere despite my ex-wife's warnings. Instead, Scarlett patted my back and followed Angela out of the room. Though Francesco remained, I couldn't confide in him. Where would I even begin? He knew the foundation, the history of me and Claudia, but there were too many chapters he'd skipped, ones I didn't have the time or energy to catch him up on.

"Come on," I said, forcing myself to stand. "Let's have a nice meal and forget this ever happened."

Francesco put his hand on my shoulder to stop me. For the first time in what felt like years, we made eye contact.

"Nella will come around," Francesco said. He leaned over, propped the fallen chair over, and sunk into it, his large frame consuming the whole thing.

"I don't know." Tossing my hands up, I sat back down on my desk, pressing my lips together. "Kid's had it in for me since I moved down here. Little Enzo's living out at the beach. All I've got is Maria."

"And Angela."

"Right. And Angela."

Francesco hunched over, propping his elbows on his thighs. "She can cook."

I let out a weak smile. "She can. Put on ten pounds since we met."

"That's what happens when you're with someone you're comfortable with."

The way Francesco leaned back in his chair with an easy confidence suggested such a notion was a good one, but I took it as the opposite. I had been comfortable with Claudia and look where that led me. No, I was of the other school of thought, that someone who kept you on your toes was the more suitable partner. Someone to continuously shape and mold you into something new, someone better than you were yesterday.

An awkward quiet settled between us, punctuated by the distant chatter of the children and the occasional clatter of pots and pans from the kitchen. I was desperate to burst the odd bubble we were trapped in.

"So, *che dice?*" I tossed out, jutting my chin toward him. "How you been feeling?"

"Scarlett doesn't know," he started, his gaze taking on an intensity, "but my heart's been going in and out of rhythm. We upped all my meds. They're confident it's going to keep things under control, so I don't want you to worry."

"But you're worried." All at once, our walls fell, and we were once again brothers whose bond couldn't be broken by time or distance. "Why didn't you tell her?"

"I don't want her to freak out." Francesco ran his palms along his thighs. "Then she's going to make me cut back my hours at work, or give up the show, or turn down the book deal on the table—"

"So why don't you?" I stood up and started pacing. "You've done it already, Fran. You've proven yourself. You've got more money than God. And you keep killing yourself, for what?"

Francesco glared up at me, silent.

"You like the fame," I guessed.

He nodded. "Yeah, I do. I like being famous."

"I guess I don't understand it. You've got a wife and kids. Two homes. And you don't enjoy any of it because you're too infatuated with a bunch of strangers?"

Francesco looked away, his jaw tight as he let out a humorless laugh. "I've lived most of my adult life in a cage. Trapped in the kitchen, behind the line, cooking whatever it was you told me to." He glanced up at me. "You were always the one calling the shots, shaking hands with people, receiving all the praise. I never understood why you loved it so much. Why you stood up straighter than me. But now I do. It's my turn now. I'm the guy people come to see. People come up to me when I walk down the street and tell me they love me. You should know as well as me how great that feels." He shrugged as if to say, *it is what it is.* "I love it. And I'm not ready to give it up."

A heaviness settled in my chest. Yes, that feeling, that attention, had been important to me when I was younger, but once I grew up, I realized how frivolous fleeting attention was. When would my brother do the same? Or was he so far gone, that he wouldn't?

"I'm, uh, I'm gonna die, Enz," Francesco said, rising to his feet. A pit formed in my stomach as he dug his hands into the pockets of his designer jeans. "I know you don't want to hear that, but it's the truth."

"We're all gonna die."

"Yeah, but the odds are, I've got less time than everybody else. But when I'm so busy my head spins, I don't have time to think about that. When my show's on TV, and when I see my book on shelves, it feels like I'm never gonna die. I'll always be out there, somehow."

My jaw clenched. I was the older brother, and though my heart was strong like a bull, it was my destiny to die first. "You're not going anywhere, you hear me? And since you won't tell your wife, I'm gonna make sure you slow down."

Reaching his arm behind him, he massaged the nape of his neck. "I get antsy when I'm home. Makes me feel like I'm suffocating."

"Why?" I lowered my voice. "You fooling around on her again?"

He dismissed me with a wave. "There's always somebody."

"Fran—"

"Hey, you've got no room to talk."

Yet another zinger. From Claudia, I expected these types of comments. But from Francesco, they stung even harder. I wasn't chiding Francesco; I was only trying to save him from the same mistakes I'd made. Look at the consequences I was paying as a result. Couldn't he see that no fleeting moment of passion, nor chasing what felt good in the moment, was worth it?

"That was a long time ago, and I regret it, alright? But I also didn't have a bad heart to worry about. You don't think the guilt, and the sneaking around takes a toll on you? You don't think all that adrenaline makes your heart go out of whack?"

"I don't know," he said with a dry laugh.

"This isn't funny. You think not taking care of yourself only affects you. But it affects all of us. And what you're doing, the way you're living, it's selfish."

He drew in a breath through his nose, his chest rising, though he chose to ignore my sentiment. "Look, the reason I wanted to talk to you is because I get the sense you're not too happy here. Am I right?"

"Captain fucking obvious."

"I want you to know you can come home. Anytime."

"Home to what?" I snapped. "I've got nothing left in New York."

"You've got me," he said, his voice suddenly softer. Weaker. "You've got my family, and you've got our restaurant. The place is insane now, Enz. You wouldn't believe it. You'd love it." He paused, the glint in his eyes disappearing. "It's not the same without you. Every night, when I look around the packed dining room, I think of you. You're the one who brought me here to this country. You should be right there with me, enjoying it." He took a deep breath. For the first time in a long time, he looked like the brother I remembered. The real Francesco, before fame and flashy watches and leather loafers swallowed him up. "I know it looks like I got all the success. But you're my brother, and I wouldn't be here if it weren't for you. Everything I have is ours."

I was flattered. Truly, I was, and I wanted to grab the opportunity to run back to New York with both hands. But I was also resentful. I'd been in Maryland for six years now, and I'd been happy for none of it. Why had he waited all this time to make me such an offer?

"Please," Francesco said before I could answer, "come home."

Home. The singular word echoed in my ear like a delicious, addictive melody.

"Enzo?" Angela's voice trailed down the hall and her footsteps neared, breaking whatever spell had fallen over us. "Dinner's ready," she said from the other side of the door.

Like a real family, we sat around the table, a lavish meal prepared by my bride-to-be topping the table. Like an actor, I nodded and laughed on cue, but my mind was elsewhere. It was in New York. I was a few mere feet from Angela, the woman who held the keys to my new life, yet I was already envisioning where I'd live, how I'd return to the restaurant, how my second chapter in the city I so adored might take shape. It was all only a figment of my imagination, yet the thought alone sent a rush through my veins, that I might have reason to live again.

Still, my Maria. She had four years left until she graduated. My fiancée, Angela, who doted on me with the care and concern I'd always craved. By the end of our meal, I was torn in two.

One half of me, sitting at this table. The other, already on its way home.

―――

"TELL ME YOU HAVE some cigarettes lying around," Scarlett said. At the sink, her hands were submerged in sudsy water, while an easy quiet lingered in the house. Francesco had taken the kids for ice cream, while Angela had gone upstairs to shower before bed.

I pulled open a drawer, sifted out a pack of cigarettes, and lit one for Scarlett. She lifted a wet hand from the water to take the cigarette, but instead, I placed it between her pursed lips. The faucet ran a constant stream, and the scents of garlic and tomatoes still clung to the air.

"God, that's good," she tried to say, though it came out stilted, the words obstructed by the cigarette.

I smirked and plucked it from her lips, taking a slow drag, my first true deep breath of the night. I let my head fall back as I exhaled, smoke curling from my lips, thinking about how I felt more comfortable with Scarlett than with the woman I was going to marry.

"Tell Angela she can come work at the restaurant anytime," Scarlett said as she scrubbed the sauce pot. "Fran was seriously impressed. So was I."

"She's a good old-fashioned Italian girl," I said, though I recognized my voice didn't sound too thrilled about that.

"Unlike me," Scarlett cracked. She flipped the pot upside down after rinsing it and set it to dry on a clean *mappina*. Then, she started scrubbing tongs and egg turnovers, all the tools Angela had used to craft a meal to welcome my family. As the cookware clanked and clattered, she looked at me with a dare in her eyes. A dare to drop the façade.

"What?" I asked.

"Nothing," she said with a shrug, briefly looking down to rinse a serving spoon. "Just have the sense you want to tell me something."

I washed my face with my palm. We were alone, not for long, and I had my chance to talk to her face to face rather than through a letter. A rarity in recent years, something I hadn't realized I'd missed so much.

"Do you think I'm happy?" I asked, regretting the question as soon as it was out of my mouth.

She shut the faucet, dried her hands, and turned to face me, leaning her hip against the counter. "I think if you have to ask me that, you already know you're not."

I looked away, fidgeting with my watch, anything to distract myself from the answer I didn't want to hear. The one that was obvious.

"Why?" Scarlett asked, breaking me out of my thoughts. "I mean, is she a supermodel? No, but you don't need a supermodel. You need a good wife."

"It's got nothing to do with looks."

"Then what is it?" At my silence, Scarlett crossed her arms and looked past me. "Fran and the kids are going to walk through that door any minute now, and you and I aren't going to get to finish this conversation. And I think you'd like to finish this conversation."

"She wants kids," I started, suddenly in a rush to get it all out. "She's thirty-two. She's in a rush. Wants them like yesterday. She wants two, maybe three, but said she'd settle for one."

"I think that's what comes with dating a woman almost fifteen years younger than you."

"I'm forty-six, Scar." My hands flew to my head, shoving my hair backwards. "Forty-fucking-six, and I'm starting all over again. Little Enzo's been on his own for years now. Nella, even though she hates my guts, is about to graduate, and Maria's right behind her. I should be thinking about retiring to Florida and playing golf, but instead, we're talking about wedding favors and nursery décor."

"And that's not what you want?"

"It's what I'm supposed to want."

"Claudia was what you were supposed to want, too, and look how that panned out." Scarlett dropped her arms and stood up straight. "What are you punishing yourself for? Do you think suffering makes you a better man? I mean, really, not everyone's cut out for marriage. Maybe it's not for you. Would that really be the worst thing in the world?"

"I wanted this to work. I wanted to turn my life around, and be a good guy and a good father, and not be the selfish bastard everybody thinks I am."

Scarlett exhaled a poignant smile. "What's so bad about being a selfish bastard, hm? It's your life. You deserve to be happy. Not just pretending to be happy."

"Isn't that what you do? Pretend?"

She flinched, as if my words stung. "We're not talking about me right now."

Silence enveloped us, cut only by the drip of the spicket and Angela's footsteps upstairs. I could tell she wanted to be angry with me, but she let go of it before I could ask her forgiveness.

"I see what you're doing, Enzo," she said, her voice breaking. "I see right through this. All of it. You're trapped in a penance you've already paid. So you cheated on your wife. You gambled. You drank. You screwed up. But you tried to make things right. You've spent six miserable years here, trying to pay for your sins. Punishing yourself. There comes a point when enough is enough."

"You forget," I whispered, "I see right through you, too. All I'm doing is exactly what you're doing. We're staying in places we've never belonged."

A tear rolled down her cheek. She quickly swiped it away. "I don't want this for you. It's no way to live."

My gaze fell to my hands. "Fran asked me to come home."

"And what did you say?"

"Didn't have the chance to answer." I rocked on my heels, trying to read her expression. I wanted to know if she wanted me to come home, too. "He asked me to come back to the restaurant."

Clearly unimpressed, she bit her bottom lip and nodded. "So he made you a job offer. We're drowning over there. Did he mention we've fired six managers in ten months?"

I swallowed the bitter truth, that my brother's offer was a request made for his own benefit, wrapped in all the words I wanted to hear.

"Scarlett," I exhaled her name as I took a few steps back, running my palms along my hair, "I don't know what the hell I'm doing. Whether I'm coming or going. And you know what's worse? I don't think anyone really cares. I'm in the way for Claudia and my kids. Fran only wants me back if he's still the king."

Her face wrinkled with something indistinguishable. "I care." She squeezed the words out, her throat sounding tight, like it was trying to keep the words bottled inside of her. "Maybe nothing else makes sense. Claudia's a bitch, and my husband's a master manipulator, and you've got a fiancée you don't even want, and you don't fit in with any of that. But I'm right here. I care. I've always cared. I've always missed you and I've always wished you'd come home." This time, she didn't bother wiping away her tears. "Even if you've got nothing else, you've got me."

My heart raced at her admission. At the way she so effortlessly saw me. Got me. Was just like me, like my mirror in female form. Feeling like we were against a stopwatch that was almost out of time, I forced myself to go on. "What about Maria? She's only thirteen."

"Take her in the summers. Bring her to Montauk. You and Fran can go back and forth to the city, and I'll take care of the kids at the beach. But Enzo, enough is enough." She and I both turned around as the headlights of Francesco's car beamed through the dark house. Her hand on my arm startled me, but she looked at me with urgency in her eyes, letting me know whatever she was about to say was important. "You've punished yourself enough. Don't lock yourself in a prison you don't deserve to be in."

And as Francesco and our rambunctious children, devoid of adult worries, barreled in, I heard the rest of her unspoken sentence.

The way I have.

CHAPTER SEVENTEEN

SCARLETT

Summer, 2011

"**G**od bless you," Pia says as I sneeze for the umpteenth time. My body evidently has an aversion to Windex. And yet, I persevere, wiping down the screen door with precise strokes. The house must look as perfect as it did in Tinsley's listing photos.

We have a showing today, and according to Tinsley, this could be *the one.*

As I vacuum the living room, pausing every so often to straighten a pillow or artfully drape a throw blanket, it all feels like an ersatz version of the home I've spent eighteen summers in. Like madmen, the four of us cover every corner of this house with critical eyes in a vain attempt to erase the history we've made here. Emilio has taken outdoor duties, staging the deck to look prime for cookouts and making the front wraparound porch look warm and inviting with rocking chairs he picked up special for the occasion. Pia has arranged the dining area to look like something out of a Restoration Hardware catalog where it used to be topped with Francesco's old-school Neapolitan fare. The gallery wall of family photos has been replaced with generic beachy artwork from Home Goods, and the kitchen countertops gleam as if we'd never once prepared a meal on them. The entire act of staging grates my nerves. What's so bad about living in a house once occupied—once enjoyed—by another family? Aren't homes havens for memories?

Enzo moves about with his usual panache, making the whole ordeal feel like less of a chore and more like a production, in the same way he used to prepare Amanti for a busy dinner service. I wonder if he feels detached from the house, having missed the last four summers, or if it tugs at him the way it does me, like something inextricable from who we are.

Satisfied with the pattern I've left in the carpet from the vacuum, I shut it off, its loud drone fading to silence. With flushed cheeks and beads of sweat decorating his forehead, Emilio comes in from the deck and announces everything's set up.

"Alright," Enzo says, taking command. He glances at the shiplap clock on the wall. "Let's do one final sweep through and try to be out of here in twenty. Can you ladies be ready by then?"

"My bathing suit and I are ready to go," Pia says. She claps her hands, her excitement cutting through the tension. Today is her big yacht day—her birthday gift that's truly a gift to all of us.

After doing one last sweep of the second level, I quickly shower and slick my hair back into a ponytail. I opt for a muted leopard-print bikini with gold accents, though I conceal most of my body beneath a black crocheted coverup. I've already transferred my essentials to a large raffia tote, and as I head downstairs, my flip-flops clacking with each step, I slide a pair of shield sunglasses onto my face.

"Everyone ready?" I ask.

"Duh," Pia retorts.

"Let's go have some fun," Enzo says. Dressed in black swim trunks that hit above his knees and a white linen button down, Enzo gives me a wink and a reassuring smile as the kids shuffle onto the porch. He locks the door behind us like he's closing a chapter and I can feel my smile faltering. But his palm lands on the small of my back, and the spark in his eye and his bright smile lift me back up.

A half hour later, we're aboard a forty-foot cruiser yacht that glides smoothly along Montauk's bay. For now, the strangers touring our home feel a world away. The sun is suspended high above us, the midafternoon rays warming me from the inside out. Pia has spent the first fifteen minutes of the ride marveling over the luxurious fixtures and furnishings inside, the plush beds on the sundeck, and the pair of jet skis attached to the swim platform. I can't count how many times she's thanked Enzo. While Emilio, who has the patience of a saint, plays Pia's personal photographer, snapping photos of her in every area of the boat for the viewing pleasure of her numerous Facebook friends, I join Enzo on the sundeck. I want to thank him myself.

"The timing couldn't have been more perfect," I say, leaning my arms on the guardrail. We drift past Sag Harbor, its historic, nautical skyline rising in the distance. Masts of sailboats punctuate the horizon, bobbing gently in the breeze, while grand waterfront homes are perched like silent sentinels, a testament to the exclusivity of this slice of the world. "You're a good ..." I pause, stopping short of letting *Dad* slip out. "No, you're a *great* guy."

"You sure you didn't put her up to asking for this?" Enzo teases. He lazily drapes his arm around my waist and pulls me in for a second, just long enough to kiss my temple. "Her reaction was the best."

"Priceless," I say, laughter rising from my throat.

"It's our last summer out here," Enzo says, the playfulness in his voice gone. "Just wanted to do something special for us all to remember."

The wind whips my ponytail in all directions as I look into his eyes, through the barrier of my sunglasses. His sentiment settles in my bones and I'm left to wonder, is this really it? When this summer fades, will we fade with it, left to become one of those families who see one another only at weddings and funerals?

"Hey, Zio," Emilio says as he and Pia pad their way around to the sundeck. Between his fingers is a deck of cards. "You up for a game?"

"Ah, what are we betting for today?" Enzo says, already champing at the bit.

"Wait a minute," Pia huffs, hands on her hips. Her black hair shines beneath the sun, the wind blowing her straight locks behind her shoulders. She's borrowed a pair of my shield sunglasses, lending her an air of maturity she doesn't ordinarily possess, a contrast against her neon bikini trimmed with black stitching. "This is *my* boat day. You can't play poker without me."

"Since when do you know how to play?" Enzo asks.

"I don't." She puts on a smile and says, "You're going to teach me."

We sit around the dining area at the rear of the boat. Pia focuses intently on Enzo's cards. He and Emilio have played a few hands, hoping Pia might catch on, but my daughter is an artist. Numbers aren't her bag.

"Are you getting it?" Enzo asks as he wins his third hand in a row.

"No," Pia complains. "I don't get how you decide when to bet and when to fold."

I reach for two cards and sit back in my seat. "Let *me* teach you."

Pia wears an expression that says *yeah right,* while Enzo looks bemused by my efforts. My hand is unplayable, but Enzo's not teaching Pia the most important part of the game.

Bluffing.

I reach for chips and play my hand as if I've got the makings of a royal flush. Emilio folds, leaving just me and Enzo. He narrows his eyes and calls, tossing in a few chips. Emilio, our acting dealer, flips the river card that does nothing to help my hand. Still, I bet again, pressing harder. Enzo studies me, fingers drumming against his cards. A long beat passes between us as he holds my gaze, trying to read my mind and my hand before he folds.

With a gloating grin, I turn my crappy hand around. A two and a six. Off suit. Nothing. It's met with confused, impressed expressions.

"Wait." Pia puts her hands up, blinking as she tries to make sense of things. "What did you just do?"

Enzo's dark eyes dart my way. "She pretended."

His dig makes my stomach hollow out. "It's called bluffing, P. And you can win a hell of a lot more hands by bluffing than you can waiting for a good hand."

"That's, like, cheating," Emilio says as he gathers our cards and chips to restart the game.

"No, that's, like, how you play the game," I quip back.

"Yeah, I'm going with Mom's strategy," Pia says.

But before we can play another hand, the stewards serve us a traditional Hamptons lunch of lobster rolls, fish and chips, oysters on beds of crushed ice, shrimp cocktail, and a variety of other fried sea creatures. The sun and sea have revved our appetites, and as the stewards pour us glasses of ice-cold sparkling water, we're quiet, savoring the delicious fare.

I allow myself the splurge of a few French fries as Pia stares out at the bay that glitters beneath the hazy golden sun.

"What's on your mind, chickadee?" I ask, reaching for a piece of shrimp.

"This is so much fun," she says, returning to the present from wherever it is her mind had wandered. She nudges Enzo with her elbow. "See what you've been missing out on these last four years?"

A melancholy grin splits Enzo's face. "What was I thinking, hm?"

"That's a good question." Pia leans her elbows on the table and casts a side glance in Enzo's direction. "What *were* you thinking?"

Enzo stops chewing. He eyes me quickly, as if he's asking permission to answer. A pit of dread forms in my gut, though surely Enzo has enough sense to give Pia a falsified recollection of events. As I nod, I try to convey that he should blame his grief, that he missed his brother too much to stay in a place that reminded him of Francesco. Anything but the real reason.

Me.

Us.

"You know," Enzo starts, leaning his back against his seat, "my parents died when I was in my twenties. A year apart from each other."

"That's awful," Pia remarks, looking stricken.

"Your father was all I had. Even before our parents died, it always felt like he was my only family. Papà was busy earning a living, and Mamma didn't like me. Used to call me her *piccolo diavolo*. Little devil. And not in an endearing way."

"You must've done something to earn that nickname," I tease.

"I was just my charming self," he says, stiffly, before turning back to Pia. "Anyway, your father and I had a special bond. We didn't always see eye to eye. What am I saying? Most of the time we didn't see things the same way. But I always said that I'd die for him, and I always meant it. If a train was coming right at him, I'd pull him aside and jump on the tracks in his place. I was the older brother. It was my job to protect him." Enzo's eyes shifted around the table, the weight of his tale settling between us. "But I couldn't trade hearts with him."

"So you left because you were sad?" Pia inquires, trying to calculate Enzo's conclusion.

Enzo takes a deep breath and shifts in his seat. "Sad's not the word, P. It felt like someone ripped an organ out of my body. My mind, maybe. Felt like I lost it. It was so disorienting to walk into the restaurant and not see him there in his chef's coat. To just *know* that I'd never see him again. So I left. Thought if I got far away enough from him, and the restaurant, and everything we used to enjoy together, I'd feel normal again."

Pia's brows furrow and after a moment of appearing deep in thought, she nods. "I get it."

Now, I lean in. "What do you get?"

"Wanting to just run away," Pia says with a shrug. "Not wanting to be surrounded by reminders. Mom used to watch Daddy's old shows after he died. I hated it. It freaked me out so bad. It was like Daddy was frozen in that TV, and I was on the outside, growing up."

"You never told me that." But more, why does Pia feel comfortable sharing this little secret of hers with Enzo and not me?

"Emi didn't like it either," Pia confesses.

"It was just kind of strange," Emilio chimes in with a shrug, trying to brush it off. "I mean, imagine the only way to see your dad is through a screen, saying the same lines, smiling the same way, over and over. Made me feel like he was trapped there in that studio, while we were moving on."

"Well, I must grieve differently than all of you," I say in my defense, folding my hands over my empty plate. "I was just trying to keep his memory alive. His smile. His voice. His laugh. You'd be surprised how quickly you can forget those types of things." I knew, because while I had video reminders of Francesco, I clung to my memories of Enzo with all my might for fear that the little details he was comprised of would slip away.

"Sounds like you were trying to *pretend*," Pia jokes, sharing a smirk with Enzo.

It makes my stomach lurch as I take in their nuanced, identical expressions. As Pia can relate to Enzo's rationale, can she too recognize herself in his face? But as the stewards reappear and reset the table for dessert, Pia settles back into her seat, drawing her knees to her chest.

"Thanks for being honest," Pia says, though something tugs at her voice. She's got a placid smile on her face, but when she doesn't immediately dig into the dessert that's been laid out before us, I know this conversation has stirred up more emotions than she'd like to let on. "But we did miss you."

Enzo's hand that rests on the table curls into a fist. I know him as well as I know myself. I know guilt is gnawing at him, as it is me. Him, for leaving; me, for lying about why he did.

"You have no idea how much I missed you guys, too," Enzo admits, his voice thick.

We finish dessert with light chatter, musing about the day, how we all prefer the charm of East Hampton to the flashiness of South, as the yacht glides past its quiet, manicured suburbs. Pia and I lounge in the sun for a while, the warmth sinking into our skin, the lull of the water beneath us rocking us nearly to sleep. Eventually, we loop our way back to Montauk's Navy Beach where we anchor just in time for the slow, dramatic descent of the sun.

From the sundeck, Enzo and I watch as the kids take the jet skis for their second spin of the day, their laughter carrying across the bay.

It's one of those moments that's so perfect, you try to commit every last detail of it to memory as you're living it. But as this idyllic day is heading for its grand finale, my phone rings.

Tinsley.

"Hi, Tinsley. How did it go?" I ask, putting the phone on speaker so Enzo can hear. We huddle closer so we can hear her voice through the breeze, and as she relays that the showing went well and she's certain there's an offer on the way, my breath catches.

"Try to close them, Tinsley," Enzo says, leaning down so his mouth is closer to the speaker. "If it's a cash offer, tell them we can do a two-week close."

Two weeks? How fast does he want this summer—our time together—to end? The boat feels rocky beneath me, though I know it's not the current. It's as if someone has turned an hourglass upside down and sand is slipping so fast, I don't think I'll be able to salvage even a handful.

"You got it, Enzo," she says before clicking off.

"Isn't that great?" Enzo says. His optimism is so palpable, I could choke on it. Is he relieved at the prospect of finally being free from our very last link?

Or at least, the last link he knows about.

"Ma!" Emilio calls out. He's brought his jet ski to a halt right beside the boat. "Come on. Just for a minute."

"I said no," I yell back.

"Get her down here," Emilio yells up to Enzo, who wastes no time wrangling me toward the main deck.

"You're supposed to be on *my* side," I mutter as I peel off my cover-up and toss it aside.

But Enzo is nice and smug as he helps me onto the jet ski. As soon as I'm on, I wrap my arms around Emilio's waist; he has yet to take off, and I'm already clutching on for dear life.

"You don't want to join Pia?" I ask Enzo, but he waves me off and before I know what's happening, Emilio takes off.

My screams and pleas for him to slow down are get carried away in the wind as salt spray soaks me, my hair whipping wildly around my face. He hasn't gone this fast all day, but now, as he glances over his shoulder with a wide, mischievous grin, I know he's taking great pleasure in torturing his mother.

Pia, floating nearby on her own jet ski, is in hysterics as we tear past her.

"Emilio Gaetano," I start in my best warning tones when he slows down. But as soon as his full name leaves my lips, he revs the engine again, faster this time.

Feeling like I might really fly off this time, weightless, breathless, I hold on tight and close my eyes. The cold water shocks my sun-kissed skin, sending a shiver up my spine. My grip tightens and my pulse pounds. And when Emilio finally eases off the throttle, my entire body feels like Jell-O.

I hear Emilio's laugh, so genuine, like it might never end. After a moment, it meshes with Enzo's and Pia's. I peel one eye open, then the other.

"I don't think I've ever seen you so scared," Emilio says, twisting his body around to get a good look at the damage he's done. I don't need a mirror to know I'm a complete disaster. I'm surprised I'm still in one piece.

I narrow my eyes. "I so wish I could ground you right now."

"Admit it. You had fun."

"Get me off of this godforsaken invention."

Enzo helps us all back onto the boat, along with the stewards who hand us fresh towels and bottles of water. With my legs as wobbly as they are, I all but collapse into the plush sofa at the rear of the deck, the towel wrapped around my body doing little to take away the chill. The kids join me, still laughing, basking in the golden haze of the stunning sunset. Enzo approaches with another towel and drapes it around my shoulders before settling down next to me. He extends his arms to either side, stretching out, glancing toward the orange ball in the sky that's diving for the flat horizon. It casts a dreamlike glow on his bronze features, and I wish I had a camera to snap a photograph.

Of him, looking so at ease, so content. Of my children, the embodiment of the brother-sister bond I always hoped they'd share. Of myself, a living, breathing remnant of the very thing my mother wanted me to do. Let go.

I was scared out of my mind, but I have to admit. I had fun.

I forgot how good it feels to have fun. How important something so seemingly trivial truly is.

"Thank you, Zio," Pia says. Her sweet voice is soft, lilting, heavy with emotion. She, too, is sun-kissed and bronzed, and free from makeup, she looks like the little girl I wish she still was. Her knees are hugged to her chest, arms wrapped around her legs.

"Anything for you, pretty Pia," Enzo says, tearing his gaze from the sunset.

We bob with the current, anchored in place, and the sun's pace tells us the day is almost over. But in true Valenti fashion, there's a plot twist before the grand finale.

Pia is crying.

At first, a few silent tears spill out of her eyes, but then, it's like a monsoon. Her chest heaves and sobs catch in her throat. I toss the towel off my shoulders and reach for her.

"Are you having a panic attack?" I ask, brushing damp, stringy strands of hair from her face.

"No," she wails.

"What's wrong, P?" Emilio asks, his voice clipped with concern.

Enzo joins in, leaning over us, his body blocking the last of the sunlight. "Honey, what is it?"

She looks up at Enzo, and Enzo alone, her tear-streaked face like a hammer to my heart. "You're going to leave."

"What?" He sinks into the spot beside Pia. "What do you mean?"

"At the end of this summer," she chokes out. "You're going to leave, and our house will be gone, and we'll never see you again."

Enzo's lips part like a reflex, but he presses them back together. His jaw clenches, and his throat bobs with a hard swallow. He looks like he wants to speak, but no words come.

A long, heavy beat hangs between us. I wait. I watch. Because like my daughter, I'm plagued with the same worry. The same dread, that this is the series finale of a show that had a good run. I don't know if he'll reassure her; if he'll lie or if he'll tell the truth. What even is the truth? Do either of us know what the future holds? Pia's sniffles are like little pleas for Enzo to say something, anything. Her body trembles and she's so different from the wild, confident girl she was just a few minutes ago.

"Pia," he starts, but the two syllables of her name sound like a question. He has no idea what to say. "Pia, it's a house. It's just a house. Just because we're selling it doesn't mean we're not going to see each other. I've got my place in Florida. You all can come visit anytime. I'm still crazy about the city. I can come visit you. Hell, we can vacation in Italy next summer if you'd like, or we can rent a place out here. The point is, P, house or no house, we're family."

I want to believe him. Especially when he opens his arms and Pia folds into him, unable to tame her emotion, I hope he won't let her down. I try not to think about how good Enzo is at walking away, and remind myself that, even though it always takes him a while, he does come back.

The sun is gone and all that's left is a periwinkle sky and an evening chill whose breeze takes the fun of our day with it. Reality has swooped back in and snatched us up. While Emilio and Enzo chat it up with our captain who slowly steers us toward the marina, I wrap an arm around Pia and squeeze her close.

"Is it too much for you," I ask, "having Enzo around? You brought up how he left. Are you angry with him still?"

She shakes her head, vehemently. Whatever her answer is, she's sure of it. Her chin trembles as she slowly turns to look at me, but I don't just see melancholy in her eyes. I see realization.

"I love him," she says.

The words slip out so easily, it's as if they've lived on the tip of her tongue all this time and she's just been holding them inside. I go completely still, studying my daughter who has no idea what she's just admitted. With just three little words, I'm crushed for no other reason than this: that like her mother, Pia has an Enzo-shaped hole in her heart.

And as I wrap my arms around her and kiss the top of her head to let her know she's safe, I close my eyes, exhausted from eighteen years of secret keeping, wishing I could tell her why.

CHAPTER EIGHTEEN

SCARLETT

2000

As I painted my face with creams and powders, making myself up, I could already see the places pregnancy had claimed.

Ten weeks in, and I was still trying to wrap my mind around it. Pregnant. With my third child. It wasn't a surprise; Francesco had all but begged me for another baby. Another chance for him to get parenting right.

I had to give credit where credit was due. When it came to being a parent, Francesco and I had different talents. He could sit down on the floor beside Emilio and play Nintendo for hours before popping some popcorn and flopping on the sofa to watch superhero movies. He and Pia could dissect music, drawing conclusions about intent and emotions I'd never be able to hear. He knew how to make the kids laugh, how to be their built-in best friend. But that didn't make him reliable.

Both kids griped about their father's absence at their respective school events, and when Francesco skipped out on Pia's last recital, it made her so nervous, her voice cracked during her solo. Emilio adored baseball, was talented at it, but he considered switching to his father's favorite sport of soccer in the hopes that Francesco might attend a game or two.

But when it came to baby number three, Francesco vowed to *get it right this time.*

Like Emilio and Pia were his trial runs. His warm-ups before the big game. His sentiment proved that fatherhood might not have been his strong suit, but maybe we both were hoping the third time would be the charm.

Leaning in toward the mirror, taking stock of the way the bridge of my nose was already expanding, I had the fleeting thought that it was a boy. But I swiped the thought away with a stroke of my powder brush. It was too soon to get too invested; this pregnancy was high risk. I was thirty-nine, and I'd had postpartum complications after I gave birth to Pia. I felt like I had to hold my breath until the twelve-week mark, but I worried deep down that even then, I wouldn't be safe to admire my growing belly and wonder if I was carrying a baby girl or boy.

The doorbell rang, startling out of my thoughts. Setting down my brush, I abandoned my vanity and carefully padded my way downstairs. The last of the afternoon sunlight streamed through the bay window as I smoothed down my dress, my small bump just slightly pulling the fabric, but not noticeable enough for anyone to start asking questions. I went on my tiptoes and peeked through the peephole before answering.

"Enzo!" I swung open the door and drew him into a hug. "I wasn't expecting you so soon."

"Beat the traffic," he said, exhaling. "Got lucky."

I stepped aside to let him in. He gathered his suitcase and duffle and trailed into the entryway. After our visit just a few months ago, shortly after, he'd ended things with Angela and put his house on the market. We let him know that our home was his, for as long as he needed.

We might've had another child on the way, and our house may have already been in the throes of chaos, but I didn't care. He was back. He was out of that nightmare, out of that life that wasn't working for him, and he was home. With us. Where he belonged.

"How'd the kids take it when you said goodbye?" I asked.

"Nella was thrilled." His brows raised and his voice sounded clipped. He took a deep sigh. "Maria was sad, but she's excited for the summers. That was a great idea on your part. Have to thank you."

"No you don't. Oh, I'm just so glad you're back. Fran will be so excited to see you." Barefoot, I led the way to the kitchen where I brewed him an espresso.

Resting his palms on the counter, he hinged his hips back. "Where are the kids?"

"With my mother. I've been working non-stop. It's been nuts." I served him the espresso in a Versace cup and saucer, an extravagant gift from the network executives at PBS. "So your timing is impeccable."

He smiled before leaning his head back and taking a long sip, letting out a satisfied exhale as he replaced the cup to its saucer with a light clink. Taking a good look at him, I wanted to believe he looked more relaxed, more *himself,* now that he was back in Manhattan, but there was still something tense about him. Something unsettled.

"I'll be out of your hair in no time," Enzo said. "Going to start looking for a place tomorrow."

"Nonsense. You stay here as long as you need to. You're family."

He gave me a tight, unreadable smile.

"Your room is all set up. Fresh towels in the bathroom, toothbrush, toothpaste, hair gel. I even bought you a new set of pajamas. Couldn't help myself." I drummed my fingertips against the cold counter. "You sure you're okay with the basement, right?"

"Do I have another option?" Enzo teased.

"I know, right? We're going to have to move when the new baby comes."

The air stilled. Enzo had been reaching for his espresso cup, but his hand froze mid-air. My eyes widened. *Shit.*

"New baby?" Enzo finally said. His mouth twisted into a smirk, not quite happy, not quite smug, and he let out a short exhale through his nose. "You definitely left that out of your letters."

I pressed my lips together and tried to swallow. "It's still early—"

"Scar, I'm kidding. It's none of my business."

"Don't say that," I protested. "I'm only ten weeks, and it's high risk. I had some complications I never told you about after I had Pia. That, and I'm old." My shoulders crept higher toward my ears, and I wrung my hands around each other. I could feel *forty* whispering in my ear, saying, *I'm just around the corner, and you'll be taking care of a newborn.* "Too old to be having another baby, but Fran really wanted this. What was I gonna do?"

Enzo nodded, finally getting around to taking that second sip of his espresso he'd been going for. He didn't speak, but his eyes said it all.

"Please, just say whatever it is your holding back," I said, tossing up my hands. "Like you have to have any inhibitions around me."

He set his cup back down, with a louder clink this time. "Congratulations, Scarlett."

"Enzo—"

"What do you want me to say, hm?" Enzo raised his voice. "You spent the last seven years writing me letters every week, complaining about your husband. That he cheats on you, and treats you like shit, and is an absentee father. And yet you still let him call the shots in your life. Why waste your breath, or in our case, your pages, if you're not going to change anything?"

His words made me take a few steps back. They were the last thing I expected from Enzo of all people, one of the only people I felt comfortable confiding in because he listened but he didn't judge.

"Do you think it'd be that simple?" I asked, my voice rising. "You think I can just walk away from my life because I'm not happy?"

"Isn't that what I just did? Isn't that what you told me to do?"

"Oh, don't give me that. You held onto that life until it was choking you."

"And you're not running out of breath?"

His eyes fell to my chest. I looked down to find it heaving up and down with shallow breaths that refused to reach my lungs. Before either of us could speak, the phone hanging on the wall rang. Its song sounded louder than usual against the thick silence. As I answered and pressed the phone to my ear, all I heard was the pounding of my own heart.

"Oh, hi, Fran," I said, glancing at Enzo, trying to gauge his state of mind. He looked like he wished he'd held his tongue. "Guess who's here." I relayed the news of Enzo's arrival to Francesco before he told us to head over to the restaurant for a celebratory meal. As soon as the phone hit the receiver, I turned on my heel and started down the hall.

"Follow me," I said without looking back.

His footsteps trailed me. "I'm sorry."

"No, you're not. Don't try to bullshit me. It won't work." When we reached my bedroom, he hung outside the door. "Come in."

I went into my closet and retrieved the gift Francesco and I had put together for Enzo when he told us he was listing his house in Maryland. On my bed, I laid out a suit, still in its garment bag, a red Ferragamo box containing a shiny new pair of loafers, and diamond monogram cuff links Francesco had purchased from our jeweler. The sound of the zipper cut the quiet, slowly revealing the pinstripe suit we'd custom ordered from Brioni.

"What is all this?" Enzo asked.

I put my hands on my hips, taking a step back. "It's your welcome home gift. Sorry I didn't get a chance to put a bow on it."

"I didn't think pinstripes were still in style," Enzo said as he approached the bed, tepidly, and ran his fingers along the lapels of the suit jacket. "You didn't have to do this."

"I know. But we run a fine dining joint, and we want you to look the part." Enzo looked lost in thought until finally, I caught his eye. "Look," I said with a sigh, "I know our situations might *seem* similar. But they're not. You were never in love with Claudia. I was madly in love with Francesco when we got married. You were there. You know that. And sometimes, despite everything, I still am." I adjusted the watch on my wrist as Enzo shifted his weight, listening. "I guess that's why they call it *falling*. You fall in, you fall out. That's marriage, right?" I let out a nervous laugh. When he didn't join me, I cleared my throat. "It doesn't have to make sense to you, Enz. It probably doesn't. But it would mean a lot to me if you could respect it."

He looked at me with a softness in his eyes, with the very thing I so craved from him. Not forgiveness. Not even understanding. But respect. Then, his eyes fell to the suit, and a smile tugged at his lips. "I feel like it's the eighties again. You're in love with Fran, and I'm back in pinstripes."

"Oh, honey, I said *sometimes*. I'm definitely not in love with him right now." Though my smile faltered as I thought about just how *not in love* Francesco and I were at the moment, I playfully pressed my hands against his chest. "Go get dressed. Come on. Fran can't wait to see you."

And so, he gathered his gifts, and I shooed him out of my bedroom. I dressed in a hurry, eager to get to Amanti.

What was in store now that the family was back together again?

"*Bello guaglione*," Francesco said, too loudly, as Enzo and I entered the restaurant. Enzo's head pulled back like a reflex, as if the boom of Francesco's voice had physical weight. He clapped his hands together once before opening his arms wide and drawing Enzo into a hug. Then, he cupped Enzo's face in his hands. "*Come stai*, hm? You look great."

"*Tutto a posto*," Enzo said, his voice several notches lower in volume and excitement. "You look great, too."

I wondered if Enzo meant it. Francesco was clad in one of his numerous customized chef's jackets. This one was navy blue and had his name embroidered in gold thread, though the fit was off. He always gained a solid five pounds during menu change season, as he and his sous chefs worked through the kinks until they crafted the perfect recipe, but the way the fabric of his coat stretched and pulled suggested he'd put on ten to fifteen. They studied each other a moment longer before Francesco cupped my shoulder and leaned down to kiss me.

"Did you see the Lambo out front?" Francesco asked Enzo with the same eagerness of a child showing off his Christmas gifts. "I gotta take you for a spin later."

"Looks sick," Enzo replied, his tone just polite enough to pass as interest.

"There's someone I want you to meet," Francesco said to me. "Enz, you come, too."

Francesco led the way to a round table at the center of the dining room. Four men clad in suits sat around the table, two bottles of an expensive label of Brunello resting between them.

"Gentlemen," Francesco said as we approached, "I want you to meet my beautiful wife, Scarlett."

He pushed me forward an inch with his hand on the small of my back. I swallowed down my irritation. I'd been doing this for years now. Did he really think I needed him to cue me in? Flashing a smile, I slipped into the role of Mrs. Francesco Valenti with practiced ease.

"Pleasure to meet you, gentlemen," I said, sounding every bit the hostess that I was.

"So this is the Pasta King's wife, hm? You're clearly his better half," one of the men said, raising his glass to me. "Your husband's got quite the talent."

"They would know," Francesco said, eyeing me. "These men work for Food Network."

"Oh," I said, suddenly understanding Francesco's big show. It was no secret his ratings at PBS were dismal. I wondered if he'd invited these men here, trying to pitch his own show to their up-and-coming network, or if they'd chosen to dine here by chance. "We love to watch Emeril!"

"He's a character, isn't he?" another one of the men agreed.

"And this is my brother, Enzo," Francesco said, motioning for Enzo to join us, as he'd been hanging behind me.

"And might there be a brotherly cooking rivalry between you two?" the first man inquired.

"Rivalry, definitely," Francesco answered with a gleeful grin. "Just not when it comes to food. Enzo runs the front-of-house operations with my wife."

"Well," the eldest of the men chimed in, "you all certainly have mastered the art of a family-run business."

"Thank you all so much," Francesco said. He opened his arms wide, like a maestro, and said, "And now, we'll be bringing out your main courses. *Risotto allo zafferano con ricci di mare e burrata affumicata, filetto di branzino con limoni d'Amalfi e fiori di zucchini, e finalmente, agnolotti ripieni di astice blu, con pomodorini gialli e caviar.*"

"I understood none of that," one of the men remarked.

"Except caviar," another pointed out.

"Whatever it is, it all sounds great," a third chimed in.

It took all of my will not to whip my head around and shoot Enzo a questioning glare. Yes, Francesco was a Michelin star recipient. Yes, he had penned five cookbooks that coincided with each of the five seasons of his TV show. But right now, he was acting like a used car salesman, putting on a show that was one bad note away from being embarrassing. My husband was an artist, that I would never deny. But charisma never came easy to him the way it did to Enzo. No matter how many times Francesco had been on camera, being a showman always felt like a part he was trying to play, when he'd been born for the role of a chef. A prolific one at that. And when he strayed from that, it didn't translate well. We left the executives with some pleasantries before retreating to our table at the rear of the dining room.

"We got new menu covers," Francesco said as soon as we sat down, showing off the embossed leather folios to Enzo. "And check holders to match."

"Very nice." Enzo nodded as a waitress named Agata approached our table. She was a new hire, a Sicilian native, and Francesco was making no bones about hiding his attraction to her.

"Agata, *questo è mio fratello maggiore,* Lorenzo," Francesco said.

While I stifled an eye roll, Enzo leaned over and offered his hand for a shake. "You can call me Enzo."

"*Piacere di conoscerti,*" Agata said before looking at me. "*Ciao,* Signora Valenti."

"*Ciao,* Agata." I forced the greeting out, though I kept my eyes fixed on the menu as if I didn't have the thing memorized. "Please bring us one bottle of still, one bottle of sparkling, and a breadbasket."

"*A presto,*" she said with a slight bow before turning away.

Francesco's eyes trailed after her, or rather, her sultry backside that sashayed toward the kitchen. Across the table, Enzo caught my eye, though I darted my gaze away.

"Enzo's wearing his new suit," I said, nudging Francesco with my elbow.

He came to and examined his brother's attire. "Oh good. I sort of guessed on the size, but looks like it fits perfectly."

Enzo patted his stomach. "Gotta keep things in check."

"Ah, not me." Francesco smacked his own gut, noticeably thicker than Enzo's. "It's impossible to stay in shape around all this good food."

Agata dropped off the breadbasket and started pouring our waters—sparkling for me and Enzo, flat for Francesco.

"Must be menu change season," Enzo teased, reaching for a breadstick.

"Oh, yes!" Agata lit up as she poured, one arm behind her just like I taught her. "Francesco was testing a new take on *osso buco* last night. I thought it was so wonderful, but he thinks it still needs some changes."

"Oh, really?" I murmured, reaching for a piece of olive bread and sliding it through the glistening olive oil. "Eat anything else of his recently?"

Agata missed my double entendre, but it was not lost on Enzo and Francesco. While I chewed, Francesco cleared his throat.

"*Porta lo speciale di oggi,*" Francesco told Agata, in a boss-like tone that I knew was put on.

This time, when Agata strutted away, Francesco looked at me. No, glared at me.

I smiled so big, all my teeth showed. "Don't worry, honey," I said, wiping my hands on my napkin. "Your little Sicilian sweetheart didn't catch my dig."

"She doesn't need to speak English to know you're being a bitch."

I flipped him the bird in response.

Enzo's eyes darted between us. I grabbed another piece of bread, lathering it in olive oil before tearing off a bite with my teeth. Ordinarily, I wouldn't have indulged in such a large amount of carbs, but I was eating for two. Francesco's fingers drummed against the white table-cloth, creating an antsy rhythm as a thick, awkward silence enveloped the three of us.

"So, Enzo," I started, adjusting the napkin over my lap, "what are you most looking forward to now that you're home?"

Enzo's brows shot up. "Staying the hell away from you two. *Madonna mia.*"

"You know what it's like," Francesco remarked. "Warned me not to get married."

"Yes, just like he warned me what a bastard you really are," I added with yet another forced smile.

Enzo was reduced to laughter, though I wasn't sure if it was so much humorous as it was out of nerves, and he covered his face with his hands.

"You sure about staying with us?" I teased. "Because if you think this is bad, you should hear us at home."

But Francesco didn't find any of it a laughing matter. He sat there like a Roman soldier, stoic and still, until Agata dropped off our appetizer without a word or a glance. Francesco slid the plate closer to him and grabbed a spoon and a fork to serve Enzo a helping of the *langoustine carpaccio* with citrus zest and caviar.

"I've decided I'm going to try for another Michelin star," Francesco said as he delicately deposited the small helping on Enzo's plate.

"Yeah?" I chimed in. I raised my index finger to grab Agata's attention. "Have you started screwing the Michelin inspector yet?"

Before Francesco could respond, Agata approached.

"Yes, Signora?"

"Could you please bring me out an eggplant parmesan, as my husband seems to have forgotten pregnant women can't consume raw seafood?" I said, loud enough to get my point across to Francesco.

"Right away, Signora."

I glanced around the restaurant for a moment. It was humming with life and conviviality, a sharp contrast to the tension that lived at my table. Did Francesco even realize how abhorrent his behavior was? That his brother—his only living relative in this country, might I add—had just returned home, and yet Francesco failed to ask even one question about how he was doing? He didn't bother to try and hide his attraction to the Sicilian beauty in front of his pregnant wife, though that didn't come as a surprise to me. I could handle it. But I felt bad for Enzo, that he'd returned home under the guise of picking up where he left off. The truth was, we were so far gone from that place, I could barely remember it.

The heat of Francesco's stare made me crane my neck.

"Yes?" I asked.

"What the hell's gotten into you?" Francesco said.

I grabbed my glass of water and leaned back against the booth, taking a sip. "If you want the answer to that question, just take a look in the mirror, *Pasta King*."

"EVERYONE THINKS THEY'RE A gangster," Enzo said with a *tsk* of his tongue.

A *Sopranos* rerun flashed on screen in the living room as I straightened up stray pillows and blankets, picking up empty cups the kids had left behind before I sent them to the kitchen to do their homework.

"Hey, Enzo?" I said. He glanced up. "You used to act just like those guys."

We laughed at the memory of who he used to be. "I did, didn't I?"

"I'm gonna go check on the kids." I started down the hall, arms laden with cups that I deposited in the sink. Cartoon Network was on mute in the kitchen, its innocence clashing with the debauchery on screen in the next room. I glanced up at the clock. It was well after nine. On a Saturday night, things would've been just getting started at the restaurant. But it was Tuesday, and Enzo had come home about twenty minutes ago after seating the last of our guests. I couldn't help but wonder if Francesco was tied up with Agata. After loading the dishwasher and closing it with my hip, I dried my hands and walked over to the kids.

"Mommy?" Pia asked, looking up at me.

"Yes, sugar?"

"You're a grown-up. Do you do math?"

"I know how to do math."

"No," she said, stretching out the word. "Emi said I won't use this kind of math in real life. Is that true?"

Emilio shot her a look of betrayal. I smoothed back his hair and fought a smile. Then, I crouched down next to Pia and looked at her homework. Word problems.

"Well, actually, P, these are real-life scenarios." I ran my index finger along one of the paragraphs. "When you grow up, you might have to do things like split the check with your friends at a restaurant, and that's kind of like one of these word problems. So yes, you will use math when you're a grown-up."

She sighed and rested her arms atop her textbook. "That's too bad. I *hate* math."

I laughed and pushed myself up from the ground, letting out laborious sigh. Just as I was heading down the hall, the front door opened. Francesco walked in. He slammed the door behind him. It reverberated like a gunshot.

I tossed my arms up. "Any one of us could've been sleeping."

But then, I studied him. His hair was windblown, and his chest moved up and down with rapid, shallow breaths, as if he'd run the whole way home, though I knew that was an impossibility. It didn't matter if Francesco was traveling two blocks or ten—he was taking his Lamborghini. His chef's coat was unbuttoned halfway, the sleeves rolled up, uneven on either side, revealing trembling hands. Had he been with Agata? Or had something worse happened?

"Francesco," I said, trying to keep my voice even, "is everything alright?"

He didn't answer. He dropped his messenger bag to the ground and headed straight for the bar cart, ignoring Enzo. Before I could get a handle on the kids, they appeared behind me, all curious eyes and ears. I drew them close as Francesco poured himself a shot of Louis XIII. It had been a gift from the PBS executives last year. He downed it, then poured himself another.

"Hey," Enzo said, rising to his feet, still clad in his work suit, sans jacket. "Take it easy."

After downing the second shot, Francesco forewent the shot glass and took a swig straight from the bottle.

"You two," I said to my children, "go upstairs."

"But, Mom," Emilio tried, but I turned them around toward the staircase.

"Now. Go to your rooms." I watched them trek upstairs, reluctantly, and only turned away when I heard their bedroom doors close. In the entryway, however, I noticed a thick document sticking out of his messenger bag. I squatted down, scooped it up, and scanned over it.

Termination of agreement. From PBS.

My stomach dropped. I glanced up at him; he was already watching me, holding the tangible proof of his failure.

"You happy now?" he shot at me.

"Am I *happy*?" I walked into the living room, the document still in my hands. Closer to him now, I saw just how badly he was taking this news. His eyes weren't sad or disappointed. They were wild. Absolutely maniacal. "Francesco, I'm so sorry."

"Are you, Scarlett?" Another swig. "Because you're the one who always bitched and moaned about how much my career *changed* me. Maybe if you had been a more supportive wife, I would've been more confident at work, and I could've done a better job. Maybe I wouldn't have gotten *this* today. Cancelled. Cancelled! Me. The fucking Pasta King." He turned toward the bar cart and set the bottle down with a thud. "Cancelled. Imagine that."

My throat burned. How did Francesco always manage to twist the truth and turn the blame on me? But I wouldn't take it. I had nothing to do with his show at all.

"Fran," I said, "you still have your cookbooks, and the restaurant—"

"The restaurant," he huffed with a humorless laugh. "I'm a television star, Scarlett. What am I going to do? Go back to kissing customers' asses every time I serve them a lousy meal? Make the rounds like I'm just some average restaurateur?"

"Oh, you mean like what me and him do." I gestured between me and Enzo. "That's right. I forgot how beneath you we are."

"You have no idea what this is like! None!" Francesco exploded. Did I imagine the creak of Emilio's bedroom door, or had he snuck out to get a better listen to his father's tantrum? "I'm a star. I'm better than this. I'm bigger than this!" He turned around and grabbed the bottle of ridiculously expensive cognac again and took an even longer swig this time. "That was our main source of income, by the way. So all those diamonds and handbags you like? You can kiss them goodbye."

I blinked, unfazed. "I don't need diamonds to live, Fran. I have no problem scaling back, and you know it."

"Scaling back," he scoffed. "You will never understand what this feels like. To lose everything."

"Fran," Enzo interjected, "you're overreacting. It's a TV show. You had a good run, and now you move on to something else. You still have your family—"

"Don't talk to me about family," Francesco hissed. "You screwed every whore in Manhattan, including my wife, you animal. You destroyed your family."

How dare you, I thought. I thought it over and over again as I ripped the bottle from his hands and smashed it against the floor, the glass exploding on impact, the scent of cognac rising like smoke from ashes. How dare he bring something like that up in our home, mere feet from our children, knowing full well the details. Knowing that I hadn't had an affair with Enzo when I was a young girl out of sheer attraction, but because I was desperate to feel like I mattered in this world.

The irony was not lost on me that not much had changed between me and my twenty-three-year-old self.

Francesco's jagged breath was audible as he glanced down at the shards pooled in the brown liquid on the ground. His eyes, looking like they were lit on fire, slowly met mine.

"That was a gift. You knew that was a gift from the PBS executives."

"Yes, I did," I said, defiant.

"You're nothing but a selfish *puttana*," he spat out. "That's all you've ever been, and I'm the fool for thinking you were anything more than my brother's lousy whore."

Francesco's words were so low, I had to wonder if I'd heard him right. But the pain was loud. I flinched as if he'd slapped me; that was how bad it hurt. I wanted to throw something. To scream and kick and fight. But then I looked at him. At those wild, seething eyes, and I knew this fight wasn't fair. I couldn't win against him. I'd never been able to.

"I'm glad my mother never got to meet you," he went on like he was enjoying twisting the knife. "She'd be so ashamed that I ended up with a wife who wanted me to fail."

"That's enough, Fran," Enzo snapped, grabbing Francesco's arm. "You've crossed the line now."

"You think she's so great?" Francesco yelled, yanking his arm free. "Take her. See if you can afford her."

"I've earned all of *this*," I shouted, my arms flung wide, gesturing to the marble floors, the chandeliers, the life that looked so glittering on the outside. "Haven't I? That's how you pay me, right? Every time you cheat or scream or shut me out, you buy me back with diamonds and handbags. Isn't that the deal?"

Francesco leaned in, inching toward me, looming. Enzo put his hand on Francesco's chest to stop him, but it was too late. I already felt the threat.

"What are you gonna do, Fran? You wanna hit me again?" I was screaming, sounding every bit as off my hinges as I was. "Go ahead. Hit me in front of your brother and our kids. Why don't you show them who you really are?"

"I'm out of here," Francesco muttered under his breath. He raised his palms in surrender as he maneuvered his way around me. Whisking his messenger bag from the floor, he stormed out. A few moments later, that damned Lamborghini roared to life, shaking the house. But a figure on the stairwell caught my attention. Emilio sat on a step, halfway down. Pia had reached the landing, peering around the corner, like she was afraid to look. My heart hammered against my chest. In all my years of motherhood, I'd always found a way to handle whatever situation came my way. But for the first time, I had no idea what to do.

"Baby," I started. Emilio locked eyes with me from across the room. Those beautiful caramel-colored eyes he'd stolen from his father. Was I imagining that they were broken, that something had been forever changed in my son? I wondered if he was going to question anything, but then they both ran up the stairs, their footsteps heavy, their bedroom doors slamming behind them. I wanted to run up there and wrap my arms around them and promise them they were safe, but I didn't have it in me.

Francesco hadn't hit me, but I could barely stand up.

The house was heavy with silence, only peppered with the faint sound of Carmela Soprano's nagging voice. My trembling hands flew to my belly. The baby. Stress wasn't good for the baby, and this was so much more than stress.

"Scarlett," Enzo whispered.

"Maybe it is all my fault." I sank into the sofa. "I'm a bitch to him. No wonder he cheats on me."

When I took in Enzo's sympathetic expression, I lost it. As a girl, I'd believed Enzo could save me. But now I was a woman who knew better. No one was coming to save me. That was how I'd ended up here. I'd waited and waited for someone to pull me out of this mess, but now it was plain as day. No one could do that because I had chosen this. Every time I'd stayed, brushed his abuse under the rug, I was heading toward this.

"I'm so tired," I finally said as Enzo held my arms.

"It's gonna be okay. You two always work it out."

I curled my knees to my chest and wiped my face dry. My eyes glazed over as I stared at the TV. There sat Tony Soprano's endlessly forgiving wife, all alone at the kitchen table in her silent mansion. Despondent. Detached. Yet I knew no matter what wars raged in her mind, though the next episode had yet to air, she'd stay. Because she was me and I was her. Two wives who couldn't find it in themselves to walk away.

"I'm really worried, Enzo."

"About?"

I looked into his eyes. "Desperate people do desperate things."

And as the words hung in the air, I wondered if I was talking about Francesco or myself.

CHAPTER NINETEEN

SCARLETT

Summer, 2011

Rain pounds against the windows and thunder rumbles low in the distance. Clouds hang like heavy shadows above the water, swallowing the sky in an ominous gray haze, while the wind howls, rattling the glass as if it, too, is protesting the end of something. A shiver crawls down my spine, and I grab a sweatshirt and tug it overhead. The storm is fitting. The perfect backdrop for today's activity.

Packing.

We've received an all-cash offer, with just two weeks to close. Just like that, our time here is up.

I shouldn't be surprised. Of course someone wants it. This house and everything it promises is a dream. Ocean views. Direct beach access. Wide open, sun-drenched spaces meant for late-morning coffee and sandy, barefoot summers. A place where memories are meant to be made. It had been my dream.

And now, it's over. Faster than I thought. I presumed we'd have until mid-August. Now, we could be out of here before the first. I want to imagine we'll spend these final days savoring lazy beach days and cookouts on the deck, but the truth is, we should've started packing weeks ago. This is a huge undertaking, storing away eighteen years' worth of belongings.

We've each started in our respective rooms, and we'll tackle the common areas in a few days, a task I'm dreading. I'm a sentimental woman. Always have been. But as I stand in my closet, staring at dresses I haven't worn in years but kept because they remind me of a particular time and place, I wonder if I've taken it too far. Trash bag in hand, I want to be relentless, but worry tugs at me. If I let go of these garments, will I lose the memories, too?

Or worse. If I toss aside these belongings, will the old versions of myself go with them? The young woman I was, so full of hope, when we moved into this house? The woman I became who learned how to hold everything together, to pretend?

I start with the easy stuff. Shoes. Tattered flip-flops and sandals, scuffed wedges, strappy heels with peeling leather all go in the bag. I already feel lighter as I move onto costume jewelry, then handbags and clutches, and I even make a dent into my swimwear. Without a beach house or any disposable income to travel, I won't be needing all these bikinis and coverups. I'm on a roll, proud of myself, until I get to the locked cabinet. I stop cold. I know exactly what's inside.

My fingers hover over the handle. I tell myself I shouldn't. I need to keep moving and stay on task. Our time is so limited. But before I even register what I'm doing, I'm kneeling on the floor and reaching for the key.

Enzo's letters.

They spill out of the cabinet like they're alive, like they've been waiting for me to let them out and breathe again. His angular, sharp handwriting stares back at me, whispering, *Don't you remember me?* And of course I do.

That doesn't stop me from reaching for one and unfolding it. I tell myself I'll just take a quick skim of one, maybe two, but I know it's a lie. If I have it my way, I'll be in this closet all night, obsessing over every one of his words like I'm trying to prove to myself that this is real. Me and Enzo. That this secret thing of ours does, in fact, exist.

The letter I've unfolded is from 1993. Cross-legged, I lean my back against the cabinets and read.

Dear Scarlett,

I don't know how to tell you this, but I didn't get to read your last letter. You're not going to like this. Shit. I don't even know if I should tell you this. Claudia read it. I know. Now you're probably never going to write to me again, but before you get ahead of yourself, I can promise you she'll never read another one of your letters again. Trust me.

When Little Enzo ran off, it brought Claudia and me closer together. It was amazing how we pushed aside our differences and came together, sharing the worrying about our son. I'm not going to lie, Scar. I've been lonely since I left New York. Maybe that loneliness is what attracted me to Claudia. I thought we could give things another try. No matter what, she'll always be the mother of my kids. I thought it would be best for all of us if we could just work it out and get back together. Was I ever madly in love with her? No. But that's not what marriage is about. You know what marriage is. It's an arrangement. Two people who come together to build a safe and stable home and make a family to fill it. It's an institution. I thought, you know what? I'm gonna push aside my feelings and go for it again.

And then, your letter.

Claudia got the mail that morning. By the time I came downstairs for breakfast, she was sitting at the kitchen table, your words in her hands. She leaned into me, hard. Asked me why I'd start something with her when I had something going on with you. I didn't think I had anything going on with you, but in Claudia's eyes, I did. She said something that I can't stop thinking about, Scar.

She thinks you're the love of my life.

It's insane. You're married to my kid brother. You can't be the love of my life. So we keep in touch. Is that so bad? I tried explaining this to her and I even went so far as to rip up your letter before I had the chance to read it. But it proved nothing to her, and she left, closing the door of us ever getting back together. I'm sure it's for the best. I'd probably hurt her again. I guess, when it comes to being in love, you can't force it. Same can be said for falling out of love. Which really, is too bad. That would make my life a hell of a lot easier.

So, I hope you're not mad at me, Scar. If I could have pieced together that letter, I would have. You don't know how much I look forward to hearing from you.

And I'm sure if Claudia read that sentence, she'd wave her finger in my face and say, See, she is the love of your life. What the hell was I thinking, trying to get back with her? She drives me nuts. You keep me sane.

Write me back, Scar. Please.

All my love,

Always,

Enzo

The letter strikes me differently than it did eighteen years ago. Back then, we were both trying to stuff our feelings as far down as they would go. Lying to ourselves, telling each other these letters were nothing more than a means of communication. But reading it now, it's so apparent, how little we believed our own lies. How our feelings for each other were right there, at the surface, dangerously close to boiling over. How naïve we were to think that no one else would notice.

She thinks you're the love of my life.

Am I? More, is he mine?

The question is still ringing in my ears when footsteps thunder down the hallway. I barely have time to shove the letters away before my bedroom door bursts open.

"Mom," Pia says. No. Cries.

I press myself up, rush out of my closet, and close the door behind me. "Yes, honey," I say, out of breath despite having barely moved. It was a close call. Too close. But my thoughts are pulled away from the letter when I take in my daughter's state. Her eyes are wide and frantic, and her shaky breath is shallow, barely there. "Oh no," I mutter.

A panic attack.

She turns as white as the sheets on my bed as she sinks to the ground. Her forehead is covered in sweat, though her teeth start chattering with shivers.

"I'm gonna pass out," Pia tells me.

"Emilio," I call out, not leaving Pia's side. "Emilio!"

"What's going on?" Emilio appears in the doorway. He takes one glance at his sister and he knows.

"Go get some orange juice," I instruct.

He dashes off, and Enzo takes his place.

"Hey," Enzo whispers as he approaches. Gently, he sinks down to the other side of her and wraps one arm around her.

"Pia." I clasp her hands in mine. "Come on, let's do our deep breathing. In for four—"

"Got the OJ," Emilio announces, slightly out of breath. He, too, sinks down to the ground and hands Pia the carton, having not bothered for a glass.

With shaking hands, she lifts it to her lips, takes a sip, and hands it back to him. She's still struggling for breath, and her entire face is covered in sweat.

"Breath work, Pia," I say, louder this time. I have to get her out of this. "I'm right here, honey. You're safe. You're with me."

She erupts into tears. Heavy sobs that come straight from her gut. I reach for her, but instead, she leans into Enzo. He kisses the top of her head and rubs her back with his palm.

"It's just a feeling, P," Enzo says as he rocks her back and forth. "It's not real. That's what you have to tell yourself. There's nothing wrong with you, and whatever you're worried about can be fixed."

I do a double-take. Who is this mental health guru, and what has he done with Enzo?

"Is it the house, sweetie?" I ask, smoothing her hair away from her face. "I can pack your stuff if it's too much for you."

But she shakes her head against Enzo's chest. Her sobs intensify, and she claws at her chest. "I can't breathe."

My own breath goes shallow. What if I can't help her? What if she passes out and we have to take her to the hospital? Before I can figure out my next move, Enzo leans his face in close to hers.

"I want you to do something for me," he tells her, looking directly

246 Sarah Arcuri

into her eyes. "I want you to tell me five things you can see or hear. Right now."

Her face wrinkles.

"Want me to help you?" Enzo asks, and Pia nods. He looks around. "Okay. I see a carton of orange juice. Emilio's messy hair. That's two." His eyes shift to mine and he gives me a wink. "Your mom, in that sweatshirt she stole from your dad that's about ten sizes too big." He glances down at Pia, trying to procure a smile. "I see the storm outside. I hear the wind, and the rain. The thunder and the ocean. I hear "O Surdato 'Nnamurato" playing from my room. And from what I remember, you know the words." And then, he starts singing. Soft, in his beautiful baritone, the old Neapolitan song he and Francesco used to blare like it was their anthem. After a few lines, Pia joins in, her strong voice reduced to breathy notes.

But a few lyrics in, and a sob bursts from Pia's throat instead of a song, raw and guttural.

On the verge of tears myself, I reach for my daughter. "Honey, it's okay. Everything's okay."

"I have to tell you something." The words tumble out in a single breath. "But you're going to be upset."

"I promise," I say, my voice sounding much steadier than I feel. "I won't. I'm your mother, Pia. You can tell me anything."

She looks at Emilio. Whatever's gnawing at her, he knows about it.

"College starts in a few weeks," Pia says, her voice small and wobbly, so different from the operatic voice those same vocal chords can produce.

"If you don't want to live in a dorm," I say, "I'll figure out a way to get you out of it, and you can live at home."

"It's not the dorm," Pia says. Silence filled with anticipation hangs between us as my daughter works up the courage to confess. "I don't want to sing anymore. I don't want to major in music, and if you say no, then I'm not going to college at all."

Not this again. I told myself it was a phase, her wanting to quit the very thing that's consumed her entire life. I thought she would realize she has a God-given gift that shouldn't be squandered. Evidently, I thought wrong. Pia's brows knit as she blinks, waiting. I can feel the weight of Enzo's and Emilio's eyes on me as I try to think.

"Can you at least tell me why?" I ask, hoping I'm not pushing her back into an attack. Outside, the storm rages, the wind picking up, whipping against the windows. Pia looks like a kettle, ready to boil over. Whatever her reason is, it's big. I brace myself.

"Just tell her, P," Emilio chimes in.

"You know how Daddy used to miss my recitals sometimes?" Pia's voice comes out even higher pitched than usual. She glances at Enzo. "You would fill in for him and come instead."

Enzo and I lock eyes. Of course we remember. I certainly can recall each time I sat beside an empty seat designated for Francesco, or beside Enzo who played his understudy; I remember being flooded with anger and disappointment toward my husband, when I should've been focused on my daughter's budding talent. I also remember how he'd come home the next day with a lavish bouquet of roses for Pia, praising the talent he didn't get to see in action, promising to be there the next time.

My eyes flutter closed for a moment. "I remember, Pia."

"I just … I felt like every time I had a performance, I was just singing to get Daddy's attention. To get him to love me." Her voice cracks, and she doesn't bother to swipe away the tears streaming down her face. "He's gone. What's the point now?"

I lean over, cup my daughter's face in my hands, and look her in the eye. Now, I know exactly what to say. "The point is *God* gave you that voice of yours, Pia. Not your father. He could've made you anything, but He decided to make you a singer. You got that gift to share with the world, to prove that He's real. Not to get your father's attention. Your voice is so much bigger than you realize, sweetheart. And the last thing I want is for your father to steal that from you. You don't have to decide right now, but before you change your major, I just want you to think about that."

We all go quiet for a moment, only the patter of the rain breaking the silence.

"Dad hated baseball," Emilio finally says. "But I kept on playing. Did it bug me he didn't come to my games? Of course. But I loved it. And Mom was always there."

I reach over and squeeze Emilio's hand. I wish I could raise Francesco from the dead just so I could kill him, for his lingering effects on my kids, for hurting them in irreparable ways.

"It's kind of like how I felt," Enzo says, gaining Pia's full attention, "when I left New York. What was the point of being there, when I'd lost my brother? But you know what I did have? You three. I was just too focused on your father to realize it. And I regret it, P. Look at all the time I wasted because I was looking at the wrong thing. We could've spent the last four summers here together, had I not left. If you really don't love singing, that's one thing. But if you do, and you're letting your old man hold you back, that's another."

All signs indicate the attack is over. Pia's skin has returned to normal color. Her shivers have stopped, and she's no longer sweating. Amazing, I find it, how the body reacts to holding a secret.

I can't help but wonder, if I wasn't pumped up on tranquilizers and antidepressants, would my body do the same?

Enzo's phone buzzes in his pocket, breaking the moment. He reaches for it and shows the screen to Pia.

"Look at that. Nightmare Nella."

Pia laughs, a sound that is nothing short of glorious to my ears. Enzo presses a button that stops the vibration and shoves the phone back in his pocket.

"I used to have these attacks, too," Enzo tells all of us. I'm shocked by this news, that this man made of bravado and confidence has experience with anything of the sort. "When I moved away, after Fran died. Felt so lost, like I was out of my skin. I went to the hospital after my first attack. Thought my *papà's* bad heart finally got me. They sent me home with Prozac and a referral to a therapist. I flushed the pills, but I went to the therapist. Once. And that's where I learned that trick."

Pia looks around at us and tucks a lock of hair behind her ear. "Thanks for putting up with me, guys."

As Enzo draws her close, I let out a long exhale and close my eyes. It's over. Maybe this was the last one. I try to push away thoughts of her having an attack all alone in her dorm room, without me to keep her safe, or Emilio to fetch her orange juice, without Enzo to talk her through it. When I open my eyes, Pia is all smiles.

"I'm okay, Mom. Sorry."

"You have nothing to be sorry for."

"So," Emilio says, "I guess we're just going to get back to packing and pretend this didn't happen?"

I draw in a jagged breath and run my palms up and down my thighs. "You know what? Let's be good old-fashioned procrastinators and leave it for tomorrow. How about a movie night, hm?" I look at Pia. "Your pick."

"*Goodfellas*," she says with zero hesitation.

We all erupt into laughter, and I reach over to squeeze her hand. "That's my girl."

My girl, who has no idea that she's been clawing for the love of a man who wasn't even her father.

We all curl up on my bed and turn on Pia's mob movie of choice, the storm outside finally giving way to stillness. Rain fades to mist, thunder to quiet, and all that remains is the crunch of popcorn and the illusion of calm. But I can't settle. My chest is tight, and I feel like I'm the one on the verge of a panic attack now. I glance at Pia, her body relaxed, laughing freely, and I think of the one phrase that's always haunted me.

The truth always comes out.

How much longer can I do this?

How much longer can I let my family live a life that's built on my lies?

CHAPTER TWENTY

SCARLETT

Spring, 2000

I told him he could go. He was desperate. Even more desperate than I'd thought.

Francesco was in L.A., pleading with the PBS network executives to keep his show on the air, while I was mere weeks away from giving birth to the child he'd begged me for.

I tried to push him from my thoughts to match the distance he'd already put between us. But with the kids gone, away on spring break with their friends, the house was still and silent. I didn't do well with stillness and silence. I didn't have a dish to clean, a blanket to fold, an impossible homework question to tackle. Everything was in its place, ironically, except for my family members.

I decided ice cream and my favorite show would ease my racing mind. I grabbed a pint of pistachio gelato and a spoon and sank into the couch. I flipped the channels until *Will & Grace* appeared, the laugh track a small, artificial comfort. Savoring the green sweet treat, I tried to distract myself from how hollow the house felt with just me, the hum of the refrigerator, the distant tick of the grandfather clock upstairs.

The sudden, sharp pain in my lower belly.

It took my breath away. I leaned over and set my gelato down on the coffee table. Had I imagined it? I shifted, adjusting to relieve any pressure from my belly, though at thirty-four weeks, it was a difficult feat. Just as I was about to relax again, the pain came back, more intense this time. Like knives stabbing my lower abdomen. Laughter burst from the television. I turned the volume down and rested my hands on my bump. When was the last time I felt the baby kick?

I stood up and rushed toward the kitchen. The pain continued like a slow-moving, torturous wave. I'd been joking this entire time that I was too old to have another child, but maybe instinctively I knew it was the truth. I'd brought two children into this world, and neither time did I experience such a feeling.

Taking a gulp of water, I tried to shake off my worry. Maybe this baby was just eager to get out of my womb. Then, I felt something wet.

I looked down at the floor. My water must have broken.

"Oh my God," I whispered. Because it wasn't just water.

There was blood.

I let out a scream. A cry for help, though no one was there to answer it. My breath hitched and I knew time was of the essence. With trembling hands, I reached for the phone and instinctively began dialing Francesco, though I hit the end button before I could finish. My husband was three hours behind and three thousand miles away. My mother lived on Long Island. Julie, down the shore. Blood continued to trickle down my inner thigh until I realized the only person who was close enough was Enzo.

And so, I dialed the ten digits I knew by heart and closed my eyes, praying he'd answer.

"Enzo," I said as soon as I heard his voice. Another wave of pain hit me, and I hunched over. It was excruciating now. "I think I'm losing the baby."

I didn't stop crying, not when Enzo rushed into the house, when he sank to the ground and held me until the paramedics arrived, not when they whisked me on a gurney to the labor and delivery floor, and certainly not now, as I lay under bright florescent lights, hooked to a hospital bed. Nurses moved all around me, attaching monitors and chords to me and my belly.

To my baby.

I was only half aware of what was going on. I recognized the pain of contractions; they'd started in the ambulance, and they were only happening closer together now. Sweat covered my entire body. Enzo paced next to my bed, stroking his chin, communicating with the nurses and doctors, none of which were familiar to me. The room was a frenzy of activity, with nurses rustling around one another, monitors beeping at competing rhythms, but it all stilled when a doctor entered with the ultrasound machine. A nurse approached the bed and exposed my belly, applying the cold gel to my stomach.

I glanced over at Enzo. I didn't say a word, but my face must've conveyed that I needed him. He came to my side and gripped my hand. Moments later, the ultrasound wand pressed against my skin.

The screen flickered to life. My baby did not.

I suddenly came out of my trance, willing the fast pulse of my unborn child's heartbeat to sound through. Everyone's faces remained irritatingly stoic, as if this were routine. The doctor shifted the wand a few inches. No sound. I glanced up at the doctor, at the nurse, at Enzo. I felt like I was fading, like I was outside of my body watching this nightmare scene happen. And then, everything happened in a blur. A quick, unbelievable blur.

The next thing I knew, my legs were hooked into stirrups, and Enzo was calling my name.

"Scar," Enzo said, his fingers still intertwined with mine. "The doctor's talking to you."

I blinked a few times, shifting my gaze to the doctor who was adjusting a latex glove around his wrist. "We're going to start pushing."

"The baby's okay?" I asked, my insides lighting up. Maybe that ultrasound machine had been broken. Maybe my baby had just been taking a rest.

"We just need you to push," was all he said.

My eyes widened. "The epidural. I'm supposed to get an epidural."

"There's no time," the doctor explained as nurses moved all around him, preparing for the familiar agony they witnessed every day. "You're fully dilated, and we need to get this baby out as soon as we can."

I snapped my head around to look at Enzo. He could fix this. He could fix anything. "I can't do this without the epidural."

Enzo's eyes were always dark, but they appeared dim. Dimensionless. "You have to, Scar. You have to start *now*."

Panic bubbled in my chest. A drowning sensation took over. I had lost all control, of absolutely everything, even my own body. "Enzo, I can't. I can't do this. Fran's not even here."

With force, Enzo grabbed my face and leaned down until our noses touched. His gaze intensified, and I knew I'd have to do whatever he instructed me to do. "I am. And I'm going to do this with you, alright? You can do it."

"Dad," a nurse called out to Enzo. Neither of us had the where-withal to correct her. "Take her left leg. Mom, you hold the right."

I exchanged a glance with Enzo, letting him know it was okay. He placed his hand on my right leg just beneath my kneecap and pressed it backwards, while I did the same with my right leg. And with my head pressed against the back of the plastic bed, I began.

Children were blessings, motherhood a gift, but giving birth was a conundrum to me. Why must women go through so much pain to produce something so wonderful? How could something so torturous produce something so indescribably miraculous?

As I screamed through my first push, bloodcurdling, piercing, I took my first brief break and attempted to breathe. My body felt like it was breaking in half. Enzo caught my eye. Worry was written in every line and crease of his face. He was scared. Maybe more scared than me. I'd been through this before, but Enzo, though he thought he was experiencing this with me, would never be able to fathom the depths to which this pained me. Pained all women.

"Come on," Enzo said, keeping his gaze fixed on my face. "Come on, Scar. You got it."

The words were utterly simplistic, but they landed where they needed to. *Come on,* I told myself as I welled up my strength, clenched my teeth, and pushed again. *I got this,* I repeated as I suppressed a scream. Two more pushes and a calmness fell over the room. Or rather, a quiet. An eerie, deafening quiet.

I felt faint, like everything was fading to black as my weak legs fell from the labor position. I couldn't breathe. Everything was excruciating. Already sobbing, I looked at Enzo.

"Why isn't my baby crying?"

I began to hyperventilate when no one answered. I longed for sound. I silently begged God for a cry. A whimper. For any sign of life. Though I had no strength left in me, I lifted my head, trying to get a glimpse of the child I'd just birthed, desperate for even the smallest movement.

But there was nothing. The baby lay still, silent, without breath in its lungs, without a heartbeat. And soon after, the doctor confirmed what I already knew.

"No," I wailed, falling back into the bed. "No, no, no." My arms flailed out to my sides and tears poured down to my breasts. My cries came out in ugly screams that I didn't try to tame or suppress. Enzo turned his back to me, his hand covering his mouth, his shoulders shaking up and down as he muffled his tears. Someone uttered that they were sorry, but what was the use in condolences? Nothing was ever going to make me feel better. Nothing could rectify this loss.

Enzo once more cupped my face in his hands and leaned his forehead against mine that was slick and sweaty. I could feel his hands trembling against the flesh of my face, and his eyes were clouded with tears.

"You're gonna be okay," he whispered.

"I won't," I said, my eyes boring into his. "Not this time."

I thought back to my other two births. When I breezed through a few hours of labor that brough my bright-eyed, beautiful baby boy into the world. When I was tortured by the long hours it took to birth Pia. Two completely different experiences to produce the two vastly different creatures I was blessed to call my babies. Tonight, however, was one of life's worst transactions.

Agony for agony.

Swaddled in a blanket and head covered in a pink hat, a nurse approached with the baby in her arms. "Would you like to hold her?"

My eyes fluttered closed. It was a girl. Of course it was. This was my punishment, wasn't it? For having Pia. For conceiving a child in sin, in the arms of a man who wasn't my husband. For carrying that sin every day since, thinking my penance was the lying, the pretending, the emotional rollercoaster that was my marriage.

But evidently, that wasn't enough. I got to keep Pia, my beautiful secret.

But this daughter, the one I did everything right for, I didn't deserve her. She was taken from me.

My stomach convulsed in another sob as the nurse gently placed the baby in my arms. I didn't want to look. I wasn't ready. But I had to. I forced myself to lower my gaze, and there she was.

She was beautiful. Perfect, with pouty lips and a sweet button nose. I dreamed of discovering her in every way, of seeing how she'd grown into her features, if she would get Francesco's curly tendrils, if she'd have dark eyes like me. I'd never get the chance to see how her face would mold and change day after day, year after year. I'd never get to tell her how much I love her; I'd never get to dress her in pink outfits and take her to ballet classes like I did with Pia. I'd never get to know the daughter who was half of me and half of the man, for all his faults, I'd chosen to share my life with.

I turned to Enzo. He was there. He always was. But he couldn't fix this.

No one could. My debt had finally come due, and my daughter was the price.

———

"Let's go to your place," I said, seated in the passenger seat of Enzo's car.

He glanced at me, his hand resting on the gear shift, looking like he wanted to say something. Instead, he put the car in drive and took off.

I was pumped up on all kinds of meds, though I wasn't sure what was the point when nothing could ease my pain. As Enzo navigated us through lower Manhattan, I thought of Emilio and Pia. I wondered if they'd called home to check in, how they were blissfully unaware of the hell I now found myself in. I thought of my husband, who left under the guise of returning home to a still-pregnant wife. He would never get to lay eyes upon the angelic life we created together, and I knew he'd hate himself for it.

But most of all, I thought of my baby. Francesca Marie. The little girl I'd never know but the one I'd never forget.

Enzo helped me to his bedroom, where he laid me down on one side of the bed and situated me beneath the covers. His plush bed felt like a cloud to my sore body. He left for a few minutes and returned with a mug of tea that he set on the nightstand. Then, he pulled up a chair beside the bed, propping his feet up. In our silence, I heard our shared question: *what happens now?*

I curled up on my side, my hands beneath my cheek, and I stared straight at Enzo. He looked as worn out as I felt. I wanted to believe that Enzo couldn't possibly be sharing in my grief; he wasn't the baby's father and he wasn't my husband. But I knew it was a lie. Enzo *knew* me. I could always feel him, as if he were a living, breathing part of me, and I knew he had to feel the same way about me. That he loved me.

And when you love someone, their pain becomes yours.

Without a word, he reached his hand out, his palm up, awaiting mine. I reached for him, squeezing his hand tight. Tears spilled down to my lips, and I licked them away, the salt burning my tongue. Enzo had gotten me through one of the ugliest days of my life. And no matter what Francesco would do after this to try and remedy the situation, I would never forget how Enzo was there for me, how his quiet assurance was the only thing keeping me together.

"Do you want me to call him?" Enzo asked after a while, his voice hoarse as he leaned his head back against the chair.

I shook my head against the pillow, its fabric rustling beneath my ear.

"I don't know how I'm gonna tell him," I said, recognizing how weak my voice sounded. "He begged me for this baby. He wanted to get it right this time. Wanted to be a better father, and this was his second chance. I'm worried. What this will do to his heart."

Enzo pressed his lips together. I knew it was a fear of his, too. But another bout of tears welled up in me, and the image of Enzo blurred.

"It's all my fault," I cried, sinking into the pillow, trying to hide.

Enzo leaned forward and caressed my back. "It's not your fault. Things like this happen in life, Scar, but it's no one's fault."

I looked into his eyes. I could have told him. I knew he would keep my secret. But more, he would've understood why I thought I brought this horrible happenstance upon myself. But I couldn't bring myself to do it. What if he didn't want to share the burden with me? What if he wanted to be a father to Pia instead of playing along with my carefully constructed façade? It was a risk I wasn't willing to take.

"I'm scared," I admitted in a whisper.

"Of what?"

"You know what my marriage is like," I said in even more hushed tones, my eyes darting all around the room as if Francesco were on the other side of the bedroom door, waiting to poke his head in at any given moment. "It's already so fragile. So up and down, and this is a big *down*. What if we don't survive it? What if he's mad at me? It was my job to bring this baby into the world. That's what a good wife does. That's what a good mother does. And I failed. I failed at both."

Enzo's eyes fell to the ground. "I'm gonna tell you something I probably should've told you a long time ago." Squeezing my hand a little tighter, he looked into my eyes with a vulnerability I wasn't sure I'd seen in him before. "For as long as I've known you, you've put my brother on this pedestal. And don't get me wrong. I love him. But he's not who you've been making him out to be all this time. He's insecure. Painfully so. When he was a kid, he'd try to be like the rest of us, all rough and tumble, but he wasn't. He's always been *him*. And for a long time, he hated that. And I don't think feelings like that ever really go away, no matter how successful somebody is.

"I don't think he can believe he snagged you, Scar, and I'm not trying to blow smoke up your ass. You're everything a man could want. Beautiful. Smart. Funny. Loyal. Tough. Caring. Fran knows what kind of woman he got. He knows that if anything were to happen between you two, you'd be okay. You'd survive. You're a hell of a lot tougher than you give yourself credit. He knows there'd be a line of men waiting to get with you. That's why he hurts you. That's why he tries to make you feel small, so you'll think as little of yourself as he thinks of himself. And I *hate* that he does this to you. I hate that he takes advantage of a woman someone else would die to have."

He didn't say it, but as our eye contact intensified, we both knew that the *someone else* he was referring to was him.

"Even if everything you're saying is true," I said, my breath shaky as I braced myself to defend my husband the way I always did, "he loves me. He has a funny way of showing it, but I know he does."

Enzo licked his lips and slowly nodded. His gaze fell to the floor. "'Course he does, Scar. He's nothing without you."

"I feel like it's the other way around. Even when we're at our lowest, I can't imagine my life without him. I know it's crazy, Enz. I know it makes no sense. And I don't know if that's his doing or mine, but that's the way it is. No matter what he does, no matter how much I hate him sometimes, I can't bring myself to leave."

Enzo leaned back into his chair, his hand slipping from mine. My skin turned cold without his touch, and I almost reached for him again. He looked at me like I was a puzzle he couldn't solve, and in truth, he couldn't. I was keeping the most important piece a secret.

Our daughter.

"Can I get you anything else?" he asked, standing to his feet.

I lifted my eyes to meet his gaze. "Will you just lay with me?"

I could tell he didn't want to. Maybe he'd had it, with me always running back to Francesco no matter what amount of immense pain he caused me. Maybe he needed a breather after what we went through at the hospital. He wandered around to his side of the bed, drew back the covers, and propped himself up on his side with one elbow. I turned to face him. Sunlight beamed through the slats of the closed blinds, and New York City kept on singing its constant song, but the world felt as small as the space between the two of us.

As a sob caught in my throat, he smoothed my hair away from my face.

"I'm sorry, Enzo." The words leapt out of me before I could think them through. "I'm so sorry."

"For what?"

The list was eternal. I was sorry that we'd started something so long ago, something we couldn't finish, something we couldn't have. I was sorry that I'd given birth to his baby girl, our Pia Rose, and I was sorry I couldn't tell him about it. But most of all, I was sorry I couldn't choose him. I wanted to. More times than I could count. And I hated that my own guilt and my complicated relationship with Francesco bled so far out that they affected Enzo.

"I'm sorry you had to go through that with me," I finally said. Of all the things I could've apologized for, it was the only one I could manage. "It wasn't your job. It was Francesco's."

His brows furrowed and his lips formed a thin line. There was a look of defeat in his eyes, one of resignation. "I don't mind filling in whenever you need me to."

His words were loaded with things he couldn't say. He wasn't just talking about holding my hand as I gave birth to a baby with no breath in its lungs. He was talking about all the times before that, when he made up for what Francesco lacked, and he was speaking about all the times we still had ahead of us, where he might have to fill in the spaces Francesco would leave blank. Yes, I knew exactly how he felt. When I was young and crazy about him, I was content to take his crumbs than go without him entirely.

I wasn't sure a more desperate kind of love existed.

He gave me a soft smile before I tucked myself into his chest.

Safe and sound, I was, left with one looping thought.

I don't know what I'd do if I lost you.

And yet here I was, lying beside him, losing him over and over again, all by my own hand.

MY SUSPICIONS HAD BEEN right. The miscarriage became a wedge, driven precisely between me and Francesco. In the weeks that followed, we became something closer to enemies rather than husband and wife. I wondered how we'd ever been in love, how we'd once seen eye to eye on big things when now, we couldn't even agree on the volume of the television.

I wondered how I was going to keep going when our new status quo was crushing me. I was no longer walking on eggshells; I was walking on all the shards of our broken marriage. Our home was no longer filled with laughter and love. Instead, only silence, tense and tight, the sharp edges of arguments waiting to happen slashing me at every turn. The future that once seemed so sprawling felt suffocating and claustrophobic. My days blurred together, dull and gray, each one bleeding into the next like an endless loop of nothingness.

That was why I decided I needed an escape. I needed to see if I could, in fact, bring some color back into my life.

I was in our bedroom packing when Francesco walked in. I'd called him at work, requesting just a moment of his time. Just long enough for me to tell him I was leaving.

"Hey," he said, sounding gruff as he closed the door behind him. He was dressed in a plaid button down and khakis, his hair unruly. Stubble clung to his jawline. From the looks of it, he wasn't doing much better than me. To add salt to his wounds, his trip to LA had been in vain; his show was good as dead, and the book deals had dried up. Francesco's life was now all about learning how to live as a faded star. A has-been. His eyes fell to my open suitcase on the bed. "What's going on?"

I finished rolling up a sundress and looked at him. "Sit down."

He did as he was told, sinking into his side of the bed. He looked into my eyes, and like a dog, I could smell his fear. He swallowed and ran a palm over his mop of curls. Then, he gestured toward my bag. "You wanna tell me what's going on?"

"Yes, I do. That's why I called you over here." I folded a pair of shorts and placed them in my suitcase before looking into his eyes. He was a few feet away from me, but I could feel the lightyears between us. Like a movie reel, everything that got us to this point ran through my mind's eye. A heavy sadness settled in my chest.

"We've been dancing around this for weeks, Fran, but this clearly isn't working anymore."

"This being?"

"Us. Our marriage."

"Scarlett," he huffed, rolling his eyes. "You lost a *baby.* We're both grieving right now. Of course nothing's working. But it's not going to be like this forever. With time, we'll get over this."

I gnawed on the inside of my cheek and let my gaze fall to the ground. "It's more than that." I scoffed. "It's so much more than the baby."

"I'm not a mind reader, Scarlett," he said with a sharp edge to my name. "If you want to get something out, let's get it out now."

Winding myself up, I nodded until I finally forced myself to look at him. I searched his face, looking for the man I married. For the man I believed in and loved and gave my heart and soul to. Gave my life to. All my years, my best ones, I'd given him every last ounce of me until we were here. With nothing left.

"I hate myself, Fran." My words were so vigorous, pouring straight out my gut, that I shook. "I hate that I've let you make me into someone I don't recognize. You have broken me down and beaten me up with the way you treat me, and all that's left of me is a shell. A worthless, useless shell who's only good enough when you need something from me, or when you want to show me off like I'm some fucking trophy. You love to parade me around, don't you? To say, *Look at the life I give her. She's so lucky to have me.* And I always play my part, don't I? No matter who you're fucking behind my back, or how shitty you treat me, I play the part of Mrs. Francesco Valenti, and I do it well. But I can't do it anymore, Fran. I'm tired. I'm so, so tired."

"Of what?" he muttered.

"Of being your wife," I yelled.

"Scarlett." He pushed himself up and off the bed. Standing just inches from me, his arms dangled at his sides before he reached up and gently touched my cheek with his knuckles. My eyes fluttered closed. There had been a time when his touch was enough to soften my heart. There had been a time when his touch made my spine stiffen with fear. "Scarlett, don't say that."

"I'm tired of going to school functions alone, being surrounded by couples while I feel like a single mother," I went on, wanting to get it all out. "I'm tired of lying to our kids to cover your ass. I'm sick of watching you break their hearts, over and over again. Our children deserve a father who's *invested* in them."

"I'm not invested in them?"

I scoffed and started pacing. "Do you know what your son's favorite TV show is? His favorite band? What kind of cereal he prefers?" Raising my brows, I waited, though I was only met with silence. "His favorite show is *Hey Arnold* on Nickelodeon. They have marathons every Tuesday and Friday. Blink-182 is his favorite band. He likes Cocoa Puffs because it turns the milk chocolate, and he likes to drink it after he eats all the cereal." Feeling like I was on a roll and couldn't be stopped, the rest tumbled out of me in quick succession. "Pia's worst subject is math. I had to hire a tutor last month because she can't grasp negative numbers, and if she doesn't pass, she'll have to go to summer school. She still sleeps with her Eloise doll that I bought for her at Plaza when she was four. Her favorite book is *Charlotte's Web*; she's read it six times cover to cover. Whenever I take her on drives, she hums until she falls asleep."

"Why are you telling me all of this? To make me feel guilty?"

"To show you that you might be their father," I snapped, pointing at him, "but I'm their *everything*. And I have given up everything for them. My happiness. My sanity. I have no idea who I am anymore. I can't remember who I was before I was *this*. This shell who's chasing around a ghost." I gestured to Francesco, who sat there, absorbing every word. "I still want to believe that the man I fell in love with is still inside you, but he's gone. He's been gone for a long time. You've shown me who you are time and time again, and it's time I believe you. Maybe you think this is like all the other times, when a handbag or a piece of jewelry or a house will smooth it over, but it's not. I can't do it anymore. I'm running on fumes, Fran. Our kids need me, and I can't be there for them because you've taken everything from me. There's nothing left. I should hate you. But I hate myself because I'm the one who allowed it. I'm the one who gave you all these chances to erase me."

As he wrapped his arms around me and drew me into his chest, I thought of my mother's warning. That this man whom I'd vowed to be faithful to in front of God when I was just twenty-four was stealing my life. I'd lived in denial for years. I'd covered for him, defended him. But the truth was out now and I couldn't take it back.

"I'm still me," he whispered in my ear. "And you're still you. We can figure this out."

"This isn't me," I said into his shoulder. "This is who I'm supposed to be. This is who I pretend to be to keep our family together."

"You can't leave me," he said, his voice desperate as he reached for my hands. Tears filled his eyes, and for a moment, the lines around them disappeared and he was the young man I married. "You're my whole life, Scarlett. My whole heart. You're everything to me."

"You don't treat me like I'm everything to you."

"Because I don't know how," he admitted. His chest moved up

and down with spurts of uneven breath as he interlaced his fingers with mine. "Do you remember what I said to you before I asked you to marry me? I told you that someday, I'd disappoint you. That I'd make you angry. That I wouldn't be any good at marriage. And look at me." He tossed his arms up. "I'm not. I've screwed everything up. In every way. And I've always been afraid that you're going to wake up one day and think about all the time you've wasted on me, and say you've had enough." He looked down at my suitcase. "And I guess that day is today."

Downstairs, I heard the front door open and the familiar sounds of my children's strides. Two thumping sounds suggested they'd dropped their backpacks by the door as they did every day. I'd miss those sounds.

"I'm going to Italy," I spit out, for fear that our time was running out before the kids barged in. "I booked a one-way ticket to Naples. I'm staying at the Palazzo Domenico, in Positano, and I don't know how long I'm staying, so don't ask me. I just need some time to myself. To heal, from the baby, and to think clearly. Or at least try to."

"Please don't leave," Francesco begged, pulling me closer to him.

I tilted my head up to look into his eyes. "My mother's going to take care of the kids. She'll make sure their homework is done, pack their lunches, and have food ready for them when they get home from school. All you have to handle is breakfast."

"Scarlett." My name was uttered even softer than a whisper. Like a vapor that could vanish at any second.

He cupped my face in his hands and his face wrinkled into an expression of pain. I worried, for a second, that I was damaging his heart by leaving. But I was done putting him before me, no matter how much it hurt me, no matter how difficult I found it to choose myself. I was owed this trip, for all the years I put him and his needs first.

"I know I'm not perfect. I know I don't deserve you," he said, "but I'm still here."

His voice cracked on the last word. I felt it in my bones. He was still here, but I wasn't.

"Doesn't that count for anything?"

It was an impossible question, one I wasn't sure I'd ever have an answer to.

"I just," Francesco started, his face clouded with absolute disbelief, "I never thought this day would come. I never thought we'd split up."

Gnawing on the inside of my cheek, I nodded. "The biggest mistake a man can make is thinking he'll always have his woman."

My face still in his hands, tears trickled down my cheeks, landing on his fingertips. I opened my mouth to speak, but Pia's voice carried up the stairs.

"Mom," she yelled. "Where are you?"

"I'll be right down," I yelled back, hoping to buy Francesco and I another minute. "We're gonna go downstairs and tell them, okay? And you're not going to act upset. We'll say you gave me the gift of this trip. They know I've been having a hard time since I lost the baby."

"Scarlett," he said with force, "I'll be a better husband. I'll change. I'll do anything. I can be who you want me to be, babe. I promise."

I looked at him with a fresh lens. Pity. Everything Enzo had said about him was true. It was playing out right before my eyes. "Stop making promises you can't keep."

The bedroom door opened. Our children poured in, curiosity in their big eyes as they quietly analyzed their parents. I drew in a breath and put on the biggest smile I could manage.

"Hi, sugar," I said, bending down to wrap my arms around Pia.

"Hey, bud," Francesco said as he ruffled Emilio's hair. "How was school?"

Pia put her hands on her hips. "Daddy, I'm starving."

"*Staje sempe murénn' 'e famme doppo 'a scola*," Francesco replied. *You're always dying of hunger after school.*

"Are we going on a trip?" Emilio interjected. He was standing near the bed, his eyes fixed on my suitcase that was propped open on the bed.

My mouth hung open. My eyes darted to Francesco. I'd wanted to buy myself some more time, to prepare the perfect upbeat speech, but both of my kids were staring at me. Pia, with excitement in her eyes, but Emilio's look was one of suspicion; his maturity far surpassed his eleven years.

I swallowed as my hands clenched into fists at my sides. "I, um, *I'm* going on a trip." My eyes fell to the ground, as I suddenly felt ashamed for my selfishness. "Mommy's going to Italy."

"With Dad?" Emilio asked.

I shook my head and pressed my lips together. "Nope. Just me."

When no one said a word, I slowly lifted my gaze. Emilio appeared perplexed. Pia's bottom lip quivered.

"You can't do that," she said, in an instant fit of tears.

I crouched to my knees and drew her into a hug. "Honey, I promise, I'll be back before you even realize I'm gone."

"But who's going to take me to school? And ballet?" She tightened her hug. "Mommy, I'll miss you. *I* want to go to Italy, too."

A lump lodged in my throat. What the hell was I doing, leaving my two beautiful children? If I couldn't heal here in New York, could I really gain some special insight in Italy? As I rubbed my daughter's back, I pictured Francesca. My other daughter. Was she the force tugging me to go?

"Babydoll, I promise, when you're bigger, I'll take you to Italy. Just you and me, okay?"

I parted from her and cupped her face, giving her a reassuring smile. "And I also promise that I'm going to bring you home *so* many presents." I pinched her cheek for good measure, and finally, she smiled. As I stood, I shot Francesco a look that he should take her downstairs before she changed her mind. Understanding me, he crouched down, and Pia crawled onto his back, wrapping her arms around his neck.

"So," he said as they started out of the room, "what are you craving today?"

I looked at my son. "You must be starving, too."

"How long are you going away for?" The words spilled out of him like he was in a hurry as he lingered near my suitcase. His concern was apparent, in his furrowed brow, in the pout of his mouth. I could smooth things over with my daughter, with promises of far-off trips and gifts, but I couldn't get one over on my son. I didn't know how, but he could see right through me.

"I'm not sure, honey." I reached for his hand and together, we sat on the edge of the bed. "You know Mommy's been having a hard time since ... since Francesca." He nodded. "Even though she's in heaven, Mommy's still sad. I wish she was here, with us."

His eyes moved all around, searching my face. "Are you and Dad getting a divorce?"

My heart sank to depths I had not known before. How did my son even know what that word meant?

"I know you think I'm just a kid, Ma," he went on, "but I hear you two fighting. All the time."

My grip on his hands tightened as my heart rate quickened. I had to fix this. I couldn't let my baby worry. I smoothed his hair back and rested my palm on his hot, rosy cheek. It must've taken a lot of courage for him to ask such a thing.

"Absolutely not." I sounded so convincing, even I believed it. "Married couples fight sometimes, Emi, but I love your father so much. Almost as much as I love you." His mouth twitched, though he wouldn't allow himself to smile. "I don't ever want to hear you use that word again, you hear me? Under no circumstance are your father and I splitting up. I just …" I sighed, relaxing slightly. "I need to get away just for a little bit. To get over this whole Francesca thing so I can be the best mommy to you and your sister. You're almost a grown-up. You understand that, don't you?"

He straightened at my compliment, his chest puffing. "I do."

"Okay then." We stood and I wrapped my arm around him, leading us out of the bedroom. "Now, do you still like Maradona? Or should I buy another player's jersey for you?"

He laughed, a sound I cherished. "Maradona's a legend, Ma."

"Silly me," I said as we trekked down the steps.

We rounded the corner and headed into the kitchen where Francesco was already working on a quick sauce. The next morning, in that same kitchen, I kissed each of them goodbye. Even though doubt clawed at me, I stepped into the summer air, hailed a cab, and didn't look back.

I didn't know who I'd be on the other side of this trip.

All I knew was that something, or someone, had to change.

CHAPTER TWENTY-ONE

❦

SCARLETT

Summer, 2011

"Take care of that thing," I say to Pia. She's got the Birkin I gave her nestled in the crook of her arm. It doesn't match her outfit—a silver bandage skirt with a flowy tank and platform heels—and it's not appropriate for a house party in Southampton, but her rationale is that *it's a Birkin. It matches everything.* "I didn't give that to you so you could spill tequila on it."

In true Pia fashion, she rolls her eyes. "This is, like, my most prized possession. You think I'm going to let something happen to it?"

I draw her to my side and kiss her forehead as Emilio barrels down the steps, an overnight bag in hand. He looks painfully handsome in a crisp blue linen button down and jeans, and he's slicked his hair away from his face, something his father only did on special occasions.

"Okay, I was more worried about her," I say, pointing to Pia. "But you're going to have girls all over you."

"I'll be his bodyguard," Pia says, leaning her weight into one hip.

"What a good-looking kid," Enzo says, joining us from the kitchen in a few strides. "You two look after each other, you hear me?"

"Alright, *Dad,*" Pia retorts with a purse of her lips.

Enzo and Emilio laugh, but my gut clenches. It's a joke to everyone but me, the sole person in this house who knows the truth. For a split second, I let myself wonder if Enzo did know, if he'd be letting Pia go to a house party full of college and law school students, or if he'd be more overprotective. But just as soon as the thought comes, it vanishes as Pia tosses her blanket of black hair behind her shoulder.

Emilio looks past me. I turn around. The kitchen is still in disarray after he cooked us yet another fabulous meal. "Let me just clean that up real quick—"

"Nonsense," I say, putting my hands on his chest to stop him. "You two go have fun. But be careful. Don't drink *too* much, and absolutely no drugs. And you, missy." I point at Pia. "No boys, either."

"I swear," Pia says to Enzo, "the woman wants me to be a nun."

We all laugh as we head for the front door. The kids kiss Enzo and me goodbye, and as Pia climbs into the SUV, Emilio leaves me with one final wave and a *see you in the morning*. A weight settles in my chest, but I brush it off. They'll be fine. They're always fine. They have each other.

I, on the other hand, have Enzo. And an entire night alone with him.

We head for the kitchen and instinctively start cleaning. He gathers the last of the serving platters and stray flatware, while I dunk my hands into the sudsy water and start scrubbing. Beyond the windowsill where I've stood for eighteen summers, the beach is vacant and stars speckle the night sky, while the ocean roars, loud and mighty tonight. I steal glances at Enzo, who works beside me, drying what I've washed.

It hits me all at once, that Enzo and I have had so much, but we've never had *this*. Normalcy. The quiet moments that seem mundane, the very ones that make up a relationship. We've had dramatic highs and even more dramatic lows, fast, fleeting moments that are such well kept secrets, I have to wonder if they're real. But we've never had the *nothing* that husbands and wives get to enjoy. And right now, as a quiet settles over the house, all I want to do with him is nothing.

I shut off the tap. Silence hums between us, filled only by the crash of waves beyond the window. I should finish the dishes. We should finish the dishes.

Instead, I turn to him. "Let's leave this for later."

"Come on. We're almost done. Just have to get the pans off the stove—"

"I mean it." After drying my hands, I reach for him and only let go when he looks at me. I take a deep breath, wondering if he'll *get* it. "Would you like to watch the news with me?"

"The news?" His brows raise, but then, they arch in suspicion. "Is that code for something else?"

"No," I say earnestly. "I like to watch the news at night. Stock market predictions, political pundits, crime around New York."

"Romantic."

I push his chest. "Come on. I'm serious. We finally have the house to ourselves and we're going to spend it cleaning?"

An amused expression on his face, he tosses his *mappina* on the counter with abandon. "Hell yeah, Scar. I'd love to watch the news with you."

We settle into the couch. Somehow, my bare feet end up on his lap, and his warm hand rests on my ankle. It all feels so normal, like every night of our lives has looked like this as the news anchor drones on about a dip in the stock market, President Obama's approval rating, a subway stabbing in Times Square, and a fire in the Bronx. But soon, it all becomes white noise. As the flickering screen plays across Enzo's face, this seemingly small moment looms bigger than all the rest.

It's everything I've ever wanted.

He must feel my stare on him, because he turns to look at me. His mouth is fixed in a smirk.

"What?" he asks, sipping on his wine.

"We never got to do this," I say as I run my fingers through my strands of black hair. "The boring stuff." I sip my own wine, though I don't break our eye contact. "It's not boring with you."

Enzo shifts, looking mildly confused by my revelation. I curl my legs up and adjust so I'm seated beside him.

"You know what I mean," I continue. "The stuff normal couples get to do."

He doesn't respond right away. He watches me, like he's taking me in, gauging whether or not I want this conversation to continue, which I do. Finally, he smiles.

"There's nothing normal about us, honey."

But I'm not teasing. I lean over and set my glass of wine on the side table. His eyes follow my every move, and his smile falters into something more serious. Like a mirror, he, too, rests his wine glass down. Whatever I feel, he feels it, too.

"I get the sense you want to say something," he says, a playfulness still clinging to his voice. I, too, want to use my sarcasm as a shield, but I recognize tonight for what it is.

My last chance.

My last opportunity to tell Enzo how I really feel. Francesco is gone; I don't have to worry about keeping secrets from him anymore. The kids won't be back until morning. I can speak at full volume without fear of young, curious ears. Our house has sold, and our time together is running out, the tick, tick, tick of the clock an ever-constant ring in my ear reminding me to *let go*. It's now or never.

He lowers the volume of the TV, then stands. "You wanted to watch the news with me, and you got it," he says. He goes to the armoire that holds our stereo system and CD collection. He plucks one out and opens the case. "Now, I want you to listen to Eros with me."

"You know what's funny?" I ask, watching his back as he inserts the CD. "I don't speak Italian, but I think I know all the words to those songs."

Candlelight catches the curve of his cheek, bathing his face in a golden glow as he returns to me on the sofa. The first notes of "Un'altra Te" swell into the room, rich and aching.

As he settles back in, his eyes are locked on mine, and he gives me his full attention, something I don't think I'll ever take for granted.

I swallow, though a nervous laugh gets the best of me. My hands fly to my face, but Enzo pulls them down. His hands remain on my wrists.

"There's no escaping now," he teases, though I know he means it.

And then, I lean into him, and I let it all out.

"I never got to choose you," I start, my adrenaline soaring. "I was too scared to make a choice, but that was a choice, too. And I can't imagine what that's done to you over the years. I was so heartbroken when you broke things off with me when we were young. I was never the same. Never, in a million years, did I think I'd do the same thing to you once, let alone countless times. But it's not because I didn't want to, Enzo. I did. I dreamt of nights like this with you. I wished I could get to experience the mundane with you. I wanted to experience every moment of life with you, but I couldn't let myself. You know how I always felt. Like I came last. Keeping my family intact was everything to me. Every decision I made was based on that, no matter what it cost me. No matter what else I wanted."

Enzo remains quiet, his only movement that of interlacing his fingers with mine. Tears spill out of my eyes as I shift so close to him, I'm nearly in his lap.

"But that doesn't change the way I felt about you. *Feel* about you," I correct myself, my lips curving into a trembling smile that he mirrors. "I've always felt like you're the other half of me, Enzo. Not in the way that makes sense. Not in the traditional way, like husband and wife. The other half of me, as a person. Of my heart, or my soul, or whatever you want to call it. I can't hide from you because you can see it all. You know me without me having to explain anything. I'm safest when I'm with you. I ..." I draw in a huge breath, afraid to express my next thought aloud. "I never told anyone this before. But right before Francesco died, we talked about me moving on someday. He had one condition. That whoever I choose has to love me better than he did. And I don't think you love me more than he did, or even better. I just think you love me the right way. Whatever way I'm designed to be loved, that's how you love me. I've spent all these years feeling like something was missing from me. From my life. It's you, Enzo. It's always been you."

I hold my breath and brace myself. He says nothing, and for a split second, I go into panic mode. I don't do things like this. I don't *let go*. What if he doesn't feel the same way? What if I've made a total fool of myself, or worse, what if this *thing* between us just existed in my head?

His teeth graze his bottom lip, and he runs his thumbs up and down my hands. His eyes, those endless pools of midnight I could stare into all night, go aflame.

"Please say something," I plead, unable to take it anymore.

"I think..." Enzo starts, slow, like he's taking pleasure in torturing me. "I think that was a very long way for you to tell me that you love me."

"Oh, you bastard," I laugh. But I let out a squeal as he grabs my hips and situates me on top of him. His hands travel the plane of my back, pressing me forward until our noses touch. His eyes search mine and mine search his. I wonder if he's as scared as I am. If he's equally as relieved, that we're finally getting it out. The truth. That's what this has always been, and that's what this'll always be.

"You broke my heart, you know," Enzo says, his eyes glistening with adoration and hurt.

"I know," I whisper, tracing his cheekbones with my thumbs.

"But I kept on loving you anyway. Every day. All those years." His voice is rough. Honest. "Because no one was ever gonna be you. You're my *anima gemella,* Scarlett." His hands find my face, holding it like it's something sacred. "Nothing was ever gonna change that."

Our lips meet, fervent, sure, the kind of kissing that's going some-where. *Twin souls.* It all makes so much sense now that he's spoken it aloud. I think back to that evening when the summer first began, when Enzo didn't know what to call me. Now, we—what we have, what we've always had—finally has a name. A definition that brings forth this feeling of being complete. Yes, we're one soul split in two, two flames dancing on the same wick. I've always felt it, in the way he looks at me, how he reads me, how he knows the precise way to procure laughter from my throat, to still my falling tears. He's got scars in the same places I do, but together, we soothe what the world once split open. That's why we've always had this eternal tether, this electric connection that's transcended time and space and circumstance. He's the missing part of me that makes me whole, and every stolen glance, every moment spent wondering *what if,* they've all led us here.

To the place where we can finally be honest.

Honest. I'm hot all over, aching for him, but one snagging thought distracts me.

Our daughter.

If we're going to do this, we're going to do it with no more secrets.

"Enzo," I say, gasping for air, my face still touching his, my hands snaked around the nape of his neck. I open my mouth to tell him, to set my secret free, but he speaks first.

"I know," he says, as out of breath as I am. "I missed you, too."

A lump rises in my throat. I should say something. I should tell him the truth. But he stands and lifts me with ease, my legs wrapping around his hips like it's instinct. The song swells, flooding my ears, pulsing in my chest like a second heartbeat. And just like the lyrics say, I know there's no other Enzo. Not even if God Himself handed me the pen could I have drawn a better match, could I have invented someone who stirs me in so many ways.

I'm giving myself to him like I have nothing to hide. But I do. God, I do.

And as Enzo rushes us up the stairs, all I want to do is give into it. This fact that's shadowed my life. I want to let it go, because maybe I've had it all wrong this time and my mother was right. I let go on that one night that seems both near and far, but there's nothing disastrous about our daughter. In fact, that night produced the most glorious part of my life. I've had it all wrong, but tonight, I'm going to get it right.

I love Enzo. And maybe there's nothing wrong with that.

Maybe there never was.

My skin burns as he lays me back on my bed. His mouth is on my jaw, my shoulder, the top of my chest as he peels off my blouse, slow and deliberate. The weight of him, the warmth of his hands, of his mouth, it's intoxicating. Overwhelming. Like a flood bursting through all the walls I've built, breaking them down forever. He's familiar and new all the same, and as he strips me bare, it feels like my life has been one big roundabout to bring me back to him.

I reach up and clutch his shirt, desperate for him, and rip it off until his skin is bare. And then I see it. Enzo's secret. What he's been hiding all summer. I become aware of all my senses. My thrashing heart. The ocean's vigorous rumble outside. The tick of the clock on the wall. The words that stare back at me, in familiar cursive, in permanent ink.

My words. Over his heart.

I blink a few times to make sure I'm not imaging things. My fingers graze the ink like I need to feel it to believe it.

"*All my love, always,*" I read the inscription across his chest. It dawns on me that the ink is permanent. That he's been carrying me with him in this way, that he always will. Forever. I meet his gaze. He looks at me, both shy and daring. Waiting, completely vulnerable. I sit up and run my lips across his chest, over the ink, over the words that have bound us together all along. I glance up at him, baring my body and soul all at once.

"I meant it, Enzo," I say with conviction. "I meant it every time."

~

OUR BODIES SLICK, PRACTICALLY glued together, we try to catch our breath. My heart hammers against his and yet, as I close my eyes and rest my head in the crook of his neck, I'm not sure I've ever felt so relaxed. So safe and so sure of anything. My legs tangle with his, and all I want to do is drink up as much of Enzo as I can until I'm drunk on him. Resting on him, feeling like I could stay here forever, I indulge myself in a dream. Maybe we can find a way to save the Montauk house *and* the restaurant. Maybe we can spend our winters in the city, our summers out here, together. Maybe my kids will find this whole thing totally *not weird,* and Enzo and I can spend the rest of our days together. Yes, I know what I want. I want to choose Enzo every day from here on out, and I don't want to feel ashamed of it.

"Scarlett?" Enzo says, breaking me out of my thoughts.

"Yes?"

"I love you."

I giggle against his throat. "I wish I kept count of how many times you said it tonight." I kiss his collarbone. How free it feels to say it aloud to each other, rather than scrawling it on a secret page. "I love you, too."

As our breath slows and my adrenaline calms down, a scent wafts its way into the bedroom. I wonder if we've left a candle on downstairs, though the aroma isn't one of perfume. I want to continue mapping out my future with Enzo, but there's something wrong about this scent. Something sharp. I inhale. Once, three times.

"Enzo," I say, cutting the silence, "do you smell that?"

And then, we hear something. A pop. A crackle.

The distinct groan of wood.

Without a word, Enzo hops out of bed and slips into his sweatpants. I sit up and hug the covers to my chest. When Enzo swings open the bedroom door, an orange glow greets him. The scent overwhelms me and to my horror, I no longer have to wonder what it is.

Flames. Devastating and ferocious, consuming the foundation of our beach house, licking the staircase.

Just when I think I finally have things right, the fire's coming for me.

CHAPTER TWENTY-TWO

SCARLETT

Summer, 2000

Positano was the perfect place to run away to. I spent the first week basking in the splendor of the hot Italian sun, the sea that glittered beneath it, and the charm of the bright, vertical city. I ate pasta for every meal, started drinking Aperol Spritzes at eleven, and I purchased a beaded mini dress that I had nowhere to wear, but it was too spectacular to leave it on the rack. My real life felt a million miles away, and as I wandered the winding streets lined with buildings blanketed by magenta bougainvillea, I selfishly wished it could stay that way.

There was a whole other life here. A whole other me.

Covered in a sheen of sweat, I drank a gulp of water as the elevator took me down to the seventh floor, where my hotel room, nestled into a cliff, was located. In true Italian fashion, I would take a siesta before getting gussied up for yet another solo dinner. On the flight here, I wondered if I would feel lonely, being in a foreign country without my family. The gnaw of missing my children was constant, but stimulated by the sights and sounds and tastes, I quickly learned to live with it. My only job right now was to savor and to heal, and Positano was already proving to be the perfect helpmate.

I slipped my key into the lock and opened the door, ready to peel off my sweat-soaked clothes and sink into the cool bed lined with plush sheets and pillows. But I stopped in my tracks. There was someone on my terrace. A man. A man whose figure looked familiar. The figure turned around and it took me a moment to register that the man staring back at me was Enzo.

Enzo, who was supposed to be in New York.

We stared at each other, his smirk ever present as he opened the French door and came into the room, walking toward me at a slow, wandering pace. He was dressed in a tan linen top, brown shorts, and Gucci driving loafers to match. He looked at ease. He looked like he belonged here, like I had invited him to join me.

But I hadn't. I came here to be alone. And yet, here he was, undoing everything with his presence alone.

"Aren't you going to ask me what I'm doing here?" he said, his velvety voice so familiar, it flooded me with an emotion I couldn't quite name. Something like nostalgia. Something like melancholy.

I didn't want to, but I smiled. I felt like I could breathe again. Enzo was here. I was okay.

I gestured toward him. "What the hell are you doing here, Enzo?"

"Came to check on you."

"And how did you get into my room?"

"We do share a last name."

"Presumptuous of you to think I'll let you stay with me."

He dug in his pocket and pulled out a key. Then, he pressed his palm against his chest. "What kind of man do you take me for?"

I laughed. "The opposite of a gentleman."

He let out a long sigh, stuffing his key back into his pocket. Then it hit me. Really hit me that he was here.

Enzo had come all the way to Italy just to see me. It didn't seem real. It didn't seem right.

"Wait a minute," I said, my hands flying to my temples. "Does Fran know you're here?"

"He knows." Enzo rocked on his heels and pressed his lips together. "I told him he was an idiot to let you get on that plane."

I arched a brow. "So, what? You're here to collect me for him?"

"I'm not here for him, Scar."

"Then who are you here for?"

He walked up to me until our faces were close. "If you leave New York, that means you're leaving me, too," he said, no louder than a whisper.

I swallowed hard. "You can't just show up here. I came here to be alone."

"Alright. Then tell me to leave, and I will."

But I couldn't. I couldn't turn him away when he'd traveled thousands of miles to *check on me.* For some godforsaken reason, I couldn't resist this man. "What floor's your room on?"

"I'm down the hall from you."

Of course he was. "You jet-lagged?"

"Not even a little bit."

I nodded. Of course he wasn't.

He looked around my room. His eyes landed on the dress I'd bought the other day, hanging on the armoire door. Strung with beads of gold, it looked like champagne come to life. Then, he looked at me again.

"Be ready by eight. I'm taking you out tonight." He cocked his head toward the armoire. "And wear that dress."

He walked out, leaving both my door and my mouth agape. Finally, as it all settled in, I made my way to the armoire and ran my fingers along the fine beads of the dress, the one I didn't have an occasion for.

But as fate would have it, the occasion had found me.

<hr />

MY HEELS CLICKED AGAINST the cobblestones as Enzo threaded his fingers through mine, tugging me through the winding streets of Positano. We spent dinner twirling pasta and sipping too much wine, and much to my delight, he made no mention of home. No talk of our kids, of our responsibilities; it was like he was here to escape with me.

To experience *what if* with me.

The streets were packed with people zigzagging in all directions—men clad in linen, women in miniskirts and beaded dresses like mine. I'd worn my hair down, a rarity, though I felt lighter as the wind blew my black tendrils behind me.

"Slow down," I called out, struggling to keep up with Enzo's stride. "I'm in heels."

He came to a halt. He looked into my eyes before scanning me up and down. He shook his head, a smile planted on his face. "You look unreal."

My breath caught. We shouldn't have been there, in that dreamlike town of Positano, together, with the stars and the town twinkling all around us. I was supposed to be healing from losing my baby and figuring out a way to forgive my husband for his years of abuse. And yet, Enzo's smile, his bronze skin and his sparkling eyes made me forget about what I was supposed to be doing. Instead, all I could do was focus on what I wanted to do.

"Where are you taking me?" I asked as people shouldered past us.

He squeezed my hand. "You trust me?"

I nodded. I always had. He led the way at a slower pace this time, until we trekked down almost to the beach. A crowd was formed outside of a building built into a cliff with music pouring out, thumping and energetic. A sign came into view. "Music On the Rocks." With confidence, Enzo marched us past the waiting clubgoers and went up to the doorman, speaking loudly in his Napoletano dialect as he discreetly slipped the large man some euros folded up. After a moment, we were permitted entry and the hum of music hit me at full blast. Blue and purple strobe lights enveloped us as "Around the World" poured out of the speakers, the sexy crowd on the dance floor swaying to its intoxicating beat. He didn't bother with getting us drinks. Instead, his hand firm on my waist, he led me to the dance floor, where we became enmeshed with the rest of the crowd, instantly synchronized with the rhythm.

Our hands were all over each other as we danced and swayed to the music, but my mind was elsewhere. I'd always thought I was the one who was locked up in a life that hadn't panned out the way I'd expected. But as I moved in sync with Enzo, I realized he was no different. He, too, had to play a role that he'd outgrown. He was just as stuck as I was, and this one night, these few fleeting hours, were a precious getaway. We were one in the same, conveying with every touch and lock of our eyes, that we didn't want this night, this feeling, to end. He twirled me to two more songs before whisking me off to the side and up a few stairs to a private table overlooking the dance floor. As we sank into the leather seats to catch our breath, a server promptly brought us a bottle of champagne, uncorking it with dramatic flourish.

We locked eyes as we each took a long sip, the bubbles dancing on my tongue and down my throat with a tickle that traveled down my spine. How was this night real? I was in Italy. In a nightclub. With Enzo. As if he were having the same exact thoughts, that same moment of disbelief, he shook his head like he was trying to wake himself up from a dream, out of a trance. I drained my champagne flute, already feeling the fizz in my veins. The hypnotic music vibrated in my chest and the swirling multicolored lights pulled me in.

"I want to dance," I shouted above the music.

Amused, Enzo gestured to the area in front of our table, our own little dance floor. "So go dance."

A smile permanently fixed on my face, I hopped up without a second thought. The DJ transitioned from a heavy beat to the addictive melody of "What Is Love" and I clapped my hands together.

"I love this song," I said to no one in particular, my head falling back as I let the song take me away. My hips started swaying, my arms were above my head, and I watched Enzo watch me. It felt dangerous, like we were walking on a line that, once crossed, would lead us somewhere new and uncharted. Somewhere where our old lives would be left behind for good.

But as the song continued, the moment swallowed me whole. The beat moved through me and the strobe lights took me someplace else, and as I swayed, I became weightless. Free. Freer than I'd felt in years, maybe ever. I didn't have a role to play. I wasn't a wife, or a mother, or a restaurateur. I was a woman named Scarlett, an unwritten future in front of me. All at once, that road that had seemed so gray and grim seemed infinite with possibilities. Colors came crawling back, bright ones I'd never seen before. Maybe my life wasn't over. Maybe I didn't have to finish out the life sentence I thought I was confined to. Maybe everything was only beginning.

I felt hands on my waist. Anchoring me, slowing me, until I finally met the eyes of Enzo. Of the man I had been completely, maniacally in love with since I was a young, naïve girl. We'd both made our choices, choices we didn't want to admit we regretted. I had pretended. I had tried to be the good girl I so clearly wasn't. And where had that gotten me? I had blips of happiness. Brief peaks of bright moments. But all I could see were the valleys. The pits of despair that seemed to stretch so much longer than those rare peaks I had to fight so hard to reach. But Enzo and I were here, alone together, just like we were that night we conceived our daughter. I had let go that night. I had let myself taste the fruits that held my happiness. And as the world stilled, as it shrank to just me and Enzo the way it always did when his eyes met mine, I decided I needed another bite.

His mouth crashed into mine and I knew it, by the way he moved, feverish and hungry, that he'd been starving for me the way I'd been starving for him. For however forbidden it was, Enzo was the most addictive flavor, the one I loved more than all the rest. The one that could excite me and calm me at the same time, that was equal parts adventure and haven.

His hands cupped my face and my arms snaked around his waist as he backed me up against the railing dividing us from the dance floor. But the club faded away. Nothing else existed. It was just me, and Enzo, and the question I'd wrested with for the last fourteen years.

What if it had been us?

When we got back to my hotel room, he pressed my back against the door. We'd hurried back from the club, stopping every so often to kiss beneath the streetlights and stars. No one looked our way; it was Italy. Positano. The place romance was destined to live. But now, back in my room, as Enzo's hand lingered near the zipper of my dress, waiting to undo me, as the buzz of the champagne was wearing off, the waves of reality were crashing against me. I wasn't some free-spirited girl. I was Pia and Emilio's mommy. I was Francesco's wife of fourteen years. I was the proud co-owner of Amanti. If my family was fabric, I was the seamstress, the woman tasked with either tightening our seams or unraveling them completely.

This wasn't real. This was an escape from my real life. A temporary one. As Enzo's hard body pressed against mine that was melting from his kisses and his touch, all I could hear was Francesco's final words.

I'm still here.

I wanted Enzo. I wanted him more than I could express with words or with my body. It was on a soul level—that much I knew. Enzo was my heart's home, but Francesco was my life's home. For better or worse, he was the one I'd chosen, I'd vowed, to spend my life with. To be faithful to. I'd broken those vows once, and I'd spent all seven years of my daughter's life admonishing myself for my recklessness and lack of self-control. Was I really about to repeat the same mistake twice?

"Enzo," I said, leaning my head back against the door. His mouth made its way from my jaw, to my neck, to my collarbone. I shuddered. But I couldn't. I couldn't hurt him any more than I already had. "Enzo, stop."

He froze. As I worked to catch my breath, we slowly met each other's gaze. My body was vibrating and all I wanted to do was drag him to my bed and have him every way I pleased, but I remained steadfast in my plight to be a better woman than I used to be.

"I don't want to hurt you." The words spilled out of me in a breathless rush. "I don't want to do this with you, and start things up again, when I don't know what I'm doing. I have no clue what I'm doing, Enzo. If I'm staying here, or going home, or going somewhere else. I …" I paused, frustration trumping all the rest of my emotions. "I don't know what's going to happen between me and Francesco."

He darkened. His eyes, his demeanor—he was just as fed up as I was. He wanted to escape just like I did. But we weren't wired like that. We weren't the kind of people who put ourselves first. If we had, we'd have been together already.

I held his face in my hands and ran my eyes over every inch of his face. Those features that blended together to make the most beautiful man I'd ever known.

"I love you, Enzo," I whispered, tears blurring those beautiful features together. He didn't smile, he didn't so much as move as I drew in a shaky breath and exhaled, "But I love him, too."

The silence was piercing. It seemed to stretch forever. Outside, the cicadas' song competed with the wail of the European siren. But in this room, the air thickened. He didn't say anything. He cupped my face one last time and kissed my cheek before letting himself out. I didn't stop him or chase after him. My heart was split clean down the middle, and I was too scared to follow either half.

———

SUNLIGHT BATHED MY HOTEL suite, warming me, waking me. I blinked a few times, my eyes adjusting to the light. My gold dress now resembled a pool of beads on the floor, and my stilettos were kicked off to the side. I rolled over and instinctively reached out, half expecting to find Enzo next to me. I closed my eyes and exhaled, feeling his absence. On the one hand, I was proud of myself. I had resisted temptation. I wasn't the same reckless girl I used to be. But on the other hand, I was frustrated. Resentful. Francesco was four thousand miles and an ocean away, and I was still making my decisions based on his feelings. I was still pretending, playing my part of his dutiful wife, and I wasn't sure why.

I was caught in some strange purgatory that I couldn't escape. Not quite happy. Not quite sad. Just stuck.

Clad in pajamas, I tossed the duvet to the side and walked out to the balcony, staring out at the endless sea and flat horizon, at the cliffsides decorated with colorful buildings. Last night returned in fragments. The way Enzo had shown up like a dream. How he'd masterfully kept things light so I wouldn't drown in my grief. How he'd whisked me away, spun me on the dance floor, kissed me, made me laugh until I forgot how to be sad. How joy had been offered to me on a silver platter that I pushed away. Even with the clarity of morning, I couldn't tell if I was a fool or a saint.

A while later, when a knock eventually came from my door, I knew it was Enzo simply by the rhythm he made and the force he used. My wet hair wrapped in a towel, I padded my way to the door, the thin hotel slippers dragging across the tile. He looked boyish, standing in the doorframe. His pin-straight black hair betrayed him, sticking out like jagged pieces, and his eyes were puffy with sleep, or lack thereof.

"*Buongiorno,* Lorenzo," I teased, sounding utterly American.

It was enough to make him laugh. He rubbed his eye with his fingertips. "Stick to English. And don't call me Lorenzo."

"Come in," I laughed, motioning for him to join me. He stood close to the door, hesitant, not sure if he should go any further. I scanned him up and down, wondering where the confident man who dragged me through Positano by the hand last night had gone. "You have breakfast yet?"

"No. Just an espresso."

Hands on my hips, I drew in an inhale through my nose. "Let's order room service. We'll eat on the balcony."

A half-hour later, the balcony was drenched in sun as we ate our breakfast and sipped copious amounts of espresso in mostly silence. Pink bougainvillea spilled over the railing, attracting butterflies of all different kinds. From the sound of it—honking horns and sirens and the whizz of motorbikes—the Amalfi Coast was already awake and buzzing.

"So," I started, resting my glass of orange juice on the table, "what do you have planned today?"

"Well, I wanted to talk to you about that," Enzo said. He dabbed at the corners of his mouth with a napkin and looked into my eyes. "I have the whole day planned, but after last night, I'm not sure you'll want to come."

I raised my brows. "Does it involve nightclubs?"

"No," he said, his mouth twisting into a smirk. "No clubs."

"Then I'm in."

"Really?"

"Yes, really." I leaned my arms on the table. "What was last night? We had fun, didn't we? Maybe the most fun I've ever had. It's my fault it didn't end the way either of us wished it had. So if there's anyone who should be reluctant about spending the day together, it should be you."

"I'm not reluctant at all."

"Good," I said, leaning back into the white wrought-iron chair. "What time should I be ready?"

Enzo told me to dress casual, wear flats, and bring a swimsuit. My raffia tote was filled to the brim; from the sound of it, we were going to be out all day, and I hadn't mastered the art of traveling light. The hotel shuttle had taken us to a little slice of paradise called Marina di Praia where we boarded a boat Enzo had arranged for us. Enzo pointed out various landmarks as the boat sped us across the Tyrrhenian Sea—Sorrento, Capri, and the ever-looming Mount Vesuvius in the distance. The boat ride had led us here.

Napoli. Enzo's hometown.

As soon as we disembarked, I could feel the difference. The Amalfi Coast was like a vivacious dream by day, a serene lullaby by night. Naples, however, had a pulse. A heartbeat that instantly synced with mine as we rode in a taxi down streets lined with vendors hawking fresh seafood and *sfogliatelle*, laundry lines extending from one side to the other overhead, and scooters that zipped down the alleyways with irreverent command. It was gritty and gorgeous at the same time, rife with history and a soul that I felt like I could reach out and touch.

The taxi let us out at the start of Spaccanapoli, a tight artery of the city, pulsing with life. Team Napoli's blue flags billowed in the summer breeze, and while most shops were open, touting hand painted limoncello bottles of all different sizes, and lemon print *everything*, graffiti covered the gates shuddering the ones that were closed.

"Hold onto me," Enzo instructed, offering me his arm.

I took it, holding onto his bicep as he led us down the street. Everywhere I turned, there was life. Tourists enjoying gelato, Aperol Spritz's, fried foods and pastries. Local Neapolitans put on a show for their customers with their melodic, unmistakable dialect I'd grown so used to from being around Francesco and Enzo all this time. I watched Enzo as we traveled further down the narrow *via*, unable to ignore how proud he looked. His smile wasn't one of amusement, but of reverence. This was the place that had made him. These streets were his foundation.

Enzo led me into a small pizzeria, whose air condition I was immensely grateful for. I grabbed a napkin off the counter and wiped my forehead dry. We were greeted by a whirring fan behind the counter, and a stout woman with coils for hair.

"*Ciao, ciao,*" she greeted us absentmindedly.

"*Oi, bella mia,*" Enzo said, leaning his palms on the counter.

The lady eyed me. "What would you like?" she asked in broken English.

"No, no," Enzo took over. "*Nun songo americano. Song' nu Napoletano.*"

"Ah," the lady patted the counter. Then, she gestured toward me. "*Ma 'a mugliera toja è Americana, no?*"

"Very American," I chimed in, and her laugh let me know she understood.

"*Bella assai,*" she said, giving me a good once-over with the critical eye every Italian woman is born with.

"*Allora, stammo murenn' 'e famme,*" Enzo said. *We're dying of hunger.* "*Dó pizze fritte, per piacere. E dó acque.*"

I held up three fingers as sweat poured down my temples. "*Tre acque.*"

The woman was getting a kick out of us. She waved us off toward the small two-tops behind us. "*Jammo, jammo. Ite a pusà, ve 'a porto io.*"

"*Grazie mille,*" I offered as Enzo patted the counter in thanks.

"All these years," Enzo started as we sat down, "and you still can't speak a lick of Italian?"

"I understand," I said in my defense. "And sometimes I know what to say. I just get so embarrassed. My accent is abhorrent."

Enzo snorted and shook his head. "What kind of word is that?"

"A big, delicious English word." We laughed together as a waiter dropped off our waters. "If I'm only going to speak one language, I have to do it well."

"I think it's cute when you try to speak Italian," Enzo said.

"Oh, Enzo," I sighed. "If nothing else, at least you're entertained."

The woman came around the counter, an apron tied around her hips, carrying two large plates of *pizze fritte*. The crust was golden, still bubbling with oil from the fryer, and she set the dishes before us. The warm aroma of basil and tomatoes tickled my nose.

"*Mangiate*," the woman told us with a proud smile.

"*Come ti chiami?*" Enzo asked.

"Adelina," the woman replied.

"*Grazie pè ll'ospitalità*," he said before turning to me.

My stomach growled. I was, in fact, dying of hunger. "You heard the lady. *Mangia*."

"Be careful," Enzo warned me. "It's hot as hell inside."

But that didn't stop him from picking up his *pizza fritta*, opening his mouth wide, and taking a large bite. He closed his eyes as he savored what I imagined had to have been familiar flavors dating back to his childhood. I decided to forego his warning and take a bite myself, and when the flavors of the tomato, basil, ricotta, and pork exploded in my mouth, I closed my eyes and let out a groan.

"Good?" Enzo asked.

I nodded, breaking the stringy cheesy with my hands. "I could actually cry it's so fantastic," I said, my mouth still full.

Some of the filling spilled out as I went in for my second bite.

"These kinds of dishes were poor man's food," Enzo told me as he wiped the oil off his hands with a paper napkin. "My *mamma* used to make it just like this. Sometimes she'd throw in other ingredients.

Just depended on what we had in the fridge. And every time she made it, I'd eat it too fast and burn my tongue."

"Hence the warning," I said, laughing, imagining a young Enzo being disciplined by his mother.

"Now look at this street. Tourists come from all over the world and go crazy over these kinds of dishes."

"I thought you didn't like this kind of food," I said, recalling how back in his days of owning Valenti's, he had a strict policy against Francesco making these very same dishes. "Like the *carrozza*."

"That was before these kinds of things became *cool*," Enzo said. "Besides, I wasn't exactly proud that I came from a poor family. Now I'm older. I see things different."

"Did you grow up near here?"

Enzo's eyes lit up. "That's where we're headed next."

After consuming every last morsel of our fried pizzas, and stopping for a *crema di caffè*—a frozen espresso beverage that was better than any dessert I'd ever had—we walked ten minutes to a neighborhood called *Quartieri Spagnoli*. Looks wise, the street wasn't too different than Spaccanapoli, though the blue Napoli flags were replaced with laundry lines extending from one side of the street to the other. But the feeling here was different. Calmer. Raw. *Real*.

Home.

In the middle of the *via*, Enzo came to a halt. His gaze drifted upward, tracing the balconies, the flowerpots and chairs that decorated them, the cracks in the walls that had likely been there for decades. He didn't say anything right away, and I knew, as he stood there, absorbing our surroundings, that he was looking at something only he could see.

Finally, he turned to me, his expression a mix of awe and melancholy. He pointed to the balcony three stories up.

"That's where I grew up."

There was a lilt to his voice, and though kids on motorbikes whisked by with loud revs of their engines, and Italian women shouted at each other from opposite sides of the street, time slowed down. I slipped my arms around his waist and leaned my head against his chest. I wished I could see what he saw. His *mamma* cutting pasta or folding laundry. His *papà* chiding him to get back inside. Him and Francesco playing *calcio* along the *via*, just like the young kids who now kicked a tattered soccer ball down the street. Though I only saw a vacant balcony, my imagination ran wild with scenarios. Scenarios that had shaped the two men who had shaped my life.

"It's crazy, isn't it?" I muttered, my eyes still fixed on Enzo's childhood home.

"What is?" he asked, his voice as low as mine.

"You're from here, and I'm from where I'm from, and somehow, our paths crossed." I looked at him, feeling the weight of being here, how special it was to step into a moment we could no longer touch. "It doesn't make any sense, you know? But I guess when something's meant to be, it finds a way."

He leaned over and kissed my temple. "*Mamma* would've loved you."

"Oh, I like to think that." I gave him a knowing glance. "But something tells me she would've called me a *puttana*."

This time, my accent was spot on. It sent us both into hysterics, our faces touching as we laughed together. He traced my jaw with his thumb.

"You're right. How the hell did we find each other?"

I didn't have an answer. Enzo and I seemed so interconnected, like we transcended time and space and all the things that made up this earth. Like we were always supposed to find each other, no matter where each of us came from, we were written into the same story. It had to be destiny. Fate. They were the only plausible things that could've bound me and this man from a land so foreign from my own.

He squeezed my hand, as if he were agreeing with my unspoken thought. "Come on. Let's get out of here."

"Where are we going now?"

"Remember how I told you to pack a bathing suit?"

An hour later, we were gliding over the sapphire waters of Capri, the sea shimmering beneath the afternoon sun like crushed diamonds. The limestone cliffs seemed to touch the sky as our captain took us in and out of grottos, like the *Grotta Iannarella* with a heart mysteriously carved into its cave. The salty air tangled my hair and Enzo's skin was growing bronzer by the minute as we baked beneath the sun that seemed brighter, more powerful, here in Italy. Our captain steered us to an area near the cliffs where boats were anchored, rocking and bobbing with the rhythm of the waves. Enzo woke from his sunbathing as we anchored. He looked to his left. In the distance, three large rocks jutted out from the sea.

"*I Faraglioni*," Enzo said, his eyes fixated on the stunning formations.

"The first one is *Stella*," our captain said. He brought out a colorfully painted ceramic dish of freshly sliced fruit that looked so beautiful, I couldn't believe it was real. "The furthest one is *Scopolo*. But the middle one, that is the special one. You see the arch in the middle? When two lovers kiss beneath it as they pass through, their love will be eternal."

Though I stared ahead at the archway, I felt Enzo's stare on me.

"Please," the captain said before I could react, "try the *percoche*."

"*Percoche?*" I asked Enzo as the captain retreated to the cabin.

"Peaches," Enzo clarified. He picked up a slice and fed it to me. "But you've never had a peach like this."

My mouth watered as I chewed, the sweetness bursting across my tongue. The fruit's juice trickled down my chin, warm and sticky. Before I could wipe it away, Enzo's thumb was there, catching the syrup and bringing it to his lips.

"That's insane."

"Isn't it?" he agreed before taking his own bite. Then, as the boat rocked in place, he sprung to his feet and reached his hand out for mine. "Let's go for a swim."

The captain tossed an inner tube into the water at my request. I wasn't fond of oceans, of how little control one had while immersed in its waters. Enzo dove in headfirst like the native that he was, while I pinched my nose and jumped in. The water was cold, stunningly so, and it shocked my system. As I emerged to the sea's surface, I saw everything through fresh eyes. Instead of clinging to the tube, I wrapped my arms around Enzo's shoulders as he treaded in place, laughter rising out of my chest.

"What's so funny?" he asked, a smirk splitting his face.

I looked out at the *Faraglioni*. "I can't believe we're here. Seeing this together. I feel like I'm dreaming."

His smile softened as he swam over to the inner tube and helped me onto it. As I became one with the rhythm of the waves, he stretched his arms across my body and rested his head on my torso. I closed my eyes, the sun beaming through, so my vision was nothing but an orange haze. I let it all sink in. The saltwater clinging to my skin. The seagulls singing and swooping through the air. The relentless sun. The cloudless sky. Enzo, the ever-constant presence, now and always. How could the rest of the world exist when I was suspended here in this perfect place? Should reality come knocking, try and drag me down with it, I would claw and fight to stay. The way I saw it, Italy and I were just getting started.

Soon after, our captain started at a slow speed, steering us back to Positano. We were still drenched from our swim as the boat glided beneath the center *Faraglioni*, its archway tall and inviting. My heart thrashed around in my chest. *Eternal love.* Wasn't that what Enzo had always been to me? Hadn't I already sealed our fate when I brought our daughter into the world? Oh, but I couldn't let this moment slip away without sealing it for good, Italian style. Enzo's gaze was upward, staring at the top of the arch, when I grabbed his shoulders turned him toward me and kissed him, only letting go when I felt the sun on my back, a sign we were out of the archway. We didn't speak the rest of the boat ride. We just existed, nestled together, our limbs tangled, tired from swimming, our skin golden from our glorious, unexpected day. Still, in our silence, I could hear him. Feel him. He wanted to hang onto this as much as I did.

"You ever think about what your life would be like if you'd stayed here?" I asked once we were back in Positano, anchored near the shore. The sun was amid its grand decent into the horizon, and we were bathed in golden light. My skin was dry, but saltwater still clung to my hair, droplets falling to my lower back every so often.

Behind me, Enzo wrapped his arms around my chest, holding me close to him. "It's just a place."

"This is so *not* just a place. This is the most magical thing I've ever seen."

"I would've had a rough life here. I know me. I would've gotten tied up with the *Cammora* and ended up either dead or in jail."

"Funny," I said, craning my neck to look him in the eye. "That's almost how your life turned out in New York."

Trying to suppress a smile, he shook his head. "What the hell am I gonna do with you?"

We both turned back toward the sun. Did he, too, want to capture this moment in his memory so that he might be able to hang onto it forever? So he could revisit it any time he liked? Because I stood there, my back pressed against his chest, our breathing synchronized, trying to memorize every detail. The hue of the sunset. How the curves of his torso melded with my bare back, separated only by the string of my bikini top. The gentle rocking of the boat separating us from that gorgeous sapphire sea. Positano just to our right, beckoning us for another night of surprises. Yes, this was what I was destined for. This was who I could have been.

Me. Him. Italy. *Per sempre.*

Enzo's grip around me tightened. His mouth was near my ear, the heat of his breath making my skin tingle.

"I'm going home tomorrow," he said, his voice drowning out the chatter in the distance, the lapping waves, the upbeat music coming from another boat. My smile faded. "And you're coming with me."

I stiffened against him, but he wouldn't let me go. Somehow, I managed to turn around in his arms to look at him.

"I'm not going anywhere," I insisted.

"Yes, you are."

"No, Enzo." I wriggled free from him. "I'm not. I came here on my own, and I'll leave on my own."

"Scarlett." He drew out my name in a tone that sounded like a warning. "I promised my brother I wouldn't leave this country unless you were on the plane, in the seat next to me."

"So you did come here to collect me for him." Rage simmered just beneath my surface, ready to boil over. I backed up a few inches. "You manipulated me and made me fall in love with you all over again so I'd go home with you?"

My eyes went wide as my admission hung in the air. It was news to both me and Enzo; I hadn't realized that's what had transpired in the two days I'd spent with him, but as soon as the words left my lips, I knew they were true. I felt like a girl again, dreaming up a future with the man I dreamed of knowing in every conceivable way. Here I thought our feelings were mutual when this grand display of affection was nothing more a tactic. A tactic employed by my husband.

"Fuck you, and fuck him," I yelled. The captain was looking at us, but I didn't care. All I wanted to do was swim to shore and lock myself in my room until Enzo left Italy for good. "You know, sometimes I wish I never met you boys. All you've done is complicate my life. Both of you. And you cannot make me go home."

"Scarlett—"

"Just, stop!" My chest rose and fell with angry, shallow breaths. "If he wanted me to come home so bad, why didn't *he* come?"

I expected him to dodge the question. To say something flippant or sarcastic. But instead, Enzo hesitated. His mouth hung open for a moment before he pressed his lips together. My brows furrowed. Why was he hesitating? Why wasn't he answering me? He interlaced his fingers and pressed his palms against the top of his head.

"He couldn't," he finally said. He closed his eyes and let out a long exhale. "He can't fly."

A buzzing sound filled my ears. "What do you mean he can't fly?"

I could tell he didn't want to look at me. He didn't want to tell me what was coming next. But trapped together on that boat, he had nowhere to run.

"When he got back from LA, when you were still recovering from the stillbirth," Enzo started, "he had some routine tests scheduled for his heart. They found some blockages, Scar. They're trying to treat it with medication, but he'll probably need surgery."

The boat dipped, mirroring the way my heart sank. I was knocked unsteady, and I reached out for Enzo's arms to keep me from knocking into the guardrail. All this time, I'd thought Francesco had been drawing back because of me. I thought he looked so worn because our crumbling marriage was taking a toll on him. Even still, I was his wife. How hadn't I known? "Why didn't he tell me?"

"He didn't want to add one more thing to your plate."

"Why didn't *you* tell me?"

"He asked me not to."

I grabbed Enzo's shoulders, and though he was a man made of muscle, I shook him. "I'm his *wife*, Enzo. Someone should've told me." A sob leapt out of my throat as I backed away, my hands flying to my temples, smoothing my hair away from my face. I thought of the wrought expression Francesco wore when I told him I was leaving. When I told him I was tired of being his wife. He was sick when I said those horrible things, battling something he had no control over. I admonished myself for all the foolish, immature scenarios I'd conjured up in my head of starting fresh in Italy when I had a family who so clearly needed me.

Then, I thought of last night. "Oh my God," I muttered. "What if I had— What if *we* had—"

"Scarlett," Enzo said, his head lilting to one side as he studied me. He approached and cupped my face in his hands, leaning his forehead against mine. "I *love* you." His voice trembled, letting me know those three words weren't easy for him to say aloud. "I know I shouldn't. I know we shouldn't be the way we are with each other. But I had to get you home and sweeping you off your feet was the only way I knew how."

I pushed myself away from him. Nothing mattered now. I looked around, at the nearby boats bobbing in the sea, at the beachgoers lounging by the shore, at the tourists meandering through town without a care in the world. Five minutes ago, I was one of them. Mystified by this dreamscape of a place. But now, it all felt trivial. Unnecessary. Gluttonous, even.

"I have to go home," I declared, my voice unwavering. I looked at Enzo, at the towering cliffs surrounding us, at the golden horizon. I closed my eyes, wishing it would all go away. I didn't deserve this beauty. Not when I'd left my husband suffering in silence. I made my way into the cabin, but our captain was nowhere to be found. I opened my mouth to shout, to yell of my urgent need, but no sound came out.

Enzo appeared behind me, his hand enveloping my shoulder. "*Capità, portace subbito a Marina di Praia. Svelt', è n'urgenza.*"

Our captain appeared, and soon after, a loud, griding sound emerged from the belly of the boat, reeling in our anchor. Enzo's hands gripped my shoulders.

"He's gonna be okay," he assured me. "And whatever happens in the future happens. But right now, he needs you."

And so, that evening, I threw all my belongings in a suitcase and boarded a flight back to New York. Enzo held my hand all nine hours, like he was carrying back to my real life. As soon as we landed at JFK, reality didn't knock at my door. It banged it down. I felt the tug of my babies, the pull of my husband, of everything that made my life what it was. Suddenly, I couldn't get back to 91 Bank Street fast enough. The dream that had been my short stay in Italy slipped away like it never existed at all, like I hadn't spent all of yesterday gliding across the glittering seas of Capri.

When the cab came to a stop in front of my home, my heart pounded. What if something happened while we were in the air? What if I was too late? I felt like I was clawing my way back to my family, when all I wanted to do was hold them in my arms and keep them safe. I wanted to pore over every last test result and come up with an action plan. I wanted to save my husband.

I wanted to save our family. It wasn't the answer I expected Italy to give me, but it was the one I received.

Enzo opened the door for me and carried my bags up the few steps to my porch. I used my key to unlock the door, drew in a deep breath, and turned the knob. And when my husband and children lit up at the sight of me, the relief and longing I'd kept bottled up while I was in Italy poured out in the form of tears and a sad smile.

"Mommy's home," I announced, sinking to my knees to draw my babies into a hug. They threw their arms around me, fiercely tight, like they were afraid to let go. In my peripheral vision, I saw Enzo hug Francesco, leaving him with a pat on the back.

"Stay for dinner," Francesco suggested.

Enzo waved him off. "You all enjoy your reunion."

I saw the gratitude in Francesco's eyes as Enzo let himself out. Then, Francesco sank to the ground next to me. As my children peppered me with questions about my trip and I appeased them with answers, I caught Francesco's eye. Written on his face was one question: *Are you here to stay?*

I gave him a soft smile and nodded. Maybe Francesco and I were

306 🐞 <i>Sarah Arcuri</i>

no good for each other. Maybe all we did was ruin each other. But he was a part of me. Maybe it didn't feel like home, not in the way Enzo did, but that didn't change the fact that he was sewn into whatever fabric I was comprised of. This was the home I had made for myself. For the family I cherished above all else. If I hadn't put them first, I would have still been in Italy, starting something new. But instead, as I lavished my kids with souvenirs and gifts of Napoli soccer balls and lemon dresses, I let Francesco wrap his arms around me and whisper in my ear that things would be different from now on.

How naïve we were, to not know how different life was about to get.

CHAPTER TWENTY-THREE

SCARLETT

Summer, 2011

We made it out just in time. One second longer, one more frantic scramble for clothes or wasted breath inside, and we would have been engulfed. Now, standing on the beach, my chest heaving, I still can't catch my breath. Flames roar behind us, devouring our beach house, licking at the sky like they're trying to consume the moon and the stars while they're at it. The heat is unbearable, a searing reminder of how close we came.

Enzo, his phone clutched in his hand, had the wits to call 9-1-1 the moment we hit the sand. But it doesn't matter. It's too late.

It's gone.

Up in flames, destroyed, taking all my memories with it.

Taking my last chance with it.

"Enzo," I yell, even though he's just a few feet away from me. I run my fingers through my hair as a sob leaps from my chest. "That was my last shot. Now I'm gonna lose the restaurant, too."

"No, you're not." Enzo is on me in an instant, grabbing my hands, grounding me. "We'll get insurance money."

"That could take months. Years. I have a few *weeks* to pay Saverio."

"I'll take out some loans. We can still sell the land. We'll figure it out."

Another loud eruption from the house steals our attention. Sirens wail, and lights switch on in our neighbors' homes as they wake to see the source of the commotion. The night feels like it'll never end as we watch the second level of our home crumble.

The air is thick, acrid. My throat burns from the billowing smoke. I dissolve into a vortex of panic, of numb, trembling limbs and uncontrollable shivers, as everything blurs. Enzo, running toward the house to speak with one of the firefighters, while the rest have already started fighting the hot, yellow and orange monsters eating my house. I don't see the large hose spraying water atop the tall, growing flames. All I see is everything I've just lost.

Pia's birthdays. Late summer nights on the deck, enjoying a meal from the grill. Lazy beach days, pastel sunsets, rainstorms that drove us to cozy up by the fireplace. Watching Emilio surf through the windowsill over the kitchen sink. Brewing Francesco a cup of espresso in the morning. Feeding baby Pia in the middle of the night while Enzo held her. I can hear the laughter we shared in this house; I can feel the tears I cried there in secret as if they've just rolled down my cheek. I see the day I walked into this house for the first time, when Francesco promised me a fresh start.

I've always thought this house to be a beginning. How was I to know it would be my end?

"Scarlett," I hear, but it sounds far away. My brain finally registers that it's Enzo's voice. Clad in mismatched sweats, I sit in the sand, trapped in a trance until Enzo shakes me out of it. "Scarlett."

I blink rapidly, coming to. Crouched down to my eye level, Enzo looks at me, his eyes framed by furrowed brows.

"They think it started in the kitchen," he tells me.

"The kitchen?"

"They said it was the most heavily burned. They'll know more after the fire is out." Enzo cranes his neck to look at the devastation. The fire is still raging, but it doesn't appear quite as wild.

"The kitchen," I repeat, feeling like I'm being reeled back into a trance. Enzo and I hadn't cooked. "Emilio." His name escapes my lips like a secret I don't want to reveal. Emilio was the last one who used the stove. I close my eyes and lean back into the sand. If only I had kept my foot down, that my son would *never* cook. If only I had been more adamant.

If only I hadn't *let go.*

I want to call my mother and say, *See? Bad things do happen when I let go. I told you so.*

If the stove is, in fact, the source of the fire, I'll never tell him. I'll never place that guilt on his shoulders when I know what that feels like myself. I know I can carry this secret; it's no greater than the one I've been carrying for eighteen years. I'll say I brewed myself a cup of tea and never switched off the kettle.

"Scar, honey," Enzo says in gentle tones. He sinks to the spot next to me and I lean my head against his shoulder.

"Our house," I mutter as we watch it burn down, together.

"It's just a house," he assures me, rubbing his hand up and down my arm like he's trying to convince himself, too. "All that matters is that you and I got out in time."

By the time the flames are reduced to smoldering embers, and our home is nothing more than a mound of plywood and ashes, it's dawn. The early morning sky promises a bright, cloudless beach day, but my world feels gray. A coating of ash clings to my hair, and my skin is scented with burned wood and saltwater. Our next-door neighbors checked on us through the night, bringing us water, offering up their home for us to sit while we wait for instruction from the fire department, but we politely declined.

What is it about destruction that makes us humans incapable of looking away?

Like a mirage, one of the firemen treks down the sand toward us. Enzo stands first and helps me up, keeping me close to him with his arm around my waist. I tune out the pleasantries, but my senses go into overdrive when he discusses the cause of the fire.

"One of the burners was on low," the fireman tells us. The scent of smoke is overwhelming, and I cough, turning my head to the side as he continues. "Do you remember if there were any greasy pots or pans left on the stove? A dish towel, even?"

The fireman's voice grows distant, drowned out by the roaring in my ears. The smoke stings my throat, but I can't swallow. A pit forms in my stomach. It wasn't my son's fault at all.

It was mine.

I was the one who told Enzo we should leave the mess for later. I was the one who recklessly, selfishly decided to give into my desires. I was the sole person responsible for this devastating destruction. All because I let go, and like always, I crashed right into Enzo.

And like always, everything has been destroyed.

I chide myself while the firefighter drones on about the impending formal investigation. How foolish I was, not to have learned my lesson the first time around. Don't I know by now that Enzo is bad news? That nothing but destruction and heartbreak and secrets form from our union?

"Pia," I hear myself saying. Then, it hits me. She's standing right in front of me. So is Emilio. Their eyes are red, their cheeks stained with tears. "Emi," I whisper.

And as I take in my children's despondence, I have this feeling in my gut that the destruction has only just begun.

I throw my arms around my kids. "It's okay. Enzo and I are safe, and that's all that matters. Thank God you weren't home. I don't know what would've happened—"

Pia pushes away from me. Her eyes are as black as midnight, but right now, they look like the flames that burned down my house. The Birkin bag is fixed in the crook of her arm, and she and Emilio are dressed in the pajamas they'd packed for their overnight stay.

"Pia, I'm sorry. It was an accident." I look at Emilio for backup. "It was an accident."

Emilio draws in a breath, but he doesn't speak. Something hangs in the air. Something I'm clearly not privy to. I look between them, waiting for one of them to say something. To tell me that they're not mad at me. That they understand accidents happen. But they don't. Instead, something else lingers. Something thick and suffocating.

Something I'm afraid of.

Pia looks past me. I crane my neck; she's looking at Enzo. Enzo looks exhausted as he joins us, like every ounce of his energy has been drained. Then, I notice the look of confusion that flickers across his face. I whip my head around. Pia has an envelope in her hands.

An envelope addressed to Enzo.

My letter. *The* letter.

The one I never sent.

The one that tells him that he's my daughter's father.

A gasp escapes my throat. The Birkin. It comes back to me, the last time I wore it.

Four years ago, when I went to visit Enzo before he abandoned me. When I had planned on telling him the truth, but he had a plan of his own.

I lunge toward her. If I can just get the letter out of her hands, my whole life won't be destroyed. I won't lose everything if I can just get it away from her. Maybe she didn't read it. Maybe she doesn't know yet and maybe I can make sure she never does.

But when I notice that the lip of the envelope is ripped, all jagged and torn, I surrender. It's over. It's all over. The ocean's roar sounds like it's miles away and I don't give another thought to the fire. All I can hear is my daughter's sweet, high-pitched voice.

"Do you know?" She stares straight at Enzo. At the man who is so clearly her father. All I see, as I look between them, as silence hangs between the four of us, is their shared features. Their identical eyes. Their shared coloring. Their inky, straight jet-black hair. Is that the reason I never deviated from black locks, so that people might think she looks like me? So that I might be able to mask the truth just a little bit longer?

Who have I been kidding? The truth is plain as day, printed right on their faces.

"Do I know what?" Enzo finally says, reluctance in his tone.

Pia swallows. She extends her arm, attempting to give him the letter. Maybe he won't take it. Maybe he doesn't want to know the truth any more than I've wanted to share it. But the minute it reaches his fingertips, fear seizes me. I brace myself.

"Do you know that you're my dad?" Pia asks.

I feel faint as Enzo stares into Pia's eyes. Hard, like he's searching for himself in her. He doesn't look at me, not when he tears his eyes away from her and slowly lifts the pages of my letter out of the envelope it's lived in for eighteen years. He undoes the trifolds, and I hold my breath as he reads the words that, even after all these years, I know by heart.

My dear Enzo,

They say if you tell yourself something enough times, you'll believe it. What is fact, and what is fiction? Can we really trick ourselves into believing something false to be true? I've tried. I've tried to render those little lies I whisper to myself when no one else is listening, the ones I tell myself so often, as actual truth.

When Francesco hit me, I told myself it wasn't a big deal. It didn't hurt so bad. I told myself I could get over it and pretend it didn't happen. When I hear rumors that he's cheating on me, I tell myself he wouldn't do such a thing. That he isn't capable. When we fight, I tell myself that it'll get better. That marriage is full of ups and downs. That this is normal.

When I found out I was pregnant with the daughter I dreamed of having my whole life, I told myself there was no way she was yours. It was one night. One fleeting, forbidden night that I can't seem to forget about no matter how hard I try to blot it from my memory. I spent all nine months of my pregnancy lying to myself, hoping I'd believe it to be true.

But now she's here, Enzo. My beautiful, precious, perfect daughter, Pia Rose Valenti, the baby you named when she was just a few hours old, resting in my arms.

She's here, and she's yours.

Ours.

I'd like to say that I'm shocked, because you might be. But

I'm not. I knew, deep down, when my belly started to swell as she grew inside of my womb that she was half of you and half of me. And I wish, Enzo, that I could say I'm upset about it. That I regret that night with you. But how can I? That night gave me the greatest gift of my life. That night made my biggest dream come true. I have a beautiful, healthy baby girl, and Enzo, honey, I love her so much it hurts. I love her more than words could ever express. I would die for her. Throw myself before an oncoming train if it meant saving her life. She's the part of me that's been missing, the one I've been waiting for all my life.

And you gave her to me. I can't regret the way anything happened. She wouldn't be her without any other set of genetics, and there's not a thing I'd change about her. You and I have never been together in a real sense, not in any kind of formal fashion, but the combination of your eyes and my lips on her sweet little face is proof that somewhere, sometime, you and I loved each other. Our blend of features will be passed down to her children, and their children, so it'll always be known that you and I loved each other. We created something ever-lasting, Enzo. We needed each other that night. We tried to save each other, and maybe we did. Our daughter is forever a reminder of that.

But beyond being forever bound to our daughter, Enzo, this means that I'll forever be bound to you. I've loved you from the moment I laid eyes on you, on that fateful day in 1985 when I walked into your restaurant for the very first time. And now there's no question that I always will.

I don't know if I'll tell her. I don't plan to. I plan on bearing the burden of this secret until the good Lord takes me. But one day, our girl might recognize your features on her pretty face. When she's old enough to feel love between two people, maybe she'll feel it between us. If she ever does question me, question her origins, I'm not sure how I'll answer her. I don't know if I'll have the courage to admit my wrongdoings which led to her life. I can't predict the future, but I can promise you some things, Enzo.

I promise you, that all her life, all my life, I will give our daughter my all. I'll die for her if I have to. I'll do absolutely everything in my power to protect her from the world that you and I know to be so cold and cruel. I promise I'll work to give her everything you and I never had when we were young. I'll make life easy for her so she doesn't have to know the struggles you and I faced. I'll give her every ounce of love I have to give, Enzo, and should I run out, I'll dig deeper until I find more.

So I want to thank you, Enzo. Thank you for giving me the baby I always dreamed of having. Thank you for being there when I needed you most. For listening to me even when you were going through things that were so much worse than what I was going through. Thank you for never letting me down, and thank you for being you, Enzo. When I was young and fell in love with you, I didn't fall for the things you had or the things you said. I fell for you. Your heart and your soul. You alone, Lorenzo Michael Valenti.

You, the father of my baby girl.

All my love,

Always,

Scarlett

As he reads in silence, his jaw tightening, his fingers pressing into the paper like it might crumble in his hands, I wonder how this could be happening. How this is real. How my greatest fear is coming true right in front of me, and I can't do a damn thing to stop it.

The truth is out now. The truth I've always been so terrified of.

As my racing heart climbs into my throat, Enzo flips back to the first page. His eyes lift to the upper right corner that I know bears the date I wrote it.

"August. Nineteen-ninety-three," Enzo reads. Slowly, painfully so, he lifts his gaze to meet mine. All I see in his eyes, those familiar eyes I've always found so safe, is pure and utter heartbreak. "You've been keeping this from me all her life."

"I had to," I rush to say. "I had no choice but to live with this secret. I didn't want you to have to watch your brother raise your daughter. I didn't want you to live with this secret, Enzo. I was protecting you."

"You were protecting yourself!" Enzo's voice carries, beyond the ocean breeze, beyond its wild song. He inches closer to me, step by step, holding the letter up in his right hand. My life's greatest secret on full display. "You did what you had to do to keep that fucking façade of a marriage intact, and you didn't care who you hurt. You weren't protecting me. You weren't protecting your son, or our daughter, or Francesco. You were protecting *you*. You were making sure nothing came between you and the life you always wanted to live. You know something, Scarlett? You know why I think you tolerated his abuse? Why you let him get away with cheating on you the whole time you were married? Because you were addicted. Addicted to the life he gave you. You liked having a famous husband. You liked being his trophy. You liked being the owner's wife. You liked the homes, and the trips, and the cars, and the diamonds, and the handbags.

That's why you never gave me this letter. Because you didn't want to lose all of that."

"Enzo, you *know* me," I protest. "You know that's the farthest thing from the truth. I never gave a *shit* about any of that."

"Then why did you stay?" he hisses.

"Because I wanted a family!"

"What kind of family did you have? Hm? You had a husband who smacked you sideways and ran around on you all the time. You practically raised the kids yourself. So tell me, Scarlett, what family exactly were you trying to save?"

Veins bud out of his neck, and I can feel my own doing the same. I'm losing him. I'm losing this fight. I'm losing, *period,* because maybe he's right.

Maybe I'm not the woman I've always thought myself to be. The one willing to sacrifice anything for the people I love. The woman who puts herself last. The one who has foregone my own happiness for the sake of others.

Maybe I'm even worse than I thought. All this time, I've thought my greatest sin was cheating on my husband. Now, I see the truth. It was the morning after, and every morning after that when I woke up and chose to live a lie. When I decided to keep the cards in my hands and stay in silence while I watched my family suffer the consequences.

Pia's weeping breaks me out of my thoughts. She's all grown up, and still, all I see is the baby I stared at, sleeping peacefully in her bassinet, as I wrote the letter still in Enzo's grip.

"Pia," I say, rushing to her.

She puts her palms up and backs away. "Stay away from me," she shrieks. "Who *are* you?"

Her features blur together as tears fill my eyes. All eighteen years of her life fill my mind's eye like a rapid-fire reel. All eighteen years of my secret-keeping, of that sin I committed on that lonely New York City night, have led us here. To the place where we might be severed forever.

"I'm your mom," I say between gasps, trying to get some air into my lungs. "I know I've ruined everything, Pia, but I'm still your mom."

But deep down, I know what my daughter sees. A stranger.

"I hate you!" she yells. "You've been lying to me my entire life."

As I look at my son, my last remnant of hope, Enzo goes to Pia and consoles her. It strikes me how all the blame has fallen on my shoulders. How he's the innocent one, even though he's half the reason we're standing here right now. Emilio stands there, stoic, unwavering, though there's a new layer of vulnerability to him. He's unsure. Unsure if he can trust me. Unsure if I'm the mother he always knew. I am. I swear I am, but I don't know how I can get them to believe me when I've spent their lives lying to them.

Enzo and Pia turn toward the house and start walking away. Though my legs are still numb, unsteady beneath me, I start after them.

"Where are you going?" I call out. "You can't leave." Enzo turns his head around and shoots me an icy glare. Where was the man who'd made love to me and told me he loved me over and over again just mere hours ago? Defiantly, he tightens his grip around Pia, an act that ignites a new emotion in me. "You can't take her." Like a lion with a primal instinct to protect her cub, I find a strength I didn't know I had and catch up with them. I claw at their shoulders. "She's mine!"

They turn around. Their identical eyes stare back at me. Enzo's mouth, the mouth I'd spent all last night kissing, curves into a grimace that's laced with hate.

"She's mine, too," Enzo says. His parting words. Before I know it, they're halfway down the beach, and though I'm planted in place, I'm out of breath.

I feel Emilio's presence behind me. I whip around. My son. My son can help me.

"Emilio," I say, reaching out for him. "You understand, don't you? It was one night. Daddy had hit me, and he was cheating on me, and—"

"I really don't want to talk about it, Mom." There is no mercy or sympathy in his expression. Rightfully so. I don't deserve those things. Instead, he looks resigned, like this is something he'll have to grapple with for the rest of his life.

"Please don't leave, Emi. I need you right now."

We stand there, staring at each other. The sun is rising behind him, glorious, gold, shining. Behind me, the house is still rife with activity, with firemen putting out the last of the flames, searching for burn patterns, though I don't care about how the fire started anymore. All I care about is my family. The family I've spent all my life fighting for. The family I'd do anything to save.

The family I've completely and utterly betrayed.

Emilio reaches in his pocket and deposits a key in my hands. "You can take my car back, Ma. But I'm gonna go with them."

"Emilio," I call after him. My sweet boy's back is to me and I know I've ruined him. Disillusioned him to who I am. Forever. "I love you," I say, though it's only a whisper, lost in the summer breeze.

My ears ring. My breath won't come. The world tilts. It ends. I'm not just all alone on this beach.

I'm all alone in the world, with nothing, and no one left, and I have no one to blame but myself.

CHAPTER TWENTY-FOUR

SCARLETT

Winter, 2007

Massive.

That was the word the doctors had used to describe Francesco's latest heart attack. *He's lucky to be alive,* was what they told us. *It's a miracle.* But nothing felt miraculous, and I didn't feel lucky. I felt like a bomb had been dropped on us. We'd spent the last six years rebuilding our marriage. It was like we'd poured concrete over our past, paving a new foundation. For the first time since the beginning, Francesco saw me. He'd come back down to earth after spending years suspended in the sky, hanging among the stars. He was like the old him. The old him, just with a weakening heart.

We always knew this day would come. Still, after twenty-one years of marriage, I wasn't prepared to lose him. That was why I had to do everything in my power to fix him.

I'd called everyone in our inner circle to rally around him and welcome him home. He'd spent three weeks in the hospital, and now, as he sat on the couch, doing his best to seem positive as he chatted with Julie and Bobby, it showed. His tall frame was gaunt, those three weeks undoing all the years it took to build the muscles that sculpted his arms. Those golden eyes of his were sunken in, dim, dull. He was tired. He'd almost reached the end. But as my hands clenched into fists at my sides, I said a silent prayer that he would have enough fight left in him to stick with us a little while longer.

Or maybe by some miracle, a lot longer.

Pia was curled up, glued to his side on the couch, resting her head on his shoulder. Emilio sat in the armchair across from them, just staring, a tense smile splitting his face. Outwardly, I projected to the kids that Daddy just needed one more surgery, and he'd be fine for many years to come. That the doctors were monitoring his medications, and they'd find a solution to make sure he didn't have any more heart attacks. But I knew that surgeries and pills didn't always work. Sometimes destiny had its own plans that outsmarted the will and wishes of mankind.

When Francesco stood, I rushed to his side. "Sit down."

"I'm fine, babe," he said, touching my arm. His hands were cold; must've been the blood thinners.

"What do you need?"

Francesco looked around and cleared his throat. "I need everyone to leave," he said at an embarrassingly loud decibel.

"Honey," I chided him, letting out an awkward laugh as my cheeks burned.

"I'm sick. Sick people get whatever they want, right?" Francesco looked at Enzo, at my mother and her boyfriend, at Julie and Bobby. At our babies, who were now fully fledged teenagers. Dusk had fallen, and I considered that maybe he wanted to go to sleep and didn't want to say so. "Listen, I appreciate all of you coming over to help me get better, but I'm fine, and I have a beautiful wife I'd like to enjoy all by myself."

"What about us?" Pia asked with a frown.

I kissed her forehead. "You have school tomorrow. You and Emi are going to stay with Grandma until Daddy gets stronger."

Judging from the look on Pia's face, I knew my daughter was confused as to why she couldn't sleep at home and go to school in the morning like normal. Why I couldn't wake up early with her and drive her Uptown to campus and pick her up on time and listen to her post-school gossip like I always did. She didn't know how dire the circumstances surrounding her father's health were, but my son was another story. I couldn't hide anything from him. He was eighteen. A legal adult. He saw right through my veils, and I didn't like it.

"Give Daddy a big hug," I said to my kids. *Just in case,* I thought. *Just in case it's the last time you get to hug him.* I shook my head in an attempt to shake away my tormenting thoughts. I plastered on a bright, toothy, upbeat smile that said *Daddy's going to be fine.*

"Alright," Julie said with a clap of her hands. "You heard the man. Give him what he wants."

The grand Italian goodbye procession began. A train of kisses on cheeks and hugs and well wishes. After, I ushered everyone to the door while Francesco settled back in on the sofa. I didn't want anyone to leave, but everyone dispersed to their respective modes of transportation, save for Enzo.

"You okay?" Enzo asked once we were alone on the porch.

"I'm scared." I waved to Julie one last time and my fake smile faded. "I'm going to be all by myself with him and I'm scared something is going to happen." I put my hands on my hips. "You think he's gonna be okay?"

"What do I know?" Enzo ran his palm over his immaculate hair. "I guess we just have to wait and see."

I leaned my arms on the wrought-iron railing. "I feel like that's all life is. One big waiting game."

"You want me to stay over? I'll sleep in the basement so I'm out of your way."

"I don't want him to know how scared I am."

Enzo's head tilted to one side. "I think at this point, he knows you better than you know you."

My mouth expanded into some strange, heartbroken smile. Enzo drew me into him and kissed my forehead.

"I don't care what time it is," he said. "You can call me."

"Thanks, Enz."

Enzo jogged down the steps and headed west. Once he was out of sight, I let out an exhale. I had to go back inside, pretend like I wasn't scared shitless, and do my best to make my sick husband happy. It was easier to stand out here and stare at the pots of hydrangea bushes on either side of the stoop which bore no blossoms. Spring would arrive in a few short months, and like clockwork, they would bud into mounds of white snowballs. I prayed that my husband would be here to see them bloom, but I felt like my prayer was said in vain. No matter how hard I pleaded and bargained with God, He already had the day and hour of the end of my husband's life written somewhere I couldn't see.

"I hope you don't mind," Francesco said once I joined him in the living room. He stood as I switched on some lamps that drenched the house in a cozy warm glow. "But I just wanted to be alone with you."

"You're right. When people are sick, they get whatever they want."

"Whatever I want, hm?" Francesco kissed my lips, then my neck. One hand on my waist, he snaked the other around to squeeze my rear.

I swatted his hand away. "None of that."

He let out a frustrated groan. "Torture."

"Come on. Let's watch a movie or something."

"I'm hungry."

"Okay. What can I make you?"

"You're not making me anything." Francesco grabbed my hand and led me to the kitchen.

"Fran, you're supposed to be resting."

"I want to cook."

"No," I demanded. Francesco raised his brows at me. "I just don't want you to do anything strenuous."

"I know *you* find cooking strenuous," Francesco teased, "but I don't. It's what I love."

It dawned on me that Francesco might need this. To heal, maybe he needed to do what was most natural to him. "Okay. Let's cook. But nothing crazy. Let's make something simple."

Francesco retrieved a loaf of white bread and a box of breadcrumbs from the pantry. He stood behind the doors of the fridge for a moment before placing a carton of eggs and some sliced mozzarella that Enzo had brought over from a salumeria on the counter. I smiled, recognizing the dish even though it had yet to be assembled.

"*Carrozza*," I said. "I don't think you've made this since the kids were little."

"Cook with me." Francesco waved me over to the counter.

"I don't *do* that," I joked as I made my way over to him.

"Tonight you will. Come on. Do it for me."

I quickly realized that Francesco wasn't strong enough to do this on his own, but that he wanted to make this memory. He wanted me to know how to make this dish we used to enjoy when we first fell in love, when we had nothing but each other. Francesco leaned his hip against the counter and instructed me while I placed slices of mozzarella between two pieces of bread, submerged it in egg wash and coated it in breadcrumbs. When I went to the stove to fry the sandwiches, Francesco rested his chin on my shoulder and his hands on my waist, like he was anchoring me there forever. When I flipped them over in the hot oil, he kissed my cheek. The golden sandwiches in the pan became a blur. I wanted to stay here forever, with his heart beating against my back, with his arms snug around me. Here, in this feeling of home I'd been forever chasing.

"There," I said once the food was done. "Now you can say I cooked for you."

"Now *you* can say you cooked for me."

I took a bite of the *carrozza* and held it up. "You can only have a bite."

Francesco took it out of my hand and set it down. He squeezed my hips and drew me toward him. "Let's go on the rooftop."

"It's freezing." But he didn't listen to my protests, so I followed him. When we lived in the apartment above Valenti's, we had enjoyed what was a typical Manhattan roof made of rusty pipes and soot. There, we'd lay out blankets and Francesco would pop in one of his opera tapes, and we'd listen to arias and pretend we could see the stars. Perhaps that was what drove us to transform our rooftop into this oasis in the middle of the city. Francesco settled on a lounge chair and opened one of his arms for me to snuggle next to him. I was grateful for the warmth of his body as I fanned some blankets over us. "We're not staying out here long. It's too cold for you."

Francesco looked up at the gray sky, unfazed by the temperature. I followed his gaze.

"I hate that we can't see the stars in the city," I said.

"But we know they're there," he pointed out. Francesco had always found wonderment amid the cosmos, but tonight, I saw something else written on his face. A fear of what might become of him beyond the confinements on this earth. This earth that was not as infinite as I liked to think it was. "Dream with me."

I rested my head on his chest, listening intently to the rhythm of his heartbeat. Slow and steady, still there, but quieter than I remembered. "Okay. Let's dream. You start."

He took a sharp inhale through his nose and said, "I want to get better."

"That's my dream too." We'd started out with our biggest dream of all. We had everything, but we had nothing if Francesco wasn't healthy. If he wasn't here. "What else?"

"I think when Pia graduates and goes off to college, we should let the kids use the Montauk house in the summer, and we should go to Italy each year."

"Listen to you, Mister Big Shot," I said. "Every year?"

"Every summer," he insisted.

"We'll go broke if we spend every summer on the Amalfi Coast."

"I didn't say the Amalfi Coast." Our laughter became part of New York's melody. "I just said Italy."

"Fine. Italy it is." I scooted my body up farther so our heads rested next to each other. He tore his gaze away from the invisible stars and looked at me. "What else?"

"Don't you want to chime in?"

"You're on a roll. Keep going."

"I want to take a road trip with you. A long one. We'll take turns listening to all our favorite songs, even though I can't really stand that Fleetwood Mac you love. I hate that hippy shit."

"I think what you hate is how I sing to it at the top of my lungs, extremely off-key."

"It's cute when you sing."

"Where do you want to drive to?"

"Maybe Florida. Or Nashville."

"Nashville?" When Francesco nodded, I giggled. "I'd pay to see you in cowboy boots."

"We would stick out like sore thumbs, wouldn't we?"

"Yeah. But we'd get some good laughs out of it. That's a funny dream."

Francesco shifted so his whole body faced mine. He smoothed my hair out of my face with his palm and cupped the back of my head. "I want to meet the woman Emilio decides to marry."

"You and me both. He's worse than you when you were young."

"I know. Which is why it'll be fascinating to see who he ends up with," Francesco explained. "And I want to walk Pia down the aisle."

Tears pressed against the backs of my eyes. "I can't wait to see that."

"I want to grow old with you," Francesco said with a tenderness that took my breath away. Tears climbed their way out of his eyes and I reached out to swipe them from his cheeks. "Older than I already am, that is. I want to see wrinkles form on your face."

I laughed through my tears. "I won't have any wrinkles. I'm gonna get Botox."

Soon, his laughter died down and a softness took him over. "I want to be one of those elderly couples who shuffle everywhere together and still kiss and hold hands. The kind other people look at and say, *Wow, they were made for each other.*"

I nodded as we both lost control of our emotions. "I dream of that, too."

"Come on," Francesco said. "You have to have one dream."

My mind was blank and racing all at once. I had a million dreams. So many, I couldn't keep up with the list. And yet, I could only think of one. "Next spring," I said through quivering lips, "I want to watch the flowers bloom with you."

"That's not a very big dream," he said.

"It is." I exhaled as cold suddenly enveloped me. "All I dream about is that you're here to see everything. The big moments, and the small ones too."

I savored Francesco's hug and committed every inch of it to memory. The way his arms felt strong and solid around my body, the way his hand felt against the fabric of my sweater as he rubbed circles on my back, the way his heart beat against my chest. The road we'd traveled thus far had been filled with bumps and wrong turns and wreckage, but it had only made our love so complex, so multi-layered, that I knew it was here to stay. We'd endured the toughest of years. When we'd turned our backs on each other, somehow, we redirected and found our way back to each other. We'd picked each other up when one was down, and though we were strong for each other, there was beauty in being able to fall apart together like we were right now. We'd seen every hue of each other and now the most beautiful colors shined through.

Francesco peered into my eyes, into my soul. I searched every millimeter of his face. How his left eye was more almond-shaped than his right. The little dimple situated in his right laugh line that didn't always show, but tonight, as his lips curved, it did. The two little brown beauty marks that fell just below his left cheekbone.

"I dream," Francesco started again, "of you knowing how deeply I regret hurting you all the times I did. You don't know how bad I wish I could go back and start from scratch with you."

"You don't have to dream of that," I told him. "I already know."

"When I'm gone ..." he started, but I closed my eyes and shook my head.

"No."

"I want to tell you what I want for you when I'm gone."

"No," I insisted, firmer this time. "Because then you'll think it's okay to leave me, and it's not." I took Francesco's face in my hands. "I love you," I whispered. My teeth chattered and the cold took my breath away. "I know we weren't perfect for a long time, but we always came back to each other. We always chose each other. And in a lot of ways, I think that means more than if everything had been easy. What we have now, we've earned it. Does that make sense?"

"It makes perfect sense." His expression remained serious, as if he were focusing on an important task. "But someday, I am going to leave you. Not because I want to, but because my heart's finally had enough. And when that day comes, I know you're going to be devastated. But I don't want you to stay that way. You've given me a beautiful life, Scarlett. You've raised two incredible children, and you've given all of us a family. You're our glue. I don't want you to fall apart when I'm not here anymore. I want to leave knowing you'll still be smiling. I don't want you to forget me," he said, his voice catching, "but I don't want you to be alone, either. So when it's time for you to move on with someone new, my only condition is this: they have to love you better than I did."

Ugly cries took me over, but I closed my eyes and shook my head. "Please stop."

"Just let me say this," he said softly, stroking my jaw with his thumb. "I don't know where we go after this, but I promise, wherever we end up, I'll find you there, too."

"We go to heaven," I forced myself to say. I wasn't ready to have that conversation yet. It was premature. "And you're not going there yet. You're not going anywhere. I need you here so we can go to Italy, and Nashville, and every other place on this earth you'd like to see, and so we can become decrepit old people together."

Francesco's face wrinkled with laughter. "God, I love you, Scarlett." He kissed me before burying his face in the crook of my neck, a place he fit as if it were molded just for him. Against my skin, he murmured, "You and me."

The very words he'd used when I was twenty-four years old and he'd asked me to be his girlfriend. *You and me and me and you.* Just like we'd always been. Just like I prayed we would always be fortunate enough to be. Nothing had ever made so much sense.

———

No matter how we fell asleep, we always woke up the same way. In each other's arms, either my head on his chest or his on mine. This morning, his face rested on my bosom, his curls sprawled across my skin. His hands rested on my shoulders. The house was still, quiet, other than Manhattan's soundtrack that always managed to bleed its way inside.

"Morning, honey," I murmured, my voice still groggy with sleep. I tore my gaze away from the window where the first bits of morning light peeked through. I raked my hands through his hair, but he didn't stir. *He must be exhausted,* I thought, until another possibility seized me.

"Fran?" My voice was sharp and tight as I glanced down at him. A chill slithered up my spine as I pressed my weight against him, trying to roll him onto his back. His head lolled slightly, but his eyes didn't open.

"Fran, wake up. This isn't funny."

My breath came faster when there was no response. I didn't press my fingers against his neck to check for a pulse. That would've been ridiculous, because he was alive. He was just in a really deep sleep.

"Francesco," I screamed. "Wake up. It's me."

But he didn't wake up. His face, that face that had been my home for two decades, remained still. Perfect. Peaceful. Like a cruel joke, as if he were only sleeping.

I sat back on my legs, my hands flying to my mouth as the air left my lungs.

"No," I whispered. "No, no, no. No."

I watched him, waiting for any flicker of life. A twitch of his fingers. A flutter of his eyelids. Something. Anything.

But there was nothing. I collapsed over him, smoothing his hair back, my body convulsing as sobs tore through me. He couldn't be gone. Francesco couldn't be gone.

Wasn't it only yesterday that I walked into his restaurant? Wasn't it only a few years ago that I walked down the aisle in a white gown and met him at the altar? It wasn't too long ago that we brought our babies into this world. Wasn't it only a mere few hours ago that my husband was still breathing?

"You can still come back," I pleaded, my voice young and raw and desperate. "Please come back. Please, Fran. We still need you."

I waited a few moments before I bent down and pressed my cheek against his, his skin still clinging to the last bits of warmth. My trembling finger snaked up the side of his neck, searching, pressing.

Nothing.

A sound erupted from me, guttural and wild. A scream so raw, it felt like it had been ripped from my innermost parts. I was falling out of my own body. Half of me was gone. Half of my heart had died.

Died.

The word lodged itself in my throat like a sharp piece of glass.

My eyes roamed over his face, that gorgeous, familiar face. Would time be cruel and erase the little nuances from my memory until he became a blur? My mind played tricks on me, flashing images like an old movie. The first time I met him. The first time he cooked for me. Our wedding. The quiet, secret smiles we used to share, the stupid things that used to make us laugh. The last six years of falling back in love with each other.

We had so much ahead of us, didn't we?

I rolled onto my side of the bed, my fingers numb as I reached for the phone. My fingers hovered over the buttons, poised to dial 9-1-1. If I called, they would come. If they came, it would be real. But it was real, whether I was ready to face it or not. I didn't ask for a paramedic to try and revive the unsavable; I just asked for a coroner to confirm what I already knew. Then, with shaking fingers, I pressed the call button again. Ten digits whose sequence I knew by heart.

Enzo answered on the first ring. I opened my mouth to speak, but no words came. Only a choked, broken sound.

There was rustling on the other end. A sharp inhale.

In the silence that stretched from his line to mine, he knew. He didn't ask. He didn't need to. All we exchanged was thick, unbearable *nothing* until I heard a click. The line went dead.

I sat there, staring at nothing, having lost everything, listening to the heavy, hollow quiet that I'd grow to hate, that I'd masterfully learn to drown out. Though my time with Francesco had come to an end, my time alone with his body would soon be over, too. I lay next to him and cradled his head in my hands. How desperately I wished for one more second with him. One last chance to tell him, really tell him, how I felt about him. How I wished I could explain to him that he was absolutely everything to me; why else had he consumed my whole life?

"Things were just getting good," I whispered. "We were just getting to the good part, weren't we?" I paused as if I were waiting for him to answer me. Salty, wet tears fell to my lips. "I wasn't a perfect wife, but I loved you, Francesco. I'll always love you. Always," I promised one last time, as if it mattered. As if he could hear me. But he couldn't.

As I traced his face with my fingertips and whispered, "You and me," over and over, as my heart began to crack in ways I didn't know it could break, it hit me. He had left me for good, and he'd left me longing for all that could have been.

～

AT THE RISK OF looking, and sounding, like a lunatic, I banged my fist against Enzo's door.

Two weeks.

Two weeks had passed since we buried my husband beneath a gray sky that poured out rain as if the earth, too, were grieving the loss of Francesco Valenti. Two weeks since I collapsed next to my husband's casket, my kneecaps sinking into the wet soil beside his burial site; since I screamed a scream that I felt like no one could hear. Since I turned my head at the precise moment Enzo was speeding away from the gravesite, as if he couldn't bear to watch his brother be permanently laid to rest. Two weeks, since fans lined the streets of Little Italy, mourning a man they never truly knew.

In those two weeks, I hadn't heard a peep from Enzo. I'd called to no avail. I'd sent him three maniacal letters, to which he hadn't responded. No one from our staff had been able to make contact with him. It was like he had vanished. I was so, so angry with him for disappearing like this.

I was also incredibly worried.

After what felt like minutes of waiting, I banged again, harder, my knuckles going white. I considered breaking in; we were family. I could have gotten away with it. But then, by some stroke of luck, Enzo opened the door. But he didn't look like the Enzo I'd known for twenty years.

He was dressed in a stained T-shirt and lived-in gray sweatpants. His eyes were puffy and bloodshot. His hair was too long and it stuck out in all different directions. Black facial hair clung to his jawline, something I'd never seen on him before. I opened my mouth to yell, to demand an explanation, but his expression was cold. Vacant. I recognized it because I'd been wearing that look myself.

Grief. The kind that's like an anchor, latching onto you, dragging you down to the sea's floor where there's no light at all.

He looked like he was about to close the door in my face. Before he could, I shoved my arm against it and wedged my way inside.

"I've been trying to get a hold of you," I said.

"I'm not in the mood to talk."

"Too bad." I closed the door behind me, but before I could say anything else, the state of Enzo's apartment stopped me in my tracks. The kitchen counter was covered with takeout containers, empty liquor bottles, dirty glasses, and ashtrays mounded with cigarette butts. As my gaze swept over the rest of his apartment, my heart sank. Boxes. Lots of them.

There was not a knickknack to be seen, not a picture frame on a shelf. The walls were stripped bare. This wasn't an apartment anymore. It was a hotel room waiting for his next guest. I'd come here with a plan, rehearsed words, maybe even hope. But the boxes surrounding us whispered a warning, that this day most certainly wouldn't go as planned.

"Enzo, what's going on?" I asked, my throat closing.

My eyes were locked on the boxes. On the life he was so clearly packing up.

"Enzo," I snapped, sharp as a whip. "What the hell is this?"

He pressed his palms against the counter, his fingers splayed wide. He hinged back on his hips, exhaling slow, deliberate. "What does it look like to you?"

I slammed my purse onto the counter. Hard. Then, I marched up to him, grabbing his bicep, my nails dinging into his skin.

"Twenty years I've known you, Enzo. Twenty years. You owe me an explanation."

He laughed, a reaction I couldn't quite believe. The sound stopped me cold. It wasn't the humorous kind, but the kind that sounded like ice.

"I *owe* you?"

His words were laced with animosity, and they hung between us, their sharp edges cutting me. Something had shifted, and I didn't understand what or how. A strange sensation clawed its way into my gut, like I was standing in front of a stranger. Like Enzo wasn't Enzo anymore.

I stepped back, dizzy and disoriented. From the confusion. From my pulse slamming against my ribs. From the way Enzo was looking at me, so cold and detached, like he was already gone.

"Enzo." His name came out like a plea. Like a prayer. "I just buried my husband. I'm barely keeping things together for my kids. You can't leave me. You can't. I need you."

He nodded, his face parted by a vicious smile. "I *know.* That's what I've always been to you, right? Your backup guy. The one you call when you've got nothing and no one. I'm the thing you fall back on when your plans don't pan out, right?"

"No," I said, but it sounded like a question. I kept backing up, and Enzo kept coming toward me. "I don't know what's going on, but just please, calm down. We can talk about this. You don't have to leave."

"Oh, but I do." He dug his hands into his pockets and shrugged his shoulders to his earlobes. "Call me crazy, but I'd like to be more than that to someone."

"You are more than that to me." My hands flew to the top of my head. "God, Enzo, you're everything to me."

That laugh again. It sent a shiver down my spine. "Wake up, sweetheart. No, I'm not."

"You saved me," I started. "You've been there for me more than anyone else in my life. You listen to me, and you've cried with me—"

"I'm a selfish bastard, Scarlett." He nodded quickly, like he was reaffirming the notion to himself. "I always have been. I'm still the same guy I was who fucked around on my wife every chance I got. The guy who chose to spend nights in fancy hotel rooms with random women instead of being home with my kids."

"I know you. Better than anyone. And you're not that person."

"I am. Because what other kind of man spends twenty godforsaken years trying to win over his own brother's wife?"

A lump formed in my throat. I reached for the edge of the countertop. I didn't know where this was going, but I knew I didn't like it.

"I've had a lot of time to think these last two weeks, and I realized something. I realized I'm never gonna be enough for you, Scarlett."

"Enzo—"

"If I had been, you would've chosen me. You never would've married him in the first place."

"That's not true," I said, but my voice was small and unconvincing. "I didn't have a choice. I was already engaged. I couldn't break his heart. And you were still tied up with Claudia."

"I was as good as free, and if you really loved me, if you weren't so *blinded* by the life you thought my brother could give you ..." He paused, mere inches from me now. "You would. Have chosen. Me."

"I wanted to. And I know I've hurt you. I know you've given me more than I've given you. But only because I couldn't. I couldn't give you what I wanted to give you, and I couldn't be what I wanted to be to you."

"It doesn't matter." His hot breath was on my skin as he tucked a lock of hair behind my ear. Did he still feel the electricity between us? "Because I'm not going to do this anymore. I've put my life on hold for you long enough, Scarlett. I can't keep being something you use and throw away when you remember why you chose him. Why he's so much better than me."

"He's *gone*," I reminded him.

"He was your first choice. And whether he's here or in a pine box, he always will be."

We stared at each other. Nothing but our shaky breath filled the air between us. I wanted to dig my claws into him and tear him apart until I found the old Enzo. The one I'd known and loved for two decades. He had to be in there still. Just as I'd lost Francesco only to find him again, I could dig out the old Enzo and resuscitate him.

"Please, Enzo, you can't leave. You're so special to me. You have no idea how much you mean to me. You're—"

You're my daughter's father. I wanted to say it, but I didn't have the nerve. My eyes darted over to the counter, where my good old cognac-colored Birkin bag was perched. My plan came back to me, to give him the letter I'd written fourteen years prior. Francesco was gone. The truth wouldn't kill anyone now. Maybe if I gave him the letter now, it would change everything. Maybe it would make him stay. Maybe he'd finally understand my actions and choices.

But instead, I let anger get the best of me. If he wanted to punish me for the way I'd hurt him and made him feel like second best, so be it. If he wanted to leave, I'd let him have at it.

"Fine," I said, the single syllable echoing in his empty apartment. "You want to leave? Leave."

He opened his arms wide, like a maestro closing a show. "There's the reaction I expected."

"You're going to regret this," I yelled as I stomped over to the counter and grabbed my purse, willing myself to hold back my tears until I was out of his sight.

"My whole life is one big regret," he tossed back.

I whipped around on my heel. My chest heaved and adrenaline coursed through my veins. Adrenaline, and anger, and regret, and love and longing, and all the things I'd always felt for Enzo.

"You know what you're doing?" I raised my voice, pointing at him. "You're running. You run every time things get real. So my marriage didn't make any sense and I stayed anyway. That was my choice. I didn't tell you to put your life on hold for me. I didn't stop you from falling in love with someone else. You chose this. You chose to stay hung up on me all these years, and now that I'm finally available, you're terrified. And what doesn't make sense to me, Enzo, is that you have no reason to be. I'm the only woman who's ever truly loved you. And you want to break my heart on purpose?" As if I were sprinting, I couldn't catch my breath. "Mark my words, Enzo," I said, unsure where the promise I was about to make came from, "if you run this time, that's it. I will never, and I mean *never*, speak to you again."

He started our period of silence right then and there. He ushered me toward the door and slammed it behind me the moment my feet hit the hallway carpet. As soon as I was separated from him by so much more than a flimsy door, panic set in. I wanted to take it all back, to trap that horrible promise in my throat before it had the chance to escape. This couldn't be how we ended.

But more than an ending, it was a beginning.

The beginning of my life without the Valenti brothers in it.

CHAPTER TWENTY-FIVE

SCARLETT

Summer, 2011

My sandals scrape against the tile floor, the sound hollow beneath the vaulted ceilings. I'm in no shape to be in a church; surely, God must find my smoke-scented, baggy sweatsuit an abomination. But something has drawn me here. After Enzo drove off with my children, the firefighters walked me through the final steps of their investigation. I was numb as they confirmed their suspicions about the origin of the fire, and I felt nothing when they restricted access to what used to be my house with a row of yellow caution tape. As their loud engines headed down Old Montauk Highway, I took one last look at the scene of destruction before mindlessly unlocking Emilio's truck, hopping in, and heading to St. Therese.

I had no place else to go.

I slip into the front pew, staring ahead at a statue of the Blessed Mother. Her face is serene, untouched by fire, unscarred by ruin. Unlike me. I know she, and the other statues surrounding her, are nothing more than inanimate figurines, but I can feel them watching me. I'm not alone here and that fact alone calms my racing heart. Church is a place that welcomes both saints and sinners in tandem, and today, I'm most certainly the latter. I lower the kneeler and sink onto it. I know every Catholic prayer by heart, but only two words come to mind.

Help me.

I close my eyes, inhaling the scent of old wood, melted wax, and incense. I don't know how long I sit there, hands clasped, head bowed, unable to pray. My mind is stuck somewhere between last night and this morning, frozen. Maybe it's because there's nothing left to say. I have no more secrets to keep. I have no one left to protect. I've lost total control of everything I've been holding onto, and I have no idea what to do next.

A voice cuts through the silence. "Scarlett?"

I open my eyes, blinking against the dim light overhead. "Father Tom," I say, sitting back into the pew. "Hi."

He adjusts his rimless glasses on the bridge of his nose. "Everything alright?"

I glance down at my clothes. Are they the giveaway? Or is something written on my face that denotes how utterly broken I am? "Not really."

I slide over and, after a brief hesitation, I nod and he joins me in the pew. I expect him to fill the silence. To offer some priestly reassurance, some wisdom wrapped in a flowery scripture. But no words are exchanged. Instead, a heavy silence settles between us, like the lack of sound is anticipating something. He sits beside me, hands folded in his lap, waiting.

And soon, I can't take it anymore. I feel every ounce of the weight of what I've done and what I've been carrying. I feel the places I'm bruised and broken from bearing this burden for eighteen years. I know it's time. Time to release it.

"Bless me, Father, for I have sinned," I say. My body trembles, but my voice is sure. I stare straight ahead at the altar, unable to look at him. "It's been two months since my last confession." I exhale, shaking my head. "I … I've been keeping a secret. A big one. For eighteen years. And I need to confess it, Father."

Finally, I look at him. His face is expectant though free of any judgement. I'm safe. I can do this.

"What sins have you to confess?" Father Tom proceeds with the standard confessional dialogue.

My throat constricts, my body making one last desperate effort to keep my sins buried. My hands are cold, curled into fists in my lap. I steel myself to go on.

"Enzo," I start. At his name alone, I'm undone. "You remember him, right? You called him the *dark one*," I remind Father. He nods. "I was twenty-three when I met Enzo and Francesco. I met Enzo first, actually. Enzo was married at the time, to a woman named Claudia." I glance at the lifeless statue of the Blessed Mother. "He and I had an affair. It only lasted a few months, but it was very intense. He was my first love. Eventually, he broke things off with me. He was trying to do the right thing by his family. I was brokenhearted, Father. I loved him. But then, months later, I started seeing Francesco. It was a completely different experience. I thought he was the one I could build a real future with. And so, I married him. And I thought that was the end of me and Enzo forever."

I meet Father Tom's eyes and hold my breath.

"But it wasn't." I exhale, sinking back into the pew. My guards fall away. "Francesco became very famous, very fast, right after we got married. It changed him. I didn't know I was being abused at the time, but I was. Verbally. Emotionally. And one time, physically. I was completely isolated, and I turned to the wrong person. I turned to Enzo." I ram my eyes shut. I can't catch a deep enough breath, and my heart feels like it'll never slow down. "I slept with him. I cheated on my husband. It was one night. And that one night gave me my daughter, Pia." I open my eyes, but I keep my gaze fixed on my hands in my lap. "I found out Enzo was her father right after she was born. Only my mother and my best friend knew. I lied to Francesco. I kept it from Enzo. I never planned on telling my kids. But now," I say, lifting my gaze, "now the truth is out. Everyone knows. And they all hate me for what I've done, just like I knew they would."

Finally, the dam breaks. The altar blurs before me. "But it's more than that, Father. Enzo and I were so much more than that one night. I always loved him. *Always.* Even when I was faithful to Francesco, part of me still belonged to Enzo. I couldn't let him go. But I tried. I put all of myself into my husband and my kids and keeping our family together. But no matter what I did, I still had this tie to Enzo. Still do. And I can't forgive myself. For any of it."

His fingers lace together, resting them lightly against his knees. His chin tilts up, ever so slightly, studying me. "How do you see yourself, Scarlett?"

I scoff. "If you'd asked me that a few days ago, I would've had a completely different answer."

He motions toward me, patient. "And now?"

My gaze drops to the floor. The air conditioning hums, a cool gust washing over me. "I'm a complete and total fraud." And all at once, I want to be honest. It's a completely new feeling, one I want to experience in its entirety. I've been avoiding his gaze, but now, I meet his eyes, like if I don't, the words won't count. "I've spent most of my life pretending. No—lying. Not just to other people, but to myself. I tell myself I'm not as horrible as my actions say I am. But I am. I'm a woman who was selfish and wanted things I shouldn't have wanted. I love someone I never should have loved. I say I'd do anything to protect my family, but I've betrayed them in an unimaginable way. I'm a cheater. A liar. An adulteress. I try to make everything beautiful—my home, my restaurant, my kids, and myself—as if beauty could somehow cover up the ugliness inside of me. I pretend and pretend, not just so others will think I'm someone I'm not, but so I won't have to face who I really am. I hate myself, Father. I hate that I've hurt the people I love the most."

I lean back in the pew and lick a salty tear from my lip. "And here I've thought myself a martyr all this time. You believe that? I look at my life like it's one big sacrifice. And it's not. I didn't deny myself happiness. I stayed in a life where I could hide. There's nowhere left to hide, now, though."

Father Tom waits a beat before speaking. "You're ashamed."

I cross one leg over the other and kick my foot back and forth. "Yeah." I draw in a sharp inhale. "I've committed some pretty unforgivable sins."

"Believing your sins to be unforgivable is an act of pride," he tells me. Great. Yet another sin. "And shame? That's the devil's language. He uses it to make us forget that God made us in His image. That His blood washes away our sins. All of them, Scarlett. Even the ones that look unforgiveable to us."

"I don't understand how that's possible."

"None of us can fathom the mystery of salvation. Of God's mercy and grace. We don't deserve it, but He gives it to us freely, anyway. His love for us is unconditional. It's not something we can or have to earn. He's our Father. You're His *daughter*."

He says the word *daughter* with such emphasis, I feel a zing in my chest, like the whole point of my faith is just now hitting me at the ripe age of forty-nine.

"You have a daughter," Father Tom continues. "Isn't it safe to say that no matter what choices she makes, you'll still love her? That you'll always forgive her?"

"No matter what."

Father Tom's mouth curves into an endearing smile. "You see where I'm going with this." But his smile fades, softening into something deeper. "This might seem like a strange question, but why did you cheat on your husband?"

Tears sting my eyes. "I just wanted to feel loved."

"And if your daughter came to you with the same set of circumstances, with that same reason, would you have compassion on her? Might you understand her?"

Tears freely falling now, I nod. And suddenly, it clicks. If I, a flawed human being, would have compassion on my own child, how much more might my Maker have on me?

"You see, we think we have to be perfect," Father Tom explains. "To live up to God's standards. But what we actually need to do is lean on God *because* we're not perfect. If we were, we wouldn't need Him. But we're not. We can't be. And He knows this. That's why he sent His only son. For the liars and the cheaters and the adulterers, for all us sinners, and that's what we all are, Scarlett. Not one of us on this earth is free from sin. But when we confess and turn away from our sin, which you've done, that's when we are forgiven. The Lord doesn't want you to live in shame. He faced death so we could know freedom. He's done His part. You have to do yours."

"Which is?"

"You have to forgive yourself. Through Christ, we can all be redeemed. We're so much more than the sum of our mistakes."

I receive my penance, that I must pray, not for forgiveness, but to believe I am forgiven. Father Tom departs, leaving me alone in the sanctuary. I abandon my pew and instead, kneel directly before the Blessed Mother statue in silent reverence. I mull over Father Tom's question. How do I see myself? Who am I now that the secret is out? Now that my children know who I am? Now that Enzo's view of me is completely wrecked?

Just yesterday, I would've rattled off how caring and nurturing I am. How I'm a good listener. Compassionate. Loving. Generous. Today? I think myself a fool, that I could keep such an obvious truth hidden. But perhaps therein lays the conundrum, that I'm not just one side of the coin. Maybe I am both selfish and giving. I've been a cheat and a faithful woman. I'm many things all at once; maybe no human is entirely good or evil. Because I'm not entirely one thing, this I can now see with my veil of lies lifted.

True is what I want to be from now on. No matter the shame or guilt or regrets I've carried, no matter what difficult path lays before me to find healing with my family. As the heaviness in my chest starts to lift, I know that, from here on out, I can only be my authentic self. The ugly, the beautiful, the everything in between.

No, I'm not perfect. It's time I stop pretending to be.

JULIE WAS WAITING FOR me when I got back to my Manhattan home. I'd used the phone in the church office—my cell phone was destroyed in the fire. When I walked in, she had a martini ready for me and a pack of cigarettes on the coffee table. But now, as we lounge on the sofa, my legs curled beneath me, both vices remain untouched. They can't fix me. They can't numb me. But more, I don't want to be numbed anymore. I'm home now, and I'm done running.

Julie, on the other hand, has had a glass of wine in her hand since I got back, and she takes short sips every time I reveal a new bit of information. About my romantic night with Enzo, that feels like it was a hundred years ago. How he had to open his bedroom window, bust the screen, how we narrowly escaped breaking our necks as we jumped down to the deck. The way Pia physically recoiled from me, how Emilio left wearing a veil of heartbreak and confusion. By the time I tell her about my confession to Father Tom, she has to refill her glass.

"*Madonna mia,*" she mutters, taking a long sip. "That's why you're not drinking. You need a pill to deal with all of this."

"I haven't taken Xanax since before Pia's birthday party."

"You're a new woman."

I do feel new. I'm not entirely comfortable in this newness, but the shift has happened, and now I have to learn to live with it. I pick at my chipped nails, red nail polish falling to my lap. "I think I held on so tight because I knew one day it would come out. The truth always comes out. I was kidding myself."

"Oh, honey." She reaches over and squeezes my hand. "Just because she's Enzo's doesn't take away what she had with Francesco. He raised her. And he adored her."

"I know he did. But that doesn't make up for the fact that I lied."

"Can I ask you something?"

I purse my lips and raise my brows. "If I say no, will that stop you?"

She cracks a laugh before her expression turns serious. "Did you want to tell Enzo? Never mind Francesco's feelings. I'm talking about *you* right now. If you could go back to when Pia was born, would you have told him?"

It's a big question, and we both know it. Our eyes lock as I imagine what life might've looked like if I'd told the truth from the start. If I'd chosen honesty instead of the picture-perfect life I thought I was supposed to build.

I nod before I even register the motion. Tears spill from my eyes. "I would've told them both. Not so I could've been with Enzo instead. But so they could've decided what they wanted. If Fran wanted to leave me, if we would've stayed together but been honest, or even if they wanted to keep it a secret, I wouldn't have been the one holding all the cards. That's what I regret most. I'm sure my daughter feels like her whole life's a lie. And I know Enzo's thinking about all the years we can't get back. I love them more than I can explain, and I hate that I was selfish enough to do this to them."

"You were just doing your best," Julie says.

The softness of her voice is a reminder of my conversation with Father Tom. Of my prayers that followed. *Forgive yourself.* No, I can't excuse what I did, but I can have compassion on the thirty-year-old I was back then. A woman in survival mode.

"But I wouldn't take back my marriage with Francesco," I say. "We had a lot of bad, and I know the bad is easier to remember than the good. But I do still remember the good. I remember the beginning."

"God, so do I."

We exchange a sentimental smile, thinking back to the days when we were girls, when we had no idea what was ahead of us. But now, sitting in this house where my husband spent the last night of his life, I remember the end, too. "I still miss him sometimes."

"You spent half your life with him, honey, for better or worse. Of course you do."

A sad smile tugs at my lips as I swipe tears from beneath my eyes.

"I know this is so dumb, but he never could get into the habit of using the key hook by the front door. He'd come in, step out of his shoes, and just drop everything in a pile. His messenger bag, his chef's coat, his keys. As soon as he'd come in, I'd start cleaning up after him." I close my eyes and shake my head, the image still vivid in my mind's eye. "It used to irritate me. But sometimes I feel this ache in my chest. Like I wish he'd walk in that front door just so I could clean up after him one last time. I know that's silly."

Julie's eyes search my face, her head tilting ever so slightly. "It's not silly, Scarlett. You loved him. And when you love someone and spend as many years with them as you did with Fran, those become the things that stick out. Those weird, little quirks. I know you have this big, passionate romance with Enzo, but what you had with Fran counts, too."

For what feels like the first time all day, I exhale. "That's exactly it."

She smiles, but it's not a normal smile. It's one of relief. As if she's been waiting for this moment longer than I have. And as we stare at each other, I finally understand why.

I've let go.

Not in a reckless way, of giving into my desires. But in the way of releasing control. I can't change the past. I don't get a redo. I can't rewrite history no matter how much I pretend, and that's okay.

I can't control the future. And that's okay, too.

Laughing through my tears, Julie draws me into a hug that reaffirms what I've always known. No matter what happens, no matter where I go, she is with me. I don't know what tomorrow will bring. I don't know how I'm going to regain the trust of my children. I don't know if Enzo and I will ever speak again. I don't know if I'll be able to save my restaurant from extinction. But right now, I have my best friend, and it's all I need.

"Let's go for a ride," I suggest, wiping my face dry with my fingertips.

"Where?" Julie asks, setting her wine glass down with a chime.

"Anywhere. Nowhere."

She stands, grabs her keys, and swings them around her index finger. "Off we go."

And so, we zigzag our way all around Manhattan, no destination in mind, arms waving through the sunroof. The city is a haze of streetlights and billboards as we sing and scream along to Fleetwood Mac and Madonna, the sounds of our youth that evaded me like a balloon I wasn't ready to let go of, the timelines of then and now blurring as if they're one. Because us girls grow into women, but deep down, us women are always the girls we used to be.

CHAPTER TWENTY-SIX

SCARLETT

Summer, 2011

It takes a week to replace my driver's license and cell phone, both lost in the fire. But the days stretch like an eternal span of nothingness. I still haven't heard from the kids or Enzo, and the pit of worry in my stomach is starting to eat at me. I'd originally thought some space might be good for all of us. But have I let too much time pass so that their hearts are now forever hardened?

I press the end button on my Blackberry for the umpteenth time, my thumb starting to go raw. The kids' phones go straight to voicemail, but Enzo is simply ignoring me. I picture him, wherever he is, watching my name light up his screen as he watches the phone ring. Frustrated, I navigate to the messaging app and type away.

Scarlett: I just want to know where the kids are. As you can imagine, I'm worried sick.

My heart thuds as I wait for the response I hope he'll give me. He knows what kind of mother I am. I bite one of my nails down to the stub while I wait. Finally, a chime. I've never been so happy to receive a text. But his answer is curt and to the point. Two words.

Enzo: Emilio's place.

Scarlett: And where are you?

I wait, biting another nail in the interim. But soon, I realize he's not going to reply. I push myself up from my vanity. I don't think. I don't wonder what I'll say when I get there. I just grab my bag, hail a cab Uptown, and go to my babies.

Standing outside of Emilio's door, my courage wanes. I have no idea what awaits me. I don't know if they're home, if he'll let me in, or if they'll demand I leave and never speak to them again. I press my palm against the wood door, as if I can somehow silently communicate to them that I'm here. My hand clenches into a fist, poised to knock, but then I remember I have a key. I dig it out of my purse, the metal cold against my skin. Do I still have the right to do this? To let myself into my son's world without question, when I've spent a lifetime keeping him out of mine? The lump in my throat lodges deeper, but I push the key in and turn the lock.

I tiptoe inside, like I'm somewhere I shouldn't be, rather than my son's apartment that's leased in my name. The place is quiet, save for the low hum of the TV in front of the sofa. Large windows bathe the room in light, exposing the empty bags of potato chips and soda cans that pepper every surface.

I take it, from the silence, that neither of my children is here.

"Mom?" Emilio's voice says otherwise. There's an edge to the way he says *Mom,* but I'm too relieved to see him to care.

"Emi." I rush toward him, but I stop myself. Every muscle that makes up my body aches to draw him into a vigorous hug and never let him go. But I stand there, holding back.

This isn't about me. It's about them.

"Is Pia here, too?" I ask.

He answers by pointing to his bedroom door.

"Please," I say. "You don't have to say a word. All I ask is that you listen."

His nostrils flare. He towers over me and for the first time maybe ever, I feel small in front of my son. He's a man now. Maybe he's decided he's had enough of me. But then, he puts his hand on my back and steers me toward his bedroom, opening the door for us.

The room is like a cave bathed in darkness. Emilio flicks on the light, and Pia groans as the stark brightness washes over her. And then she sees me.

We stare at each other. It's impossible not to notice the little differences in her. How unruly and stringy her black hair is. The sharpness to her eyes. The pouty frown of her lips. How tired she looks, compared to her usual fresh-faced state. The room is in disarray, no doubt a mirror to how she must feel inside. I stand there, adjusting the sleeve of my Lululemon jacket, unsure of what to do with myself.

"Pia, sweetheart—"

But Pia raises her palms and her eyebrows and cuts me off. "Save it. I'm never speaking to you again, so you can leave."

Emilio flops down on the edge of the bed and gives his sister a pointed look. "*You* save it. Let's just hear her out."

I'm grateful. Grateful, and in a rush, like my son might change his mind at any given moment and turn me away. I let my handbag slip to the floor and I lower myself onto the edge of the bed, facing them both. As if their heartbeats are a part of mine, I can feel their anticipation. Their fear and worry and wonderment. All I want to do is fix everything.

All I can do is be honest.

"I'm so sorry." The words hang in the air. "I know that's not nearly enough. I'm not going to pretend I know how you feel, because I don't. But I do know what it's like to wake up one day and realize the life you've been living wasn't the truth. And I know I'm the reason for that. I'm sure you're angry, hurt, and confused, and you probably feel like you don't know who I really am. And you're right. You don't. Not all of me, at least. I know apologizing isn't going to fix anything, but I want you to know how sorry I am for not telling you the truth. All of you."

I draw in a deep breath and go back to the beginning. "Daddy and I always told you two a fairytale version of our love story. That when I went to work at his restaurant, we fell in love at first sight. That's only partially true. Daddy did fall in love with me as soon as he met me. And I fell in love at first sight, too. But not with him." I focus my gaze on the stack of gold bracelets that live on my right arm, feeling the familiar burn of shame. "I fell in love with Enzo."

I feel them both staring at me, and somehow, I find the courage to look at them and go on.

"He was married at the time, to Zia Claudia. But that didn't stop me. Us. We were crazy about each other. He was miserable in his marriage, and I was desperate to get away from Grandma and her drinking and start my own life. But after a few months, it ended. Enzo went back to Claudia, and he left me completely brokenhearted. Months later, Daddy and I started seeing each other. It was so different. Calm. Normal. Sweet. He was so thoughtful and attentive to me. We wanted the same things out of life. A family and a business, and we wanted to do it all together. So I married him. I married him thinking we'd always be so in love and in sync. And for a while we were. Until he became famous.

"You both read in that letter that Daddy hit me." At this, they exchange a loaded glance. I wonder how many times, if at all, they've discussed it. "Once. When you were little," I say to Emilio. "I told myself it wasn't a big deal. That I could get over it. I thought staying made me a strong woman and a great mother. Francesco loved being famous. It changed him, but I was holding out hope that he might come back down to earth. I still wanted the life he promised me. The life we were building. For a while, I pushed it down and numbed myself with vodka and tried not to think about how *different* everything was between us. All until one night." I draw in a jagged, shaky breath and say, "One night with Enzo."

Gnawing on her bottom lip, Pia looks away. Emilio doesn't. His cheeks are flushed, his discomfort evident, but he keeps his eyes fixed on me.

"It wasn't premeditated," I explain. "It wasn't right. But it wasn't meaningless either. That night gave me you, Pia, and that's why I'll never take it back. I can't regret it."

She whips her head around to look at me. "So you cheated with … with Enzo to pay Daddy back for hitting you? I'm a mistake," she cries. "I'm the result of some sort of revenge scheme."

"No, you're not," I whisper. I inch closer and rest my palm on her arm. "Neither of you have experienced this yet, but someday, you'll look into the eyes of a stranger, and you'll recognize them. It'll feel like you've known them in this lifetime and every lifetime before it. They're the missing piece that completes you, as cliché as that sounds, that's the only way to describe it. Enzo is that person for me. I have a connection with him that I can't even begin to explain, and that's what you're a result of."

I reach for Emilio's hand, so that all three of us are intertwined.

"Cheating is a sin. So is lying. I made an absolute mess of everything, but for some reason, God still gave me a gift in the midst of it all." I look into my daughter's eyes and say, "He gave me you. I always say I love you so much it hurts, and that's because every time I look at you, both of you, I feel like my heart's going to explode. I didn't have a perfect relationship with Francesco or Enzo. But I got you two. And you two are my life."

"Just, stop," Pia huffs, tears spilling from her eyes. "You make it sound like it was some kind of destiny."

"You are," I tell her gently. "You wouldn't be you if you weren't ours, and I wouldn't trade you for the world."

"And you were just never going to tell me? Tell any of us? Do you know how *crushed* Emi is? And I can't even talk about Enzo. He *cried*. You made a grown man *cry*."

She's still holding my hand; that's my only solace. I rub my thumb back and forth across her palm.

"I didn't know how to handle it, Pia. I was so scared. I was scared Daddy would leave me and divorce seemed so terrifying to me. I was scared he'd take Emilio. I thought if anyone found out, I'd lose everything. So I lied, to everyone, all the time, thinking I was protecting everyone. I thought I was lying out of love, doing what was best for you, not realizing I was doing what was best for me. The lie got so big, it seemed impossible to tell the truth. That day on the beach, when the three of you walked away from me, my biggest fear came true. I lost you. I lost your trust. I built our family and your lives on my lies and mistakes and all I wanted to do was rewind time and tell the truth.

"I always call you two my babies," I say, my eyes flicking to Emilio. "But you're all grown up now, and I want you to learn from my mistakes, so you don't have to go out and make them yourself. So your daughters, and their daughters don't. I don't want you to do things for the wrong reasons, and I don't want you to spend your life pleasing others. And yes, that includes me. The reason I want you to go to college is so you can have time to figure out who you are and what you want out of life, and whatever that is, that's what I want you to go after. I want you to have the chance to make the selfish decisions I never got to make, because I settled down so young and took on adult responsibilities when I was still a girl. I hope you end up with someone who gives you butterflies every time they walk through the door. Maybe I had to suffer so you wouldn't have to, and I'd do it all again if I had to. I'd do anything for you two. You're worth my everything."

Emilio's eyes sting with tears that don't fall. I want to pry into that mind of his and understand where he's at, but Pia speaks up, with two words that gain our full attention.

"My voice."

"What about it?" I ask.

"Is that why you pushed me into singing? So I'd bond with … him?" Pia says, unable to call Francesco *Daddy*.

"I …" I hesitate. Because on the one hand, Pia's talent has always been so undeniable, there was no way it wasn't going to be a huge part of her life. But on the other hand, I remember how relieved I was the first time I heard that pitch-perfect, gaudy voice. I knew it would be her tie to Francesco. I swallow hard, settling into the truth. "That's why I pushed it harder than dance."

"I sang for *him*, Mom," she says, shaking. "All that time, all those years, every performance. Studying music theory and making adjustments to my placement and rehearsing scales until I reached a new note. Hours listening to Maria Callas, trying to memorize the nuances in her voice. Watching Pavarotti concerts on TV when I really just wanted to watch *Lizzie McGuire*. It was all for him, to get him to love me. To pay attention to me. And all that time, Enzo was there. I wasted all that time trying to impress the wrong person."

I shake my head, barely. "No you didn't. Nothing about your life has been a waste. Enzo might be your father, but Francesco adored you, Pia. They both did. But I...I know my fears and my mistakes shaped your life. And from here on out, both of you, I don't want that to be the case anymore. I just want you to be *you*. Whatever that means and whatever that looks like."

But Pia's face crumples, her cheeks burning red. She shakes her head vehemently before exploding into tears. Whether she wants me or not, I'm still her mother. I wrap my arms around her and hold her tight. "What is it, babydoll?" She hiccups more cries as I rub circles on her back.

"I just keep thinking about him hitting you. I don't know how you could've stayed with him, Mom. Weren't you scared?"

"Yeah, weren't you?" Emilio chimes in. He stands and paces in front of the bed, washing his face with his palm. "Why the *fuck* would you stay? If Dad hit you, and you were in love with Zio Enzo, why didn't you two just break up?"

His anger spills out from his pores. It's tangible and overwhelming, permeating the space between us. I wait until his eyes find mine before I speak.

"Because you were a little boy who loved and needed his father," I tell him. "And that doesn't make me a martyr. That makes me a mother. I would *die* for you, Emilio. And when I say that, I mean it. Maybe I wasn't happy, but I made the choice I thought was best for you. And I'd do it all over again in a heartbeat. All I want is for you two to be happy."

"That's the problem, Ma," Emilio says, still pacing, talking with his hands now. "You want us to be happy? We'd like to see you be happy, too. I didn't even remember what that looked like until Zio Enzo showed up in Montauk a few weeks ago. I couldn't remember the last time I heard you really laugh or saw you with a genuine smile until he came back. At least I know why now."

I hold my breath. Pia does the same. Emilio's temper rarely flares, and when it does, it's for a reason.

"I'm angry, Ma," he continues, "because you could've been *that* all my life if you'd made a different choice. You don't think we saw through it? You don't think we heard you and Dad fighting? You don't think I remember when you ran off to Italy by yourself and you told me it was just because you lost the baby? You don't think we always felt like you were making up for all the ways he wasn't there for us? I love him." In an act of surrender, Emilio opens his arms wide. "Miss the guy like crazy. But that doesn't change the fact that he wasn't the greatest father. And you …" His arms fall as his eyes focus in on me with pity. "That's why you hold onto us so tight. Because for so long, you were all we had, and we were all you had. That's why you can't let go of us. That's why you can't let go of *me*."

His final words puzzle me. "Let go of you?"

Emilio and Pia exchange a glance. Pia gives him an encouraging nod. He pinches the bridge of his nose and closes his eyes.

"I don't want to be a lawyer, Mom. I've never wanted to be a lawyer. I've wanted to cook for as long as I can remember, but every time I tried to bring it up, you would either shoot me down or change the subject. After a while, I just gave up. *Pretended* I was okay with giving up my dream." He gives me a sharp glance. "I learned from the best."

My mind spins. All this time, I've thought Pia to be my mirror. The one who inherited so much of me, my traits. When all the while,

Emilio was the sponge who'd picked up my way of thinking and living. Like wiping a chalkboard clean, I wish I could erase the years I spent teaching him that pretending was enough. I wish he could unlearn the ways I've taught him to hide the parts of himself that don't appear to fit the life we've built. A crease forms between his brows, as if a storm is brewing inside of his mind. He looks like he's still holding back, and Pia is the one to give him one final push.

"Em, just tell her."

For the first time since Francesco's funeral, my son cries. Those gold, glittering eyes well and my heart shatters into a million pieces.

"I got into culinary school," he reveals. "It's too late now to start in the fall semester, but I can start in January."

Oddly enough, I'm not shocked. Maybe some part of me has been expecting this, waiting for this day all along. "Culinary Institute of America?"

Emilio's jaw tenses. "The school is in Florence."

I blink incessantly. Florence. Italy. Another country. Four thousand miles away. A six-hour time difference. And yet, I smile. I'd spent my life pretending, and I would never inflict that same pain on my children. My eyes go misty as I stand and cup his face in my hands. "Okay," I say softly.

"Yeah?" he asks, his wobbly voice betraying him. Still, he lets out a bright, beaming smile. "Really?"

"Really, really." I hug him so tight, I can feel his relief. I hate that my son's been bottling up his life's greatest desire all this time, all because of me. In some strange way, I'm grateful that Pia found that letter in the side pocket of her purse. Had she not, would Emilio have spent his life chasing a dream that was never his? All because I was too afraid to let him go? After a few moments, I feel Pia's arms around me, too. The three of us are a mess of tears and nervous laughter and relief as we embrace in a way we never have before. In truth.

For the first time, they see me for who I am, and I see them for who they are. They're the very best of myself and the two men I've spent my life loving.

"I missed you two so much," I say as we break apart, swiping tears from beneath my eyes. "I know you both might still be angry with me, and maybe it'll take you a long time to forgive me, but no matter what, I love you two more than I could ever explain. I'm not me without you."

Emilio draws in a breath before he draws me to his side with one arm and kisses the top of my head. Then, he turns away. "I'm going to make espresso."

As he closes the door behind him, Pia clings to me. I hold her face in my hands, the face that I can honestly see is half of me and half of Enzo. I wonder, as she stares into my eyes, if she's spent this past week searching for bits of him in her. But then, her eyes darken, and her face crumples.

"I'm so sorry," she says, her voice wobbling all over the place.

"For what?"

"For saying you had such an easy, fabulous life with Daddy when you didn't. You totally didn't. Your life sounds really, really hard, actually, but I believed—"

"You believed the story I told you. And I'm your mother. I'm supposed to be the one person you can trust more than anyone." As we stare into each other's eyes, it's not so much mother to daughter as it is woman to woman. "I'm the one who's sorry. I made you think our life was a fairytale. I loved him, Pia, but it was complicated. And the only reason I pretended it wasn't was because I didn't want you to grow up and think complicated is normal. I want better for you." I take a deep breath. "And I want you to promise me something. I never, ever want you to say you're a mistake again." I close my eyes, determined to get the words out. "I found out I was pregnant with you shortly after your father hit me. And in a lot of ways, Pia, I feel like you protected me. I knew he wouldn't touch me as long as I was pregnant. And he didn't. You saved me." I look into her eyes again, and I know, from the glint in hers, that my words have reached her. "You were right on time, and you're the best thing that's ever happened to me."

She hugs me, fiercely, with all her love, a physical way of letting me know she forgives me. That nothing, no matter what, can break our bond.

"Can I ask you something, Mom?" she asks as we part.

I inhale and nod. "Anything."

Her eyes search my face, as if she's seeing me for the first time. Understanding me for the first time. "Does Enzo give you butterflies every time he walks into a room?"

My breath hitches. I should be afraid of this question. I should want to hide from it. But the earnestness in my daughter's face lets me know that whatever my answer is, it's okay as long as it's honest.

A smile splits my face. The devastating kind. "Every single time."

CHAPTER TWENTY-SEVEN

SCARLETT

Summer, 2011

When I walk into Amanti for the first time in weeks, for the first time since I opened this restaurant, I see it through a fresh lens. The same damask wallpaper bears the same old picture frames. The dim chandeliers are still coated in dust. Sinatra still croons in the background, like a ghost of better days. The staff is still setting tables, polishing glasses, doing the very tasks I taught them.

Yes, it's all still the same. Everything but me.

Stassi bursts through the kitchen doors, heading for the bar, but she stops cold when she sees me. "Scarlett," she says, breathless, heading toward me. "Oh my God, I wasn't expecting to see you so soon, but I'm so glad you're here. We need you."

I give her a hug, though I can't ignore her greeting. Not *We missed you.* Not *How was your trip?* Just *need.* A word that holds so much weight. "Thanks for sticking around while I was gone. But I'm back now. For good." We part, and I study her. "What exactly do you mean you *need* me?"

She takes a breath to speak, but Jeffrey comes out from the kitchen, also going still at the sight of me. "Oh, thank God."

My head whips between the two of them as Jeffrey approaches. He, too, gives me a hug, but it's short lived. "That Saverio is a real *cornuto*."

"Seriously," Stassi agrees. "I don't know how you've dealt with him all this time and haven't lost your shit. He walks in here like he owns the place. I mean, I guess technically he does, but you know what I mean."

"Wait a minute." I raise my palms. "What are you two talking about?"

"This whole Buca di Beppo thing," Stassi says with an eye roll. "I don't understand how this man could want to singlehandedly ruin Little Italy."

I blink and go quiet. I have absolutely no idea what they're referring to, and soon, they realize it.

"Oh," Jeffrey says, horrified. "You don't know what we're talking about, do you?"

I shake my head. "Enlighten me, please?"

"Saverio is trying to squeeze us, *you*, out of here. Buca di Beppo is *killing it* in Times Square, and they want to open up here, in Little Italy. Saverio said there's tens of millions of dollars on the line. He told us you knew there was a buyer."

"And clearly," Jeffrey says, "the *cornuto* was lying."

"He told me there was someone interested in buying me out, but he also said he was selling the building." I trail off, my mind reeling. Was the eviction notice just some elaborate scheme to replace me with a corporate giant? I look at Jeffrey and Stassi. "I have to go."

"Scarlett, wait," Stassi says, reaching for my arm. "We're really on bare bones here with stock. A bunch of the vendors have cut back and even halted deliveries."

"I'll handle it," I promise her. I promise myself. "I'm going to handle everything, right now."

***

"BUCA DI BEPPO?" I yell across Saverio's office. It's in a warehouse-like space atop one of his properties in SoHo that used to house a custom tailor shop, but now is home to the Adidas store. I slam the door behind me and walk with purpose toward his desk. Blood doesn't course through my veins; fire does. I know how ferocious fire can be, how fast it spreads, how quickly it consumes everything in its path. And right now, my past and future are fueling the flames. Mere feet from him, in front of his desk I shove a chair out of my way, its legs scraping across the concrete floor.

Saverio sits behind his desk, unfazed, glasses perched on the bridge of his nose. I, on the other hand, am shaking. I point at him.

"How *dare* you lie to me and make me look clueless in front of my staff. How dare you try and erase my family's livelihood with some dirty *scheme*. You gave my husband and me that lease when we were kids with nothing to our names and no experience, and after we put our hearts and souls into that restaurant for twenty-five years, you're going to try and take it away from us?"

"*You*," he corrects me, his voice like steel. "Your husband is gone."

My head throbs as his words zing my chest, but I lift my chin, steadying myself. "I'm still here."

"You can't cook." He slams his palms onto the desk and rises. "And evidently, you can't run a restaurant, either. You think I'm just your landlord who sits back and collects the rent checks, but I know what's going on, Scarlett. You owe your vendors tens of thousands of dollars. Deliveries have been halted. They're going to collections. Why not play nice and get out while you can?"

"Play *nice*? We're not *playing* anything, Saverio. This is my life we're talking about here. This is my husband's legacy." Then, with desperation, I add, "And it's my future."

A sharp inhale rattles my chest. I see it now, all the things I've been too afraid to change. The same way I spent years working to save my failing marriage, I've done the same trying to preserve a restaurant that is sinking. But suddenly, it's all incredibly clear. I want to blast Italo-disco instead of those old, tired crooners. We stopped live entertainment some time in the early 2000s, but I long to bring back the energy that only live musicians can bring. I want to redecorate. I want to transport diners to the Italy I fell in love with on my travels. I want new menu covers. Hell, I want to change the menu itself. Wouldn't I love to go to my own restaurant for dinner and not feel like I'm consuming flavors from a time past? Yes, suddenly, I see it all, all the ways I've deprived myself of my own creativity. I long to pick out new dishes and flatware. New crystal glassware patterns. Change the staff uniforms and knock down those old chandeliers so I can replace them with something from this century. All the things I did when I was young, building a restaurant from scratch with Francesco, but this time, I want to do it on my terms. I want it all, and I can't let Saverio take it from me.

Because now, it's not about preserving Francesco's legacy. It's about crafting my own.

"Scarlett," Saverio says, bringing me back to the present, "I have worked my whole life for a deal like this. I'm not going to let your failing restaurant and your pride get in the way of it. So let me tell you how this is going to go. You are going to vacate my building by the end of August. Gives you enough time to throw yourself a going out of business party and place your staffers elsewhere.

If we do it like this, I'll absolve you of all your back rent. It'll be a clean break."

A clean break. The end of August. It registers not as a deadline, but as the end. The very, very end, because I can't live my life without Amanti. Not just what it is, but what it can be. My heart pounds in my ears. Lively chatter from the tourists below filters through the window, but it's not the indistinguishable background noise it typically is. It's a reminder, that I live and own a business in the greatest city in the world. That in this sea of gross, corporate abominations to the Italian culture, in my neighborhood that's shrinking with each generation, I need to make sure Amanti prevails. I lean in, my index finger still poised toward him.

"No, let *me* tell *you* how this is gonna go," I spit back. "We have a lease agreement, Saverio. A legally binding agreement that states as long as I pay you the rent that's due, I'm still your tenant. I'm going to get you your money. Before the deadline. And when I do, there won't be a damn thing you can do to get rid of me, because I'm not going anywhere."

He narrows his eyes at me. "I know your house burned down."

It feels like a slap. But I've survived a slap before. What's one more? I laugh. Not nervous. Not afraid. The kind of laugh that means this war of ours has just begun.

"Oh, Saverio." I pat his desk before backing away. "The biggest mistake you could've made is underestimating me."

———

EXCEPT SAVERIO HASN'T UNDERESTIMATED me. He's outsmarted me. Outmaneuvered me. He's pinned me against the ropes, just like he did when he presented me with an eviction notice during my children's graduation party. I have one month to come up with a quarter million dollars, and I don't have some scheme up my sleeve like he does. The insurance process on the house has only just begun; I won't see that money until sometime next year. Even if we do decide to sell the land, we still have to get the debris from the fire cleaned up before we can list it.

With my hands on my hips, I look around my townhouse. An eerie, ticking silence fills the space. This—everything in here—is all I have left.

After I call my mother, she shows up within the hour. Francesco was a big spender, and I can't lie. I had my moments, too. Surely we can scrounge up enough valuables to cover what I owe Saverio, and keep the vendors from cutting me off completely.

We start in my closet. I don't know how much my old Louis Vuitton and Gucci bags are worth, but I throw them all into a pile anyway and don't give them a second glance. I just sift, fast and sure and desperate. Designer sunglasses and scarves. Shoes I can no longer walk in. Dresses that would show an embarrassing amount of cleavage should I try and wear them again. I feel like I'm making progress until I step out of my closet and survey the pile as I swipe beads of sweat from my forehead.

"How much do you think all that's worth?" my mother asks.

"Not enough, is all I can tell you," I mutter. "I have the Versace dishes in the China cabinet. And my Lladró collection." I gnaw on the inside of my cheek. I don't want to, but I know I have to. "Let's start working on the jewelry."

I don't know why I have such sentimental attachment to gold and silver and gemstones, but it's like every piece can speak. The ruby heart drop earrings whisper of a quick trip to Palm Beach, the way I'd gasped at them through a shop window, how Francesco had them waiting on the bed for me when we returned to our hotel. The heart-shaped diamond perched on a white gold murmurs of the moment Pia entered the world; how I sobbed from exhaustion, from relief, from the most overwhelming, life-changing love. The Rolex sitting on my wrist speaks to the early blissful days of my marriage, and how Francesco proudly came home with that bulky green box as soon as he could afford it.

My Montauk home is gone, but I can still see those sweet summer nights and delicious, dreamy days spent by the beach. Enzo's letters burned, but I still know his words, the way his scrawl slanted just so, the way he wrote to me when no one else was looking. And that tells me something.

If I let go of these jewels, I will still feel the love they were supposed to denote.

"Francesco's watch," my mother says softly, joining me in front of my dresser, Francesco's gold Rolex in her hand.

It's large and weighty and it lived on his wrist for years and years. I take it from her, feeling the cold metal in my hands. I flip it over to reveal the words I'd had engraved.

All my love, always, S

I glance up at my mother, hot tears stinging my eyes. "I was saving this for Emilio."

"You think he'd really wear it? Kind of gaudy. It's so eighties."

I let out a soft laugh, knowing my mother is just trying to distract me. She knows that no matter how hard I try, this is ripping me apart in ways I'm only beginning to understand.

I sigh and set the watch down. "Let's leave this one for last, okay?"

We continue sifting through the top drawer of my dresser containing my most valuable assets, mostly in silence, save for the faint clink of metal on wood, the occasional sharp inhale as I go through my internal debates. Diamond studs and hoops, Francesco's gold chain-link bracelet, a brooch he bought me for Christmas one year all make it into the pile. I can't yet part with Francesco's gold chains, adorned with a *cornetto* and the sign of the *malocchio,* the very same ones Enzo has around his neck, but I add his money clip to the items for sale. Nestled in the back of the dresser is a bag in Tiffany & Co.'s unmistakable robin's egg blue.

"Oh, God," I say, tugging the bag out of the drawer.

I'd rather not remember how my husband removed me from our children's education trust after my slip-up surrounding Emilio's high school entrance exam. Just seeing the bag ignites something in me, something that reminds me I've never really gotten over it. At the time, I'd felt stripped of my maternal rights, not to mention the years of labor it had taken to make numerous contributions to the trust. After a week of giving each other the silent treatment, Francesco had come home with this very bag, containing a diamond tennis bracelet that I didn't really like. We then spent all night having perfunctory make-up sex that didn't make up anything but my willingness to sweep his betrayal under the proverbial rug, as I somehow always did.

The bag is still pristine, the box tucked neatly inside. I open it, waiting for a pang of nostalgia, but there's nothing. I've never liked this bracelet due to both the circumstances surrounding it, not to mention, it's not quite my style. But just as I'm about to add it to the pile to sell, I notice there's something wedged into the top of the box. It looks like a piece of paper, slightly yellowed. I wiggle it out, careful not to tear it.

"What's that?" my mother mutters as she examines a set of cuff links.

"I'm not sure." I unfold the paper, delicate, gently rustling. My heart rate multiplies as my husband's tight, formal cursive stares back at me with a note I've never seen before.

My love, you know I do my best talking through gifts, so this is just a little something to tell you that I'm sorry. Sometimes my demons get the best of me, and I take out all of my stress on you. It's not fair to you, and I don't know how you put up with me, but I'm so lucky to have a wife who can see beyond the bad times. You've brought so much good into my life, Scarlett, and our children are lucky to have a mother like you, who puts them before everything else. I'm calling Paul in the morning and adding your name back to the trust, and we can put this mistake of mine behind us. I promise to try and do better, to spare you from the darker parts of me. My beautiful wife, you deserve nothing but the best. All my love, always, Francesco.

I read it. Again and again, because I can't quite register that this is real. How had I missed this? Perhaps I'd been so unimpressed with him shutting me up with a gift that I didn't give the box a second glance to notice the note. But more, what stings me is his promise. *I'm calling Paul in the morning and adding your name back to the trust.*

Except he didn't.

And that's why I'm here. With no access to a fund I worked so hard to build. With nothing left but a mound of broken promises.

Still, I can't help but wonder if he had called Paul. Maybe Paul was the one who told him to leave his unreliable wife off such a precious fund. And if that's the case, I feel no qualms about laying into Paul the way I did Saverio.

I've had enough of men making the choices in my life.

"Hey, Mom," I say, my eyes still glued to the letter, "can you get my phone?"

She grabs it from my nightstand, hands it to me, and without putting down the note, as if it'll disappear, I dial Paul.

"Paul, it's Scarlett," I say after he answers. "Question for you. Did my husband ever tell you that he wanted to add me back to the education trust?"

He pauses for a moment. "No, he didn't. How come?"

"Because I have a letter here from him stating he did." I go on to read Paul the letter in its entirety, and afterward, recount to him how I discovered it. "So, he didn't call you that next day?"

"He didn't. But," he says, and I wonder if I'm imagining the sound of a smile in his voice, "this letter is proof enough that he had every intention of doing so. Why don't you come by my office and we'll start on the paperwork?"

I set the letter down and look at my mother. "What paperwork?"

"To add your name to the trust. Once that's done, you'll have full authority. You'll be able to withdraw funds, update the beneficiaries, modify the terms—even dissolve it if you want to move the money into a general account. It'll be entirely in your control."

"Wait, wait, wait." I grasp my mother's hand as if she has the answers to my million questions. "Emilio's decided he wants to go to culinary school instead of law school. Does that mean I can use the extra funds for my restaurant?" My breath goes shallow as I ram my eyes shut. "How much is even in the fund now anyway?"

Paul's laugh fills my ear. "We'll go over the fine print when you get here. But to answer your big picture question, you'll have more than enough to keep Amanti up and running."

My hand flies to my chest. "Oh my God. That's ... That's incredible. That's—"

"What time can I expect you?"

I glance at the clock. "Give me an hour."

I toss the phone on the bed and throw my arms around my mother. It all feels like a release, the way I sob into her shoulder, how my shoulders shake, the way I'm holding onto her as tight as I can. She'd never been Francesco's biggest fan. She'd thought he stole my life. And for a long time, that was true. But I can't help but feel like that letter, discovering it the way I did, when I did, was one last gift from him.

A parting gift that arrived right on time.

My mother cups my tear-streaked face in her hands. "What is going on, honey?"

I glance over at the letter resting on the dresser. Those few lines of cursive that haven't just saved my past, but set up my future. "The letter means I can use Emilio's law school money to save the restaurant. It's all over now."

My mother laughs in disbelief. Her hands are warm on my face and her eyes sparkle with something I haven't seen in her in a while. Hope. "I guess we can put all this jewelry back then."

I laugh with her. "I guess we can."

She reaches for my hands, her fingers strong and solid around mine. Her laughter fades and for a moment she looks at me. Really looks at me, into my heart in the way only a mother can.

"Scarlett," she starts, "our kids are the dearest things to our hearts, and then they can break them. That's how much power they have." She squeezes my hands. "My heart broke for you, over and over again, watching you love a man who couldn't love you the way you deserved.

Watching you struggle and suffer and give that man every last piece of yourself. I hated him for a long time, because he kept breaking your heart, and when you hurt, I hurt."

"I know. You tried to tell me."

"I did." She sighs, her lips curving into a knowing smile. "But when a woman's in love, you can't tell her nothing. She has to figure things out for herself."

My smile soon fades as I take it all in. How I had to live it. How I had to suffer and pretend and give Francesco my all because I believed. Right until his last breath, I believed in all that we could be.

I've spent the last twenty-five years giving everyone else all my love. Now, it's about damn time I give some to myself.

My mother tilts her head, her eyes wrinkling with excitement. "You have a second chance now."

I nod, sure of everything now. "That I do," I say, glancing at the letter, believing, this time, in all that I can be.

"I THINK THIS WHOLE education trust thing," Pia says as we share a slice of tiramisu, still in its takeout container, "and him bailing out of law school solidifies Emilio's *favorite child* status."

She slides the container closer to me. The barstools are right there, but we stand, passing the familiar dessert back and forth.

A laugh escapes my throat. "I don't have a favorite."

She rolls her eyes as she goes in for another bite. She glances at the TV where a new episode of *Jersey Shore* has just begun.

Now I'm the one to roll my eyes as the heavily spray-tanned Snooki dances so inappropriately, they've had to blur out several body parts. "How do you find this entertaining?"

"Um, it's simple. I would never act like that in public and it's fun to watch people do things you'd never have the nerve to do."

"You have no idea how happy I am to hear that."

Pia takes the last bite of tiramisu, deposits our spoons into the sink, and tosses the container. "Want to help me pack?"

"You don't want to watch your show?" I glance at the screen. The guy with spiky, glued hair is making out with two girls in a hot tub. "I can't believe I ever let you watch this debauchery."

She laughs and heads down the hall. "Come on."

Upstairs, I kick off my heels and change out of my work clothes into pajamas. It's been an eventful week, finalizing the trust paperwork, accessing the funds, and paying Saverio off once and for all. The vendors have resumed deliveries, much to the delight of Jeffrey and Stassi, and I've already begun mapping out the cosmetic changes I'm going to make to Amanti's dining room. Emilio isn't set to start culinary school until January, so I've tasked him with rewriting the menu, and he's taken to it with great focus.

But now, as I pad my way into Pia's room where she's laid out her suitcase and some denim shorts, I have another task ahead of me.

Pia is going to visit her dad.

Enzo.

"Did he say *why* he's still in Montauk?" I ask as I sink to the ground and start folding a pile of tank tops and T-shirts.

"Okay," Pia says as she switches on the TV in her room and tunes to MTV, "you can only help me pack if you don't give me the third degree on Enzo."

"Don't you know how hard that's going to be for me?"

She arches a brow at me, sass oozing out of her. Then, she yanks open a drawer, scoops out swimsuits, shorts, and dresses, and dumps them on the floor before plopping down across from me. She eyes me, and her mouth twists into a smirk, the same one I spent years pretending she didn't get from Enzo.

"Fine," she says as she rolls a floral print dress. "What do you want to know?"

Though it's only been a few weeks since I've talked to Enzo, it feels the same as when we went four years without contact. "You two have been texting and talking," I start. "Has he asked about me?"

Giggles burst from her throat. "Oh my *gosh.* You sound like a teenager with a crush!"

"Do I?" I feel my cheeks go hot. "Oh, God, I do."

Her big brown eyes meet mine. "He's asked about you."

"What exactly did he ask and what did you say?"

Her head falls back with laughter; she's clearly enjoying this. "Are you going to do this to me all weekend?"

"I would love to, but I know you'll kill me."

"Okay." She leans in like she's about to divulge some big secret. "He's still pretending he's mad, but I can tell he's dying to talk to you."

My hands fly to my face, and I hide behind my palms. This is all so new, being with Pia like this, talking about *everything.* "Pia, Pia, Pia." I shake my head, looking at her again. "How do you know that?"

She shrugs. "I can just tell."

"That's not very convincing." We laugh together as we continue to fold her clothes and stack them into her suitcase, as *Jersey Shore* drones on in the background. But I pause and hold her gaze. "I don't know what's going to happen between me and him, but I'm happy you're going to spend some time with him. And I'm sure he's over the moon."

Though her gaze flicks to the suitcase for a moment, she smiles. "I'm excited, too."

I draw in a jagged breath and hold it. "Can I ask you to do me one small favor?"

She looks surprised as she nods. I get up and tell her I'll be right back. In my bedroom, tucked in my nightstand, is a letter. One I wrote to him when my daughter announced she'd like to go visit her father who, to my surprise, is still in Montauk. The envelope is sealed and his name is written across the back of it in my swirly cursive, and when I hand it to Pia, she shoots me a look that says, *Really, Mom?*

"Will you just give it to him?" I ask as I sink back down to the floor.

"Did you have *another* kid with him?" she teases, and when she takes in my horrified expression, her laughter explodes. "I'm kidding, Mom."

"You can read it if you like. I have nothing else to hide."

"Yeah, I'm good." She gives me one last smirk before tucking the letter into her suitcase and zipping it shut. "Wanna watch the rest of the episode with me?"

"Oh, yes, Pia. This is the exact kind of mother-daughter bonding stuff I'd planned to do with you when you were born."

She rises, offering me her hand to help me up. But before we curl up on her bed to watch the admittedly addictive reality show, I hang on to her hand.

"I just want you to know I'm really proud of you. You've handled this whole thing with so much grace."

"Mom, appreciate the pep talk, but I really want to see if Sam and Ron break up this week," she teases. But then, her playful expression softens. "I love you so much, Mom. And I really, really want to regain that *favorite child* status. Why else would I be spending an entire weekend trying to get your man back?"

"Pia!" Our laughter melds together as we sink onto her bed. "Don't think about me this weekend. This trip is all about you and Enzo getting to know each other as father and daughter."

"I know," she says with a shrug. "But I really want my mom and dad to be together. And you know what they say about Daddy's girls."

"What's that?" I ask as we lean back against the pillows.

She gives me a sassy, all-knowing look and says, "We get *whatever* we want."

CHAPTER TWENTY-EIGHT

ENZO

Summer, 2011

"You sure you don't want to stay a few extra days?" I ask, rolling my daughter Antonella's suitcase behind me as we approach the train platform. After much convincing, she'd agreed to spend a few days with me here, in Montauk.

"I have to get back to work, Dad," she says in appeasing tones.

"You want to get back to that boyfriend of yours." She gives me a sheepish expression that tells me I'm not wrong as we park ourselves near a bench, the hot afternoon sun beaming down on us. "You tell him, even though I'm four states away, I'm watching everything."

Her face radiates with a smile as her long, wild, curly brown hair dances behind her from the breeze. "It was a nice visit."

"I had a great time. I'm glad you came." An announcement emits from the speakers, letting me know our time is running out. "I know you haven't wanted to talk about the past this weekend, but let me just say this before you go. I know I wasn't the father you needed, Nella," I start. She shifts her weight from one foot to the other, her eyes narrowing. Whether she wants to have this conversation or not, I have to tell her the truth. "But I'm not the same person I was when you were young. I have so many regrets. If I could go back and redo everything, I would. But I can't. I just want you to know that you can trust me. You can depend on me. Nothing matters more to me than our family."

"I wanted to be close with you, Dad. I always did. But I felt like *someone* had to be on Mom's side. Little Enzo was always pretty neutral, and Maria is still a total Daddy's girl. I think that scared Mom." Her tense expression shifts to one of worry. "I think she was terrified to lose us to you. And the only way I could let her know that I wasn't going anywhere was to dig my heels in and pretend to hate you. And yeah, she told me a lot of things you did when you were married that made me mad. But you were still my dad." As tears sting her eyes, she flicks her gaze away for a moment, as if she's wrestling with herself whether or not she should continue. "You *are* still my dad."

Are. Present tense. One syllable, one little word lets me know that there's a door between us and she's finally opened it. I'm flooded with relief. Hope that things might stay this way. That they'll only get better. That she might knock down the door completely and let me in all the way. I've lost my family before. I know that pain and sometimes I can still feel the scars opening back up. But now, standing across from my daughter, I promise myself that from here on out, I'll do anything, everything, to keep us together.

"You're still my little girl."

She scoffs, smiling. "Dad, I'm almost *thirty*. It's so *weird*."

"You wanna talk about weird?" I say, as the incoming train's horn rings in the near distance. "I'm almost sixty. I have a grandchild."

"And," Nella says, arching a brow, "you're kind of a new dad."

I shake my head. "Life's pretty wild, Nella."

"She's lucky."

"That my brother raised her instead of me?"

Her mouth falls open. "No!"

My shoulders shake as I laugh, but this time, she doesn't join me.

"She's lucky to have you as her dad. Just like I am." A stack of bangles lives on her right wrist, and they clink together as she reaches for my hand. "I know things didn't work out when you moved to Maryland. But you tried. You tried really hard. For a long time, I focused on all the other stuff. The bad things Mom said about you. But I never forgot that you moved for us. I held onto that, actually. That was proof you cared."

Just like Scarlett said. She'd been the one who promised me that my kids would never forget the sacrifice I made for them, leaving my life behind to chase them to another state. Here we are all these years later, and finally, I'm seeing the payoff.

As the train pulls into the station, its brakes hissing, I open my arms and draw Nella into a hug. "I love you. Call me when you get in, okay?"

"I will." When she smiles and looks into my eyes, I try to capture the moment, sear it into my memory, because I've spent years chasing it. Now that I have it, I don't ever want to let it go. "Love you."

She promises she'll see me soon and waves one last time from her window seat on the train. I grab a coffee sit on the bench, recounting my weekend with Nella. Going out to dinner, spending a day on the beach, having breakfast by the bay, little things that feel monumental given my history with her. Even in her absence, I feel her, like she's been reconnected to me. She's given me hope that the family I so regretted splitting up finally has a real chance at being whole again.

Maybe they're not better off without me.

That feeling only multiplies when Pia steps off a different train an hour later, and lights up when we lock eyes across the platform. The train hisses as it pulls away, and people zigzag in all directions, but all I see is her.

My daughter.

Sunlight glints off her hair that's the same shade as mine, and I barely have time to take a breath before she reaches up and draws me into a hug. She smells like raspberries and vanilla, a detail of hers I never registered before. And as she looks into my eyes, sparkling with anticipation, I know this is just the first of a thousand things I never got to know about her.

But now, I have the chance.

"How was the train ride?" I ask as I take her suitcase and roll it behind me as we make our way to my truck.

She shrugs. "Good. I just listened to music the whole way."

"Yeah?" I lug her suitcase into the trunk before opening the passenger door for her. Dressed in a T-shirt, jean shorts, and a pair of Keds, she hops in and buckles her seatbelt. Once in the driver's seat, I ask, "Do you like Italian music like me, or that hippy shit your mother likes?"

Her laugh fills the air between us. "Neither. Both of you have the *worst* taste in music."

As I steer us away from the train station, I lean over and hand her the aux chord. "Then by all means, show me what good taste sounds like."

She plugs her phone in and scrolls for a moment. I expect something that's up to her standards. She's been studying classical music since she could read. But then, she leans over, turns up the volume, and the speakers explode with a thumping bassline and a rhythmic rap.

My face wrinkles with confusion. "What the hell is this?"

She grins at me, her head bobbing to the beat, as she starts rapping along, not missing a single lyric. "It's "Super Bass,"" she yells over the music.

I steal glances at her as I navigate through Montauk, and soon she sways her upper body to the beat and throws her arms in the air like she's done this a hundred times before.

Like *we've* done this a hundred times before. She's so full of life, sunshine in human form, and I already feel more energized just being in her presence.

"That's not what I was expecting from you," I tell her when the song winds down.

"You have *a lot* to learn." She taps her phone, and a heavy techno beat fills the car. She closes her eyes, lost in the song, until I make a turn into a driveway.

The turn must feel familiar to her, because she opens her eyes. Then, she leans over and lowers the volume.

The driveway still looks the same, uncharred, unmarked by the devastation we witnessed just last month. But all remnants of the house are completely gone. As I put the car in park, all we see is a patch of land that overlooks the beach.

"What are we doing here?" Pia asks, unable to tear her eyes away from what used to be our summer home.

I get out of the car, open the passenger door, and guide her toward the empty lot. "You're about to find out."

I lead the way to a small card table I set up at the border, where the lot meets the sandy dune. Just beyond us, the ocean draws and crashes, and the sun sits high, casting a bright haze. Pia is a mix of curiosity and concern, as told by the way her lips are pursed and her eyebrows are furrowed. Once we reach the table, I run my hands along the pages that top it.

Blueprints.

I hunch over the table, my palms resting on the edges of the pages so the wind doesn't whisk them away. I stare at the rendering of the home that could very well occupy the empty lot behind me in just a few short months.

"What is that?" Pia asks, joining me, glancing over my shoulder. Her eyes that are copies of my own scan over the rendering.

"This is the house I'm planning on building." I look over my shoulder at her, trying to gauge her reaction. "Here. On this lot."

She freezes, as if it doesn't make sense. "You're building a new beach house?"

"Yeah."

"I mean, I know this is what you did in Florida and all, but…" she trails off, her smile fading. "Is this for us? Or is it an investment property?"

It's like she's plucked the questions right out of my own brain. As I took on the task of cleaning the lot and preparing it for construction, I've begged those same two questions of myself. Who am I doing this for? Am I going to build it and run, or might this house and what it could represent keep me here? Is it merely a way for me and Scarlett to recoup the money we would've made on the sale, or am I building something else entirely—a new foundation for my family?

I could tell her that's what this is. But I'm not so sure it would be true.

"I don't know what the future holds," I admit, scanning the blueprints with a critical eye. I'd done this enough times in Florida, hell, even back when I was a kid in Naples, to be able to envision what a one-dimensional drawing could become. Though the house is nothing more than an idea at this stage, I can see it all so clearly. The cedar-shingled façade, crowned with an arched dormer, its oval window peering over the property like an ever-present watchful eye. The gambrel roof will curve into flared eaves, and white, sturdy columns will flank the wraparound porch so that it appears as unwavering as I hope it'll be. If I can see it as if it already exists, does that mean it will be? Doesn't that indicate that I'm not taking on this project in vain? I stand up straight and let the blueprints coil back up into a roll. "But I'd love to see you spend your nineteenth birthday here. Wouldn't you?"

Her eyes brim as she draws in a breath and holds it. Her eyes flick to the lot, then back to the ocean. "Can we go for a walk?"

We kick off our shoes. Then, I offer her my arm and when she takes it, we start down the beach. She stays quiet, staring out at the water, and when I glance at her from the corner of my eye, she doesn't acknowledge it. I feel like she's miles away, and I worry I've done something to upset her.

But when we reach the shoreline, she stops, tilts her head up at me, and finally speaks.

"I need to talk to you about my mom," she says. "She told me to stay out of it, but I can't. Mom's always fixed everything for me, and I want to fix this for her."

"*This* being?" I ask, my heart rate already multiplying at the prospect of discussing my history with Scarlett with our daughter.

Pia puts her hands on her hips and exhales through her nose, looking utterly determined. "If I can forgive her, so can you. I know you're mad at her for not telling you, but can you blame her? Can you imagine how scared she must've been, knowing I might grow up and look just like you?"

A smile tugs at my lips. "And you do."

"And I do," she echoes, though she doesn't appear happy about it. Her face clouds with worry. "My mom really loves you. She told me she still gets butterflies every time you walk into a room. And you know what she said? She said that's the kind of love she wants me to find. That must mean it's the real thing. The *best* thing, because I know all my mom wants for me is the best of everything. I mean, don't you feel the same way about her?"

I press my lips together, fighting a smile. Digging my hands into my pockets, I rock on my bare heels. "Of course I do, P."

"Then why won't you talk to her?"

"I don't like to admit this," I say, "because I'm a tough guy, but your mother hurt me. I trusted your mother more than I trusted anyone in my life. I thought we told each other everything. I'm not just upset she kept it a secret. I'm upset because she took away my chance to be your father. I understand why she hid it while my brother was still alive. But he's been gone for four years. She could've told me. Both of you went through a bad time after Fran died, and I could've been there for you."

"You could've been there for us regardless."

As if we're ruled by the same rhythms, our mouths curve into smirks at the same time. "There's no doubting you're mine, is there?"

For a moment, she lets her guard down, her brow arching with sass before she dissolves to laughter. But then, a poignancy falls between us.

"I think it had to happen that way," she goes on. "Because I got four years with Mom that I would never take back. Yeah, I made her want to rip her hair out sometimes, and half the time I hated how strict she was with me, but we had four years of it just being the two of us. And after Daddy died, I think that was exactly what we needed."

Pia's gaze drifts out to the ocean. "I'm worried about her. And you're my dad. You're supposed to take my worries away."

"What exactly are you worried about?"

"She's going to be all alone," Pia says. "Emi's moving to Italy, and I'm moving into my dorm in a couple weeks. I know I have to leave and grow up, and I'm excited for college, but there's this part of me that isn't because I know I'm leaving my mom behind. And she's got no one there with her. I gave up a lot of my social life in high school to spend time with her because I didn't want her to be alone. But I won't be able to do that anymore."

Finally, I let myself think of Scarlett. Of the woman I've spent the last two and a half decades being in love with. I think of her vigor, of her lust for life, of her resilience. Of her sharp wit and humor, how she can turn even the darkest of moments into light. I think of how safe I feel when I'm with her, how she's this constant force in a world of uncertainty. I remember how adrift I felt during those four years we were apart, and how seeing her again felt like I was back in the center of the universe. Of my universe. She's everything, that woman, and yet I can't help but think maybe I'm not everything to her. That's always been my problem, my biggest fear.

"Pia," I say, staring at the little girl we created together, "when I think of your mother, I think of her as the one big love of my life. *Anime gemelli.* Twin souls. As embarrassing as that sounds." I slick my hair away from my face with my palm. "But I still don't know what's going to happen with us. And I'm not going to make you a promise unless I can keep it."

She looks to her right, toward the lot. Like me, can she see the house to be? "Eighteen birthdays there wasn't enough."

I wrap my arm around her shoulder, steering us toward the lot. "I think I can read between those lines."

"Can you read that I'm totally starving?"

"I'm renting a place over on the bayside. We'll cook something and watch the sunset."

She stops walking and raises her palms in disbelief. "Wait, since when do *you* cook?"

"Pretty Pia," I say with a wink, "you're not the only one who's full of surprises."

I DO THE COOKING, while she plays DJ. I've never noticed it before, just how intertwined she and music are. How it's her second language. She sets the mood with some classic Neapolitan songs she's known since her youth, while I whip up shrimp *fra diavolo* for the two of us. The shrimp hisses as it hits the hot oil, filling the air with garlic and heat. Taking after her mother, Pia sets the table, but she's consumed with the melody, humming along like she's in a trance. I wonder, as I watch her, if she even realizes she's doing it, or if music just lives inside of her and this is nothing more than second nature. Just beyond the kitchen windows, people gather on the small rocky beach to watch the gold ball in the sky begin its descent into the calm, lapping waters of the bay.

She catches my eye from the table, doing a double take. "What?" she says, blushing.

"Just admiring how musical you are."

She lets out a sigh and returns to the kitchen, setting the extra forks and knives on the counter. Then, she props herself up onto a barstool, resting her chin in her palms. "I do love music. But I still don't know if that's what I want to study in college."

"How come?"

She shrugs. "What am I going to do with a degree in music?"

"You can't look at it that way." I flip the shrimp over, revealing a golden crust. "We can try to plan our lives all we want, P, but there's always surprises. Things that shock us. What I'm more interested in is how music—singing—makes you feel."

The question stills her. She folds her arms and looks around like she's searching for the answer. Then, as if summoned by the melody itself, she latches on to the song playing from the small speaker on the counter—"Dicitencello vuje." In an instant, her gorgeous soprano soars, radiant, outshining and overpowering the sounds from the speaker. As she slips down from the barstool and paces around the kitchen, her head falling back, her eyes closing as she sings in my native tongue, I feel a swell of pride. This is what Scarlett and I created together. This stunning creature so full of talent is half of me. I'm half of the reason she exists. I'm part of the reason she can emit such a glittering, show-stopping sound from her lungs and from her throat. And for the first time in a long time, I feel like I've done something right.

My daughter overshadows all the mistakes I've made.

I switch off the burners as the song comes to its conclusion. I rest my palm on the counter, leaning my hip against it, soaking in my daughter's flushed cheeks and beaming smile as she blinks her eyes open. She looks at me, steadying her breath, waiting for my reaction.

My laugh is one of amazement. Of awe. I shake my head. "I don't know where you came from, but your mother and I are so lucky you're ours."

Her brows knit as she swallows hard, her gaze falling to her hands. "I feel like I'm free when I sing. Like I'm floating or something. I don't know how to explain it." She looks into my eyes. "I feel like it's just me and the song, and nothing can touch us. Does that make any sense at all?"

Her words linger, and something about the way she says it, how she's floating, how she's untouchable when she's one with the music, draws up memories I haven't let myself revisit in years.

My brother.

I remember how he used to go into his zone when he cooked, how the world drifted away when he had his hands sunk into ingredients that needed him as their maestro to craft the perfect medley. Food was his language, the balm that soothed his scars. Cooking wasn't merely a career, a means to earn a nice living, but rather, his life. The thing that breathed oxygen into his lungs. His first and greatest love.

I recognize those same traits in Pia, with music.

And I realize, I might be her father, but she's got so much of Francesco in her. Nothing will ever take that away.

"You remind me of him," I mutter, before I realize the words are out. Her head tilts to the side, instantly knowing who I'm referring to. "That's how he felt when he cooked. You can't buy that feeling, P. And so many people wish they could. So it seems impractical right now. You don't know what kind of career you'll have after you graduate. But so what? When you do what you love, when you give it all you've got, there's no way you won't succeed."

Her perplexed expression lingers a moment longer before a smile takes over her pretty face. She opens her arms wide and flings them around my shoulders, hugging me with all the strength she's got. Then, she draws back, rests her hands on my shoulders, and gives me her most serious expression.

"Great chat, but *seriously, stòngo murénn' 'e famme.*"

I burst into laughter at her curt, near perfect Neapolitan accent. And as I plate our dinner, as she settles into the seat next to me and tells me all about how she's going to decorate her dorm room, all I can think about is how much I love her.

Like Scarlett always says, I love her so much it hurts.

PER HER REQUEST, WE watched *The Godfather* together after dinner, and as soon as the credits started rolling, her eyes turned heavy and she turned in for the night. But now, as I fold the throw blankets and drape them over the arm of the couch, I hear her gentle footsteps padding toward me. I turn around.

"You're still up?" Then, I notice she has something in her hands.

She glances down at it, following my gaze. "I have to give you something." She extends the envelope toward me. Instantly, I recognize Scarlett's handwriting, the same loopy way she's always written my name. "It's from Mom. Obviously."

I nod and take it from her. "Thanks."

"And I swear, I didn't read it." She takes a step back and stares at me. "I had so much fun today."

"Me too." I drag my fingers along the envelope's edge. "So much fun."

Her face wrinkles, and though she hesitates, struggling, she gets the words out. "I love you, Dad."

Tears flood my eyes. I hadn't expected or even wished that she'd call me *Dad,* not for a long while, at least. But as I hug her, enveloped in her scent that I wanted to bottle up and never forget, I can't help but admit how much it means to me.

Pia accepts me. And it makes me wonder if all this time spent feeling like I'm on the outside, like I'm in the way, has been a waste.

Maybe I was never locked out to begin with. Maybe the door was always open, and all I had to do was walk through.

"I love you, too, Pia. I love you more than you know."

"And one more thing," she says, masking the sincerity in her eyes behind an arched brow. "I don't think there's anything embarrassing about you saying you and Mom are *anime gemelli*. If anything, I hope someday, someone feels that same way about me."

I let out a tight smile and nod. "They will."

She steps back and takes a deep breath, like she, too, is processing what she's just said. But as she turns away, I realize I can't let her go just yet.

"Pia," I call out. She swivels around. "Don't tell your mom about me building a new house. Let's just keep it between us for now. Okay?"

"Mm," she muses. "A *secret*. How original."

She flashes me one last smile before leaving me with Scarlett's letter. I try to tell myself that I'm tired and I'll read it in the morning, but as if Scarlett's here, tugging on my arm, whispering in my ear, I sit down and slide my thumb beneath the envelope's lip and tear it open. Crickets chirp and the fireplace crackles as I unfold the pages and sink farther into the couch.

Dear Enzo,

I need to start by saying I'm sorry. I could say it a million times and still feel like it's not enough. I'm sorry for keeping the secret. For staying silent when everyone deserved the truth. You were right. I wasn't protecting anyone but myself. And in doing so, I hurt you. I hurt our daughter. My Emilio. Francesco. The people who make my life what it is. If I could go back, I'd do it all differently. But I can't. All I can do now is ask, and pray, that you can forgive me for getting it so wrong.

You know now. I can't tell you how many times I've envisioned telling you the truth over the last eighteen years. None of my fantasy-like scenarios, however, included our house burning down, and you storming off with my children. I think that moment might be seared in my memory forever. It was my worst nightmare, Enzo, watching the three of you turn your backs on me and walk away. The three people I love most in this world.

By some miracle, Pia has handled this with so much grace. She's lighter, like something has clicked into place. Maybe deep down she always knew. Maybe she always felt like something was missing, and maybe now she realizes that missing piece was you. I know you're angry with me, Enzo, and you have every right to be, because you feel like I stole our daughter from you. But you have her now. You'll have her forever. She's marvelous in every way, and I can't wait for you to discover every last thing about her. She's wild and full of surprises and she'll melt your heart into a puddle, that I can promise you. And I think, like me, you'll cherish every second of it. The greatest joy in my life is being her mommy. I'm so happy for both of you that you're getting to know each other. If she brings you half the joy she's brought me, you'll be over the moon.

But I'm not writing to you to tell you how wonderful our baby girl is. You'll discover that all on your own. I'm writing to you to talk about us. If there even is an "us" anymore.

I'm almost fifty, Enzo. I've spent half of my life loving you.

Half of my life feeling like you're my true soulmate. I know that I'm the one who singlehandedly destroyed what we had. I'll forever be remorseful for hurting you. Not just by keeping Pia from you, but for every time I led you to believe that it was finally our time, only for me to run back to your brother. I hate knowing that I caused you enough pain to drive you away, not once, but twice.

Our relationship hasn't been perfect by any means. But when I think back on everything we've gone through, I think of how much you've given to me. A job, when I was just a girl with no experience and not a dollar to my name. A shoulder to cry on when things got rocky between me and your brother. A hand to hold when I had no strength. A listening ear I could confide in, safely. Support, when I made decisions that hurt the both of us. The daughter of my dreams.

And most recently, Enzo, on that beautiful night in Montauk before the fire ravaged everything, before the truth exploded like a bomb, you gave me a second chance.

It was like you breathed new life into my lungs. You reminded me that I'm still alive. That the best isn't behind me, but in front of me. You gave me the push I needed to keep going. To keep fighting. To live. Not just for my kids or for my business, for Francesco's memory, but for myself.

You gave me true love, and I'm not sure there's anything more important in this life than love.

After a twist of fate, a long story from which I'll spare you, I was able to access the education trust to pay off Saverio. But I'm not just saving Amanti. I'm renewing it. I'm making it everything I ever wished it could be and making it my own. I feel like I have a new lease on life, Enzo. I feel as vibrant as I did when Amanti was nothing but a shell of a building and somehow, I was able to see it all. All it could be. All it turned out to be. And now, it's going to be something else. It's going to be the first of many ways I'm going to make my life my own.

As excited as I am about that, I can't say I feel complete. I can't say I no longer feel like something is missing because I do. You're still the piece that's missing from me. I still have a hole in my heart that's shaped like you. And you know what? I always will. I know that now. And if that's something I have to learn to live with, then so be it. I'll learn. But if by some chance, you have a hole in your heart that's shaped like me, I'm happy to fill it, Enzo. It's my turn to give to you all the things you gave to me, and more. I long to show you in every way just how much you mean to me and just how much I love you. I know in my bones that I have a big, beautiful life ahead of me, and I want to share it with you. And if you decide that you want that too, I say, let's do it, Enzo. I'm not the same woman I was who kept a secret for eighteen years. I know who I am now.

I know I'm yours.

Like I always have been, I'm right here, honey. All you have to do is come home.

All my love,

Always,

Scarlett

I read it three times through before I let my eyes rest on her signature. The same words that are written in permanent ink on my chest. The way she's signed off for eighteen years. But this time, it doesn't feel like a signature. It feels like a promise, like I'll always have all of her love. And for one fleeting moment, I want to pick up the phone and hear her voice and tell her she'll have all of mine.

Just like eighteen birthdays spent in Montauk wasn't enough for Pia, twenty-five years of loving Scarlett isn't enough for me.

No, I'm going to love this woman until I take my last breath, and even after that.

I know it, in my bones, undeniably so, that I belong wherever she is. I can feel my feet slowing, like the race I've been running my whole life is finally coming to its end.

CHAPTER TWENTY-NINE

SCARLETT

Fall, 2011

I inhale the crisp air of late September, my stilettos click-clacking down Mulberry Street in time with the city's heartbeat. The Feast of San Gennaro is in full swing, and though I usually ignore the loud festivities, tonight I'm in the mood to savor everything. It's a special occasion, after all.

Tonight, we're celebrating Emilio's departure for Florence.

The streets are alive with a cacophony of laughter, the sizzle of street food, and a rhythmic rendition of "That's Amore." The rich, savory scent of sausage and peppers mingle with the sweet fragrance of *zeppole*, while festivalgoers lap up Italian novelty items sold by sidewalk vendors. It all puts a smile on my face as I finally reach Amanti.

The new and improved Amanti.

The word glows in a vintage-style script on the new neon sign I had installed last month. I pull open one of the heavy mahogany doors by its gold handle that leads me into the entryway. As soon as my stilettos hit the hardwood floors, I'm enveloped in the world I've created, where old school meets new. Hues of rich burgundy and deep emerald are blanketed by the soft glow of ornate, hand-blown chandeliers. Tufted chairs surround each table that's topped with heavy crystal glassware etched with ornate patterns. Deep teal banquettes hug the walls, while behind the bar, a mirrored wall reflects up-lighting that casts a moody glow on our stock of vintage labels and Amaros from Italy. Every iota of the Amanti experience, from the bowties worn by my servers to the Pino D'Angiò song that greets me, is a reflection of myself. And by the time I reach my family, gathered around a U-shaped table making chit-chat over drinks and *antipasti*, I'm beaming with pride.

"Hi, Mom!" Pia strides toward me and greets me with a hug. Her black hair is straight and shiny, hanging to her waist where a wide belt cinches a black bandage dress with cap sleeves. For the first time maybe ever, she's taller than me thanks to a pair of sky-high platform pumps.

"Look at you," I say, stepping back to survey her outfit. "You look stunning."

"So do you." Though she's only been at college a matter of weeks, Pia has already gained an air of maturity and self-assurance, blossoming into womanhood quicker than I can keep up with. She gestures toward the table, where miniature David statues stand proudly between Florentine-patterned dishes rented special for the occasion. "I think theme parties are afraid of you."

I cackle, having gone totally overboard with the whole "Florence" thing. Emilio has spent the last two months training with my head chef, becoming acclimated to the pace of a commercial kitchen as if it were his destiny to do so. Though his schooling doesn't commence until the new year, he's off to Italy early to get settled into his new city of residence.

"I'm just going to check on the kitchen—"

"The hell you are," Julie says as she joins us and kisses me on the cheek. "You're not supposed to lift a finger tonight." She surveys my outfit—a red, off-the-shoulder dress accented by my regular jewels and a pair of black pointy pumps that never fail me. I've opted to wear my hair down, and my black locks cascade down my shoulders in voluminous waves. "Quite the showstopping outfit."

"I don't look this way every day?" I wink as we head for the table.

I glance at the bar, where guests laugh over cocktails, their voices melding with the swirling, upbeat music. But I turn away. Tonight isn't about making sure everything and everyone is happy. Tonight is about my family. Where we've been, who we've become, and where we're headed next. Though we're gathered under the guise of celebrating Emilio's next adventure, I can't help but also celebrate the resilience of my children. Being broken apart by my secrets has only made us build back stronger. Trust one another that much more. It's made us believe that no matter what, together, we can endure. That the threads connecting us are so strong, nothing could cause them to sever.

"Chef Emilio," I say, opening my arms as my son heads toward me at a slow, wandering pace. He's got a lazy grin on his face, but I know it's just a shield for the excitement bubbling inside of him.

"Look at that smile." My mother joins us, handing me a glass of wine as she pats Emilio's cheek. "We need to send bodyguards over there to look after you."

"Remember," I say, pointing at Emilio, steeling my expression, "no girl will ever be good enough for my baby boy."

We all laugh together as he leads me to my seat. I scan over the room filled with my closest friends and family who are all enjoying Florentine cuisine, though I know my son will become accustomed to flavors only Italy can produce. As the staff buzzes around, ensuring a smooth, fluid service, I take a deep breath. This is all a product of me and me alone. My children, whom I've successfully ushered into adulthood. The restaurant, in this season of newness. Looking back now, I wonder if the restaurant faltered to near closure not because I wasn't capable, but because I was focusing on the wrong things. I was so busy looking back, that I couldn't see ahead. I believed I needed the Valenti brothers, even just their legacy, to survive, when in truth, my hands are capable all on their own.

They always have been.

"Okay," Emilio says, standing tall next to me as the rest of the party remains seated. Taking my place as hostess, he commands the attention of the room. My son, who is so clearly a man now, who is about to venture off into the most transformative chapter of his life thus far, draws in a deep breath and raises his glass. "My mom is famous for her speeches, but tonight, I'm gonna try to outdo her."

"Let's go, Emi," one of his friends calls out.

Pia hollers and cheers and a few others clap before everyone settles down, focusing on Emilio. His cheeks are flushed with excitement and the glow of too much champagne, but all I feel is the joy he radiates. The joy of living in the truth.

"I surprised my mom when I told her I wanted to go to culinary school. Between me and my sister, Mom thought I was the reliable one who would always remain here in New York. But little did my mom know, I spent my free time reaching out to schools all across Europe. And I ended up at the perfect school in Florence, as you all might be able to tell from the plastic David statues on your tables." Everyone laughs as I flash my son a sheepish grin. "I don't know what this next year will bring, but I'm excited to find out. I can't wait to come back home a year from now and cook for all of you."

I know how much can change in a second, let alone a year. I can't help but wonder what the future holds. I wonder what my son will be like upon his return; if he'll want to take over Valenti's or open up his own place, if he'll have a pretty Italian girl on his arm. I wonder what'll become of Pia in the next four years. If she'll complete her full term at NYU, if her renewed love for music will continue to flourish, or if she'll unearth a new passion.

I wonder what'll become of me in these next several years. If I'll ride out my kids' education right here at the restaurant and be perched in the same seat when they come home. If I'll continue to have the energy and grit to keep running Amanti on my own.

The beauty of being young is that everything changes. Everything changing is the scariest part about growing older.

"My Emi," I say a while later, as our guests chatter around us, waiting for the main course to be served. "What am I gonna do without you?"

Emilio purses his lips, pondering. "I think you're gonna be busier than you think." He glances behind me, and that's when I feel it. The hush in the room. The pull in my chest. I turn around, and there he is.

Emilio must've known that the sight of Enzo would render me dizzy, and that's why he's kept his hand on my back. I'm met with the same storm of feelings I had when he showed up in Montauk, unannounced. A flush of heat, a swarm of butterflies. A draw of indignation, followed by a tsunami of fondness.

"Enzo," I whisper, those two familiar syllables that never fail to make my heart race. "What are you doing here?"

"I, uh, I have this hole in my heart," he starts, placing his hand over his heart, but then he stops. He gives me a knowing glance, one filled with tenderness, as a smirk tugs at his lips. I take in the rest of him. He looks like the Enzo of days past, clad in a tailored suit made of fine fabric that fits his frame just so. He's foregone the tie, instead leaving the first few buttons of his shirt undone to reveal a tanned chest and his usual gold chains. His bronze skin remains despite autumn's arrival, and his face is freshly shaven, glowing.

He looks devastatingly handsome.

"I didn't invite you," I say, swallowing hard. I glance around, realizing we have an audience. The room has fallen quiet, save for the festivities just beyond the restaurant doors.

"I know." Enzo's eyes dart to our daughter. Our daughter, who wears a smile that of someone whose secret has just been found out. "My little girl did."

Pia reaches for my arm before I can say anything. "I didn't think Dad should miss this."

She's been calling him *Dad* in conversation, but to hear her say it aloud, here, in front of him, to his face, is a bit surreal. Heartwarming, in all honesty, to see the love they have for each other on full display.

I turn my attention back to Enzo, my heart pounding. "You're late."

"But I'm here." Enzo moves in closer so our faces nearly touch. His familiar scent overwhelms me with comfort. As he always does, Enzo makes me feel like it's just me. Not in this room, but in the world. Like his eyes can see only me, can only find mine in a sea of people. "I've always been here. I've always belonged to you, Scar, just like you've always belonged to me. Even though I wasn't supposed to, I fell in love with you when we were young and crazy and had all of this in front of us. I didn't fight for you when I should have. I wasn't there for you when you needed me most after my brother died. I tried to find a home in other people but it never worked because I've always, always loved you, Scarlett. You see, even when it wasn't supposed to be, it's always been you."

Flanked by my children, I draw in a jagged breath and hold it, my eyes locked on Enzo's. The truth becomes evident. Plain as day, as if it's always been simple. I always saw Enzo as a threat to the carefully constructed family I built. Though I've always believed him to be my true home, my soul's one true mate, in many ways, I viewed him as an outsider. I built walls I was too afraid for him to break. But in an instant, at the sound of his words, they come crashing down to smithereens, into something that can never be restored. I spent my life afraid he'd tear my world apart, but now, a veil has been lifted, and I can finally see Enzo for what he is. The final thread that will weave us all together.

Enzo won't break my family. He'll make it whole again.

"I've always loved fixing things," I start, my voice trembling, "but I've never been able to fix the way I feel about you. I think that's because it's the one thing in my life that never needed fixing. It's always been you, too, Enzo, and it always will be. Always."

As he pulls me in, our bodies fitting together like pieces of a puzzle that were perfectly designed for each other, the room erupts into cheers and applause. I barely register it. I'm overcome with a sense of belonging, of completeness, as he draws me into him by my waist and kisses me as if he's claiming me. I'm his, and he's mine, and we were always meant to end this way.

We were always meant to start this way.

"I can't believe this," I say, my smile wide. "I can't believe you're here."

"I'm staying this time," he says, tracing my jawline with his index finger, studying me as if he's missed me desperately. "I'm here to stay, whether you want me or not."

"Oh, I want you." I kiss him again. "You're not going anywhere."

Pia snakes her arms around my waist and rests her head on my shoulder. Emilio joins in too and squeezes us all a little tighter.

"Are you happy, Mom?" Emilio asks.

I look at the three of them, the pieces of my heart that live outside of my body. Tears pour down my cheeks as my chest expands with the most immense amount of love I've never felt. "This is everything. This, right here, is absolutely everything. You three are all I need in this life to be happy."

Emilio squeezes Enzo's shoulder and gives him a look that suggests we have his blessing.

Pia looks between Enzo and I, her eyes glittering, full of anticipation. "*Anime gemelli,*" she says, as if she's sealing our fate.

My head tilts as my daughter and I lock eyes. Every time I hear that beautiful Italian phrase, I feel like I've been struck by lightning. But perhaps this bolt is designed to bond me and Enzo in the places where we're torn, to put us back where we belong. On the same wick, flickering to a rhythm invented just for us, until time no longer exists.

Though the party resumes and it'll go well into the night, I pull Enzo aside, clinging to the lapels of his sport coat. I feel like we're glued together, and I know from here on out, we always will be. Across the room, my son raises a glass, his eyes filled with pride, his smile saying everything he doesn't need to put into words. My son, who is leaving, but will always be my strength. My daughter, who has brought our family closer together than ever before. My Enzo, my love, my first and my last.

"Those words you have tattooed across your chest," I say, tracing the fabric covering it, "they were always a vow, Enzo. You have all of me, always. You always did." I lean my forehead against his, smiling. "You always will."

"I know." He holds my face in his hands and stares at me like I'm the most precious thing to him. "That's why I came home."

As we seal our promises with a kiss, as I soak in the feeling of my family around me, of this sheer completeness, I look into Enzo's endless, dazzling, delicious eyes and dare to dream.

Of who we were and who we'll be.

Of who we've become.

Of who I've become.

Scarlett Marie Valenti, full and free and alive at last.

SCARLETT

Summer, 2012

"Can I please open my eyes?" I ask, seated in the passenger seat of Enzo's SUV. "I'm getting carsick."

"Two seconds," he says.

We make a turn and gravel crunches beneath the tires. I don't know where he's taking me, but I have a sneaking suspicion it's somewhere in the Hamptons, as he made me close my eyes two hours ago as soon as we hit the Long Island Expressway. I peel my eyes open, but he extends his hand.

"Not yet," he commands.

I hear the sounds of his seatbelt unbuckling, of the car door opening, of his footsteps dragging across the gravel until he reaches the passenger side. He reaches over, squeezing my hip after he unbuckles my seatbelt, before helping me out of the car. I stand there, baking beneath the summer sun, blinded by its rays, disoriented.

"Now?" I ask.

He interlaces his fingers with mine. I hear him take a deep breath and his pulse beats against my wrist. Finally, he obliges. "Now."

I blink a few times as I open my eyes, adjusting to the brightness.

We're standing before a grandiose house made of gray cedar shake shingles, white trim, and unique architectural elements. I've never seen this house before—that much I know—but something about this place feels familiar. I look around. And then, as I take in the familiar curve of the driveway, I realize.

"This is our lot."

"Yes." Enzo looks at me like he's waiting for a lightbulb to go off.

My brows knit as I stare at the house again. I try to wrap my head around how this house, this dream of a house, ended up here, but I come up dry. "I got nothing. What the hell's going on, Enz?"

"Scarlett," he sing-songs, snaking his arm around my waist, "I built it."

He starts toward the wraparound porch, but I hang back. "You *what*?"

He wears a devilish smirk as he holds my hand, pulling me inch by inch closer to the house. "You know how I sold my Florida properties?"

"Yes," I say slowly, still not connecting the dots.

"And you remember all those weekends I told you I was going to visit my girls and Little Enzo?"

"I do."

"That was kinda sorta a white lie. I was out here. Building this house. With the money from the properties I sold." My jaw hangs open, poised to unleash some sort of outrage, but he holds up his index finger. "You, the queen of secret keeping, can't be mad."

"You built a whole house and didn't tell a soul?"

"I told all our kids." Finally, he gets me to the front door. He puts the key in the lock, pushes the door open, and says, "And I told them not to tell you."

I don't have time to register any of it. How he managed to keep a secret for almost a year. How he managed to make *this*. The most spectacular thing I've ever laid eyes on. The house is wide and bright and airy, flooded with natural light, and my eye goes directly to the back of the house that's lined with floor-to-ceiling windows that frame the beach before us. The home is fully furnished, effortlessly elegant yet deeply livable. The large sectional sofa in the living room stretches like a cloud-like expanse of creamy linen, big enough for the whole family to pile onto, begging to hold movie nights and lazy Sundays. A grand stone-front fireplace anchors the room, and I long for a quiet night, just me and Enzo, with nothing but the crackle of the fire and the roar of the ocean.

The kitchen and dining area blend into one open, sunlit space. A long wood table whispers of a thousand meals to come, surrounded by breezy linen-upholstered chairs. A sideboard holds dishware and wine glasses that I suspect will be filled in the not-so-distant future. White marble countertops gleam beneath oversized glass pendant lights, and a farmhouse sink overlooks the ocean; it's like my old spot, only better. Beside it sits a built-in espresso machine, and I can already see myself there, still in pajamas, sleep in my eyes, brewing Enzo his morning cup.

"Let me show you upstairs," Enzo says as he whisks me away. We jog up the two flights and a long hallway stretches on either side of us. There are doors. Lots of them.

"How many bedrooms are there?" I ask, surveying the wide space.

"Six," he tells me. "One for each of our kids, and the big one is for us."

We tour the bedrooms and their accompanying bathrooms at rapid speed, each one spacious and decorated with queen-sized beds and dressers that suggest whoever comes will stay a while. But our bedroom is different than all the rest.

It's *us*.

I gasp as I take it in. The stone-front fireplace mirrors the one downstairs, and beside it is an oversized chair poised for cozy nights with a glass of wine and a good book. The floor-to-ceiling windows let in the most breathtaking view, the one I know I'll never grow tired of. The bed is anchored at the center of the room, topped with a linen duvet and more pillows than I can count in hues of tan and cream and ivory. But the front of the room catches my eye. A white writing desk sits before the window overlooking the driveway. Above it is a gallery wall. Photographs of us stare back at me. All the pictures and selfies we've snapped over the last ten months of being together. Snapshots of the most blissful months of my life.

"Enzo," I start, meeting him at the center of the room, "this is overwhelming. It's just … beyond. Beyond my wildest dreams. Beyond my imagination—"

"There's something for you, on the desk," he says.

I do a double take. I don't see anything right away. And then, there it is. An envelope, with my name written in his sharp handwriting. "You wrote me a letter?" I ask, heading for the desk.

"I did."

I let out a shaky breath as I reach for the envelope. I'm overcome with emotions I can't even name. This isn't just a house; this is a life. A life I never thought Enzo and I could have. I want to go through the house a hundred more times and get to know every nook and cranny, but Enzo goes behind me and anchors me in place, wrapping his arms around my waist and resting his chin on my shoulder. I look over and kiss his temple as I unfold the page. And then, I read.

My Scarlett,

Yes, I can call you that now. You're mine. I know you say you always have been, and in many ways that's true, but now you're mine like you've never been before. I get to hold hands with you when we walk down the street. I get to work side by side with you at Amanti, and I get to drive home with you, and I get to pour us some wine and listen to your breath slow as you fall asleep on me on the couch while the news drones on in the background. I get to wake up with you in my arms. I get to love you, Scarlett, in all the ways I always wished I could.

I built us this house because there's so much more I want to do with you. With our family. I want Pia to celebrate the rest of her birthdays here in this house. I want to escape here with you in the winter and make love to you by the fireplace. I want to spend the summers here with you so we can wake up and have our coffee on the deck and go for a walk along the shore in our pajamas. I want to grill us dinners at night and listen to music and talk until you can't keep your eyes open anymore. I want our kids and their kids to fill these bedrooms and hallways and kitchen, and tear everything upside down with their beautiful chaos that I wouldn't trade for the world. I want this to be our home, forever. I want you to be my home, forever. Officially.

And what I want, above all else, my beloved, beautiful Scarlett, is for you to marry me.

All my love,

Always,

Enzo

My grip on the page tightens. I read that last line again, and again, and again, until I hear Enzo's laugh in my ear. He kisses my collarbone, grounding me in the present, and he gently takes the letter out of my hand and rests it on the desk. And as he draws a little velvet box from the pocket of his jeans and sinks to one knee in front of me, I see all the versions of Enzo that I've known. I've loved every single one of them, and I love all the ones to come. Whatever life holds, however long I've got left, I want to spend it with him. The man who has had my heart since the moment I met him.

"Scarlett Marie Valenti," Enzo says, emotion catching his voice, though he forges on, "will you marry me?"

I'm a mess of tears and nervous laughter and trembling limbs, but I sink down to his level. I don't bother to look at the ring. I just wrap my arms around him and look into his eyes, wanting to start forever right this second. "It's not even a question, honey."

His lips crash into mine like he's spent his whole life waiting to ask me, and I kiss him back like I've spent my whole life waiting to answer. To give him the *yes* he's always deserved. He shifts to a seated position, taking me with him, my lips never leaving his. We're entangled now, every bit of ourselves and our lives, and nothing will undo us. When we finally part, he presents me with the ring made of baguette emerald-cut diamonds that go all the way around. It's an eternity ring.

Endless. Just like us.

As he slides it onto my ring finger, I feel its permanence. I hold his face in my hands as we kiss, but as he grips me and lifts me off the ground and lays me back on the bed, laughter escapes my throat.

"Did you propose in the bedroom just so you could have your way with me afterwards?" I tease.

He leans his body over mine. "You know me. Always with an angle."

I laugh as he winks at me, but I slip out from under him, grab his hand, and give it a tug to follow me. We run down the hall, feeling the space, its wide expanse, its endless possibilities. Home. A word with so much meaning. For me, it's always been a person, and now we have our place. Downstairs, he pops the bottle of champagne he had chilling in the fridge while I go to our entertainment system. Instead of a massive CD collection, there's an iPod and a speaker.

"This is new," I mutter.

"It's got all your favorites on there," he says from the kitchen.

I scroll in search of the perfect song to set the mood and then I find it. I press play and bars of a dreamy chime begin, twinkling, glittering, like sunlight dancing on the sea. Its brightness is an echo of how weightless I feel, how life has become a dream I never want to wake up from.

"Not this hippy shit," Enzo cracks as he hands me my glass of wine.

I take it from him and draw him close to me, our bodies instantly falling into sync as we sway. "Dance with me."

He looks into my eyes and says, "Anywhere. Anytime," as the song swells to words that explain everything I feel.

I want to be with you everywhere.

.

Dear Enzo,

You didn't really think I was going to let you write the last letter, did you? I'm the one who started this thing, and I'm the one who will end it. Or, instead of ending the letters, even though we live together now, even though we're engaged (OMG!), maybe the letters can still be our thing. Maybe if you want to tell me something embarrassing, like that I snore in my sleep and I just don't know it, you can tell me in a letter and it will be less excruciating for both of us. Or maybe, just don't tell me if I snore, and let me live in ignorant bliss.

I thought I knew you, Enzo. Every piece of you. But these last few weeks of being your fiancée—which I still can't quite get used to because it's so far beyond what I ever dreamed—I've fallen in love with the pieces of you I never knew existed. You are more thoughtful than anyone's ever given you credit for. Last week when I started to get a cough, you went to the pharmacy without me even asking and picked me up some supplements. It might not have been a big gesture to you, but it meant more to me than you know. A few weeks ago, when I finished reading a novel and you went to Barnes & Noble and came home with an entire bag filled with books—by the way, the one called The Owner & The Wife *was very good—it excited me more than a bag if diamonds would have. It shows me, Enzo, that you care, not just about the broad strokes, but about the little details that no one else might ever notice. It doesn't matter if anyone else does. We do.*

Besides our engagement, I still can't quite believe we have a new Montauk house. This one is different because this home is built on our love, Enzo. This home will be haven for that love. I love running the restaurant with you by my side. Every day we get to go to work together feels like an adventure. We don't know what awaits us behind that heavy mahogany door, but we know we've got each other to get through it with. We get to experience it all together, and don't think I take that for granted even for a second.

But just like you, my favorite thing we get to do together is the boring stuff. None of it is boring with you, honey. I get butterflies when I hear your car pull up. When you walk in the door, I light up. When we walk hand in hand down the street as the leaves fall and a breeze hits us, I love when you pull me close to keep me warm. I love sitting around the dining room table in our sweatpants, eating takeout, talking about anything that comes to mind. Sometimes, in the middle of the night when you're fast asleep, I wake up and I look at you. Sometimes I can't believe this is really happening, that I got you, Enzo. That by some stroke of destiny, I found you and you found me.

I love watching you be a father. When all of your kids, including your Nella, agreed to join us for dinner, I cried for you because I knew how long you wished for this. And my Pia, our Pia, I don't know if I've ever seen her so happy. She's thriving at school, but it's more than that. I think you swooped back in at the right time, Enzo, when me and my girl needed you the most. You being in her life, you being her father, has put new wind in her sails. I know my Emi appreciates you because he knows you make his mamma happy, and now he doesn't have to worry about me the way he used to. You see, my love, you've brought so much good into our lives. All our lives, but most of all mine.

Our love story might be twenty-five years old, but it feels new to me. Maybe it's just been twenty-five years in the making, and this is our true start. Maybe it was always supposed to be us. Maybe, Enzo, when God wrote time, He wrote us. Maybe we were always designed for this place, here and now, together. The place you and I have always longed to be. This is only the beginning, my love.

I'll be your wife soon, when we go to Positano in a few weeks and get married there, and that's when we'll make our vows. But in the meantime, there are a few things I want you to know. Know that I'll spend the rest of my days on this earth loving you. Know that when things get tough, because they inevitably will, I'll get tougher, and I know you will too. Know that your sorrows are my sorrows, your joys are my joys, your victories are my victories. Know that you are my everything, that you are the other half of who I am, that I am not complete without you. Know that you have all of me, Enzo, and know that I am holding nothing back. Know that I think you are the hottest, most gorgeous man alive, and I'm quite obsessed with you. Know that I don't care if you snore; there's no one else I'd rather share my bed with (I'm not saying you snore, but I'm also not saying you don't snore. I'm just trying to make you laugh).

My dear Enzo, my anima gemella, my twin soul and my soon-to-be husband, know that until God ends time and if He ever starts it up again, you will forever have all my love.

Always.

ACKNOWLEDGEMENTS

T he irony is not lost on me that in writing a book about truth, I discovered my own.

A year ago, I was working frantically to contort this story into a marketable, commercially viable package that could sit alongside beach reads. Now, there's nothing wrong with a great beach read—but a beach read, this story is not. Why was I trying to water it down? Because I was chasing external validation. I wanted a book deal from a major publishing house. I wanted someone to tell me I was finally good enough.

I can honestly say now: I'm so grateful that version didn't sell. Because it wasn't the truth. When I was writing that version of the Valenti family—the one crafted to fit neatly into the market—I hit wall after wall. Nothing flowed. I wanted to quit. Over and over again. But I didn't. And I'm so glad I didn't. Because now we're here, with the *real* story. The one that poured out of me when I finally surrendered. This story is the truth, and that's why it sings.

All this to say: I hope this book gives you the courage to be authentic. To be your true self, whether that's a perfectly aesthetic package or a beautifully flawed mess. In my book, authenticity and truth trump everything else. And in writing Scarlett's truth, I finally found mine.

I want to thank my many beta readers for reading early drafts of this book. Your insights helped me find the story buried beneath all those deleted scenes. Thank you for your encouragement that helped me keep going when I wanted to quit.

To you, my readers, and to my social media community, thank you for sticking with me and supporting me. I love making videos, but writing makes my soul sing. You picking up this book and reading it means more to me than you'll ever know.

To my beautiful little doggies, Chi Chi and Emma, this book is just as much mine as it is yours. Thank you for snuggling with me during every moment of writing this book. Mommy promises to use all her royalties to buy you new toys. I love you forever and ever, and even after that.

To my grandmother, Carmela, thank you for always checking in to make sure I'm still writing, and for fully believing that my books will be made into movies. To my mom, who loves to tell everyone her daughter is a *New York Times Bestselling Author* (hey, maybe someday, Mom), you are the very, very best. I can't write much more about you because I'm on the verge of tears just thinking about how much I love you. Thank you. For literally everything.

To my husband, Franco, thank you for sticking with me and supporting me, even during the nights you had to order takeout because I spent too many hours writing and forgot to make dinner. I don't know how you deal with me. Maybe it's because I'm so hilarious and gorgeous. I love you, bird.

To the Valenti family (whom I do realize is fictional and won't actually get to read this), I don't know where you came from, but thank you for choosing me to scribe your story. I know eventually I'll write other Italian American families, but you'll always be the first. You'll always be my favorite. I really don't want to write anyone else because I love you so much.

And to *you*. The woman who sees herself in Scarlett. The one who cried when she cried and laughed when she laughed. The woman who has felt every bit of her pain. The woman who understands her a little too well. Know that you are more than the things you regret. Know that you are not beyond redemption. Know that there's a Heavenly Father who will give you double for your troubles.

> *"And now, here's what I'm going to do:*
> *I'm going to start all over again.*
> *I'm taking her back out into the wilderness*
> *where we had our first date, and I'll court her.*
> *I'll give her bouquets of roses.*
> *I'll turn Heartbreak Valley into Acres of Hope.*
> *She'll respond like she did as a young girl,*
> *those days when she was fresh out of Egypt.*
> *—Hosea 2:14-15 (MSG)*

And to the Lord, my God, thank you for making me a writer. Thank you for closing the wrong doors and opening ones no human being can shut. May whoever's hands this book is in be blessed. May they know that You can do a new thing in them, too. May they feel Your unconditional love, and may they know that through You, they can start all over again. May they know without a shadow of a doubt that they are fearfully and wonderfully made, and that they are enough exactly as You created them.

God doesn't make mistakes. He has a good, good plan for you, and a future full of hope. If you take nothing else away from this book, I hope you take that.

All my love,

Always,

Sarah

Hello, Dear Reader,

It's me. Pia Rose.

I know this is technically my mom's book, and let's be honest—she's the main character of every room she walks into. But come on. Did you really think Scarlett and Enzo's kid would be a wallflower? Please. You know my parents. It's just not in my DNA.

Anyway, even though my mamma will always be the star in real life, thanks to our dear family friend Sarah Arcuri, I get to be the main character next. That's right. A whole novel. About me. (Finally! I've only waited my whole life for a moment like this).

About how I thought falling in love would fix everything.

About how it didn't.

About how sometimes the hardest lessons are the ones that make you who you're meant to be.

About how—unfortunately—our moms are pretty much right about everything.

If you thought finding out my uncle is really my dad was dramatic, buckle up. Because in true Valenti fashion, my story is full of big feelings, beautiful places, and decisions I probably should've thought through a little more carefully.

So meet me in Positano—where the sun is a little

warmer, the sea a little bluer, and life feels a little more like a dream... until it doesn't.

In the meantime—and I can't believe I'm actually saying this—you can follow my mom on TikTok @scarlettvalenti. She's thriving over there, because of course she is. She's Scarlett.

Until then, you have all my love.

Always.

Pia

AUTHOR BIO

SARAH ARCURI is a screenwriter, author, and social media sensation with a flair for bold storytelling and building worlds women want to live in. Her debut novel, *The Owner & The Wife*, became a cult favorite among thousands of readers and is currently in development for the big screen. A summa cum laude graduate of the University of Maryland, Sarah lives in New Jersey with her husband, where they own a beloved Italian eatery. When she's not writing, she's hunting for vintage treasures, curling up with her Yorkies, Chi Chi and Emma, or spending summers along the Amalfi Coast for a well-earned dose of la dolce vita.

@thesweetpaisana   @scarlettvalenti

www.ingramcontent.com/pod-product-compliance
Ingram Content Group UK Ltd.
Pitfield, Milton Keynes, MK11 3LW, UK
UKHW011151300625
6641UKWH00026B/153

9 798998 969218